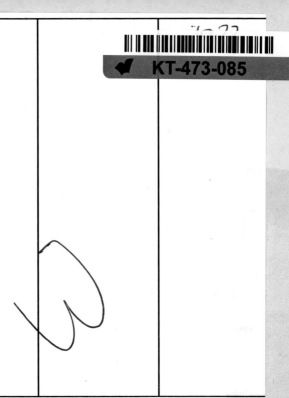

Also by Jaimie Admans

The Beekeeper at Elderflower Grove

JAIMIE ADMANS

ONE PLACE. MANY STORIES

HQ
An imprint of HarperCollins*Publishers* Ltd
1 London Bridge Street
London SE1 9GF

www.harpercollins.co.uk

HarperCollins*Publishers*
1st Floor, Watermarque Building, Ringsend Road
Dublin 4, Ireland

This paperback edition 2022

1
First published in Great Britain by
HQ, an imprint of HarperCollins*Publishers* Ltd 2022

ISBN: 9780008541538

This book is produced from independently certified FSC™ paper
to ensure responsible forest management.

For more information visit: www.harpercollins.co.uk/green

Printed and Bound in the UK using 100%
Renewable Electricity at CPI Group (UK) Ltd

For Bill.
Thank you for sharing your bee expertise with me!

Chapter 1

*The honeybee is the only insect that
produces a food eaten by humans.*

As job interviews go, it's probably the strangest one I've ever had.

I'm hunched over my mum's dining table at my laptop, having an online interview with a bee. Well, it's not really a bee, obviously. It's someone using a bee filter on the Zoom video chat. They're also using a computerised voice, so I can't see their face *or* hear their real voice. It's disconcerting not to know the first thing about the person who's interviewing me. It *should* put me off, but I'm so desperate for a job that I've certainly had more disturbing interviews than this recently, and I'm *still* jobless and staying in my mum's spare room.

But no matter the odd interview, this job was meant for me.

'Have you got a lot of beekeeping experience, Miss Harwood?'

Well, apart from that teeny-tiny detail.

'Oh yes, tons,' I say breezily. 'Bees, bees, bees, everywhere. I've kept bees here, there, and all over the place. They're very ... buzzy.'

'Buzzy?' the bee repeats. Even the computerised voice sounds surprised.

'And vitally important to the whole ecological system of the world, of course.' I try to think of something I know about bees. I thought I'd be able to wing it on this interview, but the best I can come up with on the spot is they're stripy and fuzzy.

'Why did you leave your last job as a beekeeper?'

'The bees died,' I say, glad of something I'd rehearsed earlier. And then I realise I sound far too pleased with myself and back-pedal so quickly that I go off-script. 'I mean, in an accident, not because of me or anything.' Note to self: interview is for beekeeper, not bee*killer*. 'It was an arson attack. The farmer was too upset to rebuild, so … no more job.'

I've seen that on a TV drama somewhere; it's bound to be realistic. And I'll have to text the friend who's posing as my reference and say that he needs to pretend to be a very upset farmer.

'Right. And where are these farms you worked on because I've not heard of them? Not local?'

'No. They were far away. Very far away.' I rack my brain for faraway places. 'The Outer Hebrides!' I add to my note that my friend needs to pretend to be a very upset *Scottish* farmer.

'Oh, really? How unusual. I thought honeybees were scarce so far north, where there isn't much shelter or pollen for them …'

Oh, cockgoblins. 'Well, you have to try these things, don't you?' I sound like I'm trying a new ice cream flavour, not insulting this cartoon bee's life's work.

'Hmm.' The bee sounds unconvinced. 'And according to the CV you sent over, you left beekeeping for … candle-making, is that right?'

Of all the things I've lied about on that CV, that's the one thing that's true. I just hope this bee doesn't ask about the abrupt ending and months of joblessness since.

'Yeah, my other half and I started a candle-making business, but …' I sigh. It's been a year and I still can't talk about it without getting upset. 'It didn't work out. With the business *or* the other half.'

'I'm sorry.' The bee gives me a few moments to get myself under control. 'But you've gone back into beekeeping now?'

'Yes! I'm fully committed to the bees now. Who doesn't love bees, right? And it's important to save them.' I try to think of some fact I know about bees when the closest I've ever come to a bee is batting away one that decided it wanted a share of my sandwiches on a summer picnic.

'And you know your duties will involve weekly hive inspections, watching out for diseases or mites and treating accordingly, keeping the bees calm and happy, and of course, harvesting the honey, and then preparing the hives for winter. You will report to the head of the Nectar Inspectors – a "Friends of Elderflower Grove" group, a charity set up to support the bees and their habitat in the wake of the owner's … disappearance. And you're local to Little Kettling, aren't you? So you know how important the bees are to the villagers?'

'Yes, of course.'

'Right, and I do have to ask you about the premises. This job takes place at Elderflower Grove. You must be aware of the stories that swirl around the village about the old mansion?'

I love Elderflower Grove. It's the main reason I want this job. The burnt-out manor house on the edge of the village where I grew up. I've always felt drawn to the place, although I've never been inside. When I was younger, it was owned by an old witch of a woman – the local gossip mill claimed she was an actual witch of the bubbling cauldrons and black cats type – a wicked spinster who lived alone and cast a spell on anyone who dared set foot on her land.

She's long gone now. Presumed dead in the fire that gutted Elderflower Grove seven years ago, nothing left behind but the shell of a beautiful old manor house, a cross between Pemberley and Downton Abbey, a building that watches me through empty window frames every time I walk past its overgrown grounds. The only sign of life is the buzzing that emanates from the rooftop beehives on summer evenings.

'Yes, of course. I live about ten minutes' walk away, down the side streets. You can see the roof from my bedroom window …' Why did I say that? No job interviewer cares about the view from my window.

'And you're not bothered by the ghost stories? You're not afraid of ghosts?'

There have always been ghost stories about Elderflower Grove. When I was little, all the local children were afraid of the 'old witch'. There were campfire tales of venturing past the gate of Elderflower Grove and never being seen again. Any football that accidentally went over her wall would be returned in shreds. The dog walkers who accidentally stumbled into her grounds and were chased off by a woman wielding a knife. There was probably a headless horseman in there somewhere too. There's usually a headless horseman in ghost stories for good measure.

I can honestly say I've never had a job interview where ghosts came into the equation before. 'No.'

'Only our last beekeeper had a close encounter of the spirit kind and ran off screaming into the night, never to be seen again. I could do without a repeat of that. What would you do if you saw a ghost?'

This really is the strangest interview. I'm half convinced it's a joke or prank of some kind, and yet I get the sense that my potential employment hinges on my answer to this question and that it might be more important than my extensive beekeeping experience or lack thereof. 'Offer it a cup of tea and a chocolate Hobnob?'

The bee laughs.

'It's dead – it's going to need a cup of tea. Can you imagine how long it would have been since its last cuppa? If anything calls for tea and a biscuit, it's being dead.'

The bee is laughing too hard to speak, and I'm barely able to restrain myself from singing the *Ghostbusters* theme tune. I knew it would be a strange one as soon as the bee filter popped

4

onscreen and a message came up saying the filter was to protect the interviewer's privacy, and if I had a problem with conducting the interview like this, it clearly wasn't the job for me.

The stories about Elderflower Grove have always been just that – stories. A fire-damaged house, grounds that haven't been disturbed for years, and a question mark over what happened to the owner. It would be more surprising if there *weren't* ghost stories about the place.

The gossip has amped up lately, mind. Every time I go into the village, someone or other is talking about hearing 'things that go bump in the night' and mysterious lights have been spotted in the building when there's no one there.

The bee is still laughing, so I barrel on ahead. 'Look, I love Elderflower Grove. I've just moved back here after being away for a while, and it's still here, unchanged, unloved, like a monster, caged in and looking out, but a good monster. A friendly monster.'

Oh good lord, why have I gone from ghosts to monsters? I sound like I'm writing a children's book, not applying for a serious job. I've never blown a job interview this badly before in my life, and I've blown a *lot* of job interviews.

'A friendly monster?' The bee sounds bemused.

There's no pulling it back now. May as well go all in, at least it'll give the bee a funny story to recount to its colleagues. Or use as video training for how *not* to do a job interview. 'I feel like that's Elderflower Grove – a misjudged monster. It just needs someone to love it. To see it as something other than old and damaged.'

'Don't we all?'

The seriousness in the computerised voice makes my breath catch for a second. 'It must have so many stories to tell. People make up stories about it, but no one ever listens to what it has to say.' Oh great, now I've gone from monsters to sentient buildings. This is going *so* well.

'I know that feeling.' It's a mutter I'm fairly sure the bee didn't mean to say out loud.

'My mum always says that when she was young, the stories about Elderflower Grove were more like fairy tales. Far from ghosts and witches, the rumours back in those days were that pixies hid in the woods, fairies flitted through the trees, mermaids sang in the lake, and there was a wishing well that really granted wishes. Do you know the song "Dear Jessie" by Madonna? I always thought it would be like that – like walking into a lullaby.'

The bee makes an unidentifiable noise.

I try to steer the conversation away from all things supernatural. 'This job was meant for me. I've been looking for a job for ages and there's nothing going. Every week I do the demoralising trek to the job centre to apply for jobs I have no interest in, and every week I get nothing back – not even a "sorry, your application has been unsuccessful". It's soul-destroying out there. And when I walked to the job centre this morning, that notice wasn't on the gate, and when I walked back two hours later, there it was. Fate – like it was posted just for me. Like it was waiting.'

'Hmm.'

I'm not sure if it's a good hmm or a bad hmm. Are there different categories of hmms? 'And what are the chances of you posting a job for a beekeeper and an actual beekeeper happening along at just the right moment?'

Another hmm. The bee is quiet for a moment. 'What is it you want out of this job, Miss Harwood?'

I decide to be honest. Well, apart from the whole pretending to be a beekeeper thing. Not *that* honest, obviously. But I've been to a ton of job interviews in the last few months and been well-practised and word-perfect. I've studied the companies and been the well-put-together epitome of the ideal employee, and it's got me nowhere. If you can't try a different approach in a video-chat interview with an unseen bee, when can you?

'Things have spiralled lately, and I'm constantly chasing my tail, trying to make ends meet, living in my mum's spare room after a break-up, and I need to do *something* to take back control of my life. I've been trying *so* hard to find a job. I've been doing everything "right" but no one wants me. Life is moving on around me and dragging me with it like I'm clinging to a pair of water skis at the back of the boat, being thrown into rocks occasionally. I want to *live* again, not just be pulled along for the ride. I feel like everything I do is dictated by someone else. I need to do something for *me* again. I need to feel important to someone, somewhere, because I feel forgotten … like Elderflower Grove.'

From the silence, I can tell the bee didn't expect me to say that. Neither did I, to be honest.

'You know what,' it says eventually. 'I appreciate someone being honest instead of saying what they think I want to hear. And we've all felt like that at some point – like we have no agency over our own lives. If Elderflower Grove can help with that then so *bee* it.' The bee deliberately extends the 'e', making it clear that it's a pun. 'And I'll be honest with you in return. We've got a big honey harvest due this Friday and, quite frankly, I need a beekeeper *now*. I'm sure you know of the rumour around Little Kettling that they're special bees. It's a miracle of nature that they survived the fire that destroyed the manor house, and now the locals think their honey must have magical healing properties. I've got villagers chomping at the bit for this year's first honey. It's like a village full of Winnie-the-Poohs.'

The unexpected laugh catches me by surprise, and then I realise what it's saying. 'You're giving me the job? Seriously?' I barely refrain from adding, 'What is *wrong* with you?' By no one's standards has this interview gone well. It's been a disaster from start to finish, and I cannot *believe* anyone would be daft enough to give me a job as a beekeeper.

'You're a beekeeper, you're local, and you can start straight away, right?'

'All true,' I lie. *Mostly* true, apart from the beekeeper bit. My false smile is so bright that the bee is going to need sunglasses.

'And one thing I value above all else is honesty, and you've clearly got that in spades. The job's yours, Miss Harwood.'

I squeal in delight and jump up to do a victory punch, and then realise the bee can still see me and sit back down quickly. I feel a huge pang of guilt about the lie, but I can learn, right? I haven't got the faintest clue about what's involved in beekeeping, but surely it can't be impossible to pick up as I go along?

'This job is for one season only. Your contract will terminate in October once you've prepared the hives for winter. Your services will not be required next year.'

I murmur an agreement, but I can't help thinking that's odd. The bees have been at Elderflower Grove for decades – it's not like they're going anywhere. If they're so desperate for a beekeeper, I wouldn't have thought they'd be keen to get rid of one so quickly.

'The apiary is on the roof,' the bee continues.

Apiary … What on earth is an apiary? 'Apes?' I suggest. They say there are unexpected things in Elderflower Grove, but a gang of apes would be taking the biscuit.

'Apiary,' the bee says. I can *hear* the expression on its face. 'Where the bees are kept?'

'Oh, of course!' Is that what they call it? Who knew? 'Sorry, the internet must've dropped out for a second. I missed what you said.'

The bee filter doesn't change its expression, but I can tell it looks unconvinced.

'There's an outside set of steps to the rooftop where you'll find sixty hives …'

I choke on my own tongue. *Sixty* beehives? How the heck am I supposed to take care of *sixty* hives?

'There's one rule and one rule only, Miss Harwood – you must never go inside. *Never*. The Elderflower Grove manor house is unsafe due to damage from the fire and many years of neglect. It is *not* for poking around inside. The roof where the hives stand has been made safe by structural engineers, but the rest of the building is not so lucky. It's damaged beyond repair, a severe hazard, and *no one* is allowed in. You *must* stay outside where it's safe. Do you agree?'

'Yes, of course.' I try to hide the sting of disappointment. I was looking forward to a good poke around inside.

'Good. Now, the head of the Nectar Inspectors will meet you at the gate tomorrow with the keys and whatever equipment was salvaged from the last beekeeper. Say 10 a.m.?'

I make a noise of agreement. 'Salvaged' is *not* a good word. I dread to think of what happened to the last beekeeper.

'We will never meet, but it's been a joy to speak with you, Miss Harwood.'

I detect a hint of sarcasm in the bee's tone.

'I wish you the best of luck in your first week. I suspect you're in for a baptism of fire.'

With that, the call ends. Which is good because hopefully the bee missed the look of horror on my face. Why are first weeks at new jobs *always* like that? Couldn't we just ease into things gradually?

It doesn't change the sheer excitement that fizzes through me. I've often stood at the gate and looked in, wondering what secrets the crumbling, fire-damaged manor and overgrown grounds hide.

A half-naked man chooses that moment to walk into the kitchen and open the fridge. Unfortunately, it's the *wrong* half that's naked – the half you'd generally prefer to remain covered. When I squeak in horror, he spins around in surprise and grabs a milk bottle to cover his modesty.

'Oh, sorry, love. Didn't see you there.'

I'm sitting at the dining table with a computer in front of me, am I really that invisible? It's a good thing the call ended when it did, or that bee would've seen something it couldn't unsee.

'Katrina, isn't it?'

'Kayleigh,' I correct him. At least he got the K right. One of the others thinks I'm called Maud.

Most men would scurry away in embarrassment at being

caught half-naked by their date's daughter, but not this one. 'Your mum tells me about your *predicament*.'

'Predicament?'

'With the husband, or you know, *without* a husband. I've heard about that nasty break-up.' He taps his nose like it'll be our little secret. 'But not to worry, we'll soon find you a new one. I've got a son, he's *much* younger than you and married, of course, but I'll ask if he's got any older friends and we'll set you up on a nice date. How does that sound?'

'That won't be neces—'

'Yes, yes, we can't have the older generation having more sex than the younger generation, can we?' He laughs so hard that he comes worryingly close to dropping the milk bottle. 'Well, I must dash, mustn't keep Mother Dearest waiting.' He turns back to the fridge, replaces the milk bottle, picks up the squirty cream, and sidles frontwards out of the room, his sixty-something-year-old wrinkled bum cheeks wobbling as he goes. 'Nice to meet you, Katrina. No point holding out for Mr Willoughby, you'll be an old spinster by the time he comes along. Got to be sensible at your age.'

'Mr Darcy!' I shout after him. 'Believe me, no one wants Mr Willoughby!'

My mum always complains about my love of Jane Austen, but she can't even get the characters straight when moaning about my non-existent love life to one of her multiple boyfriends. 'Mr Darcy and Mr Willoughby aren't even in the same book.'

I hear the bedroom door shut behind the half-naked man. I'd say I wonder where my mum finds them, but I don't want to know.

This is why I need a job so badly – so I can move out and leave my mum to her afternoon dalliances without being scarred for life. After a disaster of a break-up and losing my candle-making business last year, I moved back in with my mum, right around the same time that one of her friends found a new man via Tinder and introduced my mum to the wonders of app dating, and now she's got more boyfriends than you can shake a stick at, and she can't understand why I'd rather be single than trust another man *ever*.

But to get my own place, I've got to be able to *afford* my own place, and that's where a job comes in. And now I have one.

The beekeeper at Elderflower Grove. Me. I guess stranger things have happened …

Thank god Amazon offers same-day delivery, because I need a book about beekeeping and I need it *now*, or this is going to be an unmitigated disaster. It can't be that hard to keep a few bees happy … can it?

Chapter 2

*In the autumn, the female worker bees evict all
the male drones from the hive, leaving them
to die when the cold weather sets in.*

Little Kettling is a quiet village in the Hampshire countryside.
Trafficless cobblestone streets with a shop, a post office, a café, an
antiques shop, and a couple of other tiny independent boutiques.
It's not far from Chawton, where Jane Austen lived for the last
eight years of her life, and a few tourists come through now and
again. Elderflower Grove is ten minutes away – halfway between
the town itself and the leafy outskirts where my mum lives.

The wrought-iron gates hide a sprawling estate that very few
people have ever seen, and lead to a tumbledown manor house
that's half castle and half stately home. I nervously approach
the gate at ten o'clock the next morning, a crossbody bag on my
shoulder that conceals my just-delivered copy of a book touted
as a 'beekeeping bible' and hastily ordered yesterday.

'Helloooo!' The woman waiting for me pops out from behind
a poster she's tying onto the gate and gives me a Mrs Doubtfire–
esque greeting. She's dressed as a bee. She's wearing yellow tights, a
black skirt, and a black-and-yellow-striped T-shirt with a cartoon

bee motif and the words 'bee kind' on the front; her hair is fluffy around her ears and dyed a bright yellow, and she's wearing black-and-yellow fuzzy deely boppers. 'I'm Gracie, leader of the Nectar Inspectors. You must be Kayleigh, the new beekeeper?'

'I am,' I confirm. 'Are you who I spoke to yesterday?' I know the bee said we'd never meet, but surely she is, what with the bee filter and then coming dressed as an actual bee.

'Oh, heaven's no, petal. We don't know who that is either. We've never known.'

'So you get your instructions from an unseen bee too?'

'Yes, always have done. Texts, emails, and the occasional video call with the filter on. The bee manages the Elderflower Grove fund – where all the money from honey sales and our fundraising efforts goes and where your wages come from – and myself and a few other villagers volunteer to maintain the wellbeing of the bees and provide the locals with their supply of honey. It was the bee who put us together.'

I close my hands around the iron bars of the gate and peer into the huge estate. The sandy-coloured stonework of the Elderflower Grove manor house is mostly hidden from view by weeds that have grown into triffids and overhanging trees. It's the kind of place they'd film live-action Disney movies, and I always think that if I look hard enough, I'll see Belle inside with her nose in a book while the Beast skulks around the courtyard, feeding birds or tending his rose garden.

'Between you and me, I think it might be *her*.'

'Her who?' I ask without looking away from the manor house, bricks toppling from one side of its roof, the beehives obscured from down here.

'Josie Garringham.'

Josie Garringham. A name to strike fear into the hearts of all children who grew up in Little Kettling. The spinster who used to own Elderflower Grove. A common threat from parents trying to coerce their children into good behaviour was that

Josie Garringham would be on the warpath if we didn't brush our teeth, clean our rooms, or whatever else kids object to doing without a protest first. As we grew older and parents were disappointed by our dating lives, there was always a cautionary tale of 'You'll end up like Josie Garringham if you don't find a man and settle down soon'.

Like it's a bad thing. I'd rather live alone with a load of beehives than ever let a man take advantage of me again. I feel a sudden affinity for the old woman. When I was young, I used to watch from my bedroom window as she spent hours on her rooftop, tending to her bees. She seemed the opposite of the spell-casting witch the local children made up stories about.

I realise what Gracie means and drop my hands from the gate with a gasp of shock. 'You don't think she's dead?'

So many years have passed since the November night that the building went up in flames. I still lived with my mum then, but was about to move in with my *now* ex-boyfriend. The fire brigade doused the flames as I watched from my bedroom window, surrounded by boxes ready to be moved out. A lifetime ago for me.

Josie Garringham's body was never found, but there was no doubt that she perished in the fire. Many of the stories that swirl around the village are about her unquiet spirit haunting the grounds of Elderflower Grove, seeking revenge on the arsonists who caused her death. No one's ever been caught in relation to the fire, but it's widely believed that it was kids playing a trick on the 'old witch' of the village and the fire simply got out of hand, as fires tend to do.

'I know it sounds daft, but I don't know who else it could be. Who else would hide their identity? Who else would care so much about the bees of Elderflower Grove? And then there's me. I was her best friend when she was alive, her *only* friend some might say, and I was the first person who was approached. The bee got in touch with me and asked if I'd be responsible for overseeing

14

the care of the bees. Once word got out that they'd survived the fire, the villagers thought they were miraculous. There were break-ins to attempt to steal the honey from the hives, and then that first summer, the charity was set up by an unseen benefactor, and a beekeeper was employed to care for the bees and harvest their honey to sell locally.'

I didn't know any of this. 'I've lived away for a while.'

'Oh, I know. Your mother told me everything. Nasty business with your husband swindling you like that.'

I'll never get used to it. That village life thing of *everyone* knowing more about you than you know about yourself. An ant couldn't walk into this village without several people looking up its family tree on Ancestry.com.

'I wasn't married,' I mutter, like it makes any difference.

I don't think she hears me. 'Your mum's never mentioned you having a talent for beekeeping though.'

Surprise, surprise. I steer the conversation back towards the ghosts. 'But how? Why? If Josie Garringham isn't dead, where is she?'

Gracie shrugs. 'I never said it made sense. I just don't know who else would do it. Josie *loved* those bees. More than she loved anything else. She didn't have any family who would care for them in her absence, so who *else* would the bee be?'

'I didn't know there was ever a question over her death.'

'Oh, there wasn't. It's silly, really. My husband thinks I'm imagining it as a way of keeping my friend alive. Sorry to keep harping on when you must be keen to get on with your job. This is for you.' She fishes in her pocket and deposits something smooth and heavy in my palm – a pebble with a bee handpainted onto it with a banner saying 'Bee-st of luck'. 'My granddaughter made it for you. We all do everything we can to draw attention to the bees of Elderflower Grove. The Nectar Inspectors are all *of a certain age* and we like to get our grandchildren involved, pass on our love of wildlife to the next generation.'

15

'Wow, that's lovely.' I look down at the stone in my hand and fight not to well up. 'Tell your granddaughter thank you so much.'

'We hide them around the village for people to find. We paint a positive message on them and I like to believe that the people who find them are the people who most need a word of encouragement at that particular moment. We're all mostly retired so we have plenty of time to do this sort of thing.'

'Couldn't you be the beekeeper?'

'Oh goodness me, no.' She titters as she goes over to her trolley bag and digs down inside it. 'I'm not going in *there*.'

I glance at Elderflower Grove as she crackles out a huge carrier bag and comes over to deposit it into my arms. 'Why not?'

'It seems like hallowed ground. When she was alive, Josie never *ever* let me inside. She would always meet me in town. She never allowed people in, not even the postman. She'd be angry with me for not respecting her rules now, even after being gone for so many years.'

'You have the keys and you've never gone in, even for a look?'

'Why would I? The police crawled all over the place after the fire, but there was nothing to find. I don't want to disrespect my friend, even if she isn't still with us.'

I gulp and try not to think about an angry ghost turning in its grave at the thought of me going against its cardinal rule. From the stories, it seems like Josie Garringham was angry enough when she was alive. Being dead certainly won't have improved matters.

I'd assumed Gracie was going to show me the ropes, and a tingle of apprehension about being alone makes the hairs on the back of my neck stand on end.

'What is all this stuff?' I rustle the heavy bag open and peer inside.

'The equipment we managed to recover from the last beekeeper. Your beekeeping suit and gloves. Her husband returned it a few days later, said she'd gone to stay with her sister outside Hampshire due to not wanting to be in the same county as

16

the ghosts, and would be emigrating from England itself with immediate effect.'

I let out a laugh and quickly realise Gracie isn't joking. I swallow. 'The bee said something about a spirit encounter?'

'She never spoke about what happened, but people say she ran screaming into the night with the wheelie bin chasing after her.'

I nearly choke as I try to hold back laughter. 'The wheelie bin?'

'Right out in the middle of the road, it was. And when someone went to return it, it was *gone*.' She speaks with a tone of a child sitting around a campfire and shining a torch on their face.

'I'll be sure to watch out for any possessed rubbish containers.'

'You can laugh, Kayleigh, but the ghostly activity has amped up in recent months. Do be careful in there, won't you? Things have not just been going bump in the night, but people have reported things going crash, bang, *and* wallop, and dog walkers have spotted mysterious lights on.'

'I'm not afraid of ghosts,' I say, without adding that I *am* afraid of living in my mum's spare room for the rest of forever and never managing to get back on my own feet and claw some modicum of dignity back, and if it's between that and the ghosts, I'll take the ghosts. I'd rather them than half-naked old men with whipped cream, and never escaping the pitying looks and sympathetic 'your mum told me what happened with the ex' speeches.

'There's an air about the place. It's like you're never *quite* alone. Here are the keys.' She switches from sombre and foreboding to cheerful in an instant. 'Don't forget, you must *never* go inside. Never, never, never. The building was badly damaged in the fire and is extremely unsafe. The beehives are on the roof, and there's a rooftop shed where you'll find all your equipment and whatnot. You know where my little shop is, so come and ask if you need anything.'

I've hidden away in my mum's spare bedroom since I moved back here, so I don't know the villagers very well, but I can already tell she's one of the people who is the absolute centre of village gossip and if a feather landed in Little Kettling, she'd know about it.

I nod to the half-hanging poster she was attaching to the gate when I arrived, and lift a corner to see the whole thing. It reveals a black-and-white photo of a man with a shiny bald head, and a big 'no entry' road sign stamped across his face in red. 'Who's that?'

'Leader of the local council, Kingsley Munroe. He's a bee *murderer*. A despicable man. Nice as pie to your face, but always seems a bit *too* overly interested in the Nectar Inspectors and what we're doing. I'm sure there's an ulterior motive; I just haven't worked out what it is yet. I wanted to give you a warning. That vile man does everything he can to harm our bees. The Nectar Inspectors sow wildflower seeds in every available space around Little Kettling and he orders every single one to be strimmed and sends his minions out to do it. Most local authorities are embracing wildflower meadows and letting parts of their land go wild to help the bees, but not him. He's doing the opposite. Cutting their much-needed sources of nectar and spraying pesticides here, there, and everywhere. If there's a way to damage wildlife, he'll find it. We make our own seed bombs and throw them everywhere we can to counteract his cruelty. He always cuts down the flowers as soon as they've grown, but we keep doing it. A silent war. He cuts, we seed bomb, repeat to infinity. We went into local schools last month and showed the children how to make the seed bombs. Thank god for Elderflower Grove, eh? Land he has no authority over and can't destroy. *Our* bees get to feed on the elderflower hedgerows and forage on the wildflowers that have taken over since Josie died. If you see him skulking around here, don't let him in.' She waggles a warning finger at me, the keys dangling from it and jangling around. 'Always make sure you lock up behind you. He'll get in any little gap!'

I almost laugh at how serious she sounds. 'I'll hand them back in October.'

'Hand them back? Why would you do that?'

'The bee said my services won't be required next year?' I say questioningly. Is it odd that she doesn't know that?

She nods thoughtfully. 'Maybe they're trying to play it safe after the last beekeeper *incident*, but I can't see why your role wouldn't be ongoing. I'll give that bee a piece of my mind next time I speak to it.'

I can't help grinning at the thought of that virtual bee being put in its place by a woman dressed as a bee who must be well into her eighties.

She finally stops jangling the keys and encloses them into my hand, pointing out a large metal one for the gate itself and several smaller keys for the heavy-duty padlocks fastening weighty chains around it.

'Don't forget to tell the bees!' she trills as I start undoing locks. Houdini would've struggled with this gate.

'Tell the bees what?' I'm distracted by trying to get a key into a rusty padlock.

'Everything, of course. You must know the old folktale.'

I shake my head, and then she shakes hers in dismay. 'I've never met a beekeeper who didn't know it. You have to tell the bees everything. They'll produce more honey if they know all your secrets. And you must *always* tell them when you take over a colony. If something has happened to their old beekeeper, you need to tap on each hive three times and tell them their friend has died and introduce yourself to them. They'll desert you, otherwise. The last beekeeper point-blank refused to believe the old wives' tales and she never spoke to them. The honey was bitter last year because of it.'

'I'm sur—'

'Bees grieve, you know. They're a living, breathing, feeling entity. You need to become friends with them. If they feel like you trust them, they'll trust you in return.'

'Friends with the bees. Right. I can do that.' May as well – I don't exactly have a lot of other friends around here.

19

'Tell the bees your secrets and they'll tell you their secrets in return,' she says as the last chain falls away, and it takes the both of us to push one side of the heavy double-gate open, so unused that it makes a screeching sound as rusted metal grinds against rusted metal.

'This is where I leave you.' Gracie takes a step back. 'Good luck on your first day. Bee-st of luck, even.'

I pat my pocket where I've put the pebble and thank her for all her help, even though between ghost stories, sentient wheelie bins, and talking to the bees, I'm almost positive this is some sort of wind-up and someone filming a prank TV show is going to jump out of the undergrowth at any moment.

**

It's like stepping into a different world. Even though Gracie is only a few feet behind me, waving from the gate, her fuzzy bee headband bouncing with every movement. I feel like I've looked into a painting and accidentally fallen through it.

I'm on what was once a wide tarmac driveway lined by neat walls and trimmed Buddleia bushes, but the walls have started to crumble and the bushes have grown so out of hand that they're more than double my height and toppling over. The tarmac is cracked and weeds have grown through every fracture, spiky thistles and clumps of stinging nettles leer towards me, thorny brambles are winding through tall grass-like weeds and self-sown trees of unidentifiable varieties. Nature's own barbed wire, keeping people out. *Anything* could be lurking in here, and no one would ever know. The answers to the mysteries of the world could lie in this garden. The Bermuda Triangle of Hampshire.

It should probably be foreboding, but I've always thought it would be amazing to be inside Elderflower Grove. In my Disney-loving childhood, I used to think a prince turned into a Beast might live inside. Between my mum's stories of mermaids and fairies and wish-granting wells, and the rumour that did the rounds about a library inside the manor – as a child who loved books, I dreamed of seeing it for real, but this … This is more like the start of a horror film than a Disney film.

It's so quiet. The traffic noise from a distant road is dulled by the number of trees that have been allowed to grow un-pruned, their leaves rustling in the gentle breeze, and when I stop worrying about what creatures might be living here, I realise the branches around me are *alive* with birdsong, and there's the gentle burbling of a river that runs right through the grounds.

Elderflower Grove manor is even more impressive. I feel like Jane Bennet approaching Netherfield Hall for the first time in my favourite book, and it feels so much like I've stepped into a Jane Austen novel that I half expect Mr Bingley to pop up in one of the windows. It feels like a grand old French château in the middle of the English countryside – there's even a dry fountain in what was once the courtyard, but instead of an angel or a cherub on top, there's a moss-covered statue of a gargoyle. An angry gargoyle.

I look up at the house in awe. A heavy-looking double door is padlocked and chained shut, and judging by the keys on the keyring, I don't have the means to open it, which I wouldn't, obviously, because of the whole not-being-allowed-to-go-inside thing.

The courtyard was paved once, but like the driveway, it's cracked and grass has started growing at random spots through the cracks. There's ivy scrambling up most of the building, and what were once neat elderflower hedgerows around the back and sides of the house are now so tall that some of them have started growing *in* through the missing windows.

I find the narrow stone staircase set into the brickwork at the side of the house and start the steep climb upwards, finally emerging from the shadow of the elderflower trees and into the spring sunshine on the rooftop.

It's one of those May days where it already feels like summer,

21

and the content hum from the hives gets louder up here. The rooftop is paved with light-coloured slabs, and set out across the wide-open space are beehives. Many, many beehives. Ten rows with six beehives in each row, all painstakingly positioned at perfectly even intervals, each one a small house-shaped structure with a gable roof, and built of different sections that form each part of the hive.

The rooftop is surrounded by a battlement wall that makes me feel like I'm standing on the top of a castle. There's a full-size brick shed on the right side, away from the hives, and behind me in a corner, there's a door that must lead down into the manor house. There are two stone benches at this end and I drop my shoulder bag and Gracie's carrier bag onto the nearest one, feeling utterly amazed that anyone could build all this on a *rooftop*.

I stand at the wall and look out at the view, and it would take my breath away if my breath wasn't already taken away by every moment since I stepped through the gate. From up here, the view is a panorama that looks out across the entire estate. I can see tops of elderflower trees frothing with the white blossom that gives Elderflower Grove its name, and across the greenery, there's a gap in the trees that reveals a lake. It wasn't made up! Josie Garringham had her own lake! It really *is* like Pemberley. The only thing missing is a giant statue of a wet Colin Firth in a see-through white shirt.

I'm far enough away that no bees are bothering me from this distance, but the buzz is constant and bees are zipping back and forth to the hives without a moment of rest. I open Gracie's carrier bag and pull out the baby-blue jumpsuit I've seen beekeepers wearing on TV. I open my beekeeping bible to the chapter about clothing and take note of the big warning printed beneath the chapter header, that reads, '*Be careful! Bees will find any tiny hole. Make sure every centimetre of your suit is sealed.*'

I shrug my way into the thick cotton-canvas material and then zip it up to my neck. I make sure my boots are tight around my calves, then I pull the hood over my head and straighten out the net veil, and zip that up so it joins the front of the suit. I find a pair of elbow-length gloves in Gracie's bag and pull them on.

There. At least I look like a beekeeper.

I double-check myself again for holes, because although I've never been particularly bothered by bees, and I'm not outdoorsy enough to come across them too often, I don't fancy being stung if I can possibly help it.

I decide to ease myself into things by talking to the bees. It's a bit daft, but Gracie seemed invested in it, and whatever befell the last beekeeper … Well, I don't want any crazed bins to get the hump with me too.

I know she said something about knocking three times on each hive, but with sixty of them, I'd be here all day, so I walk across the roof and do three gentle taps on the side of the nearest hive.

'Hello, bees. How are you ladies today?' I rethink it. I *really* wish I'd had more time to read the book. 'Wait, bees aren't all female, are they? Are some of you male? In that case, hello, bee ladies and bee gentlemen. I'm Kayleigh and I'm your new beekeeper.'

I'm standing near enough to the hive that a few of them are flying around my face, thankfully on the other side of my hooded net, and I tell myself they've come to say hello.

'Apparently I need to introduce myself and let you know that something's happened to your last beekeeper. Well, if there's any truth in the wheelie bin story, you probably saw that for yourself. And before that, apparently there was some old man keeping you, and then before that was Josie Garringham, the lady of the house, and you almost definitely know something's happened to her by now, it was years ago.'

I'm grateful that it *is* an abandoned estate and at least there are only a few ghosts to hear me.

'I'm a very experienced beekeeper. I've been keeping bees in the Outer Hebrides for *years* now and …' No, I can't do it. I can't lie to the bees. 'Okay, as you've probably noticed because I needed an instruction manual to put the suit on, I'm *not* a beekeeper. But I've had to move back home and stay in my mum's spare room, and she's started dating again and there are all these random men wandering around the house … Oh wait, that makes it sound like a brothel, doesn't it? Not at the same time or anything. She sees them all individually. Apparently she's trying to decide between them and doesn't want to limit her options before she makes a decision …'

What do you know, talking to bees *is* therapeutic. When I was younger, I used to see Josie Garringham up here from my bedroom window. She used to spend hours on this rooftop, talking to her bees. Sometimes she used to sing to them, and she often danced with an imaginary partner as the sun went down on warm evenings. It always intrigued me because there was such a difference between the knife-wielding, football-stabbing, spell-casting evil witch the villagers spoke about and the woman in a floaty dress who used to sway around her rooftop garden.

'So, long story short, the best way to take back control of my life *has* to be getting a job so I can save up for a deposit and find my own place to live. It's really humiliating to be thirty-six and have your life together, to be proud of turning a love of candles into a business, and then for it all to go tits-up, and have to turn up on your mum's doorstep and beg to stay. Maybe I can learn a thing or two from you. Bees have it together, don't they? They don't fall for dishonest men who take everything and leave them with nothing. I will learn everything I can about you and be the best beekeeper you've ever had.'

The last one is pushing it a bit, if I'm honest.

'Thank you for listening, bees.' I decide to be polite. I've no idea if bees respond to manners, but I'll err on the side of caution.

The buzzing is continual, the bees seemingly unaffected by my presence or rambling introduction. I stand and watch for a while, unsure of what else to do when faced with so many hives. I can't begin to imagine the number of bees in each house-shaped box.

24

I'm going to have to familiarise myself with all of this, and fast. There's a honey harvest due, and if Gracie's expecting the first jars on Friday, that gives me less than three days to *become* a beekeeper.

I go across to the shed. 'Elderflower Grove Honey House' is etched on the door, and when I use my key and let myself in, it's quite possibly the thing that has surprised me the most so far today.

It's a small-scale honey production factory. A long building with a low ceiling, shelves around the walls and a worktop going around the room. There are bright overhead lights and a sink with running water, and the worktop is littered with tools and equipment, like someone left in a rush.

I walk around with the book in hand, attempting to match up which tools are which by comparing them to the photos on the pages. There's a big extractor and various knives and scrapers, and boxes upon boxes of new honey jars, sterile and sealed, ready for the next harvest.

I read what you're supposed to do for a hive inspection and pick up the smoker – a bellows attached to a fire chamber, used to puff smoke into the hive before you open it to make the bees more docile while you work. If I'd ever thought it might be scary to be alone in an overgrown estate the size of Elderflower Grove, as I stand there and scan the book for instructions on how to use something so simple, I'm immensely grateful for my solitude.

I pick up torn cardboard and set a match to it in the smoker, and once it's burning and I've added a handful of wood shavings, I take that and a hive tool, which looks like a big metal spatula with a hook on one end, and cautiously approach the nearest hive, paranoid that I've missed a gap in my suit and the bees will be lining up to sting me.

I squeeze three puffs of smoke into the entrance hole of the hive and give it a couple of minutes to work before I lift the roof from the wooden box. Inside I'm greeted by a crown board with a few bees walking across it, and I have to prise that off with the hive tool because the bees have glued everything together with propolis, a sticky substance they produce to plug holes and keep the hive secure. Under that is the first honey super – a box that holds nine wooden frames, and I can't help the intake of breath at the sheer number of bees. I knew there'd be a lot, but there must be thousands here … *tens* of thousands, even, and if each hive houses a similar amount … the maths is un-doable and overwhelming. That is a *lot* of bees.

Despite the smoke, the bees are everywhere, crawling all over my hands, up my arms, buzzing around my face, and I fight the urge to bat them away. Most people's natural instinct when a stinging insect gets too close is to flap and run, and I have to force myself to remain calm. People do this for fun. Beekeeping is a supposedly relaxing hobby. They die if they sting, I know that much. They don't want to sting me any more than I want them to.

'Good morning, ladies.' According to the book, the male bees will be in the lower level of the hive attending the queen, and the ones in this layer will be mostly female workers. 'Don't mean you any harm, just having a look at how this all works. So I take out the frames one at a time …' I talk to myself as I loosen the first frame with the hive tool, urging bees out of the way as I prise it free, surprised by the weight when I grip it at both sides and pull it out of the box.

'Flipping 'eck, you lot have been busy.'

The frame is absolutely loaded with sealed honeycomb, so much so that it's hanging from the bottom like humongous waxy icicles. I thought the sight of *so* many bees would give me the heebie-jeebies, but I watch in fascination as they carry on sealing more honeycomb, meaning the honey inside is ready.

Eventually I slide it back into place and lift the honey super away to look into the lower level of the hive. There's a separator grid that stops the queen getting into the upper level, so she can lay her eggs down here, and the honey is stored above.

I'm doing a hive inspection without even realising. I'm trying to familiarise myself with everything about beehives, but I've got the book open and it shows me what I should be looking out for, and I get quite excited when I spot capped brood about to hatch and eggs in the honeycomb cells. The queen bee is obviously at home, but I'm not experienced enough to recognise her.

I put the hive back together and move to the next one. It looks the same. Just as healthy and just as lively. I inspect hive after hive, choosing a random few in each row rather than doing the whole lot. I puff the smoke around and pull out frame after frame thronging with bees, looking for deformed wings or signs of mites or disease, but either they're all healthy or I don't know what I'm looking for.

Sixty hives is too many to inspect in one day. It's probably a bit like painting the Forth Bridge and if I start at one end, it'll take me all week, and by the time I'm done, the first one will need doing again.

Instead, I brush off the few bees that are walking across my suit and take my beekeeping bible back to the bench to read up on how to extract the honey, but the call of the door at the far side of the roof has been getting louder.

It's time for a break anyway, and I could go and have a look, couldn't I? I'm *sure* it will be locked, but it wouldn't hurt to check … I'm not doing any harm or breaking any rules by checking the security of a door … Like when you buy hot cross buns in January to 'check' their suitability before Easter arrives, and then do it every week just to be sure.

My footsteps sound hollow as I get further away from the beehives and the constant buzz diminishes. The door is old and looks like it's been a decent snack for several hungry generations of woodworm. I push against it and rattle the handle, but it is, indeed, locked. Disappointed, I go to walk away, but the lock glints in the sunlight and catches my eye. It's a remarkably modern lock for a door that looks like it's been here since Edwardian times …

like it's been replaced in recent years … It looks like the same lock on the Honey House door. I try my key in it, and let out a gasp of surprise when it opens.

Whoever replaced the Honey House door must've replaced this one at the same time … with the same lock. Hurrah! I mean … no, that's bad, isn't it? Terrible security. It's a good job I found out, really. Someone should be told. But … the open door gives nothing away. It leads into a stairwell that smells musty and damp. I duck my head in a bit further, hoping my eyes will adjust to the darkness inside.

'Hello?' I call quietly, my voice echoing through the empty stone tower with a staircase that spirals down. Unsurprisingly, I get no response.

I should leave it alone, I know that. I've been told not to go inside, but the thought of what this old manor might be hiding is overpowering. With the rumours that have always swirled around Elderflower Grove, I've wanted to see inside for years. I could just have a little peek, couldn't I? No one's going to know … There are only a few bees here to see me, and they're not going to tell anyone, are they?

Chapter 3

*Bees communicate through a waggle dance. When
a worker bee has found a good source of pollen, she
returns to the hive and dances in a figure of eight,
waggling her abdomen to show the other bees where to
go in terms of distance, direction, and position of the sun.*

The staircase is narrow and cold, and each footstep sounds like a boom as I go downwards. I run my fingers along dusty stone walls, disturbing cobwebs and sending woodlice scuttling for cover, until I come to another door. Surely this one will be locked, and all my dreams of seeing what Elderflower Grove looks like inside are about to turn into dust, but when I reach the wooden door, swollen with dampness but not locked, the handle turns and opens with a bit of gentle persuasion. I blink in surprise when I emerge onto a bright landing. The daylight that was missing from the tower returns, the broken windows letting in the late-May sun and flooding the building with light.

The landing area is huge, a faded red carpet, a grandfather clock at one wall, and doors that lead to rooms unknown. Every step sends dust motes dancing in the sunshine as I walk over to the window and peer out. I'm on the third floor and there isn't any sign of fire damage this far up. It just looks like an old house that hasn't been cleaned in many, many years.

'Hello?' I call out again. Why do I keep saying that? Who do I think is in here? Am I announcing my presence to the ghosts? It just seems weird to enter a house without a greeting, even if it is empty.

I push open the nearest door and discover it leads to a bedroom. The lavish four-poster bed in the middle of the room, covered by a pink damask bedspread, must have been Josie Garringham's when she was alive. A chaise longue sits at the opposite end and the walls, a sumptuous deep pink colour, are lined with gold-framed oil paintings showing landscape scenes. There's an ornate wardrobe that's so much like the singing one in *Beauty and the Beast* that I watch it for a moment in case it *is* about to burst into song.

It feels like an intrusion being here though. From what I know of Josie Garringham, she was a blisteringly private woman, and whether she's alive or dead now, she wouldn't want me in her bedroom.

The next room reveals a bathroom, big and tiled, with a luxurious Victorian-style claw-foot bathtub and cupboards full of products that are no longer made. M&S soaps with faded labels. Tiny bottles of shampoo and body creams, the kind of thing you'd have got your grandma for Christmas when you were a child in the Nineties and she'd have been overjoyed with, even though she already had seven unused M&S floral gift sets from previous years.

My fingers leave marks in the dust on the banister as I descend the next flight of stairs. When I come to a corner, I turn twice before arriving on the second floor. I'm in a huge banquet hall. The floor is tiled in what was probably once black and white, and I have to scrape the toe of my boot through the grime to confirm the floor tiles are diamond-patterned and grouted with gold. There's a long dining table down the centre, big enough that you could have the entire village over for dinner if you were so inclined. A heavy silk table runner, so dusty that it looks more grey than the cream it once was, leads to two place settings, opposite each other. A dainty plate, a cup and saucer, cutlery, all laid out like Josie was waiting for someone else to join her and that person never came. It's like something Pip would find in Miss Havisham's house and it makes me shiver, and not *just* because I accidentally knock the table runner and I'm unsure what might run out after so many years of not being disturbed, but it would undoubtedly have eight legs.

There's a piano in one corner, and two huge archways lead through to a ballroom. It's exactly the sort of place you'd expect to see a blue-suited Beast spinning around Belle in her yellow dress. There are columns around the edges, supporting a domed ceiling with a mural painted on it. There's sweeping gold decorative mouldings and more gold-framed pictures lining burgundy walls, brightened by the huge windows. Three chandeliers hang at equal intervals across the room that's so enormous, you could do with hopping on a bus to reach the other side. One of the chandeliers is hanging at a haphazard angle that suggests it could fall down at any moment and I fear that my footsteps might be the final nail in its coffin. I imagine it in its heyday, a glitzy ballroom where Elizabeth Bennet and Mr Darcy are doing a stiff Regency dance. This is so much like a Jane Austen novel that it makes me tingle. Scenes from every TV adaptation I've ever seen could've been filmed here.

Between the banquet hall and the ballroom, there's a grand staircase going downwards. The wood is burnt, and I'm not certain my foot won't plunge straight through it with every step, but I'm almost relieved to find some hint of the fire that took hold of Elderflower Grove all those years ago. From how bad it looked that night to the severe warnings I've had to stay outside, I was expecting so much worse, and from the upper floors and the roof, it doesn't seem like there ever was a fire.

At the bottom of the staircase, the house changes again. Far from the glitz and glamour that was once upstairs, this feels like a cosy home, and I can see the dark shadows of soot stains on the walls and the flame-licked remnants of floral wallpaper and singed remains of what once were carpets.

I'm not sure whereabouts I am in the house. Somewhere at the centre of the ground floor because there's only a hint of daylight filtering in from either end of a long and narrow hallway, and it's so dark and dingy that I could easily believe I'd bypassed the ground floor and was in the basement level.

The hallway leads into what must have been a living room. There's a marble fireplace along one wall, with the metal frame of a broken mirror above it, and there are skeletons of burnt armchairs and a couple of sofas gathered in front of the fireplace, an exploded TV on a melted and twisted stand near it. Picture frames hang on the walls, but whatever was inside them didn't survive the fire.

The living room makes me sad so I continue on, and then come to such an abrupt halt that I nearly trip over my own feet and have to grab the bare plaster sides of the doorframe to stay upright.

There's a body on the floor.

I go to scream but the oxygen has left my lungs so fast that no sound comes out. Oh my god. It's going to be Josie Garringham, isn't it? Her dead body. I've never seen a dead body before and I *really* had no desire to start now. I go to clamp my hand over my mouth but it gets tangled in the beekeeping veil I've forgotten I still have on.

What am I going to do? I'll have to call the police, and then they'll know I've been inside. *Everyone* will know I've been inside and I'll lose my new job before I've even begun. All because I'm too nosy to keep my head out of places where it doesn't belong. Why did I come in here? This is the *last* thing I wanted to see.

Maybe it's *not* a body. It's a human-shaped pile of ripped-up carpets or something. My foot scuffs against the concrete floor

– the carpets *have* been pulled up in this room. I'm going to look a right fool calling the police to report a pile of carpets.

I tiptoe back into the room I've just come from, looking for something I can use to make sure. I spot a smoke-blackened companion set on the edge of the hearth and carefully extract the fire poker. That'll do.

I creep back towards the body. It *can't* be a body. Rescue crews searched the house top to bottom after the fire – there's no way they would've missed it. It's my imagination playing tricks on me. I'm expecting ghosts and ghouls and I'm inventing my own horror movie, like some macabre version of seeing clouds in the shape of Scooby-Doo.

A body would smell, right? It's definitely going to be a rolled-up carpet that someone's thrown a sheet over, and I tell myself to stop being so ridiculous as I approach the body-shaped lump on knocking knees, my hand trembling as I use the fire poker to push at it.

I don't know which one of us screams louder – me or the man who wakes up with such a start that he falls off what I now realise is a mattress.

It's not a dead body. Someone's actually here. Asleep. At three o'clock in the afternoon. My mind rushes through scenario after scenario of who this could be, but it can only be something bad. A drug addict, perhaps. A murderer on the run. A rapist hiding out. Some sort of escaped criminal or someone running a drugs gang. An actual ghost?

A ghost would be the preferable option.

I picked up my bag before I came in, thinking I should have my phone on me in case the building fell down around my ears and I got trapped, and I can feel the weight of the beekeeping book against my hip. I grab it instinctively and brandish it at him, waving the fire poker in front of me. 'Who are you and what are you doing here?' I think I sound confident and self-assured, but I probably sound shaky and a bit squeaky.

His lower half is encased in a zipped-up sleeping bag, and he stumbles to get to his feet and slips again, scrambling backwards on the floor to get away from me.

'Don't hurt me! Take whatever you want! What are you? Some kind of ... monster?' He scrubs a hand over his face. His body is heaving from the shock and he's panting for breath. 'Are you ... human?'

'Yes!' I snap, offended at the idea I might not be. 'Who are you? Are you ... alive?'

'I was last time I checked, but now I'm starting to wonder.' His hand is on his chest, clearly trying to will his heart rate into slowing down. 'You can't sneak up on someone in a haunted house!'

'I thought you were dead!'

'Do dead people usually have a nightlight and a good book?' He gestures angrily towards the things on the floor beside the mattress.

'I don't know, I've never seen a dead person before!'

'Wait ...' His eyes run over me as he blinks himself awake. 'Are you the new beekeeper?'

'No! I always walk around like this for the fun of it. Like carrying around your own personal sauna on a daily basis. Of course I'm the beekeeper, why *else* would I be dressed like this?'

'You weren't supposed to come inside!'

'You weren't supposed to *be* inside!'

'So what are you going to do? Brain me with a fire poker and a copy of ...' He squints at the book in my hand. '*A Complete Idiot's Guide to Beekeeping*?'

My heart was already pounding from the adrenaline, but now it's pounding for an altogether different reason.

'I thought you were ... I mean, I thought they'd get an expert, not an ...' He trails off before openly suggesting I might be an idiot.

I look between him and the book. 'It's a good-luck charm!'

I'm so excited at thinking up a good excuse that I nearly drop the poker. 'It got me my first job as a beekeeper and now I carry it around to all new jobs for good luck.'

Adrenaline must make me think fast or something. Usually it takes me a good couple of weeks to come up with a clever retort.

Even in the dark and through the beekeeper's veil, I can see that he's giving me a doubtful look.

'Never mind all that. Who are you and what are you doing in here?' I ask again.

'I'm not doing anything wrong. I have a legitimate reason for being here.' He holds his hand against the back of his head like I've already hit him. 'Can you put down the fire poker? You're scaring me and, quite frankly, you seem a little unhinged.'

'*I* seem a little unhinged?' I screech, sounding quite unhinged. 'I've just stumbled across you sleeping in an abandoned haunted mansion at three o'clock in the afternoon! What are you – a drunk? An addict? A squatter? A murderer on the run?'

'None of the above. Can you put down the deadly weapon? I'm not going to hurt you, I swear.'

'That's exactly what someone who was going to hurt me would say!'

'I'm trapped inside a sleeping bag and you've terrified me half to death, but *you're* the one who needs self-defence.'

'I'm alone on an abandoned estate with a stranger who's obviously up to no good, where no one can hear me scream!' I realise before the end of the sentence that reiterating that to a potential murderer may not have been the *best* plan.

He's still panting for breath and his chest is *still* heaving. I really did frighten the life out of him.

He pinches the bridge of his nose. 'Yeah, you're absolutely right. I'm sorry. I realise how this must look, but I mean you absolutely no harm.'

I go to speak but he cuts me off. 'I know, I know, that's exactly what someone who did mean you harm would say. What I mean

35

is … Look, there's a light switch right around this corner, will you let me get out of this sleeping bag and put a light on without inserting that into my spinal cord?'

His seriousness almost makes me laugh, but I take a step backwards and nod.

He's still sitting on the floor, and he leans forward to unzip the bag around his legs and pushes himself upright. Leaving one foot in the room, he leans around the wall until there's the click of a switch and the room is lit up by the yellowy light of a bare bulb hanging from the ceiling.

He peers back around the wall, looking wary, and when he steps back into the light …

If Elderflower Grove really is anything like the Beast's castle, the enchantress has got here early and turned him back into a prince.

He's tall with light eyes, a clean-shaven, smooth jawline, and light brown hair that's long enough to flop to one side. The lack of sleeping bag reveals bare feet, black jogging bottoms, and a T-shirt with *The Wombles* on it. The randomness of it makes me start giggling and now I really *do* sound unhinged. I can feel some of my fear and adrenaline slipping away. It's almost impossible to feel threatened by a man wearing a Wombles T-shirt.

'I think we got off on the wrong foot,' he says cautiously. 'I'm Carey. Carey Paxton. I honestly don't mean any harm and I'm not doing anything wrong by being here. I didn't mean to sound so harsh, but I've never been on the verge of a heart attack before and I'm still ninety-five per cent sure I'm about to have one.'

His face does look pale and when he holds a hand out in front of him, it's shaking.

'I'm sorry. I thought you were a pile of carpets.' I tuck the book under one arm and unzip my hood and push it back. 'Kayleigh Harwood. The new beekeeper.'

'You haven't brought any of those sting-y little blighters inside, have you?' He flaps a hand around, his eyes darting to every corner of the room.

'What do I look like? Some Pied Piper of the insect world? Where I go, the bees will follow?'

'They'll hide in your folds!'

I raise an eyebrow and he goes red.

'Of your suit! They'll crawl and swarm all over you!' He shudders.

'There are no windows. The bees could get in anywhere.'

'The bees and I have got an understanding. They don't come inside the house and I don't go near them. I give them space, they give me space. If they don't sting me, they don't die. That's the fairest thing you can say to a bee – no stinging, no death.'

'You don't like them?'

'No, I'm absolutely terrified of them. Scared to death.'

'This is not the ideal place for you to stay then,' I say, but his honesty intrigues me. 'You could've just told me you were allergic or something.'

His eyes narrow. 'Why would I say something that's not true? I'm scared of bees, end of story.'

'I don't know. Most men don't admit to stuff like that.' I shake my head at myself. 'I'm sorry, I'm not used to men being honest with me. It's … refreshing.'

He tilts his head to the side, the light catching on natural highlights in his straight hair. 'Kayleigh, I have no wish to pretend to be something I'm not. I have nothing to gain by trying to be all macho and unafraid. I'm scared of those little fuzzy creatures that you obviously love. You bringing bees in here with you would be the icing on top of a very crappy cake of a morning. Afternoon. Ugh.' He rubs a hand over his face again. 'I'm sorry. I'm totally discombobulated after that. I think I'm still in the middle of a nightmare about veiled monsters and bees. Wake up, Carey.' He slaps his own cheek and overbalances, stumbling against the wall.

I actually feel a bit sorry for him. He doesn't seem like he's any kind of threat and if I'd realised he *wasn't* either dead or a rolled-up carpet, I'd have been nicer about waking him up. 'Why are you asleep in the middle of the afternoon?'

'I was working last night.' He hesitates. 'Here. On this place. I've been doing a bit of work to make it liveable, and I knew I wouldn't be able to make any noise because you were starting, so I worked all night and thought I could catch up on sleep undisturbed today. Which, obviously, went *so* well. What is it with you beekeepers always poking around where you're not meant to be? Is there something about the job that makes you exceptionally nosy people or what?'

'Did the last beekeeper come in here too? The one who was chased off by a possessed wheelie bin?'

He bursts out laughing and drops his head into his hands. '*How* do people know about that?'

Things suddenly start to make sense. 'Did you have something to do with that? It wasn't ghosts at all, it was *you*?'

He goes to protest and then holds his hands up and sighs. 'Yeah, it was me. Bit of writing on a mirror, the rubbish bin on a string of fishing line. It worked a treat. I'm surprised the woman wasn't back here the next day with the *Most Haunted* team.'

'By all accounts, that poor woman is leaving the country because you scared her so much. Why would you do that?' I think about it. 'Is that what you're going to do to me? Pretend to be a ghost and scare me into leaving?'

'No, of course not.' He glances at me. 'It loses its appeal if the person knows. What's the point in pretending to be a ghost pretending not to be a ghost? Even I don't understand what I just said, which proves how pointless it is.'

'That's good. I think. But *that's* not. That's a *really* horrible thing to do.' I tighten my grip on the poker. Maybe Wombles T-shirts can be deceiving after all.

'There are two sides to every story.' He sighs and leans against the wall. 'The last beekeeper was stealing. I caught her going through the bedrooms upstairs, turning out Josie Garringham's jewellery boxes and pocketing anything that looked valuable. She didn't see me, so I dived into the bathroom she was sure to ransack next; there are still toiletries in the cupboards so I wrote on the mirror in lipstick, saying to give back what she'd stolen, did a bit of banging the pipes and clattering like an angry ghost might, and she burst into tears, emptied her pockets, and ran away screaming. The wheelie bin was just for fun.'

'Well, that changes things. An angry ghost with a sense of humour.'

He grins. 'I know it wasn't very nice, but what was I supposed to do? Let her get away with it? Let her take a whole load of stuff that wasn't hers and come back next time for more? People like that don't belong here.'

'When you put it like that …'

'I take it the gossip mill hasn't heard *that* side of the story.'

I shake my head. His accent is local. English. Well-spoken. A nice, soft voice. 'If you're homeless, there are charities that can help …'

'I have a home. I'm about forty minutes that way.' He waves a finger over his shoulder in the opposite direction from where my mum's house is.

'If you're not homeless and you're not an escaped convict hiding out, what are you do—'

'Look, I can't tell anyone you're here because I'm not supposed to be here, and you can't tell anyone I'm here because you're not supposed to be here either, so can we just … be not supposed to be here in our trespassing solitudes? I won't tell anyone you've been poking around and you won't tell anyone you've seen me, and that's the end of it.'

'No.' I fold my arms, which is a seriously impressive feat with a book tucked under one arm and a poker in the other hand. 'And I wasn't poking around. I've always felt drawn to Elderflower Grove and I wanted to see what it was like inside. I'm not doing any harm.'

'Neither am I.'

'So what *are* you doing then?' Now the light is on, and I don't feel like he's about to imminently attack me, I look around the room. It's not part of the main living room I came through, it's more like a part of the hallway but wider, carefully positioned to be away from any windows. There's a rucksack and a couple of holdall bags in one corner, and an armchair with clothes laid out across it like they've just come in from the washing line. It's also clean. Other rooms I've seen so far are dusty and cobwebby, but not this one. 'You've been here for a while …' I deduce. 'And you said you were doing work on the place?'

He sighs. His hair is mussed-up from sleeping and he shoves a hand through it, smoothing it down. 'It's a long and complicated story, and I'll tell you, but I *really* need a cuppa. Do you want one?'

Of all the ways I expected this confrontation to go, this was certainly not one of them.

He holds both hands up again. 'I'll keep my distance and you can keep your fire poker. The kitchen's just through there.' He points to a closed door on the left. He sounds defeated and he looks tired – more tired than the unexpected wake-up call would've left him – and everything he's said so far intrigues me, and I couldn't say no if I wanted to.

He wedges the door open and flicks on a light to illuminate the big room, and goes across to the far unit to pick up the kettle and fill it. I follow him into what could best be described as a retro kitchen. It's got faded lino flooring, brown veneered cupboards, and a big island in the middle with stools along two sides of it. There's wallpaper peeling from the walls and mould stains in the corners, but it's obviously lived in. A fruit bowl is piled high with apples and oranges in the centre of the island, and next to the kettle is a box of teabags, a jar of instant coffee, latte sachets, and a sugar bowl. A fridge-freezer is humming in one corner, and there's an old-fashioned microwave on the unit, and an upside-down cereal bowl and spoon on the draining board.

'Are you actually living here?'

'Kind of.' He speaks over his shoulder without turning away from making the drinks. 'Temporarily.'

I partially unzip the bee suit to loosen it and sit down on one of the stools nearest the door, where I can keep my eyes on him at all times, but instead of on him, I find myself looking longingly at the fruit bowl. I didn't have the forethought to bring lunch with me, and the adrenaline of the last half-hour has dissipated and left me feeling exhausted and absolutely starving.

Carey finishes clinking the spoon against the mugs and throws it into the washing-up bowl. He carries both mugs across to the island, and like he can read my mind, he returns to get a packet of biscuits out of a cupboard and puts that down on the island countertop and rolls it across to me.

Do murderers offer tea and biscuits? I wasn't intending to put the fire poker down, but I slide it onto the unit beside me, still within easy grabbing reach, but the tea and biscuits combined with the Wombles T-shirt make me feel utterly unthreatened despite the circumstances.

I tear into the packet of chocolate Digestives like a wild animal, shoving the first one into my mouth whole, as he sits down on the opposite side of the island, leaving a wide distance between us.

'Thank you,' I say guiltily, putting my hand up to cover my full mouth. 'I hadn't brought any lunch. I was starving.'

'So I see.' He raises an eyebrow.

I take another biscuit and push the packet across the island to him. He takes a biscuit, snaps it in half, and dunks it in his tea.

Potential murderers definitely don't dunk biscuits. He takes another one and pushes the packet back towards me. My eyes fall on a closed laptop on the other side of the island and an official-looking document folder. I reach out and pull the file towards me and lift the cover.

Carey doesn't say anything or try to stop me.

A photocopied picture of Josie Garringham stares out at me,

and underneath is a police report in tiny print, and some photos of the building.

More things start to make sense. 'Are you a private investigator? Here to find out what really happened to Josie Garringham?'

'No. Not really.'

'Then why do you have this?' I tap the file.

'Friends in the right places?' He rubs the back of his neck awkwardly and answers like it's more of a question than an answer. 'If I tell you, it *has* to stay a secret. I can't have anyone knowing I'm here, or why. I'm not kidding, Kayleigh. You know what people are like in this village. Gossip is a more important life source than oxygen. This has to stay between us. You can't tell *anyone*.'

He seems serious and genuinely concerned.

'I won't. I haven't long moved back here and everyone knows everything about my life. I have no wish to be part of that gossip-mongering. Whatever you're doing is up to you, as long as it's nothing evil. Or illegal,' I add as an afterthought.

He might be good at making tea and adept at seeing off light-fingered beekeepers, but he could still be running a drugs gang or some kind of money-laundering operation from the abandoned manor house.

'I think Josie Garringham might've been my grandmother.'

I choke on the tea I've just made the mistake of sipping. 'Seriously? She didn't have any family, did she?'

'I don't know. I mean, not that we know of, but … it's a long story. The short version is that my father was adopted when he was a baby. He had a wonderful adoptive family, my grandma and granddad are both long gone now, but they were incredible people. He'd never known any other parents. It was never an issue within the family, and he quickly shut down any rare mention of his birth family because he had no interest in who he was born to. As far as he was concerned, they hadn't wanted him and his parents were his parents, and that was the end of it. He died last September.'

'I'm sorry.'

He gives me a gentle smile. 'It had always fascinated me. I'd often pestered him to tell me what he knew of his birth parents, but he wouldn't speak of it. He felt it would be disrespectful to my grandma and granddad to even think about it. They were his parents and he never wanted them to think he considered that they weren't – does that make sense?'

I nod.

'He got very reflective in his last few weeks. On his last day, he admitted the one thing he'd always regretted was not finding his birth mother. He told me that the only thing he knew about her was that she was an eccentric beekeeper from Hampshire.'

'And you think that could be Josie Garringham? It's kind of a tenuous link.'

'I know.' He pulls the biscuit packet closer, takes another one, and pushes it back towards me. 'But I've always felt a pull towards Elderflower Grove. Every time I'm in this area, I find myself standing outside looking in, wondering what secrets it hides. And let's face it, the only thing anyone really knows about Josie Garringham is that she was eccentric, was from Hampshire, and kept bees. I put two and two together and got … probably not four, but … I don't know. I thought maybe there's a reason I've always felt drawn to this place. It made more sense when I thought about it, but you're the first person I've had to say it aloud to. There must be hundreds of beekeepers in Hampshire. I'm clutching at straws, I know, but I have to follow this hunch while there's still time.'

'You know they think she could still be alive, right?'

'I've heard, yes.'

'They think she might be secretly running the Nectar Inspectors group.'

One of his eyebrows goes up and the other one goes down. 'That would be *very* impossible.'

'Her body was never found. She could've got away.'

43

'Kayleigh, you do realise she was ninety-two years old at the time of the fire, right? She was alone in this huge house and it burnt down around her. It was late at night – the police report suggests she was in bed and was probably overcome with smoke inhalation before she even realised what was happening. It started through there.' He points to his right, an area at the back of the house I haven't got around to exploring yet. 'It was Bonfire Night. The remains of a firework were found inside a broken window. Kids playing tricks on the "old witch" of the village.'

'But the bedrooms on the third floor are untouched by fire damage. If that's true, her body would've been easily discoverable. And the house *didn't* "burn down around her" as evidenced by the fact we're sitting *in* the house. And from what I've seen so far, it seems remarkably undamaged, considering. There's more damage from the water used to put the fire *out*.'

His mouth opens and then closes. It opens again but nothing comes out.

'Even her best friend thinks it's possible.'

'Do you know, you've actually got a point about the damage. It's much less severe than I thought it would be. That end of the house is worse.' He inclines his head to the right again. 'Part of the roof collapsed and caved in the rooms beneath it, but the fire was caught before it did much more damage.'

'I know. It was me who called the fire brigade that night.'

He does a double-take. 'Seriously?'

'I can see the roof of the house from my window. It was hard to get the operator to listen because it was Bonfire Night, they thought it was a hoax.'

'And now you're working here. That's a weird full-circle thing, right?'

'The point is, I watched the police crawling all over this place for days afterwards. Surely they would've found something.'

He shrugs and takes another biscuit and pushes the packet back towards me. 'I can honestly say I've never given it much

44

thought. It's well-known that she died in the fire. The key fact the Nectar Inspectors are missing is that *if* she did somehow survive, where is she? Why hasn't she been heard from in the years since? Everything ceased that night. There's no more use of her bank account, no sightings, no elderly ladies who have lost their memories in nearby hospitals or whatever other fairy-stories you're dreaming up. It's tragic, but those are the facts of the case. She vanished on the night her house burnt down. It's not a stretch to believe she died in the fire. No remains being found doesn't mean she survived – it means they just haven't been found *yet*.'

'Is that what you're doing then? Looking for the body?'

'Noooo.' He half-laughs and half-shudders. 'Nothing that macabre, thankfully. I'm looking for evidence that she might've been my biological grandmother. Paperwork or something – anything to suggest she had a child who she gave up for adoption in 1947.'

'Have you found anything?'

He shakes his head. 'There's nothing lying around, but there wouldn't be, would there? Information like that would be hidden, and the house seems, I don't know, closed off, I guess. It doesn't want to share its secrets with me.'

'So you're going to stay here until you find something?'

'It's my last chance. I had to do *something* this summer, and it's forty minutes each way. That's valuable time wasted commuting when I could spend it searching. It's easier to stay. I didn't fancy it earlier in the year, but the weather's nice no—'

'What do you mean by it's your last chance?' I connect it with something he said before. 'And earlier you said something about while there's still time. You're not dying, are you?'

'I'm not, but Elderflower Grove is.'

'What?'

'Oh, hell.' His blue eyes go wide as he looks at me. 'I wasn't supposed to say that. Can you pretend you didn't hear that?'

He looks like he knows that's as unlikely as James Corden *not* being cast in the next movie-musical adaptation that hits our screens.

'Are you kidding me? No, I can *not*. What do you mean?'

He groans and drops his head into his hands and then clonks it down onto the table. 'I *really* wasn't supposed to say that. I'm going to be in a *ridiculous* amount of trouble if this gets out.' His words are muffled where he hasn't lifted his head yet.

'I won't tell anyone.'

He groans again, and raises his head enough for his eyes to shift to the fire poker. 'And if I don't explain myself, you're going to insert that in somewhere I don't want it inserted, right?'

It makes me laugh out loud, despite the feeling of unease that's settled in my stomach at his words. Whatever he means, it can't be anything good. 'Well, now you've suggested it ...'

My fingers jokingly creep towards the poker and he laughs and sits back upright. 'Okay, I'm pleading with you here. Kayleigh, you *can't* tell anyone this. Not a soul. You can't even *think* about it in public in case there are any mind-readers about.'

I'm sure he's joking on the last point, but it makes me worry about what on earth he knows. He must have friends in more than one right place.

His fingers massage his forehead, and he really does look annoyed at himself for saying too much.

'I won't tell anyone. I have no friends here. No loyalty to anyone except my mum, and she couldn't care less about Elderflower Grove. I hate the way gossip spreads in this village. I get looks of pity from people I've never even met, who have no business knowing *my* business. I don't want to be part of sharing anyone else's business with people who have no business knowing it in the first place.'

Way to go, Kayleigh. Make the gorgeous man think you're a complete and total friendless loser and rabbit on using the word 'business' twenty-six times in the same sentence. He'll probably

46

trust me not to share his secrets because I can barely string a sentence together.

His mouth has moved into a half-smile as he watches me, and I attempt to give him a smile back, because I am *not* leaving this room without knowing what he meant. Even if it means getting creative with the fire poker.

He pushes a hand through his hair, worry lines crinkling across his forehead. 'This November will be seven years since the fire.' Even his voice has dropped, like there's a possibility of someone overhearing us.

'Okay,' I say when he pauses like he's waiting for me to get it.

'When a person has been missing for seven years, they can be officially declared dead. With no family and no heirs to inherit it, the land Elderflower Grove stands on will be handed back to the local council.'

'Okay …' I say again, slowly this time, like I'm missing something.

He sighs. 'They're intending to knock it down and build a theme park.'

'What?' I say in horror. 'They can't do that! It isn't theirs!'

'It will be – that's the point. When Josie Garringham is declared dead, the land will become theirs to do what they want with.'

'But … but …' This is *awful*. I had no idea something like this could happen. 'But who would build a theme park here? Who would *want* a theme park here? What kind of a theme park?'

'An Alton Towers–type place, as far as I know.'

I make a noise of horror. 'But this is Hampshire! It's quiet and green and leafy! This is Jane Austen country. Jane Austen doesn't want a rollercoaster full of people screaming past her as she walks down the road, does she?'

His blue eyes are shining with amusement. 'I don't think Jane Austen's opinion is hugely valued when it comes to making planning permission decisions. We're a couple of hundred years too late for it to count for much.'

I give him a scathing look. 'You know what I mean. This is a tiny, peaceful village. A theme park doesn't belong here. If they're going to do anything with Elderflower Grove, it should be to restore it and open it up to the public. People pay to visit stately homes like this. A nose around the house, a wander round the gardens, a picnic by the lake. Why on earth would they want to destroy this beautiful place and put in a horrible theme park?'

'Because it's profitable, obviously. I'm totally with you, the thought of it is abhorrent, but the council aren't going to make much money through whatever small entry fee they could charge if they kept it as it is, but they're going to make a shedload of money from a theme park, and it'll be a hell of a lot easier to flatten the land and rebuild something big and flashy than it would be to restore and maintain this. They've already got "donations" from companies wanting to buy in.' He does the inverted quotes.

'That's bribery!'

'Keep your voice down. No matter how horrified you are, you're not supposed to know.'

'They can't do that. This place is beautiful. How could they want to destroy it?' It's a rhetorical question, of course. Like everything else, these things are decided by people in fancy offices who only see figures on a spreadsheet, not the lush greenery teeming with wildlife they'd see if they came here. 'What are they going to do with the bees?'

'Move them, I would think. Probably sell them to some commercial honey manufacturer looking to expand their apiary.'

I sigh. 'At least that explains why my job is strictly one season only. I couldn't get my head around that, but whoever that bee is, it obviously knows this too.'

'What bee?'

'Job interview.' I go to explain and then wave my hand instead. 'Don't worry about it. The point is that we have to do something.'

'There's nothing we *can* do. This has been planned for many years.'

48

'You!'

He looks alarmed. 'Me what?'

'*That's* why you're here! If you're Josie Garringham's grandson, *you're* the heir! *You* inherit all of this.'

He puts both his hands up and pushes his stool back like I've got the fire poker trained on him again. 'Woah, woah, woah. It's nothing to do with that. I'm not interested in any inheritance. All I want is proof of whether my hunch is right. It's not about anything else. I know how unlikely that sounds, but it *is* the truth. All I want from this place is what it can tell me about someone who I think was my grandmother, because come November, everything inside Elderflower Grove will be destroyed.'

We hold eye contact for a long few moments across the table, and I feel a little bit guilty for thinking the worst of him. 'But it *is* right though, isn't it? If you are Josie Garringham's grandson, you *will* inherit this place. Do you want to build a theme park here?'

'God, no. Never. What this place needs is someone to love and care for it.'

Somewhere above us, a pipe contracts inside a wall and makes a banging sound. Our eyes meet again and we both let out a nervous giggle.

'I think the house agrees with you,' I say, laughing until we turn serious again. 'In that case, I *really* hope you're her grandson, Carey. It would be unthinkable for anyone to shove a theme park in place of this beautiful estate.'

He looks awkward and uncomfortable, and I'm not a hundred per cent sure I trust him. I can't imagine how much a manor house with grounds like these must be worth, but it's a *lot*. There isn't much someone *wouldn't* say to secure themselves that kind of windfall, but at the same time, there's something genuine about him. Something quiet and trustworthy.

'What have you found so far?'

'Dead mice, mainly.' He makes a face. 'And the occasional living one. I'm not sure which is preferable.'

49

It makes me laugh again. 'I'm serious. You've been here a while, what have you found?'

'Nothing. I've been concentrating on making it liveable. As in, cleaning the kitchen and living area.' He waves a hand towards the room we came from. 'The electrics down here needed some work, and the plumbing leaves much to be desired, and I've been looking around. I found blueprints of the house, but most of the rooms are closed off, doors swollen shut with dampness and I can't get them open, no matter how hard I try.'

'Have you seen any ghosts?'

He laughs. 'No. And I don't think I'd be staying if I had.'

'So you're scared of ghosts and bees and you choose to stay in a haunted house with sixty beehives on the roof …'

'Well, when you put it like that …' He repeats my words from earlier with a grin.

'You don't think it's haunted then?'

'It's an *old* house, it has some quirks – creaky floorboards, clanging pipes, draughts from all the missing windows, but actual ghosts?' He makes a face. 'The most haunted thing about this place is the stories the villagers tell about it. How about you?'

'I think I've just found the most recent "ghost" the villagers talk about. They keep saying the ghostly activity has amped up lately, what with the beekeeper running away, and people hearing noises and seeing lights on. That must be you – you *are* the thing that goes bump in the night.'

'I can honestly say I've never been called that before.' He laughs out loud. 'That makes me sound like a *Goosebumps* book. Do you remember them?'

I grin. 'I loved them. My mum didn't like me reading them when I was young because she thought they were too scary, but I devoured them.'

'Me too! I used to swap them with my friends and read them under the covers by torchlight …'

We're smiling at each other for no reason again. If the Wombles

50

T-shirt and the dunking biscuits weren't enough to convince me he's unlikely to be a murderer, then being a reader definitely does.

'There's a library here, you know.'

'Seriously? The rumours about Elderflower Grove having its own library are true? It really *is* like the Beast's castle.'

'There's a surprising lack of sentient cutlery that makes dinner for you though.'

I snort out another laugh and then try to swallow it down. I'm pretty sure you *should* be scared of men you find sleeping in haunted houses in the middle of the afternoon, but there's something about him that's impossible not to like, whether it's his honesty, his dimples, or his cheeky smile. 'Well, that settles it, they cannot bulldoze a place that has its own library. No books are being destroyed on my watch. You simply *have* to be Josie Garringham's grandson. It's the only chance of saving Elderflower Grove.'

'It's not exactly a roaring success so far.'

'Well, there are two of us now. I'll help you look. We can cover more ground between us.'

'Don't you have a job to do?' He raises an eyebrow and looks pointedly down at my beekeeping suit, which I'd conveniently forgotten I was wearing. When talking to a handsome man, it's always handy to forget you're wearing the most unflattering garment of all time.

'Oh, right. That.' I wave a hand again. 'That won't take long.'

'Don't you have to harvest five hundred jars of honey by Friday?'

I'd just swallowed the last of my tea and choke on the biscuit crumbs that were lurking in the bottom. 'Five *hundred*? You're having a laugh.'

I really, *really* hope he's having a laugh.

'The order from Gracie's shop is five hundred jars by nine o'clock on Friday morning, at which point the villagers will be beating down her door because this harvest is already late after the last beekeeper kerfuffle.'

Kerfuffle. There is something about a guy who uses the word 'kerfuffle'. And if I focus on that, I don't have to focus on what he's saying.

'By my calculations, that's 250 jars tomorrow and 250 jars on Thursday … I don't think you have time to poke around down here.'

'Five *hundred* jars …' I repeat in horror. 'I can't do—' I stop myself before admitting aloud that I can't do that. We might have trespassing in common, but I can't trust him with a secret like that, no matter what secrets he's shared with me. 'Is there even going to be *that* much honey in the hives?'

I can't get my head around that number. When I was told the jars of honey had to be delivered to the shop, I imagined it would be something small and manageable, like ten jars, twenty at a push.

'I would guess so. I'm not going anywhere *near* those hives to find out, but the bees are busy at this time of year, and the elderflower is out in force, so there's a *lot* of pollen for them to forage on. How many jars do you usually get from your hives?'

'My hives?'

He looks at me curiously.

'Oh, right! *My* hives! Um … certainly not five hundred jars. And how come *you* know more about my job than I do? No one told *me* that five hundred jars of honey are due on Friday morning.'

'I overheard the last beekeeper talking. Before she started stealing the valuables, that is. The interviewer not telling you is clearly an oversight on someone's part …'

'How am I supposed to …' I trail off again.

250 jars tomorrow and 250 jars the next day. That's *impossible*. I suddenly feel overwhelmingly sick. What have I got myself into here? I thought I'd be checking on a few bees and merrily harvesting honey as and when, not churning out jar after jar of the stuff like a one-woman factory.

'It's just a one-off. Everything's been delayed by the …

52

departure … of the last beekeeper. They've been left in the lurch. So I've garnered from my eavesdropping skills.'

Personally, I'd rather the last beekeeper had stayed. A few valuables are a small price to pay in exchange for me *not* having to somehow produce five hundred jars of honey. I don't even know *how* to produce a jar of honey.

'You okay? You've gone a bit pale.'

'Bad lighting,' I murmur, pointing towards the bare bulb swinging above us even though there's no draught. 'I'm fine. Maybe I should go though … Prepare myself for tomorrow.'

'Well, I'd say it's been nice to meet you, but it's been an *experience* to meet you and I'm not sure I've quite recovered yet. Thank you though, it's been interesting to have a conversation with a *living* person.'

'As opposed to the dead people you converse with all the time?'

He laughs again as he gets off his stool, and I like that he stands back and lets me go first, keeping a distance between us at all times. There's something about a guy in a Wombles T-shirt, who uses words like 'kerfuffle', *and* realises that being alone on an abandoned estate with a stranger could be intimidating.

I can't help looking around his living area again as we walk back through it. 'I'm sorry again for the wake-up call. I hadn't seen your things there.' I glance down at the lamp, book, phone, and bottle of water in a corner beside the mattress. 'What are you reading?'

'Stephen King. *The Shining*.'

It makes me laugh yet again. 'A book about ghosts while staying in a haunted house. You're brave.'

He laughs too. 'I got it out of the library here. Didn't actually think through the ghost aspect. I suppose I should've looked for a romcom or something to take my mind off it.'

'I need to see this library, you know.'

'I would never keep a book lover from a library.'

Neither of us mentions the five hundred jars of honey. He

offers to escort me back to the staircase to the roof, and I let him because it feels nicer walking through this house not-alone.

On the way out, I put the fire poker back on the hearth where I got it from.

I'm pretty sure there's nothing to be afraid of here.

Chapter 4

*To produce honey, a forager bee stores nectar from flowers
in her 'honey stomach' where the enzymes start to change
the chemical composition. When she returns to the hive,
it's regurgitated and passed mouth to mouth by many
bees, until it's eventually deposited in a honeycomb cell.
The bees beat their wings to evaporate the water content
and it becomes the honey we know and love. Finally, they
cap it with beeswax to keep it clean and store it for winter.*

Five hundred jars of honey.

It *must* be doable. They only employed *one* beekeeper, so it must be achievable by only one person. That's what I keep telling myself anyway.

I've been up half the night studying the beekeeping bible, and as I walk over to Elderflower Grove the next morning, I'm doing a mental run-through in my head. 'Frames that are fully sealed only. Brush off bees. Take to shed. Cut off beeswax. Put in centrifugal extractor, spin honey out, put through double filter. Jar. Label.'

I don't realise I'm muttering to myself until a dog walker gives me a wary look and a wide berth as we pass.

I repeat it over and over again. I have to know what I'm doing, and I don't have time to waste in trying to figure it out on the go, but all I can really think about is Carey. Will he be there? Should I take him breakfast so I've got an excuse to go in and say good morning? Maybe lunchtime would be more appropriate. I've actually had the sense to bring sandwiches today, so going inside to see him at lunchtime seems like a reasonable plan. It would be rude to know he's there and not bother to say hello.

I'm still running through the honey extraction process as I walk through the grounds of Elderflower Grove and start climbing the steps to the roof, imagining each stage I'll have to get right, when there's a voice from above me.

'Good morning, Queen Bee.'

It's quite possibly the nicest thing anyone's ever called me, and makes me feel a bit like Beyoncé, and doesn't everyone want to feel like Beyoncé, especially when it's 8 a.m. and they've barely run a brush through their hair, and can't even be sure they've got their socks on the right way round?

I start taking the steps two at a time. And I shut up, because I'm fairly sure I was still talking to myself.

'Carey!' I say when I reach the top of the steps and see him sitting on one of the benches with two steaming mugs of coffee beside him. 'I thought you never went on the roof.'

'Well, I told you I was scared of ghosts and bees, so I thought I'd better prove my manhood by showing you I'm not afraid of heights too.' He squints in the morning sunlight glinting behind me as he picks up one of the coffee mugs, turns it in his hand, and holds it out for me to take by the handle. It's such a simple gesture, but it says a lot about him, and I take it gratefully, my fingers brushing his hand as he holds the mug out.

'Thank you.'

Even though it's early, he looks less dishevelled than he did yesterday. His light brown hair is full of natural highlights, blond strands being picked out by the sunlight, and it looks straight and smooth today instead of the hastily finger-combed mess it was yesterday. He's wearing dark navy jeans and a blue T-shirt with yet another old children's show motif on the chest.

'Okay, I thought *The Wombles* was some kind of pyjama thing, but if *Fraggle Rock* is daywear too, you clearly have excellent taste in TV shows. And fashion.'

He lets out a loud laugh. 'Thank you. You're never too old to rewatch the shows you grew up with, even when you are, in fact, too old and definitely too old to be seen in public wearing their merchandise.'

'No such thing as too old for anything,' I mumble, because I've looked at his T-shirt and got distracted by the muscles hidden underneath. There's something about the way he's dressed – jeans and a T-shirt and a pair of well-worn trainers – that makes him look totally at home here.

I sip the coffee he's made and sigh in pleasure. 'What's in that? It's lovely.'

'Elderflower syrup. How could I *not* use it while staying here?' He pats the empty space on the bench beside him and shifts along to give me more room, and I shrug my bag off my shoulder and sit down.

'You can't deny *that's* a good view to have with your coffee,' he murmurs, his blue eyes on the horizon, the rising sun visible through the branches of overgrown elderflower trees.

I sit back and relax as I sip my drink again. I've always thought Elderflower Grove was special, but it's even more special than I imagined. I've been stressed out since the mention of five hundred jars and I didn't get a lot of sleep last night for fretting and studying the bee book. This is the first time I've taken a breath since yesterday, and just sitting here in silence with Carey is really nice.

His eyes are closed and his face is turned towards the sun, laughter lines crinkled at the edges of his eyes, not bothered by the bees at this distance from the hives.

'No ghosts overnight then?'

'Not that I know of. I did have weird dreams about a veiled

monster in a beekeeping suit poking me with a long metal stick though … don't know what could've kicked that off?'

It makes me laugh too. 'So, what are you doing up here this morning? Facing your fear of bees via the fortifying medium of coffee?'

'Actually I thought you might need a second pair of hands. You seemed daunted yesterday, and it wouldn't be right for me to be hiding downstairs while you're trying to get to grips with all that honey. Maybe I could help.'

'Awww.' I don't mean to say it aloud but it bursts out before I can stop it. 'That's really sweet of you. Thanks, Carey.'

Although I'm touched, I'm also horrified. I have *no* idea what I'm doing. I thought I could learn as I went, but if he's around, he's surely going to notice that I've never done this before. 'But … bees.' I point towards the hives like he might not have seen them.

He laughs. 'I can help from the safety of the Honey House where absolutely no bees are allowed to come in. If you want me to, that is.'

'Yes, yes, yes!' I say quickly. Although the option of him real-ising I'm not a beekeeper isn't a good one, neither is trying to produce five hundred jars of honey by myself.

He grins as he looks back out at the view and slowly drinks his coffee, and I can't help smiling to myself when I take another sip too. When it comes to unexpected things in Elderflower Grove, so far, *he* is the most unexpected of them all.

Eventually he drains his mug and stands up, taking my empty one as well and walking over to leave them by the door down into the manor house, and I take the opportunity to pull the beekeeping suit on, because if it's not the most unflattering thing for a hot guy to see you in, it definitely *is* the most unflattering thing for a hot guy to see you wriggle and flap and yank and grunt your way in to. Instead of watching, he takes the keys from where I've left them on the bench and goes into the shed, giving me a moment of privacy.

By the time I get into the Honey House, he's put kindling in the smoker and is standing in the doorway to light it.

'Man make fire,' he says in a caveman-style grunt as he stands the smoker on the ground outside and comes back in, quickly closing the door to keep any bees out.

'Go on then, boss, where do you want me?' He holds his hands open, offering himself up.

Every time I see the *Fraggle Rock* characters on his T-shirt, it makes me smile. And I try not to panic at the question and think about what I read so many times last night that my eyes were blurring with tiredness by the time I eventually gave in and went to bed.

'If you're sure, that is. It sounded like you were practising just now.'

I go blisteringly red. I *knew* he would've heard that. 'Just getting my head in the game. Shaving minutes off my time. Like running a marathon but with bees.'

He nods like he doesn't believe me.

I look around the shed. I've already forgotten everything I read last night. 'Right. First we need to …'

I run my hand along the countertop, trying to repeat the mantra in my head. 'We need a bowl and a bit of wood to rest each frame on when we cut off the wax …'

I sound unsure even to my own ears, but Carey locates an empty washing-up bowl with a baton of wood beside it, and I find a couple of food-grade buckets, rest a filter inside them, and he gets a cutting knife and a scraping tool from a drawer under the unit.

'Everything's got to be sterilised, can you do that?'

He nods and salutes me.

I pull on my gloves and double-check myself for gaps in the bee suit, pull the hood over my head and zip it closed. I pick up the hive tool and take a couple of empty hive supers to put the honey-filled frames in and go to walk out.

'You're going to need this.'

Carey's holding out a soft brush. 'You *have* to make sure *every* bee is gone before you bring the frames in here. I can't deal with 'em, Kayl.'

Kayl. In less than twenty-four hours, he's shortening my name. People I've known for years don't call me Kayl.

Like he can tell what I'm thinking, he's gone red. 'Sorry, Kayleigh, I didn't mean to …'

'It's fine, *Care*,' I say pointedly. I've never met anyone called Carey before, but I like it.

He smiles as I take the brush, wishing that beekeeper romper suits made you look effortlessly sexy rather than like a cross between a gas boiler engineer and an adult baby.

'*Bee* careful.' He looks ridiculously pleased with the pun as he picks up the smoker and hands it to me.

I'm still laughing as I close the door firmly behind me.

'Good morning, bee ladies and bee gents.' I lift the roof off the first hive I looked in yesterday and lean it against the wall, and give the bees a few puffs of smoke to calm them down, and while I wait for it to work, I glance back at the Honey House.

Carey's standing at the window and I give him a wave and a smile, but when I turn back to the bees, it turns into a grimace.

I really *am* going to have to look like I know what I'm doing. I lift the lid and use the hive tool to lever the crown board off, sealed up with propolis even in the hours since I last looked.

Bees are crawling all over the tops of the frames and I puff more smoke around, just in case. The last thing I need at the moment is angry bees.

'Right then, ladies. We've got an audience today, and that audience is *very* gorgeous and thankfully out of earshot otherwise I'd die of embarrassment, so could you all do me a favour and *beehave* yourselves while I nick all this honey you've worked so hard on …' Maybe I should apologise for that dreadful pun or they'll sting me out of second-hand embarrassment.

I glance back at Carey again. He smiles when he catches my eyes.

I brush bees away and insert the hive tool under the edge of the first frame and lever it up. How do people do this without squashing bees? They're *everywhere* and I hate the idea of accidentally hurting even one.

I lift the frame out, and although the bees have been busy building honeycomb, it isn't full yet, so I put it back. Once I reach the middle frames, they start to get heavy with honey. When I come to one that looks like each hexagonal section of honeycomb has been capped, I know it's ready.

I hold the frame with both hands above the hive and give it a sharp shake, and the mass of bees slide off like a wave, dropping back into the hive. I was scared of hurting them, but they instantly carry on, beetling about, getting on with what they were doing like I was never here.

A few bees are still clinging on to the frame, so I use the bee brush to gently wipe them off and then slot the frame into the empty box and get the next one from the hive, but I didn't put the lid on and the bees have found the box and are already trying to take back their honey.

I lift out the frame and once again brush the bees off it, and by the time it's clear, the second one is swarming with bees too. 'This is not what I meant when I said *beehave*,' I tell the bees loudly.

Like they can understand me, a swarm from the two frames suddenly gets angry and a whole load of them fly at my face, and I drop both the frames and do the dance of the crazy bee lady – running away and flapping around, trying to disperse them and shake them off the netting of my hood.

When they decide they've punished me enough, I look up and Carey's laughing inside the window. He mouths, 'You okay?' and I give him a thumbs-up in return, glad he can't see how red my face has gone.

I try to compose myself and pick up each frame again, brush

the bees from them *again*, and slot them back into the empty box, and this time, I put the lid on securely. That was probably a horrifically amateur mistake, and I get the feeling he knows that.

I get another frame from the same hive, but the rest of them aren't filled yet so I put the hive back together and move on to the next one.

Once the box is full and so heavy I can barely lift it, I haul it across the roof to the Honey House. The door opens a crack and another brush is pushed through it, a long one, a bit like a loofah. 'You're not coming in until you've brushed yourself off. No bees in here, Kayl. Not even one.'

Even though I mutter as I brush myself down, I like the fact he openly admits to being scared of them. Most men are too macho and obsessed with saving face to admit a phobia, and there's something refreshing about a guy who isn't.

I lift each frame out one by one and give them all a final brush-down as his hand snakes out of the barely open door and takes each honey-heavy frame in. When the box is empty, he makes me turn in a circle to confirm there are no bees hiding about my person before letting me in and shutting the door.

I push my hood down and look around. One food-grade bucket is set up with a filter in it and a baton of wood across the top, another one is set up beside the honey extractor. I *really* could have done with a dress rehearsal to learn all this before I had to show someone else what to do.

'So we cut the beeswax off to uncap the honey …' I run the knife under the hot tap to heat it and then pick up a frame and rest it on the baton of wood, settle the bevel of the knife into the grooves in the wooden edges, and slice downwards.

'Hah!' I'm so amazed when it actually works that I let out a noise of surprise and punch the air victoriously. The wax falls away in a sheet and light-coloured honey glistens inside the frame. I watched someone do it on YouTube last night, but I still didn't expect to be able to do it myself.

Carey looks at me curiously and I compose myself. 'Good knife,' I say by way of explanation. 'My one at home is rubbish compared to that.'

I feel horrible for lying to him. He's told me things he didn't intend to tell me, but I can't bring myself to admit I'm not a beekeeper.

The beeswax collects in the filter and the few drips of honey seep through into the bucket below, and I turn the frame around and cut the wax from the other side too.

And then it's the extractor. I've read about how they work, but actually using one is like being faced with the control panel of a spaceship. Carey's watching like a model student, but the extractor lid has slidey bits and knobs and I fiddle with it for a silly amount of time, unable to get it open.

Eventually he takes pity on me and leans across to lift one half of the lid in a simple move.

I give him a grateful smile. 'I've not used one like this before.'

'What do you usually use?'

'Oh, um … much smaller. This one takes four frames.' I glance down at the compartments inside. I have no idea how many frames it takes.

'Eight frames,' he corrects me, sounding nonjudgemental.

'Right, of course.' I peer down into it with the honey-filled frame ready in my hand. I can't work out how *one* fits in, never mind eight.

There's clanging and banging as I slot the frame in, realise I've gone wrong, and try to turn it around halfway through, pull it out again and try the other way round, the sound of wood knocking against metal reverberating through the room, each inept clonk driving up my embarrassment.

'Can I …' Carey takes the frame out of my hand and slots it neatly into one of the baskets in the cylindrical extractor.

Of course. That's how you do it. He makes it look ridiculously easy.

'Thanks. Bad angle.'

'So I see.'

I like how keen he is to help, because instead of waiting, he finds another knife from a drawer, cleans it, heats it, and picks up another frame and we dance around each other, moving smoothly from station to station like a well-oiled machine.

'So, what do you do?' I ask, interest piqued because yesterday I caught him napping in the afternoon and he clearly doesn't have anywhere to be today either.

'I'm kind of between jobs at the moment.' He doesn't hide the groan. 'I'm a garden designer. At least, I *was.* I designed an outside area for a start-up company's new office and I got it wrong. They wanted a sharp, modern, concrete garden with fake grass and artificial plants, but it was a *beautiful* space, full of bumblebees and butterflies and birds, and I couldn't bring myself to destroy it. I ignored the brief and made it a wildlife garden. I re-wilded parts of it so it wouldn't need maintenance, and saving the bees is cool now, so it was modern in its own way. I genuinely thought that when they saw it, they'd love it, even though it wasn't what was planned ... but they didn't. So now I'm an out-of-work garden designer whose references will say, "Can't follow instructions".'

'You didn't deserve to be fired for that.'

'One of those things,' he says with a shrug. 'I knew it wasn't what they wanted, but I thought I'd get away with re-interpreting the plan. The company were *supposed* to be ecologically inclined – keen to market with that strategy, not so keen to actually put it into practice.'

'So you're a friend to bees *and* beekeepers then?'

He laughs. 'Well, I haven't been stabbed by a fire poker yet today, so I must *bee* doing something right.'

'You're never going to let me forget that, are you?'

When his eyes meet mine, his face breaks into a wide grin. 'It's certainly a first meeting I'm never going to forget. And one of the worst ways I've ever been woken up. And I used to have a cat – I once woke up to half a mouse being dropped on my face.'

I burst out laughing so hard that I bump into him as we pass on the way to the extractor, and I realise how good he smells. Fruity, like tart apple cut with some kind of spice. I move away quickly in case he notices how hot and sweaty I'm getting inside the bee suit. It's absolutely roasting when the sun is beating down on the roof.

'How about you?'

'I've never been woken up by any form of rodent life.'

'I meant your job. How'd you get into beekeeping?'

'I, er, kept bees …' I hate this lie, but I don't know how else to respond. 'I kind of fell into it. I *really* needed a job and beekeeper was the only one going.'

It's not *exactly* a lie. He just thinks I'm talking about years ago, not the day before yesterday.

His lips form an 'o' shape. 'So you started this with *no* experience? Wow. You really are brave. Bees are not something you want to tackle unprepared.'

'Well, everyone's got to start somewhere, haven't they?'

He glances doubtfully out the window towards the hives. 'That's what you meant about the book helping you get your first job?'

'Mmm hmm.' I sound more unbalanced by the second. If he doesn't know there's something wrong with my story, the squeak in my voice will definitely tip him off.

My hand is shaking so much as I'm cutting beeswax off a frame that I miss half the caps and have to pick up an uncapping fork and start scraping at it and making the biggest mess I've made so far today.

'Like this.' Carey does a motion with his hand, showing me that you're supposed to slide it under and lift the capping off instead.

'Ones I've used before are different,' I mutter.

He nods without looking up. He probably knows as well as I do that they're all the same.

When all eight uncapped frames are loaded into the extractor, Carey closes the lid and starts turning the handle. Slowly at first, and then faster, winding it until the frames are a blur through the transparent lid. It's a much more physical job than I'd imagined, and he spins it faster and faster, his *extremely* muscular arms working hard, flexing, showing off tanned skin where the sleeves of his blue T-shirt have ridden up with the exertion. He really is a *gorgeous* man. Lines at the edges of his eyes are crinkled up as he looks down in concentration, his forehead starting to glisten with sweat from the effort, spinning it so fast that he's getting out of breath, and when he looks up and meets my eyes, he starts laughing and slows down to a stop.

'You're obviously used to spinning these things and I'm not, so let's pretend I'm not as unfit as I look right now.' He releases the handle and steps back. 'My turn to watch the master at work.'

I take over the handle of the extractor and peer in. The honey is splashed all over the sides and slowly dripping down to the basin at the bottom. There's still honey in the frames, and I get the impression this is a much harder job than it looks. I start turning the handle slowly, and Carey goes across to the sink for a glass of water.

I nearly break my fingers when I lose my grip on the handle and it carries on turning without me because I can't take my eyes off him. It's like my own personal Diet Coke ad, and I'd be surprised if I'm not drooling.

I never look at men now. Since I broke up with my ex and moved back in with my mum, the only men I've even thought about are fictional ones from the nineteenth century. I've lost myself in Jane Austen classics when men were dashing and debonair and treated women with respect. I've had enough of modern-day men for one lifetime.

'Kayleigh?' He sounds like it's not the first time he's said it.

'Sorry, what? I'm, um … must be the sugar overload from the honey fumes.' I hadn't even known honey fumes were a thing, but the whole shed smells of a mix of honey and beeswax and it's definitely a reasonable excuse for not being able to concentrate.

Who knew focusing would be so hard? I take the handle of the extractor and wind it again and again, starting slowly and building up speed. This is *exhausting*. Who knew bees did such a good job of storing their honey?

After a few minutes, Carey takes over again, and I go to get a drink of water and get my breath back. All in all, it takes under ten minutes, and then the frames have to be turned around and spun again to get every last drop out. Once the frames are empty, I zip my netted hood back up, return the empty frames to the hives for the bees to fill again, and go to get another eight from the next few hives.

We get into a rhythm. I get the frames, make sure and double-sure they're clear of bees; we take it in turns to cut the beeswax off, load each frame into the extractor, and spin the frames until each lot is empty, squeezing past each other in space that suddenly seems a lot more cramped than it did earlier.

'Don't you have a wife who's missing you while you're staying here?' I blurt out.

I don't even know why I'm interested, but he seems like the kind of guy who'd have a wife – gorgeous, funny, and at a guess, late thirties – a couple of years older than me. Men like him have *always* got wives. And why am I holding my breath as I wait for him to answer?

'Heck, *no*. Did have, once. Not anymore. And never, never, never again. Been there, got the T-shirt, definitely don't want another T-shirt. I'm done with love and relationships. What's the male equivalent of a crotchety old spinster?' He thinks for a moment. 'Whatever it is, that's me.'

'But you're so—' There are many ways I could end that sentence, but he cuts me off before I decide which one to use.

'How about you? Boyfriend who's going to be angry about you spending the day with the "ghost" of Elderflower Grove?'

'Heck, *no*.' I deliberately repeat his words, wondering if my answer is emphatic enough. 'I live with my mum. Moved back in after a break-up last year. I could never trust anyone again.'

'Me neither.' He holds his water glass out and I clink mine against it. 'Cheers to bad break-ups that traumatise you for life.'

'Not traditionally something you toast to.'

He laughs. 'I like to be different. People are really horrible, aren't they?'

'I seem to have a knack for picking the worst ones.'

'Cheers to that.' He clinks his glass against mine again and we both down the water like it's something much stronger, but there's a sadness in his eyes that doesn't shift when he smiles at me again.

Once we've done another few rounds of spinning, the basin at the bottom of the extractor is getting full, so I pull over one of the food-grade buckets, put the fine mesh filter in the top, and position it under the tap of the extractor.

'Moment of truth.' Carey's watching in anticipation as I unlock the tap and flip the gate up, and liquid gold pours out.

He cheers, and I'm laughing in elation as a steady stream of honey runs from the tap on the extractor and into the bucket, filtering out the remaining bits of wax and body parts of dead bees. Lovely.

He nudges my arm with his elbow. 'We did it!'

I can't help beaming back at his wide grin. I hadn't realised how satisfying this moment would be.

He bends down to swipe his finger through the stream of honey and then sucks it clean. 'That's *really* good.'

I do the same, letting the honey pour over the tip of my index finger and then licking it. 'Oh my god, that's actual honey! It tastes like honey and everything! Wow.' I can't quite cover my surprise.

He's laughing as he watches me. 'What did you think it was going to be?'

'I don't know. I didn't think it was …' I trail off before I say something I shouldn't. Until yesterday, I had *no* idea how honey was produced, and I didn't expect it to come out of the extractor ready to eat, just as simple as filtering and putting into jars.

'You act like you've never done this before.'

'Well, every job is new,' I stutter out. 'And this is Elderflower Grove. I've never done anything as prestigious as this before. This is special honey.'

'Ah, the magical, mystical cure for all ills? Most important honey the world has ever known or something.' He leans down to swipe his finger through the running stream again. 'I can feel myself getting younger already.'

I swipe another finger of it too. 'It's really nice, actually. Floral and delicate.'

'That's the elderflower. It's the closest thing for the bees to forage on.'

The trees surrounding us are a mass of delicate white sprays of blossom, and the scent fills the air outside. I can taste in the honey the same thing I can smell all around me.

When the stream starts to run slowly, Carey tips the extractor forwards until we get every last drop out, and we wait while it runs through the filters, and then it's jarring time.

The shelves are full of empty jars in unopened sterile packaging, and we once again form a tag team. I kneel on the floor by the bucket and fill each jar from the tap at the front of it, pass each one up to Carey, who puts the lids on and cleans them of any spillages, sticks labels on the front, and loads them into the waiting wooden crates.

It's starting to get dark before we're done, and I stand next to Carey and look at the crates of our handiwork. Each crate holds twenty jars, and we're at least one crate over the target 250 jars, and there are still the other thirty hives to do tomorrow. I'm consumed by the scent of honey, like it's seeped inside my pores and if you pressed my skin, it would start oozing sticky sweetness. It will be a miracle if I get home without a trail of ants following me.

'See you tomorrow for the next 250 jars then?' He nudges his elbow against mine with a grin.

I laugh at his optimism. 'Of course.'

He drags his fingers across his forearm, drawing my eyes to the fine hair covering his tanned skin. 'God, I need a shower. Every inch of me feels sticky. I'm probably going to smell of honey until August.'

I laugh because it's exactly what I was thinking, but the thought of Carey and showers is *not* a good one. It brings to mind all sorts of mental images that I can't get rid of.

'We should …' He gestures vaguely towards the door down into the house. 'I'm going to have that shower.'

'Yeah, me too. I mean, not *that* shower, my own shower, obviously. In my own home, that I'm going back to now …' The thought of Carey and showers has made my brain sputter to a halt. You can see the muscle under the thin T-shirt; he's obviously strong and fit from outdoor work, and if there *are* any ghosts in Elderflower Grove, they are seriously lucky. I wouldn't mind being invisible when Carey's in the shower either.

I get out of the beekeeping suit and leave it folded up for tomorrow's work, and we both leave the Honey House to the wider rooftop outside.

'See you tomorrow, Kayl.'

I *should* be annoyed at him for shortening my name, but everything seems cheeky and good-natured and easy-going with him. He's the kind of guy it's difficult to be annoyed at, even if you want to. Which I don't.

'Carey, thank you. I don't know what I would've done without you.'

'You're welcome.' He grins, and looks … sort of proud, like he's trying to hide a smile but he can't quite manage it. 'And thank *you*. It was fun. It's been a while since I felt useful. I don't have much of a purpose these days.'

His cheeks redden and I take a step towards him, and there's an awkward moment of lingering and hovering because I'm not sure what to say to that, and I want to hug him goodbye, but I don't know him well enough yet. His face goes redder as we stand there for too long, and he lifts an arm like he might be about to offer a goodbye hug but then he drops it again.

'So, tomorrow then, yeah?' He scratches the back of his neck.

I nod and bite my lip as I watch him walk backwards, keeping his eyes on mine until he reaches the door, when he waves and ducks inside. I go down the steps from the rooftop apiary and through the weeds towards the gate, but it takes a while to get his words out of my head.

Chapter 5

*Bees can vote. When a new nest site is found, scout bees use
the waggle dance to inform the other bees of the location,
and when enough bees have checked it out and agreed,
they do a dance of approval until a majority is reached.*

The second day is pretty much the same. The only thing that's
changed is that Carey's wearing a different, but no less impressive, T-shirt.

'*Bagpuss* today.' I point at his chest when he meets me on
the roof the next morning with two cups of coffee. 'You have
excellent taste.'

'Thank you, Queen Bee.' He does a mock bow and hands me
one of the mugs. 'And good morning.'

I mumble a good morning as I sit down on the bench next
to him. It's earlier today. One of the Nectar Inspectors will be
here at five o'clock this afternoon to pick up the crates of honey
and deliver them to Gracie's shop in time for tomorrow's rush,
and I thought I'd better get a timely start. 'I didn't expect you
to be here so early.'

'Why? You weren't waiting for the opportunity to jab me awake
by ramming a fire poker into my kidney, were you?'

I reach over and smack at his leg.

He grins. 'I love mornings.'

'You weird, weird person.'

It makes him laugh out loud. '*Bee* never too busy for a morning coffee. And it's different here. Peaceful and quiet. I feel like the only person on the planet when I'm here. Early mornings, you can watch the bunnies bouncing around and the birds coming over to the feeders for their breakfast. I feel like an intruder in the daytime, but in those post-dawn early morning hours, I can sit unseen and watch the grounds coming to life around me, and I feel like Elderflower Grove doesn't mind me being here.'

'You're really into nature and wildlife and stuff then?'

'I'm a gardener – of course I am. You must be too with the bees and all.'

'Oh yeah, totally. Yay nature.' I wave an imaginary pompom. I can't say I'm into nature either way – only enough to know that a place like this should stay as natural and wildlife-friendly as it is now, and not be replaced by a theme park.

I open the Honey House and pull my bee suit on while Carey's still outside and not watching every time I stumble over because a leg is stuck in an arm hole. Babies wear romper suits because they have a parent to dress them – no one ever mentions how complicated it is getting into one as an adult.

We quickly fall back into the routine of yesterday, and the day passes in a blur of honey and companionable silence. Before I know it, there's the honk of a horn and a pick-up truck pulls up outside the gate.

'It can't be five already!' I look at Carey in horror. 'We're not done!'

'We're close enough.' He pushes himself onto tiptoes and peers through the window. 'You go and stall him, I'll do a final count.'

I race down the steps from the roof and forge my way through the trampled brambles and weeds that are getting more trodden down every day.

'Hello!' The man who climbs out of the pick-up greets me. 'You must be Kayleigh. I'm Wilbur, second-in-command of the Nectar Inspectors. Come to pick up Gracie's honey order.'

He's a tall guy, probably in his sixties, with arms like tree trunks and salt-and-pepper short hair. He's also wearing a pair of bee deely boppers on his head, and a black vest top with a tiny bee embroidered on the chest pocket.

'Did you get all the jars done? It must've made for a busy week!'

'Ah, I wasn't alone. I had—' I remember I'm not supposed to mention Carey and amend quickly. 'Help from the bees! You could say the bees did a vast majority of the work!'

I laugh much louder than anything is actually funny, until he starts looking at me like I've not got all my cornflakes in one box, and I tell him I'll start bringing the honey down.

When I get back to the rooftop, Carey's hefting the second crate outside the Honey House door.

I pick it up, surprised at the weight of twenty jars, especially because he's moving them with no trouble. I use a knee to push it up into my arms properly and stumble backwards under the weight.

'I'd help but I can't be seen.' He sighs and takes pity on me. 'I'll bring them to the bottom of the steps, the wall is high enough to hide behind. You'll have to take them from there. Just don't let him come in.'

Letting him come in isn't a problem. Sweat is beading on my forehead by the time I get back to the gate where Wilbur is waiting, but like Gracie, he stays outside and peers in worriedly, looking like he's expecting a ghost to jump out at any moment or a wheelie bin to roll past of its own accord.

I let him take the crate out of my hands and load it into the back of the truck, and when I get back to the house, Carey's standing on the bottom step, waiting to hand the next crate over to me. He's hidden by the tall wall the steps are built into and holding the crate against one hip like it weighs nothing.

'Thank you,' I mouth at him, my arms nearly being pulled from their sockets as I almost drop the thing.

After I've brought a few more crates down to the gate and stacked them on the pavement for Wilbur to load in, I take a breather. 'Will Gracie really sell all this?'

'Probably by Monday.'

'What?' He's winding me up. There aren't five hundred people *in* Little Kettling, and surely not *all* of them want jars of honey.

'She'll ration a few crates over the next couple of months, until the big harvest at the end of the season, but the locals are getting desperate. They were allowed only a maximum of two jars each last autumn, so they've had to eke it out. It's the cure for everything, you know? Coughs and colds, digestive issues, ulcers, cuts and burns. It's anti-ageing. It's a moisturiser or an antiseptic. My wife's paranoid about her wrinkles, she ran out in January and the mass-produced supermarket stuff is no match for genuine Elderflower Grove honey. My mother-in-law even put it on a bunion once and she swears it disappeared.'

'That sounds … uncomfortably sticky.' The mental image of honey on feet is not a good one.

'They're such special bees from this special place. Raw honey straight from the hives – nature's cure for everything, nothing more powerful than that.'

Hanging from the mirror in Wilbur's truck is a crocheted bee with a 'bee kind' flag, and a honey jar charm. People *really* love these bees.

'Elderflower Grove honey has got a cult following online,' he says when he sees me looking. 'When the big harvest arrives in the autumn, Gracie starts shipping internationally. She's got hundreds of pre-orders already.'

Big harvest? Was five hundred jars *not* the big harvest?

He points to the poster of the local councillor that's still on the gate where Gracie put it. 'He was at it again last night. The grass verges and central islands on the nearby motorway. The flowers had just started to open, and now they're all gone again. Last week he filled in the pond in the local park. A hazard, so he said. A haven for wildlife, more like. Thank god for people like us trying to help. At least the Elderflower Grove bees will never be short of pollen, eh?' He nods towards the elderflower trees.

It makes that little thread of dismay feel like it's being yanked through me. No one has *any* idea about Elderflower Grove being repossessed.

By the time I get back, Carey's stacked crate after crate at the bottom of the steps, and I collect them one by one, feeling ridiculously grateful. I don't know how unlikely it is to stumble across someone living in an abandoned manor house, but it's definitely unlikely that the person also turns out to be so kind and willing to help.

When Wilbur has finished loading the crates into the back of his truck, he beckons me over, still unwilling to take even a step inside the gate.

He fishes something from his pocket and holds his hand out, and when I open my palm, another smooth stone is dropped into it, this one with a painted bee and the words 'bee-lieve in magic' and some sprigs of elderflower blossom.

'Thank you on behalf of the Nectar Inspectors,' Wilbur says. 'We know it was a tall order on short notice.'

I'm inexplicably welling up. 'Oh, it's fine, no problem at all,' I stutter, feeling guilty for taking the credit when Carey's done half the work. I stroke my fingers over the smooth stone. 'Thank you.'

'My granddaughter painted it especially for you. She thinks you're some kind of superhero.'

'Superheroes have more attractive outfits than this.' I shake one of the sleeves of the bee suit, the hood hanging down over my back.

'Well, we all think you're very brave to face the ghosts. No sightings yet?'

'None at all.'

'Poor Josie.' He shakes his head, looking up at the house. 'Breaks my heart to imagine what she must've gone through.'

'Did you know her well?'

'Used to, when we were younger, but not in the later years. She was always such a big part of village life, and then she stopped. Pulled away. Wouldn't let anyone in or speak to any of us. No one had seen her for ages before she died.'

He doesn't mention there being any question over her death.

I thank him again for the stone, still blushing at the idea of being a superhero in a beekeeping suit. Best not start wearing my knickers on the outside though.

He says goodbye and gets into his truck, and I wait until he pulls away and then lock the gate and plod back up the stone steps to the rooftop.

Carey's leaning in one of the notches of the battlement roof. 'We did it!'

He holds his hand out to give me a high five. I slap my hand against his and his fingers close around mine and tug our joined hands downwards before letting go. 'That was fun.'

'That was amazing. I didn't think we could do it.' I couldn't get the smile off my face if I wanted to. I was *so* daunted when I got here on Tuesday, and to have actually managed to extract and jar *that* much honey is unreal, and I *still* think this might be some kind of dream.

'Thank you, bees, you amazing little creatures!' I call to the hives on the opposite end of the roof. 'You little stars! I'm sorry for every time I've batted you away when you wanted to share a picnic with me!'

Carey laughs. 'How can you be so surprised? You must have done this hundreds of times.'

I gulp, and not just because my mouth is still dry from lack of oxygen. 'Well, yeah, but … not here. Not on this scale. Not with a two-day deadline. Not with hives I don't know and an extractor I've never used before. And, more importantly, not with your help.'

'Probably more of a hindrance than a help with the fear of bees.'

'Not at all, you were invaluable.' I really am embarrassingly out of breath, and he hasn't even broken a sweat.

Carey reaches across the wall and picks up a glass of water that he's put ready for me and hands it over.

'Thanks.' I slurp it gratefully.

'You're going to ache in places you didn't know you had. C'mere.' Before I realise what he's doing, he's stepped nearer and turned me around. His hands are on my shoulders, massaging gently through the thick material of the bee suit. 'I'm sorry about having to hide. You know what the gossip will be like if anyone finds out I'm here.'

It's the closest I've got to him so far. I can feel his height behind me, the strength of his gorgeous hands pressing into my shoulders, rubbing gently. They *are* going to ache tomorrow, I can tell that much, but with Carey's hands on them and his apple-like aftershave so close, it doesn't matter.

I enjoy the massage for a few moments before he jumps backwards like he's been burnt. 'I'm sorry, I didn't mean to do that. I've been on my own for so long that I've forgotten how to act around other people. I'm forgetting I don't know you well enough to touch you without permission yet.' He shakes his head at himself. 'No wonder you wanted that fire poker nearby.'

'Care, it's fine.' In my head, I cling onto the 'yet' part of that sentence. I'd like to say something fun and flirty, like 'carry on if you want to', but he looks embarrassed and the moment is gone.

It wasn't an intimate touch, but the atmosphere between us is awkward and odd, and I'm absolutely sure he's not going to expand on exactly how long he's been alone, which is what I really want to know, especially after the comments about past relationships yesterday.

'Thanks for noticing my level of unfitness,' I say to break the tension, glad when it works because he laughs and goes back to looking out across the grounds.

I walk around him and lean on the wall in the next notch along, and reach out and touch the back of my fingers against his bare forearm. 'Thank you.' I pull my hand away quickly. 'Couldn't have done it without you. Literally could *not* have done it without you, Carey.'

He glances at me and smiles. 'How was that for a baptism of fire?'

'Why does everyone keep saying that? That's what the interviewing bee said too.' I try to groan, but I'm still so buoyant that I can't stop smiling. 'It was fun, actually. Did we make the quota? If not, I'll have to take however many we were short on over to Gracie in the morning.'

'Five hundred and seven jars to be exact.'

I let out a whoop and he smiles again, those dimples at the corners of his lips making me feel more fluttery than the thought of actually succeeding in a job I didn't think I could do. 'That's brilliant. *Bee*-rilliant, even. Getting things right hasn't been my strong point lately.'

'Mine neither.' His wide smile turns into a small, lopsided smile with only one dimple – an expression of solidarity. It intrigues me. While I believe he could be Josie Garringham's grandson and that it's easier to stay here while he looks for evidence, it also seems odd to lock yourself away in a crumbling old manor with only a few ghosts for company, and I get the feeling he's holding back.

He walks across the roof and ducks inside the Honey House before returning with a jar of honey in each hand.

'You kept the extras,' I say, laughing. Of *course* he did. 'Seven jars! The villagers will have the police on us. At the rate the honey seems to go around here, we could sell them on eBay for £200 a pop.'

'The worst part is, we'd probably get it too. I've never known a village so obsessed with honey.' He hands me one of the jars. 'Don't know about you, but I'm taking one of these. Thank you, bees. Terrifying, scary bees.'

I use the jar of honey to salute towards the hives. 'Thank you, bees. Sweet, fuzzy, environmental geniuses.'

I never eat honey. There's always a jar in Mum's cupboard in case anyone gets a cold, and it's usually been there for so long that it's set solid. Honey reminds me of being ill when I was little and drinking hot honey and lemon to soothe a sore throat.

'I've got to ask an expert – what's your favourite honey-based dish? I never buy the stuff, but now I want to make the most of this … fountain of eternal youth or whatever it is.'

The laugh distracts me from trying to think of an answer. I'm supposed to be an expert on all things honey, and the most exciting thing I can think of is a Lemsip.

'Bagels!' I say in a burst of inspiration so sudden that it makes him jump. I remember a friend saying she was enjoying honey on a toasted bagel for breakfast, which is just about the most inventive honey use I can think of at such short notice.

'That sounds remarkably … simple. I was expecting the honey expert to say something you'd be charged eighty-five quid for in a posh restaurant … Just plain bagels and honey?' He sounds confused.

And I'm *really* hoping my friend's throwaway comment about her breakfast one day a few months ago is right. 'I'll prove it. I'll be here in time for breakfast tomorrow morning, and I'll bring the bagels.'

He laughs because I sound so serious that I should be in a Robert De Niro film, and then he uses the honey jar to indicate back across the roof. 'Do you usually use the beeswax? There's loads of it leftover.'

'*Use* the beeswax?'

'Well, people make things with it, don't they? Didn't you mention something about candles yesterday?'

Did I? 'No.' My voice is too sharp and wasn't meant to sound that snappy. I don't ever want to *think* about making candles again, but that's not his fault. I sigh. 'I used to. But now I don't.'

There are a few chapters towards the end of the bee bible

about beeswax, but reading them wasn't a priority, but maybe it should be. Should *bee*. The pun makes me think of the stone Wilbur gave me, and I dig it out of my pocket and put it down on the wall between us.

'Aww.' Carey pushes his bottom lip out, and although he sounds mocking, he traces his finger across the design with a wistful look on his face. 'That's sweet.'

He sighs and rests his chin on his hands on the wall, sounding thoughtful and faraway as he gazes out across the grounds.

The white sprays of the elderflower trees rustle in the early evening breeze and unseen birds in nearby trees are singing their hearts out. It's something you hear often in a leafy, quiet village like this, but I've never really stopped to appreciate it before, to listen to the distinct melody each bird sings.

'I think you could here.' His voice makes me jump from where I was lost in a reverie. 'Believe in magic,' he adds when I glance over at him.

He goes back to looking out, his chin leaning so heavily on his hands that he has to speak from the side of his mouth. 'I wish I could stay here forever. It's like a different world. Like nothing bad has ever happened here, even though something bad obviously did happen here. It's an escape in the middle of real life. Stepping through the gate is like pressing the pause button. We all need to do that sometimes.'

Now we've hit the honey target, I can't wait to go and explore the grounds. Walk by the lake to make sure Mr Darcy *isn't* about to emerge from it. He's right though. Things seem different here. Even when racing to make five hundred jars of honey, I've found there's a peacefulness about Elderflower Grove, and it seems to be a part of Carey too. Not once in the past two days has he got riled or snapped or rushed.

I take a deep breath and let it out slowly, enjoying the way the air fills my lungs to an almost uncomfortable capacity.

It feels like the first time I've breathed in over a year.

Chapter 6

*The buzz of a bee is caused by their wings beating
200 times per second – 12,000 times per minute.*

It's only my fourth day at Elderflower Grove, and if I thought
about it, I'd notice I've been systematically earlier every day so
far. It's a whisker past eight o'clock now, and I've only left it this
late because I had to pick up bagels on the way and the village
shop doesn't open until eight.

I've never had a job where I was eager to get to work. Even in
jobs I've enjoyed, I've still hit the snooze button a few times and
groaned and grunted my way to work in a caffeine-fuelled haze,
but everything feels good this morning. I walk along empty pave-
ments and grassy verges glisten with early morning dew. There's
not even a dog walker about – it's just me and the birdsong.

Something's different as soon as I approach Elderflower Grove.
Yesterday, the driveway was covered with spiky weeds that had a
narrow path trodden through them, but now it's clear, and Carey's
cut down the nasty, thorny, stinging weeds and painstakingly
trimmed around patches of celandines, daisies, and sprawling
buttercups because the bees might feed on them. He's even left
the dandelions, and *no one* likes dandelions, apart from bees.

The driveway – slightly downhill from the manor house, and wide enough to accommodate three cars side by side – is so much bigger than it seemed and seeing it makes me feel all glowy inside. Carey is so … thoughtful. Helpful. I didn't think men could be like that, and it makes me want to throw my arms out and spin around in circles on the newly uncovered driveway, but I restrain myself by *only* walking up to the house with a little bit of an extra skip in my step.

I dump my bag and shrug off my coat and leave them on one of the rooftop benches and say good morning to the bees before I go down the spiral staircase into the house.

'Good morning!' I shout as I emerge onto the upper landing area, my voice echoing loudly through the empty home.

'Sorry,' I say to the nearest wall. 'Just trying not to startle him.'

And then I realise I'm talking to a building and hurry on.

I go down the other two flights of stairs and find my way to the kitchen, and it's mere minutes before Carey appears from the bathroom, rubbing a towel over his just-shaved face.

'Good morning, Queen Bee,' he says with a bright grin. 'You're early.'

For just a sec, I think he's going to bend down and hug me, and the seconds stretch on while we hover, but then he swiftly sidesteps and goes around the island in the opposite direction, and I set about slicing and toasting two bagels.

When they're done, Carey sets two coffees down on the kitchen island and puts two plates ready, side by side instead of opposite like we sat the other day, and I use a spoon to drizzle honey over the bagel halves and watch it soak in.

'Cheers.' He knocks his bagel against mine.

'It takes twelve honeybees their whole lifetime to make one teaspoon of honey. Thank the bees, not me.'

He grins around the piece of bagel he's just ripped off with his teeth. 'I still don't like them, but thank you, bees.'

'Thanks for doing the driveway. You didn't have to do that.'

'You're in and out all the time now. It's no fun walking through brambles and god knows what else. Although I've missed a trick by not saying it wasn't me and leaving you to wonder if the ghosts did it.'

'Last I checked, ghosts weren't big on garden tools.' I flash my eyebrows at him and use my bagel half to indicate to his grey marl *Tom and Jerry* top. 'Good T-shirt choice today. One of my childhood favourites.'

'Mine too,' he says with a grin.

'You've become the highlight of my day.' I suddenly realise what I've said and start backpedalling *fast*. 'I meant your T-shirts. Your T-shirts have become the highlight of my day. *Just* your T-shirts.'

I try to hide my red cheeks behind the coffee mug as I take a swallow, but it hits the back of my throat at the wrong angle and makes me start coughing.

Why do I go to bits in front of this man? Yeah, he's good-looking and he seems nice, but it's like it's been so long that I've forgotten how to act around a man who *isn't* from a Jane Austen novel.

'You looking at my T-shirts has become the highlight of my day too.'

We've both gone red for no reason. It sounds like flirting even though it isn't, and I *really* need to change the subject. 'So, where are we going to start today?'

'You really don't have to help me, you know. You've got all those bees to deal with, and I've got the rest of the summer to find *something*. I don't even know what I'm looking for.'

'Firstly, the bees are fine. I checked them all yesterday, and I don't want to disrupt them unnecessarily, and secondly, you're our only hope of saving Elderflower Grove. *That* is the most important thing. If there's something in this house that proves you're an heir to the estate, and you solemnly swear not to turn it into a theme park, then that has got to be worth trying for.'

'I swear. Solemnly.' He says it in such a solemn voice that it makes me giggle.

'Besides, you're looking for something like paperwork, and there's a distinct possibility that something like paperwork could be kept in the library.'

It's his turn to laugh out loud. 'You really are only in it for the library, aren't you?'

My grin matches his. He's not wrong there.

***

'I have looked, you know,' he says as we go up the stairs to the second-floor landing. 'There's an office-type room upstairs with a big desk that looks like a place where someone might've done paperwork, but there's nothing there, nothing in the bedrooms, and other than that, there's the rooms with doors that won't open. The house feels cold and closed off to me, like it doesn't want me here, even though I'm trying to save it.'

The door on the second floor is plain aged wood, and when Carey leans past me to push it open, it gives a heavy-sounding creak and swings back inch by inch, and the scent of musty paper filters out of the chilly room.

'I've never been in a place that had its own library before.'

'Me neither.' He edges around me to reach a pull cord with a dangling crystal on the end, and a chandelier illuminates the room with bulbs that aren't nearly bright enough.

'Oh. My. God.' I unintentionally do my best Janice-from-*Friends* impression. 'I know there are unexpected things in Elderflower Grove, but this tops the lot of them.'

The library is ridiculous in the best way possible. The floor-boards under our feet are warm mahogany, and covered in such a layer of dust that I can still see the footprints from Carey's earlier visit, but it gives way to a gigantic room, so tall that I have to strain my neck to see the ceiling, which must go all the way up to the third floor. At the opposite end, there's an open-tread spiral staircase leading up to a second storey with a balustrade around it, so the library must cover both upper floors of the manor house. Dark mahogany shelves are the same wood as the floor and the staircase, and there are matching ladders to reach the highest shelves. 'This is incredible. Can you imagine owning a house with a library bigger than the actual local library? It's like the Beast's castle, but better.'

'Can *you* imagine someone wanting to tear this down?'

'We're going to find that proof.' I point an assertive finger at him. 'That rotten councilman is *not* having all these books.'

Although I do realise why he seems so daunted. There must be thousands of books on these shelves. If something was hidden here, how would we ever find it?

I trail my fingers along the spines on the nearest shelf. 'I wonder who's lived here over the years. Josie Garringham was in her nineties – *that's* an unthinkable amount of time for us, but someone must've been here for centuries before her. Families. Look at this.' I move up a shelf and pull out a copy of Sherlock Holmes, and immediately choke on the cloud of dust it brings with it. 'This looks like a first edition. How many other books are there like this? This house must hold so many stories.'

'Literally.'

I give him a sarcastic look. 'You know what I mean. It's seen so many things over the decades, and now it's left here to rot. All of these books are just sitting here, waiting for what? A bulldozer to arrive? Moths to get them? Mould to finally break through the walls? They deserve better than this. Elderflower Grove deserves better than this.'

Somewhere above us, there's a creaking noise, and my eyes meet Carey's and we dissolve into nervous laughter.

'This house seems to agree with a lot of things you say.'

I cross the aisle and look at another shelf. 'Jane Austen! Look at this, Josie had all of Jane Austen's books, multiple editions!'

I pull out a copy of *Pride and Prejudice*, a hardcover released in 1995 with Colin Firth on the front. 'I knew she was a woman of good taste.' I carefully brush the dust off it and give it a gentle shake. 'Oh, you poor darling, shut away for all these years. I bet you were once read by a little girl who took you outside and sat reading by the lake, dreaming of Mr Darcy emerging from the water …'

And then I realise I'm talking to a book and ram it quickly back onto the shelf. When I pluck up the courage to look at Carey, he's biting his lip in a valiant effort not to laugh. 'I like books, okay?'

He finally fails in his attempt and lets out a warm laugh. 'I know. Me too. I just don't often have full-blown conversations with them.'

I resist the urge to poke my tongue out at him.

'So what is it about Jane Austen?' Carey asks as I wander around, rucking up threadbare rugs that need a good wash, brushing away cobwebs that stick to my fingers, and dusting off dust bunnies lurking in the corners of every shelf.

'It's a snapshot into a different time of life.'

'A time when no one had first names?'

I burst out laughing.

'Seriously,' he says. 'It's all Miss Dashwood and Miss Bennet and Mr Darcy and Mr Wickham. Not one of them has a first name.'

Despite the fact he's insulting my favourite author, I'm actually quite impressed that he knows Jane Austen well enough to be able to name characters. 'Men were a different breed back then. They treated women like ladies. They were chivalrous and respectful and they looked after us.'

'Yes, because women were unequal, weren't allowed to work or earn their own money, and it was all about dowries and fortunes. A woman's sole goal in life was to do embroidery, play the piano, and find a rich man. That's not aspirational.'

'It's the principle. Even in this day and age … I want someone to treat me with respect. To look at me like Fitzwilliam Darcy looks at Elizabeth Bennet.' I say it pointedly to prove that they *do* have first names. 'And I love the glamour of the Regency-era balls and the way everyone did the English country dances. It's a time that doesn't exist anymore, but it's my lifelong dream to attend a party like that.'

'Where you have to "take a turn around the room" to attract a man's attention in the hopes of securing a dance, and a man is forbidden from introducing himself but must be introduced by a chaperone, and then if he asks you to dance, you're not allowed to say no?'

'It was romantic and chivalrous. I even have a Regency dress that I'll probably never get to wear. It was fifty quid in a charity shop a few years ago. It takes up loads of space, and my mum keeps saying I should throw it away, but I can't bring myself to. I fell in love the moment I saw it.' My cheeks burn red because I'm sure he isn't even vaguely interested in a dress I should never have bought that *does* take up a chunk of much-needed wardrobe space. 'And the letters too. I love the romance of the letters. What could be more romantic than the letter Captain Wentworth writes to Anne Elliot in *Persuasion*? No one communicates anymore, but back then, it was all horse-drawn carriages delivering carefully written fountain-pen letters. Nowadays if you try to communicate with a guy, you're lucky to get a text that says "'k" back in response, or a text with the poo emoji in it. You know – how was your day? His response – one poo emoji. On a bad day, three poo emojis.'

He's laughing so hard. 'Okay, I've been off the dating scene for a while, but I can honestly say I've never sent a poo emoji to a lady. Or at all, actually. And I think I should speak up on behalf of all men who don't communicate via the medium of poo emojis.'

I cannot stop laughing either. 'You must be more verbose than my ex then, because he *loved* a poo emoji.'

'I can see why "ex" comes into it.'

'Oh, if only it had been as simple as the overuse of poo emojis.'

'Yeah, poo-emoji-related break-ups don't traumatise you for

life.' He references our toast a couple of days ago. 'And we really have talked about poo emojis an abnormal amount now.'

Even though any mention of my ex never leaves me with a smile on my face, somehow giggling with Carey makes it feel less raw than it usually does.

I trail my hand along another shelf, wishing there was enough time to clean this library up and give it the love it deserves, but if Elderflower Grove is to be demolished in November … what would be the point?

'If I ever own this place, Kayl, I'll get it restored and throw a Jane Austen–themed ball just for you,' Carey says. 'And I promise there won't be a poo emoji in sight.'

'Aww, that's probably the most romantic thing anyone's ever said to me.'

'Feel free to call me Mr Paxton and curtsey every time I enter or leave a room. I wouldn't complain, even though Mr Paxton sounds more schoolteacher than dashing gentleman in this day and age.'

'It's a good job these books are valuable or I'd throw one at you. Where'd you find Stephen King in this lot?'

He points out an aisle of books that contains horror titles. I wander further and find every sort of book you can imagine, from novels in a selection of genres to non-fiction manuals, cookbooks, craft books, and everything in between. It's like entering a Waterstones from decades ago.

'I feel like I should start pulling out books to see if the wall opens and there's a secret passage.'

'I can honestly say I hadn't thought of that. There *is* a passage though.'

'What?' I spin around to face him in surprise. 'I've known you for four days and you're staying in a place with a secret library passage and you're only *now* telling me? Four days, Carey!'

He grins. 'A, forgive me. B, I've had other things on my mind, for example, five hundred jars of honey. C, it's not secret, it's on the blueprints, and D, it's jammed shut and I can't get it open from either side.'

I follow him to the furthest end of the library where, tucked into a corner, there's a small wooden door that really does look like an entrance to Wonderland and I'm surprised not to find a 'drink me' potion nearby.

'It's stuck fast,' Carey says. 'There's no lock, so the wood must've swollen and got stuck in the frame. It's un-openable. If it still won't open in a couple more weeks, I'll get my chainsaw on it and cut my way in.'

I reach out and try the door handle, and although it's a bit stiff, the wooden door opens with a slow creak.

I raise an eyebrow, my voice *dripping* with teasing pride. 'What, this door?'

His mouth is open in shock. 'How did you … I've been pushing at that for weeks!'

'Maybe you haven't got the biceps …' I trail off because I've made the mistake of looking pointedly at his biceps, and he's too close for that, and all I can see is smooth, tanned skin where his T-shirt sleeves are taut around his upper arms, which are a lot more capable of door-opening than my flabby ones. I swallow hard. 'You must've loosened it. The weather's been dry for weeks now, maybe it's had a chance to dry out and un-swell.' I'm pretty sure 'un-swell' isn't a word, but Carey's biceps and his fresh mint-and-apple aftershave has short-circuited my brain and I can barely remember where we are, never mind what my name is.

'Yeah, maybe.' He sounds dubious.

'Thank you!' I call to the house, just in case it *is* listening.

'Do you think that's where I'm going wrong? Not being polite enough to a building?'

'Elderflower Grove isn't just a building.' I reach out and pat the doorframe. 'It's a keeper of hundreds of years of memories. You blundering in with your muscles and threatening it with power tools isn't going to do any good.'

'So the solution is to be nice to it? It's a *building*.'

'It's a better solution than menacing it with a chainsaw. And you're clearly not off to a good start.'

He mutters as he gets his phone out of his pocket, switches on the torch, and shines it past the open door. It does nothing but illuminate cobwebs and a narrow passageway. 'What do you know, the secret passage is literally just a passage. You disappoint me, Elderflower Grove.'

'He didn't mean that!' I say to the house and smack his arm for good measure.

The passage has the musty, damp smell of a room that hasn't been opened for many years, and I wonder what we're going to find in there, other than several species of spider previously unknown in the UK. I hover by the small doorway, but Carey's already taken a step inside and at my hesitation, he holds a hand out to me.

Secret passages in movies are always fun and exciting, but this one seems decidedly inhospitable and not the kind of place you voluntarily go into.

'Hang on.' I grab a stack of books from a nearby shelf and use them to prop the door open in case it decides to slam shut and trap us inside, and then I put on the light on my phone as well and step in gingerly. I don't intend to take Carey's hand, but when a man that gorgeous is holding a hand out, it's impossible to refuse, and his warm fingers close around mine.

It's dark and hollow and I'm almost positive I can hear the 'ooooh' of a ghost, but it's probably just my own intake of breath. The wooden floor underneath us feels crumbly and makes splintery noises with each step, and both our phone lights don't do much to illuminate the tight passage.

'Be careful, this floor doesn't feel good.' Carey shines his torch downwards, but most of the floor is buried by a layer of indistinct grime.

We go a few more steps before the passageway widens, and

in the beam of our torchlights, I can make out the silhouettes of … furniture.

Furniture? In a secret corridor?

There are semi-circular uplighter lamps at intervals around the wall, and he looks for a switch and reaches over to press it without letting go of my hand. The room slowly flickers into … well, light would be pushing it, but you can almost hear the fizzle of electricity as the light bulbs ping on one by one, filling the small room with the tonsil-clenching smell of burning dust as the bulbs get warm. Each light casts a yellow glow upwards, onto sumptuous but faded plum-coloured walls, slowly brightening the small room.

I honestly expect to see a skeleton sitting in the chair. It's the kind of secret room where you'd find a skeleton sitting in a chair.

'It's a reading room!' My hand falls out of his in relief. 'There's a reading room attached to the library. It's a scientific fact that nothing bad has ever happened in a reading room.'

The air is cloying and has the mildewy stench you'd expect from something so shut away, and it's tiny. I reckon Carey's about six-foot-one, and his head is at an angle to avoid the ceiling. There's another moth-eaten circular rug in the centre of the floor, a two-seater sofa, and two armchairs, each with a Tiffany lamp on an end table beside it. There are stacks of books on each table, and a load more piled on the coffee table in front of the small sofa.

I reach down and pull out a yellowed newspaper with curled edges and faded print, a crossword half-completed by a dried-up Biro pen. '1979, Care.' I hold it up to show him.

He's looking through the book stacks on one of the end tables. 'Did Josie have a husband?'

'Not that I know of.' I think about it. 'No, she was known as the "lonely old witch". Our parents used to tell us we'd end up like her if we didn't find a man. She couldn't have.'

'Only this looks very … his and hers. Look, by this chair, there are horror books and true-life war stories, and by this chair, there's … Sophie Kinsella, which is a lot more modern than that crossword.' He taps the dust-covered book that's facedown on top of the pile nearest to the right armchair.

'Josie liked Sophie Kinsella. I *knew* she was a woman of taste,' I repeat. 'Everyone loves a good romcom. Something to unite generations.'

'Well, she must've liked to mix things up because she also had George Orwell on the go.' He points to a bookmark inside a fraying book on the opposite table. 'These to-read piles don't look like they belong to the same person.'

He's got a point. It looks like a reading nook for a couple. An armchair each, a sofa to share. But who? Surely the village would have known if Josie had a partner … 'If she *was* seeing someone, this is the most romantic thing I've ever seen. Can you imagine curling up together and reading? Picking a book from your own library, bringing a cup of tea into your reading nook, and sitting here in a warm glow with the person you love? Talk about relationship goals.' I laugh and spin around, but I step backwards and shriek as my foot plunges straight through a crumbling floorboard with a scraping, splintering sound.

'One way to ruin the romance.' Carey offers me his arm to hold on to as I pull my foot free, leaving my trainer still stuck in the hole. I put my foot down on the dirty rug as he crouches to free my shoe as well, the wood so decayed that he can break it away with his fingers. I pull at the shoe while he pushes and eventually it comes out with a tearing pop and the momentum sends me sprawling backwards. My leg hits the armchair, which knocks into the table and sends the Sophie Kinsella book tumbling to the floor. I pick it up, but the page is lost.

'I'm so sorry, I lost your place,' I say to the house itself. 'That was an accident, please don't strike me down.'

As I dust myself off and brush splinters from my shoe, Carey's looking at me with a quirked eyebrow from where he's still crouched on the floor.

'That could be a ghost's reading material!'

He doesn't say anything, but he shines his phone light across the floor and examines the wood. 'Deathwatch beetle in the floorboards. No wonder it feels so dodgy.'

'Deathwatch?' I repeat. 'That sounds friendly and welcoming. Why is there never a "warm and cuddly" beetle?'

'A beetle that comes in and says, "Hello, I'll be your beetle for the day, what can I do to make your stay more comfortable?"'

My laugh sounds even louder in the small room. 'Exactly!'

'Well, this is the kind of beetle that destroys floorboards beyond repair, and if anyone was trying to save this house, they'd have a large bill to have their flooring torn up and replaced.'

I like how he seems to know something about everything. He's outdoorsy and obviously an expert at gardens, but he seems able to do everything inside the house too, and he's fearless when it comes to walking down dark, possibly haunted passages.

'So where does this lead to? You said you'd been trying to get it open from the other side too?'

'That office I was saying about earlier. Big desk, filing cabinets, looks like the kind of place someone would keep paperwo— Kayl, there's something down here.'

'Don't tell me, a gang of "I want to kill you" beetles? Poisonous beetles? Beetles crossed with wasps or something pleasant like that?'

'No, some sort of … box.' He pushes his hand through the hole in the floorboard and I shine my phone light downwards. There's a cavity underneath, and I can see something dull and metal. He tries to get hold of it, but the hole is too small, and he pulls his wrist out, wincing as splinters catch.

He looks around for something we can use, and I pick up his hand and brush the splinters off without really thinking about it. 'There must be an easier way. There's no way a ninety-two-year-old put this here and then laid the floorboard. We're missing a way in somewhere.'

I shift aside the rug and use my knees to push an armchair back … Ah ha! 'Or we could just use this handy trapdoor.'

'Well, would you look at that!' He makes a noise of joy. 'Secret passages *and* secret trapdoors. I love this house.'

The small ring handle on the trapdoor has a loop of wool tied around it, and when Carey crouches down again to pull it, it lifts without any fuss. 'Almost like it wanted to be opened.'

He plunges his hand straight into the pitch-dark hole without even looking, ignoring the catch of cobwebs, and feels around, straining until he can reach the metal of the tin and pull it out inch by inch.

He stands up and brushes the dust off the lid carefully, revealing a rusty metal logo of a gardening tin you'd keep packets of seeds in. He's looking at it like it's about to spontaneously shatter at any moment. 'This could be a memory tin, couldn't it? This is the kind of thing you'd find, I don't know, mementos of a childhood in, right?'

I nod.

'And it's in a hidden hidey-hole in a hidden room. It's the kind of place you'd hide something you didn't want to be found …'

I nod again.

'So this could be it, right?' His voice is quiet and he seems genuinely emotional, and even though I've wondered about his motivations over the past few days, I can see this means something to him. He's fearless when it comes to walking down dark corridors or plunging his hands into dark places that look more like a bushtucker trial on *I'm a Celebrity … Get Me Out of Here* than somewhere you'd willingly insert body parts, but he's staring at the box like he's hoping it might unexpectedly open itself.

Eventually he shakes his head and holds it out to me. 'I can't do it. You open it.'

I take it from him and sit down in the dusty armchair with the tin on my lap. 'This means a lot to you, doesn't it?'

'Yeah. I mean, I'm not searching for some great grandmotherly love or anything – I'm lucky in that respect, I grew up with two incredible grandparents – but this … this was my father's last wish. The one thing he'd always wanted to do and never admitted until it was too late. I owe it to him to find out if my hunch about Josie is right.'

I bite my lip, mainly to stop myself prodding for more information. Carey seems bold and outgoing, but he's guarded and I get the feeling that he doesn't open up much. It feels important that he wants me to do this.

I'm holding my breath as I pop the lid open and lift it stiffly back on its rusty hinges, revealing a lot of yellowed envelopes.

'They're unsent letters. They're not stamped or addressed, but the envelopes are all open.' I start rifling through them in the neat row they're in inside the tin. 'They're to someone called Guillaume.'

One letter after another has the name scrawled across the envelope in looped handwriting, and none of them are sealed, so I pull a letter from the first one, and start reading it out.

June 23rd, 1984

My dearest Guillaume,

I'm on the roof of Notre Dame Cathedral in Paris. The deacon was gifted some beehives and has personally requested my services to take care of them. I never imagined I'd get the chance to visit your home country. It was a dream for so long, but we never could, of course. The city is beautiful. Talk about a summer to remember.

The bees are well-behaved. They have been very nice to me and their honey is excellent. The deacon has been kind enough to gift me several jars. You would've liked it. The hum of the hives is my constant companion since you left.

I keep looking down at the square in front of the cathedral

*and thinking I see you looking back at me, but then I blink,
and it's never you. I'm convinced I'm going to find you here.
The universe wouldn't allow me to be in your country without
somehow throwing us into each other's path. Around every
street corner, I expect to bump into you. Every tall chap in
a queue at the boulangerie, I am certain it will be you. Why
isn't it you, Guillaume? Why am I living out a dream we
shared, but alone? Is this where you went? Back home? I can't
see anywhere you could have gone in England. I feel like you
would've come home, but maybe I am wrong.*

I seem to have been wrong about a lot of things in my life.
Forever love,
Josie

'Notre Dame ...' I run my fingers over the crisp page. 'She kept
bees on the roof of Notre Dame Cathedral. That's incredible. I've
always wanted to go there.'

I tuck the envelope back into the tin where it came from
because they look like they're in some kind of order and I don't
want to mess it up. 'That's so sad. Who was this Guillaume? Why
doesn't she know where he is?'

I take another envelope and pull out the letter.

July 9th, 1987

My dearest Guillaume,

*I'm writing from the grounds of the Taj Mahal. It's so
very beautiful. I'm spending the summer as a beekeeper here.
Whoever thought my bees would bring me the opportunity to
travel the world and meet so many people? It's so hot here,
the heat is unbearable some days, and the nights are stifling.
It makes me think of you – the way you always loved the
warm weather, and I preferred the autumn and winter. We
always wanted to travel, and now I travel, but without you.*

It is wrong, somehow. The joy I should take from it is negated by the fact you are not with me.

I know you're unlikely to be here in India, but I look for you wherever I go, just in case. I keep thinking I'll find you one day. Maybe in the most unexpected place. I can't imagine my life ending without ever seeing you again. I'm old now, 64 this year. Do you still remember my birthday? I make you a cake every year on yours, but I don't even know if you're still alive. In my mind, you are always the age you were when I last saw you. I can't remember what it was like to be young. I can't remember a time before you.

Forever love,
Josie

Carey's crouched down beside me, his hand resting across my knee as his little finger keeps the place in the row of letters in the tin. 'These are heartbreaking. *She* was heartbroken. Whoever this guy was, he must've left her with no explanation.'

I put that letter back inside the envelope and move Carey's finger so I can return it to the tin and take another one.

December 20th, 1990

My dearest Guillaume,

Instead of a far-off place, today I'm writing to you from the kitchen. It's nearly Christmas. My eleventh without you. I haven't bothered with any decorations again. This house used to be a wonderland, but without you, it feels pointless. I've been drinking tonight. One of those vintage wines we were saving for a special occasion. I don't think there'll ever be a special occasion again. I should be tipsy and happy, but I'm drunk and angry. How could you do it? Did I mean nothing to you? Did our home and our life together mean so little that you could walk away without a second thought? Without

*even so much as a word? The more time that goes by, the less
I understand.*

*Maybe I'll get a Christmas miracle this year and you'll
come home.*

*I used to decorate because I thought you'd be disappointed if
you came back and the house wasn't decorated. I keep making
bargains with fate – if I do this thing or that thing, some law
of the universe will bring you back to me. It never works. The
bargains are only ever one-sided. Fate has no interest in me.*

Even my beloved bees are quiet now.

*Maybe I will go away for a while. I travel to take my mind
off you, but half the time, I'm scared to leave the house for
too long in case you come back while I'm not here. I've left
the spare key in our usual spot.*

*Wishing for a Christmas miracle and a hangover cure. It's
been a long time since I indulged this much. There is nothing
to celebrate any more. Happy Christmas, indeed.*

Forever love,

Josie

I return the envelope to its place and put my hand on my chest.
My heart feels like it's breaking on behalf of Josie Garringham.
I'm on the verge of tears and have to swallow hard and blink as
my eyes readjust to the low light in the room. 'She's looking for
him, *searching* for him. Writing letters she'll never send because
she doesn't have anywhere to send them *to*.'

'So she hides them in a box under the floor where no one
will ever find them?'

I look down into his blue eyes, closer than they have been up
until now, and we blink at each other for a few long moments.
Carey looks touched and I'm stupidly emotional over decades-
old letters written by someone I didn't even know, but Josie's
heartache is tangible in every inch of Elderflower Grove, and
these letters start to explain what I feel here. Beauty but sadness.

Love but abandonment. She must have lost the love of her life and had no idea where he'd gone.

'Maybe the house wanted us to find them …' I whisper. Speaking in a normal voice feels wrong. The air is heavy with heartbreak, like opening the tin has reopened old wounds for the house itself, and Carey's fingers slip from the tin to my knee and tighten gently, and without losing eye contact, his mouth starts to quirk up at one side, the start of a smile, and I'm smiling back despite the sadness those letters have evoked.

And then he overbalances where he's crouching and only manages to stay upright by clasping a hand on my knee and one on the arm of the chair, sending up a cloud of dust that chokes us both.

He pushes himself upright and walks across the rug, and I put the lid back on the tin. These letters feel valuable somehow. Josie's jewellery and ornaments and other possessions are scattered around the house as they were when she died. Nothing of monetary value is hidden, but these are.

Carey shoves a hand through his hair. 'Do you think she was married? Because I've checked the archives and there's no record of a marriage.'

'I don't know. She was known as a spinster. I've never heard mention of a partner of any kind, and you know what the gossip mill is like around here. If Josie's husband had left her, people would know, wouldn't they?' I bite my lip as I watch him pacing. 'I'm sorry it's not exactly what you were hoping would be hidden in this tin.'

'Well, no, but it's all part of her life. The mystery of who she was. We have to read the rest of those letters. They might explain something. They might mention a baby.' He looks between my face and the tin. 'It doesn't have to be today.'

'I want to read them with you. I'm part of this now. We're in it together.'

'Maybe we'll read on and find this ended happily. He could've come back and she hid them there because she didn't want him to see them.'

'No.' I shake my head even though I like his optimism. 'She lived here alone, with the villagers calling her a witch and children making up horror stories about her. It wasn't the life of a happy woman. I used to see her when I was younger, talking to her bees on the rooftop. She always seemed so strange – she wore floaty dresses and danced around the roof with an imaginary partner. Maybe it was him – maybe she was imagining Guillaume. She sang songs to the bees and spoke to them for hours. My mum used to say she was lonely and had no one else to talk to.'

'And now we know something happened. There's a story here. And I don't know about you, but I'm *desperate* to find out what happened to Guillaume.'

I nod so hard I'm surprised my head doesn't fall off and wobble across the floor.

'There must be a lot more to Elderflower Grove than we think, and we are *going* to find out before they raze this place to the ground.' Carey offers his hand to pull me up, and we head back towards the library, the tin clutched tightly in my other hand.

I always thought there was more to Josie Garringham than the 'old witch' tales that followed her around Little Kettling, and I can't help thinking the mysterious recipient of these unsent letters might be the reason.

Chapter 7

In 1984, honeybees on the space shuttle Challenger
constructed honeycomb in zero gravity.

Once again, I'm early the next morning, but when I get inside the Elderflower Grove gates, instead of walking around the side and up to the rooftop, I stop in front of the main door.

In my mind is the letter where Josie told Guillaume she'd left the key for him. Where would it be? It's got to be somewhere near the front door, and surely hidden somewhere, like under a doormat or a plant pot. There's nothing of either sort, not even a stone or a paving slab, and I stand back, looking up at the house and willing it to reveal another secret to me.

'Good morning, Queen Bee.' Carey appears in one of the ground-floor windows with his face covered in shaving foam.

'Good morning, my favourite ghost.' I can't help smiling at the sight of him and the *Pinky and the Brain* T-shirt he's wearing today.

I explain about the idea of finding the key to the main door, and he watches me stalking around the courtyard, but there's nowhere a key could be.

'Do you have much beekeeping work to do today?'

'I … er …' The truth is, as far as I can work out, there's *not* much beekeeping work to do now. With the initial honey harvest completed, the bees can be left to their own devices to make more honey and raise their brood. I must do weekly hive inspections to make sure there are no signs of mites, disease, or intruders, which I can definitely put off for another day or so.

'I was wondering if you wanted to go for a walk around the grounds? It's a beautiful day and yesterday was a bit intense. I thought we could take lunch and eat by the lake or something. Take the tin and go through the rest of the letters – they might feel brighter in the sunshine.'

'I'd love to. I've been dying to see what it's like out there.' I glance through the screen of elderflower trees into the unknown mass of weeds and brambles beyond. 'It looks a tad overgrown …'

'It's not too bad. I've forged a few paths to get around, but I haven't seen anywhere near all of it. I thought you might want to explore too, and it would be nice to go … not-alone.'

'I agree.' As soon as I got this job, I couldn't wait to wander around the grounds, but once I saw how overgrown it is, I had visions of getting lost and being eaten by wolves.

All right, the wolves are probably unlikely, but it's still impossible to fathom just how large the grounds of Elderflower Grove are. There's a genuine possibility they extend into the next county.

He grins, the sunlight shining through the trees and making his eyes glint, and for just a second, something melts inside me that someone looks *that* happy about me saying yes.

'Things could have moved since she wrote that letter,' he says, going back to the key, but my eyes are still scanning the courtyard for potential hiding spots. 'She must have given up on him ever coming back eventually.'

He's right, of course. It's silly to think it would still be here. The only thing in this courtyard that *would* have been here in 1979 is the fountain. I walk a circle around it. The gargoyle on the top where the water once poured from is growing moss at an alarming rate, and the basin, made of mosaicked blue tiles, is dry and cracked and cultivating some form of algae from rainwater collected in it.

Carey's leaning on his elbows inside the window with his chin in his hands, a grin on his face as he watches me.

'Josie Garringham doesn't seem like a woman who would've given up.' I climb up on the wall around the fountain edge. I can imagine Josie and Guillaume sitting here with a glass of wine, watching the sun set as the water burbled behind them, but the curved-edge bricks have broken over the years and now it's all cracks and sharp corners. I don't know what I'm looking for – a false brick, a hidey-hole, anywhere that a key could be pushed in, but there's nothing. Maybe I'm barking up the wrong—

The gargoyle didn't move, I *know* it didn't actually move, but something draws my attention to it. It's freestanding on its stone plinth, and I lean over but I'm too short and have to step down into the fountain and reach up, trying to rock it backwards with one hand while using the other to grope blindly underneath it.

'I'd help, but I haven't got a TV in here and this is the best entertainment I've had for weeks,' Carey calls from the window.

Like a true adult, I poke my tongue out at him.

My fingers touch something smooth and … moveable. I shove the heavy stone gargoyle back once more and my fingers tighten on whatever the thing is, and I pull out a polythene bag, brittle, disintegrating at the edges, but still sealed and relatively intact. Inside the weather-clouded plastic, there's a key and a piece of paper.

'Hah!' I hold it up in victory in Carey's direction and he starts laughing.

Instead of opening it straight away, I shove it into my pocket and put one foot on the centre column, which has all the potential to go horribly wrong, and end up doing a midair version of the splits so I can reach across to the gargoyle. I push it back into place and use the flat of my hand to scrub the moss away and uncover its eyes.

'So it can see out again?'

'Obviously.' I give Carey a scathing look. 'Don't tell me it's just an inanimate object. That *wanted* to be found. It did something nice for us, we should do something nice for it in return.'

I turn back to the gargoyle and give it a pat. 'There you go, mate. Now you can enjoy the scenery again. If it was up to me, I'd have water running through you again in a heartbeat.'

I can't be certain, but I think the gargoyle's wing moves just a little, but I'm sure it was just a trick of the light. I jump down off the wall and undo the bag while walking towards the front door.

'Thank you!' I call to the house, holding up the key.

It's rusty and far from the shining metal it once was, but when I insert it into the lock on the old fortress-like door, it crunches and grinds, and eventually turns.

I push it cautiously. It looks more like the doorway to a dungeon than a manor house, and although we don't *need* it open to get inside, it still feels significant somehow, like the house is letting us in.

'Let me help.' Carey's voice is muffled from the other side as he inches it from its frame until it swings backwards, leaving a once-dark entrance hallway brightened by daylight.

'Wow.' Carey stands in the doorway, looking out at the court-yard and surrounding greenery. 'You're amazing, Kayl. I didn't think you could do that. Lesson to self – don't underestimate women who like Jane Austen.'

I laugh, unsure how Jane Austen comes into it, but it's a nice compliment when compliments have been few and far between lately.

Instead of concentrating on the scent of his peppery apple aftershave as he stands next to me, I unfold the paper from the bag.

It's much older than the other letters, and even though I can sense Carey standing close enough to read it over my shoulder, I read it aloud.

My dearest Guillaume,

If you are reading this, it means you've come back and I am not here. If you find this, I've gone to look for you. Stay here, please. I will always return. Go in, make yourself at home. It is your home and it always will be. I've left some letters in the spot where we shared our last kiss. If you ever come back, please read them. Please know what you meant to me.

I will spend the rest of my life looking for you.

Forever love,

Josie

'Do you think that's why she travelled? She never stopped looking for him.'

'That's equal parts tragic and romantic,' he says.

'I'm sorry we're not him,' I say to the house in case it's disappointed that the first person to find the key *isn't* Guillaume. I peer in to what was once a glittering entrance hall with marble floors and moulded wall panelling, dust motes dancing through the sunlight.

Carey walks backwards and frames it between his hands. 'It could almost look welcoming when you see the door open like that. Like a palace, rather than a horror movie mansion.'

'It deserves that. It's wrong that its life will end like this. It used to be so much more. It was a happy home for a young couple in love, maybe families before them, and now it's the subject of various ghost stories, unloved and abandoned for all these years. It deserves someone to give it a second chance.'

Until now, there's been no breeze, but a gust of wind suddenly shakes the elderflower trees, and I'm almost positive the gargoyle's wing moves again in agreement. I mean, it *doesn't*, obviously, and I'd think I was imagining things, but Carey glances over his shoulder like he's seen it too.

Our eyes meet and we burst into nervous giggles.

'I guess the house agrees.'

'It does that a lot.' I go back out into the courtyard and we both look up at the house with its door open once more. A small hint of what it must've been like once, open to visitors, inviting friends inside as they walked up the impressive driveway. The thought that in a few short months, it will be bulldozed to make way for a theme park causes an overwhelming sadness to settle over me.

He obviously feels it too, because he gestures towards the grounds and says, 'Shall we ...'

'I'm just going to go and say hello to the bees.'

'I'll go and finish packing a bag. Got your lunch?'

I hand it to him and he disappears inside the house, and I make my way up the steps to the rooftop.

'Good morning, bee ladies and bee gents. Although, quite frankly, it's the women who do all the work, so maybe just good morning to the ladies.' I shrug my bag off my shoulder and leave it on the bench, and go a bit nearer to the hives, keeping my distance because I'm not suited up. 'Did you ladies know about Guillaume? I'm guessing you did because I used to see Josie talking to you all the time.' It's hard to reconcile the 'old witch' of village tales with the heartbroken Josie in the letters we've read. 'Wait, are you even the same bees? No, you wouldn't be, would you? Bees don't live that long. And you couldn't tell me even if you were *bee-cause* you're bees.'

I roll my eyes at myself. 'I'm going out for lunch with Carey today. No, wait, that sounds wrong, like it's a date or something and it is most definitely *not* a date. Just two friends taking a picnic. We are friends, aren't we? I wasn't sure I trusted his intentions at first, but he seems nice, doesn't he?'

'You know I can hear you, right?' he calls up from below.

I cringe. I thought I'd hear him coming back outside, but clearly not.

'It's a known fact that bees dislike eavesdroppers,' I call back, trying to deflect attention from myself. I suppose it's lucky I didn't tell the bees that he's quite possibly the hottest man in the known universe, and quite frankly, I can't see an alien being any hotter, so it probably covers the known *and* unknown universes.

'It's all right, I wasn't sure about your intentions at first either, but you seem nice too.' He nudges my arm with his elbow when I get back to the courtyard. 'And yes, we *are* friends. At least, I hope so.'

I like that he doesn't make it any more embarrassing than it needs to be. Instead, he pulls the front of his white T-shirt down, drawing my attention to the motif. 'You haven't commented on my shirt yet. Is *Pinky and the Brain* not to your liking?'

It eases what could've been a seriously awkward moment. 'On the contrary, I think it's one of the classics. I've just been a bit distracted by door keys and lost letters this morning.' And I really shouldn't be focusing on the curve of his chest or the way the T-shirt clings in *all* the right places.

He's got a rucksack on his back with two thick straps over his shoulders, and a machete and pair of heavy-duty loppers in one hand, and he gestures for me to go first.

Buddleia bushes taller than me spring up as the concrete of the courtyard fades into grassy, mossy ground, with patches of low-growing wild strawberry plants and creeping pimpernel covered in masses of tiny, bright yellow star-shaped flowers. Buttercups wave in the breeze and wild daisies are crying out to have daisy chains made from them. I loved wildflowers when I was younger. Mum and I used to go for walks and I'd come back with bunches of daisies and coltsfoot and cuckooflower and celandines and put them in a vase on the kitchen table, proud of my young flower-arranging skills, not having any concept that they were weeds to most people.

'Does it make you think of the Flower Fairies?' I glance back at Carey, a couple of steps behind me.

'The what?' He thinks for a moment. 'Oh, wait, those old

books from the 1920s? Yeah, I remember them. My mum used to quote them when I was young. You know, when I was into trucks and trains and would squeal, "Ewwww!" at the mention of something girly like fairies.'

I laugh out loud. 'My mum used to read one of the poems to me every night before bed. I loved them. I wished they were real.' I point out clumps of lilies of the valley that have sprung up along the path edges and quote a line from the Flower Fairies that pays tribute to their pretty white bell-shaped flowers. 'Elderflower Grove seems like the kind of place Cicely Mary Barker would have gone for inspiration. If there were going to be fairies anywhere, it would be here.'

Walking into the grounds of Elderflower Grove feels like wandering even further away from the outside world. The tallest weeds are Himalayan balsam with its pink and white flowers soon to turn into seed pods that burst when you touch them. Trees stand metres above our heads, a mix of elderflower and self-sown oaks, sycamores, and hazelnuts, and bluebells and white stems of wild garlic grow in their shade.

'My parents always used to say there were fairies in Elderflower Grove. When they were children, this was supposed to be a magical, mythical place.'

'Mermaids who combed their hair in the lake and a wishing well that really granted wishes?'

'Yes!' he says. 'What happened here? Back in the Fifties and Sixties, this was a magical wonderland, but by our generation, it's all ghouls and ghosts and murdery unpleasantness. In our parents' day, Elderflower Grove was a fairy tale. By our day, it was a horror story. What changed? It went from fairies flitting around to somewhere the local vampire population would hang out.'

'Surely Guillaume is what happened? She went from being a happy young woman to someone sad and bitter, desperately searching for her lost love. Maybe *that* is when things started to change for Elderflower Grove.'

'And yet she travelled. She earned a living as a beekeeper. The beekeeper of Elderflower Grove. Just like you.'

'Oh, I'm not …' I trail off and glance back at him. 'She travelled to look for him. Or maybe because staying here without him was too painful sometimes and she had to get out.'

The burbling of the river is getting closer, and it isn't long before Carey's hand closes around my upper arm and pulls me back. The ground turns to rocks under my feet and we're on the edge of a bank that drops down sharply, and we both stand and look out across the trickling water and stony river beach, blocked by tree branches.

He urges me backwards, and uses the nippers to cut away the thickest branches, and at the sound of his first cut, there's a quack, and from somewhere upstream, a family of ducks takes flight, swearing loudly in our direction.

'Ducks!' I squeal in excitement. 'Josie had a river in her garden with *ducks*!'

Carey's put his tools aside and started climbing down the bank, and he turns and holds his hand out to me. I don't really need the help, but I slip my hand into his anyway. His fingers close around mine and he locks his elbow, making his arm feel ridiculously strong and I lean on him and step down one foot at a time.

'I've never known anyone to get so abnormally excited about ducks.'

If there's anything worth getting excited about, it's definitely ducks. We reach the riverbank and Carey doesn't let go of my hand straight away, giving me a chance to find my footing first. The weather has been dry lately so the water level is low, but I still want to dip my toes in.

'This is incredible,' I whisper. I'm repeating myself but I say it again. 'This is *in* her garden. Her own private part of the river. Her own ducks. It's criminal that someone wants to destroy this. What about the river?'

'It'll be re-routed.' He realises he hasn't let go of my hand yet because he yanks his away and murmurs an apology, shaking his fingers like he's got pins and needles.

'Do you miss designing gardens?'

'Very much so.' He looks down the river to the point where it disappears from view and breathes like he's filling his lungs. 'Being surrounded by nature soothes my soul. It settles something inside me. It's easy to forget I've lost my job when *this* has been my home for the past few weeks.'

'Are you looking for another job?'

He hesitates before he answers. 'Yes and no. I have no other discernible talents and I can't imagine working in an office or being shut indoors somewhere all day. I've only ever worked for one company, so I don't have loads of references – only one boss who's *really* not happy with me. I don't fancy my chances of getting another job based on what his reference will say.' He looks at me and then turns away again. 'I'm holding out hope that I can get mine back if I keep my head down, don't cause any trouble, and don't rock any boats for a while.'

I pick up a flat stone and skim it across the water. It bounces twice and then sinks with a plop.

'How about you? What happens when the Elderflower Grove contract is up? Will you look for another beekeeper gig elsewhere or go back to candles?'

The thought of this being over is horrible. Even though the interviewing bee made it clear this was for one season only, I still hoped that I could prove myself and be re-employed next year. I had no idea it would be the end of Elderflower Grove for good. 'Back to looking for any job that will have me, I guess. Not candles. That's gone, along with all my savings. I can barely look at a candle now …' I stop myself when he looks at me curiously.

Instead of pursuing it, he gives me a proud grin as he picks up a flat stone and skims it so it bounces five times and only stops when it hits the boulders on the opposite side of the river. Of *course* someone so outdoorsy is a master stone skimmer.

'We should take some stones and give them to the Nectar Inspectors' grandchildren to paint. Genuine, bona fide Elderflower Grove stones.'

I feel carefree and childlike as we walk around on the dry riverbed, selecting the flattest and best shaped of the water-smoothed stones. Carey shrugs the rucksack off his shoulders and moves aside our lunches and Josie's tin of letters to let me put them in the bottom, and doesn't complain about carrying the extra weight as he hefts it onto his back.

It's gone 11 a.m. when we make our way back up the bank. Carey holds his hand out again, but drops it as soon as we reach the path this time.

We're aiming towards the lake, which is quite a way over to the left, and it's nice wandering through the immense grounds, appreciating the butterflies that flutter past, the constant sound of birdsong from the trees, the easy conversation, and the way Carey can identify every tree and wildflower we pass and every bird singing every note.

On one narrow path, we're cut off by a solid block of hawthorn hedges, the almondy scent of their white blossom filling the air. We're about to turn back and try another way when I spot something through the spiky branches.

'What's that wooden thing?'

It's impossible to get through the hedgerows until Carey cuts branches off to make a gap, and we come out in a grass-covered clearing, surrounded on all sides by a wall of prickly hawthorns.

'They're beehives!' Climbing through the hedgerow reveals there's more than one of the wooden structures that caught my eye – a *lot* more, arranged in a circle around the clearing.

Carey stumbles straight into my back and I can *feel* the fear shoot through him. 'Oh good god, no. I've got to get out of here. I don't have my—'

'They're empty.' I reach out and grab his wrist, stopping him from racing back the way we came. 'There's not a bee in sight and no sound of buzzing anywhere. These hives aren't in use.'

'Are you sure?' He sounds hesitant and like he's unsure whether to trust me or not.

'Yes,' I say confidently. These hives are totally different from the ones on the roof. There's no bee activity *at all*.

'What on earth are these doing here?' I count them. 'And there's sixty of them, the same amount as there are up there.'

'Josie had a second apiary?'

'Yeah, but it's not been used.' I let his wrist drop and go over to the nearest hive. It's weather-beaten, but there are no traces of propolis around the edges, and no debris in the long grass around the base.

I lift off the roof and the crown board cautiously, not *quite* trusting myself at recognising bee activity, but there's not a single bee inside, and the frames are clean and empty. 'They've never been used. That's really strange.'

'What was she doing with sixty hives hidden away out here? We're *miles* from the house.'

'Maybe it wasn't Josie. Maybe it was one of the beekeepers who worked here after she disappeared.' I replace the lid and walk further down the field to remove the lid of another hive and make sure they're all the same.

'Well, the one I scared away was too busy ransacking the house to go near the garden, but I knew the bloke she replaced, and he never mention—'

'You knew the last beekeeper too? How long have you been here?'

'Not in that way. I came across him occasionally. In my job. It doesn't matter. What I mean is …' He trails off like he doesn't know what he means either.

'They've obviously been here for a fair few years.' Although the wooden hives are in good condition, nothing can withstand the

113

great British weather for long without sustaining some damage, but none of them show any sign of ever housing bees. It niggles at me. There's something odd about this.

I crouch down and tip one of the hives forwards, looking for something, anything, that might give us a clue. My fingers brush over the indent of a manufacturing stamp on the base, and I tilt the hive until I can see it. 'These were manufactured in the year of the fire. That's weird, right? That's got to mean something …'

He quirks an eyebrow. 'Like what?'

'I don't know.' I can feel the cogs in my brain turning. 'But Josie must have put them here herself. Before the fire. Like she was intending to move the bees …'

I can also see the cogs in *his* mind turning. 'What are you suggesting? That she … had something to do with the fire?'

'I don't know, but you've got to admit this is pretty weird, even by Elderflower Grove's standards.'

'I'm not sure the date means much. Those hives could have been put in at any time before the November of that year. We don't know that she put them there *right* before the fire. She could have been planning to relocate her bees.'

'Then why are they still on the roof?'

'Because she died before she had a chance?' He looks genuinely confused.

'No, that can't be right. Bees are inactive in the winter. The fire was in November. If she'd been intending to relocate the bees, she'd have done it in the spring or summer. Besides, you'd move the hives themselves, not move the bees to new hives. And why so far away from the house? The one thing I know about Josie is that she *loved* her rooftop apiary. She was up there every evening. Why would she want to move her hives all the way down here?'

'Maybe she couldn't do it anymore. Whether you go up through the house or use the outside staircase, those steps up to the roof are *hard*. And I say that with the knees of a thirty-eight-year-old.

114

Josie was ninety-two. It's not hard to believe that she was struggling with those steps.'

'But *that's* a trek.' I point in the direction we've just come. 'Maybe you're right about the steps – my knees are already complaining about them and it's only been a few days – but there's plenty of space all around the house. If she wanted the hives to be more accessible, why would she hide them all the way out here? That walk was arguably harder than climbing the steps to the roof.'

'I don't know, Kayl.' He shakes his head. 'Maybe she was starting to lose her marbles. Maybe she couldn't look after the bees anymore and was going to employ a beekeeper. Maybe she needed help with moving them and she didn't have anyone to help her. And everything's hidden now. Seven years ago, these were probably neat paths and somewhere there'll be a proper entranceway that's overgrown.' He looks around doubtfully and then sighs. 'Go on then, tell me what you're thinking.'

I stand in the middle of the circle formed by the hives. So many things don't make sense, and yet, somehow a theory has formed in my head that makes more sense than anything we know so far. 'What if she *really* isn't dead? What if she really did plan the fire? What if it was a cover to disappear?'

'But why? Why would a ninety-two-year-old do that?'

'I don't know.' I falter for a moment. 'But the fire was set away from the library and away from the bees – the two things she loved the most.'

'It was set by a firework thrown through the window on Bonfire Night. Kids tormenting the old witch of the village that wasn't meant to go as far as it did.'

'A firework thrown through a window that you can't access from the road.'

'That's ridi— What?'

'That's what doesn't make sense in your police report. The fire was started by kids throwing a firework, but you've shown

115

me the window it came through – it's at the back. You can't even see it from the outside.'

'Then I suppose they thought someone got into the grounds. It's difficult but not inconceivable.'

All right, he's got a point there, but something about this doesn't add up. 'These hives are here for a reason. Smoke makes bees docile. They load up on as much honey as possible in case there's a fire that will drive them from their homes. That's *why* we use a smoker before we open the hives. Josie knew that. She must've thought that when the bees sensed smoke, they'd gather up what they needed and abandon the rooftop hives.' My voice is getting faster as my mind turns over this possibility.

I'm certain he's going to laugh at me, but he listens, and it makes me feel more confident in my theories. 'I don't think these hives were put here for humans to find – they were for the *bees* to find. She assumed the bees would be driven from their hives and need to find new homes. She put them down here, surrounded by hedges that would blossom in the spring, ready for when the bees needed them.'

'But the fire didn't spread as much as she thought it would so they never used them?'

'Exactly. Think about it. The fire was set on November the fifth. Bonfire Night. If you want to start a fire without anyone noticing, *that* is the night to do it. That's how you hide a fire in plain sight – by lighting it on the one night a year when *all* of Britain is on fire. It's too much of a coincidence.' I look at him standing with his head cocked to the side, thinking it through. 'You think I'm mad, don't you?'

'Not at all. I'm thinking I got exceptionally lucky on the day you stabbed me with a fire poker. I couldn't have found a better beekeeper to help me solve the mystery of my possible-grandmother.'

I blush and we meet each other's eyes and blink for a few long seconds, and then he continues. 'But why? Why would she do

116

something like that? And where would she go? And why hasn't there been any trace of her since?'

'I don't know.'

'I don't know either.' He shakes his head, but his expressive face shows how unlikely he thinks my theory is.

It *is* unlikely, I know that. What would a ninety-two-year-old be doing burning down houses and setting up sixty beehives in the furthest reaches of her huge estate?

We look around at the empty hives. It's like standing in some sort of bee graveyard and even though the weather is warm, a chill goes through me. I can't shake the idea that Josie is still alive and hiding behind a bee filter, running the Nectar Inspectors group, still protecting her bees from beyond the grave.

Or *not* beyond the grave.

***

Outside the forested area, the walk towards the lake is full of wildflower meadows, fields filled with waves of buttercups, and absolutely *alive* with butterflies and damselflies, and the delicate scent of elderflower is strong in the air.

'What would you do if this was all yours? If you really are Josie's grandson and you inherit this, what would you do with it?'

'Keep it exactly as it is and open it up to the public,' he says without thinking about it. 'Cut it back a bit first, obviously. Get it back to being the nice garden area it must've been once. So many people could benefit from somewhere like this. The river, the fields, the lake if we ever find it. A place you could spend a day without having to spend money – something that's rare these days. Families, dogs, even horse rides if we could uncover a trail for them. Kayaking along the river. Pedal boats on the lake. All subsidised by some huge amount of money I don't currently have, but pipe dreams aren't meant to be realistic, are they?'

I can't help smiling back when he grins at me. It sounds

perfect, including the sudden magical cash injection we could all do with.

'Everywhere you go has hidden charges these days. I'd like to throw open the gates and let people come in and wander with no other expectation. Walk their dogs, eat picnics with the family, skim stones on the river, dip their toes in the lake, run around the maze trying to find the centre …'

'Is there really a maze here?'

'I can see what would've once been the entrance to it from the upper floor windows. It's over that way.' He points in the general direction of behind the manor house.

'Mazes are so old-fashioned and charming. The height of sophistication in days gone by. Kids want, I don't know, scavenger hunts and augmented reality Pokémon things popping out of their phones now, but the simplicity and allure of a maze never goes away.'

'That means you're going to come and uncover it with me one day then, yes?'

'Yes!' I say it so quickly that I might've metaphorically bitten his hand off. 'I'd love to.'

I meet his eyes and we grin at each other.

'I know it's pointless to bother with the garden when the whole place is being demolished, but I want to see a hint of what it was like in its glory days. I can't be here and *not* try to make it a little better, even if it's only for a while. Whether I'm related to Josie or not, someone should bear witness to Elderflower Grove's last days and remember it as it was.'

It makes that overwhelming sadness resettle across us. The thought of Carey and me being the only two people to ever see this place before it's wiped from the landscape for good … 'Why don't we do that?'

'Open it up to the public?' He laughs and then looks at me with a raised eyebrow when I don't laugh too. 'Are you serious?'

I nod enthusiastically as the idea gathers speed.

'Where do you want me to start? Firstly, it's not ours *to* open up. Secondly, it's hazardously overgrown and dangerous. Thirdly—' He sounds like the list could go into the twenties, so I interrupt him.

'No, it's not ours, but it doesn't belong to anyone at the moment. Well, Josie, but if she's really dead, then it's in limbo because the council don't own it yet. And if she's not dead then she's seven years past caring what happens to Elderflower Grove. Yes, it's overgrown and hazardous, but *we* could fix that. You're a gardener. You're desperate to get stuck into sorting this chaos out, and the bees aren't a full-time job, so I can help. We're the only two people who know this is here. *Everyone* should know before they knock it down. You said someone should bear witness to its final days – why don't we let them?'

'No one can know about the theme park. I wasn't supposed to tell you, and I'm going to be in serious trouble if anyone finds out.'

'I can say I was poking around inside and found some paperwork or something. No one will know it came from you.'

'Paperwork that *I'm* not supposed to have. This is the most ridiculous thing I've ever heard. We *cannot* tell anyone any of this. And we can't throw the gates open and let people go poking around anywhere they fancy. The house genuinely is unsafe, for a start—'

'We could block that off.'

He frowns at me but I carry on. 'I'm serious, Carey. Everything you've just said is right. The *slight* trifle that we don't actually own it is irrelevant. Until November, you and I are its caretakers. We have to do what's best for it, and it's *wrong* that we are the only people who know what's behind those gates. People have a right to know there's a country park on their doorsteps, and they definitely have a right to know what the council are planning to do. The villagers would be up in arms if they knew about the theme park. What about the bees? The villagers *love* our bees. They'll never stand for them being relocated. There will be protests and petitions. They will fight for Elderflower Grove if they know what there is to fight for. Maybe if the council know that opening it as it is will be popular, they'll reconsider a theme park.'

He makes a scoffing noise. 'Believe me, they will *never* reconsider something that will bring them such a vast amount of revenue.'

'You don't know that. They might be keen to keep their local residents happy.'

'Kayleigh, there is a "no entry" sign with the council leader's face on it strapped to the gate. *That* is indicative of the relationship between our local council and their residents. Our councillors have never listened to a resident in their lives – the only people they listen to are their accountants.'

'So we have until November to prove you're Josie's grandson.'

'We don't know that I am *or* that there will be any proof.'

'Then we have until November to give Elderflower Grove the send-off it deserves. The villagers need to know what this place is like.' I think of both Wilbur and Gracie, each stopping at the gate, peering in worriedly. 'We need to debunk the ghost stories. Elderflower Grove is a good place, a nice place. We can let people see that for themselves.'

He sighs. 'You don't understand. No one can know the stuff I've told you.'

'What if we don't tell them? What if we just tidy it up and open the gates? We don't *have* to say it's the final year, but the council have got to tell them eventually, *then* they'll be up in arms and storming the offices.'

'They're not going to tell anyone until *every* last shred of paperwork is signed. There will be no time for protests when it's already too late.'

'That's horrible. That's *really* horrible, you know that, right?'

He sighs again. 'Of course I know that. I hate what they're doing. I hate that there are people in this world who can see an area like this and *want* to destroy it, but that's the world we live in. Two people can't change that.'

'How do you know if we don't try?'

'We *can't* try. For so many reasons. It's a grand idea, a dream for this place, but it's not realistic.' He sounds so finite and resolved, and there's no way it's something I could do without him onboard, and maybe it is just thinking out loud, dreaming out loud, and I *don't* know what kind of work would be involved in it or the legal ins and outs, but I do know one thing – being at Elderflower Grove makes me feel alive for the first time in years, and I'm not giving up on this.

Chapter 8

Bees can detect landmines. By exposing honeybees to the odour of chemicals used in explosives and giving them a sugar water reward, scientists have trained bees to stick their tongues out whenever they sense the correct chemical.

Up close, the lake looks less like something Mr Darcy would emerge from, and more like something some sort of swamp monster would emerge from. The water has a greenish tinge and a muddy look to it, and there are reeds all around the edges that a family of moorhens swiftly hide in.

'No mermaids then,' Carey says as we reach the clearing surrounding the lake.

'Mermaids would have more discerning taste than this. Let's face it, the only thing it's missing is an old supermarket trolley.'

'It looks inviting. When you get past all the sludge and slime, it's clear further out.' He points towards the middle of the lake where it is, indeed, clear enough that you can see the sludgy bottom with all manner of reeds and thriving slimy pond life.

'I bet it was wonderful once. Swans and ducks, and frogs on lily pads. Look.' He nods towards the edge of the water, and we both crouch down to see masses of tadpoles swimming, and further out, there's the telltale ripple of a fish coming up for air.

'Does this feel really special to you? We're the only two people in the universe who have seen this place, Carey. At least for seven years, if not more, because I can't imagine a ninety-two-year-old doing that walk often. It feels like we're a part of nature itself.'

He reaches out for my hand and I let my fingers curl around his, and we stand there looking out at the water in silence. It's a question he doesn't need to answer. I can see his awe on his face.

It feels like we're on the verge of something great, like anything could be possible at Elderflower Grove – magic, love, fairies and pixies and other things every adult stopped believing in decades ago.

There's an island in the middle of the lake with an overgrown tree on it, overhanging so low that its branches dangle across the surface of the water. It looks so much like Grandmother Willow in *Pocahontas* that I wouldn't be even vaguely surprised if it started talking. 'It's like being in a Disney movie.'

It could have been a romantic and magical moment where his lips lower to mine and we kiss as fireworks burst above our heads, but what actually happens is my stomach lets out such a loud rumble that the fish in the lake probably hears it, never mind Carey.

He finds a flat, grassy spot in amongst the tall poppies and the orangey-red star-shaped flowers of scarlet pimpernel, shrugs the rucksack off his shoulders, and gets out a fleece blanket, which he spreads carefully, avoiding squashing even a single flower. He sits down cross-legged, pulls the rucksack in front of him and starts getting our lunches out while I sit down opposite him.

I can't tear my eyes away from the lake as we eat and drink tea from the flask he's brought, enjoying the soft lap of the water on the grassy edges, listening to the buzz of bees visiting the wildflowers all around us, and watching for the occasional ripple that indicates life in the water.

'Do you think they'll keep any part of it?'

'Honestly?' He pulls his knees up and puts his arms around them. 'No. Not a chance. I've seen the plans. No part of the estate remains.'

'From your "friends in the right places"?'

'Exactly.' He rests his chin on his knees. 'The more time I spend here, the more I start to wonder if they're friends in the *wrong* places.'

When I glance at him, his cheeks have reddened.

'Your enthusiasm is inspiring. I wish we could …' He trails off and sighs again. 'I just *wish* in general. I wish it didn't have to be this way.'

I run a fingertip over the blue petals of a cornflower next to me. 'This is exactly what they're telling people to do these days. Save the bees. Don't cut your lawns. Let patches of wildflowers grow. Bees and other pollinators are in major decline. If we went public with this – if we told people, newspapers, social media, what the local council is planning – there would be backlash. The kind that couldn't be ignored.'

He doesn't say anything, and it's my turn to sigh.

Josie's tin is sticking out the top of his bag and I reach over for it, select a letter, and read it aloud.

February 2nd, 2001

My dearest Guillaume,

Someone broke in the other night. I woke up to find a man in my bedroom, rooting through my drawers. For just a moment in the barely awake haze, I thought it was you and I was overjoyed you'd come back. Glad to see a burglar, can you imagine? He had a knife, which he threatened me with. He took my money and some trinkets, nothing that mattered. I let him. I didn't call the police. I didn't want the fuss. I didn't want people poking through our house, finding your things, asking me about you.

I cried after he left. I sat at the kitchen table for hours with a knife in my hand in case he came back. God knows what I thought I was going to do with a butter knife, but I was shaking so much that I didn't trust myself to hold a proper knife. I was so scared. My private space, invaded. I don't know if I'll ever feel safe here again. I don't know why I'm telling you. You stopped being my protector long ago. It was one of those moments where your absence makes me feel weak, and I hate you for it. For the first time, I wished I had a neighbour or someone I could call on, but there's no one. I've pushed them all away. The 'old witch' of Little Kettling, alone, as always.

Forever love,
Josie

'That's horrific.' I glance at the date. 'She would have been in her late seventies then. She must have been so scared. Even her handwriting is shakier than usual.'

Carey holds his hand out for the letter. 'Does not wanting people to ask questions suggest that no one knew of him?'

'Maybe?' I look over at him. 'I'm sorry she knew what people thought of her because I don't think she was like that at all.'

'Maybe her solitude made her feel better. Like she didn't deserve anyone knowing or caring about her.'

His chin is resting on his knees again, the letter dangling from his fingers, but there's something in his voice, a hurt of his own, that makes me want to reach out and rub my fingers across his tanned forearms.

I force myself not to be so silly and take the letter from his hand, put it back in the tin and pick out another one.

August 15th, 2004

My dearest Guillaume,
You won't believe the afternoon I've had. I was minding my own business, tending the bees on the roof of the Plaza

Hotel in New York when I was called to collect a swarm from … guess where … only the Statue of Liberty's crown! We drove at top speed in a police car and dashed off on a boat to Liberty Island. I felt like I was in an action movie. The police officer who accompanied me came back tonight. He'd bought me a box of chocolates and a bottle of wine to thank me for my time. He asked if I'd go out to dinner with him, but I politely declined.

I'm an idiot, aren't I? I haven't seen you in twenty-five years. I should have said yes. It would've been nice to have some male company, even though we live on different sides of the world. We could've had a pleasant evening. Maybe he would even have stolen a kiss.

But, no. I'm still holding out for you. Thinking those kinds of thoughts about someone else makes me feel like I'm cheating on you, even after all these years. I'm an idiot, aren't I?

I should have moved on long ago.

Forever love,

Josie

The sadness pervades every letter. But there's anger now too as the dates get later. 'His disappearance must've turned her life upside down.'

'You keep saying disappearance. Do you not think he left her?'

'I don't know. Why, do you?'

'Obviously.' He scoffs. 'In my experience, love *never* lasts. He probably got a better offer from someone else and cast her aside. Ghosting someone must've been easier back then without social media and phones.'

'You can't be serious. She calls him the love of her life – her soulmate. You think he just stopped loving her and moved on?'

'What *other* way does a relationship end?' He sounds bitter and, while I think he was trying not to show the hurt in his voice, he fails at hiding it. He clonks his forehead down onto the hands holding his knees up, his light brown hair flopping forward, and I bite my lip as I look at him.

I don't know what makes me do it, but I fold Josie's letter back into its envelope, and then reach across to tuck his hair back, my fingers brushing through the light brown strands, warm in the sun, and he lets out a sigh of contentment and his eyes drift closed.

'You've really been hurt, right?'

'No, I—' He lifts his head and meets my eyes. 'For some reason, you make me not want to put on a front with you. Yeah, I have. My ex-wife—' He stops again. 'You too, I gather.'

'No one gets to thirty-six *without* being hurt, but not enough to give up on love completely. There's no way Guillaume simply decided he didn't love her anymore. Something must've happened to him.'

He grunts, but he hasn't made any move to dislodge my hand yet, so I continue tucking his hair back, the sun-warmed strands slipping through my fingers.

'Josie obviously thinks he left.' His voice sounds relaxed and not as certain as he was moments ago. 'If something had happened to him, an accident or something, she would know. She wouldn't be looking for him in places all over the world.'

'Maybe he was kidnapped,' I suggest.

Instead of answering, he shifts his head and raises an eyebrow so disbelieving that it leaves me in no doubt how likely he finds my grasping-at-straws suggestion.

Mainly, I want to push him to finish the sentence about his ex, but sitting here brushing his hair back is probably weird enough, and he clearly doesn't want to talk about it.

'Is it warm today or is it just me?'

I murmur an agreement, too distracted by his arm muscles and how peaceful his face looks with his eyes closed that I'm not really capable of following the conversation.

Like he can sense the change in atmosphere, he pushes himself onto his knees, dislodging my hand with a clunk.

'I'm going for a swim.'

'In that?' I stare at the water in horror. 'You don't know what could be living in there!'

'A few fish, I wouldn't wonder.'

'No, I mean, pond life. Pond-skaters. Leeches. Parasite things that crawl into your body parts and start eating your brain.'

Oh no, 'body parts' was *not* a good thing to mention because it draws my attention in all sorts of inappropriate directions, and he glances downwards with a raised eyebrow like he can tell what I'm thinking.

'Eels!' I say to get my mind off said inappropriate direction. 'It's exactly the sort of place there would be eels.'

'Eels don't live in British lakes, but you watch too much TV – has anyone ever told you that?'

'Freshwater sharks! Crocodiles!'

'Again, those are horror movies, not real life.' He laughs. 'What's the worst that's going to happen? I'll be eaten by an angry mermaid?'

'Well, it's not *impossible* …'

'Get your phone out then because a video clip of *that* will make us millions.' He gives me a wink as he bends down to put his phone on the blanket and unlace his walking boots. 'Are you coming?'

He cannot be serious. 'No! Not in a million ye—'

'It's a beautiful day for a swim.'

'Yeah, in water. That's not water, that's a swamp. With swamp-like things living in it that would really *welcome* the fresh blood of an intruder after all these years.'

He grins as he stuffs his socks inside his boots and then walks backwards, barefoot across the grass, which is bad enough due to the undoubted presence of stinging nettles in this wildflower meadow, never mind actually getting *in* to that water.

'You're fully clothed! Your jeans will chafe on the walk back!'

I realise I've accidentally turned into someone's mother

because he laughs out loud, his eyes twinkling as he walks away. 'If you want to see me strip, Miss Harwood, you only have to ask. However, the answer would be "no", so yes, while in polite company, I intend to swim fully clothed. Come back on a moonlit night, however …' He waggles suggestive eyebrows and I can't help giggling.

He's a total conundrum of a man. Fun and laid-back, cheeky and good-natured, serious about the things that matter, and yet sharp and standoffish too. I don't know what happened with his ex-wife, but it was obviously bad enough to leave emotional scars, and yet sometimes, he seems like a naughty schoolboy who the teachers are always trying to stop doing silly things with potential for grievous bodily harm.

Instead of wading in carefully, he reaches the edge of the bank and then dives in one smooth move, avoiding the green slime and creating a huge splash in the clearer, deeper area of the water, and there's a flurry of terrified peeping as the moorhen family scoot into a different patch of reeds.

I feel like I'm on the set of *Pride and Prejudice*, but Mr Darcy never looked *this* good. Not even when played by Colin Firth.

Carey surfaces with his wet hair stuck over his face and shakes it back. 'Water's lovely!'

He takes a breath and dives down again, and when he resurfaces this time, he calls, 'No eels!'

I watch as he swims around, and to be fair, it *does* look inviting, and I kind of wish I *was* brave enough to join him. Although maybe a better plan is to wait and see if he gets any infectious diseases or parasitic ticks in the next few days, and maybe I can join him next time.

It's probably weird to just sit here watching, so I go through the tin of Josie's letters and select the final letter in the box. There are plenty more we haven't read, and it feels like skipping to the last page of a book to see if you'll like it or not, but it also might provide some answers.

My dearest Guillaume,

I've just been asked to go to Fiji this summer to care for their bees. Do you remember how often we spoke of it being our dream honeymoon location? Sometimes I think the universe is deliberately playing tricks on me by sending me to places that remind me of you. Gracie tells me I am too old to be travelling now, but I like to travel – it makes me feel like I'm doing something rather than sitting here and waiting to rot.

I'm in the banquet hall tonight – I always set an extra place for you, even though I know you won't be here. I still dream of the nights we danced around the ballroom. The way you were so determined to get up those steps after the accident. You promised me that we would dance in the ballroom when you recovered, and we did. The moment you took those first steps is still one of the greatest of my life. The way you made me tell you where my favourite place in the house was and then refused to kiss me until you could kiss me there, and those torturous months while you learnt to walk again, so you could be strong enough to make it to the library and we could finally share that one magical kiss. There has never been a more wonderful kiss in the history of the world.

You thought my love had healing properties. You recovered so quickly after that. It wasn't long before we were dancing in the ballroom every night. The greatest years of my life. I'm grateful to you for that. I often get angry when I write these letters, but my new year's resolution is to be grateful for what I have, and I had a love greater than most people will ever be lucky enough to know. For that, I thank you.

Forever love,
Josie

Carey has made it to the island on the other side of the lake. He pushes his body up on both hands and climbs out of the water, and even from this distance, I can see how the wet T-shirt clings to well-defined back muscles, and I take another sip of my tea to hide the fact I might be drooling.

He waves from dry land. 'I think there's something living over here. Possibly Bigfoot.'

'You're hilarious,' I mutter, even though it wouldn't be a huge surprise if Bigfoot *was* living on that island. It doesn't look like it's been disturbed since the last century – *anything* could've taken up residence.

He shakes water off like a dog that's just had a bath, and although it's a mental image that shouldn't be sexy, any formation of Carey and wet undeniably *is*. He bends under dead trees with fallen branches, and disappears as he goes to look around the island, and even though internally I'm still shouting something about the dangers of being barefoot, I wish I was over there too. It looks like the kind of place you could put a little hut and sit for hours with a book, watching the wildlife all around.

Including the eels. Probably.

I can hear the snapping of branches as he moves, and suddenly there's a flurry of angry quacking, and Carey dashes into view and leaps feet-first back into the water, being chased by an enraged duck.

It stands on the bank screeching at him, staring him down until he's swum a satisfactory distance away. I'm doubled-over with laughter as the duck waddles back to its nest with a final threatening quack in Carey's direction. Of all the things to be scared of, he definitely *is* scared of infuriated ducks.

As he swims towards me, I lean back on my arms and turn my face to the sun, and I feel a sense of calm that's been missing from my life lately. With the manor house just visible through the trees behind me, a gorgeous Mr Darcy splashing around in the lake, and no sound except for the chirrup of birds, it really does feel like being on the set of a Jane Austen adaptation. All I need is a bonnet and a parasol.

He reaches the edge and finds the least sludgy part to climb out, directly in front of where I'm sitting. I go to tease him about the duck, but …

Oh, holy abs, batman.

His T-shirt *had* to be white today, and it leaves *nothing* to the imagination. *Every* muscle is showcased by the see-through wet top, which draws attention to each one in turn, from distinct abs to the slight smattering of fair hair covering his chest, to wide shoulders and a defined collarbone.

He pushes himself out of the water on both hands, arm muscles straining against wet fabric, flexing, and my mouth has gone drier than a box of Weetabix. I squint upwards and use my hand to shade my eyes from the brightness of the sunlight behind him, making him look like some golden god glistening with water, his torso carved of pure marble.

There is a *lot* to be said for outdoor work.

I down a shot of now-cold tea before I can get any words out. 'Fun?' There. One word will have to suffice for now.

'Would've been better with company.' He grins, and it makes my knees feel weak even though I'm sitting down.

He's definitely noticed my staring. 'Should I start enquiring if your family is in good health?'

An unexpected laugh bursts out. '*You* know *Pride and Prejudice*?'

'I've seen the TV adaptation. Can't forget that scene. It made me determined to dive into any lake I come across since.' He nods to the letter forgotten in my hand. 'Did you read any more?'

'There was an accident.'

'With the letters?' He looks worried.

'With Guillaume.' I read the letter aloud because I'm not having him dripping all over it. 'She's signed off on a positive note, but it's not exactly the sweeping final goodbye I was expecting.'

'Maybe it's not the last letter,' Carey says. 'Maybe it's just the last one that would fit in the tin. Maybe there are more hidden in other places, like the one you found with the key.'

'Maybe it was the last one she wrote before he came back?' I say hopefully.

I expect him to laugh and say something dismissive, but he cocks his head to the side, water dripping from his hair. 'I love your optimism. I thought it was annoying at first, but no one's looked on the bright side in my life for a very long time, and I like that you do.'

I didn't even know that I did, but something feels right about Elderflower Grove. Like we're both here exactly when we're meant to be.

'How are you scared of bees, but you'll plunge your hand into dark crevices and dive into unholy-looking water without a second thought?' I ask as he sits down on the blanket, water seeping from his jeans, and pulls his boots across, brushing water off with his socks before putting them back on.

He squeezes water out of the longish top part of his hair and thinks it over before answering. 'Because you're the first person in a really long while to care whether I hurt myself or not.'

I bite my lip to stop the intake of breath. It's such a simple answer but it feels heavy and honest. I shouldn't touch him again, I've already crossed god knows how many lines today, but I reach out and slide my hand over his as he's lacing up his boots. 'You had better get used to it.'

A look passes over his face and all his features soften. He sighs and his body loses some of his usual tension. His hand covers mine, and he meets my eyes and gives me a soft, gentle smile that makes something tingle inside me. A little fizzle that sparkles through the air between us and I don't think it has anything to do with the magic of Elderflower Grove.

Chapter 9

A queen bee lays 2,500 eggs a day in summer.

Gracie's shop stands at the corner of Little Kettling high street, a wide, traffic-free, cobblestone affair with quaint little shops, where owners display their goods outside on sunny days, and a café, with tables and chairs under a striped awning that's the central hub of village gossip.

It's a place that's stood still in time and where any of Jane Austen's nineteenth-century characters would fit right in; I can picture Edmund Bertram riding along on horseback or the Bennet sisters strolling past on an errand for Mrs Bennet.

Gracie's corner shop faces diagonally outwards, a sentinel for the rest of the row. It started off as a grocery shop, and while she still sells essentials like milk and bread and fresh fruit and veg, over the years, most of her stock has been replaced simply by things she likes, and an entire section is dedicated to selling crafts by local people.

The same sign of the local councillor's face with a 'no entry' symbol over it is laminated and stuck to her door. The bell tinkles as I go in.

'Hello!' She pops up from behind the counter, still dressed

in her yellow-and-black-striped top with fuzzy deely boppers bouncing around on her head. 'Kayleigh! It's so good to see you! Thank you for that remarkable honey harvest the other day, it's gone down a treat with the locals.'

I can't help but smile at the warm welcome. 'I hear you're hoarding some for later.'

'Shhhhh!' she shushes me quickly. 'Don't say that too loudly, they'll be in here looting the place for my secret stash!'

It's only just after eight, but I wanted to come here before going to Elderflower Grove because I can't get the thought of all those hidden hives out of my head. I produce the bag of stones that Carey and I collected yesterday, all carefully washed and bagged last night. 'We were exploring, and—'

Her ears prick up. 'We?'

'Me,' I correct, slapping my palm to my forehead. 'Me and the bees, obviously. They follow me around like a gang of … buzzy dogs.'

Buzzy dogs? What is *wrong* with me? 'Anyway, *I* found the river and thought the Nectar Inspectors' grandchildren might like some bona fide Elderflower Grove stones to paint.' I dump the heavy bag onto the counter, and Gracie oohs and ahhs as she goes through it.

'Ah, I remember that river from when I was a little 'un. Hard to imagine it's still there, meandering along, impervious to the passage of time.'

'You've been inside Elderflower Grove before then?' I ask in surprise.

'Oh, yes, petal. When I was *very* young, an embarrassing number of years ago now. We were all at school together, you see. My older sister was close to Josie's age. Her father would invite us over to play on summer evenings. He'd have the barbecue going in the courtyard – lots of village kids would come. We weren't allowed to go far – too dangerous for unsupervised children with the river and the lake and the well, but I used to come

135

home dreaming of mermaids singing and fairies flitting through the trees. My clothing used to smell of elderflower blossom for days afterwards. Her mother stopped inviting people after Josie's father died.'

'Did her family always own the house then?'

'For as many centuries as it's possible to trace back. I believe it was bought by a grandfather with a few "greats" in front of his name, lord knows how many centuries ago now. They say he was a knight riding through the village on his way elsewhere, and he locked eyes with a beautiful but impoverished maiden, and he immediately got off his horse and asked her what he'd have to do for her hand in marriage. She jokingly told him she'd accept nothing less than a mansion, and not twenty-four hours later, he arrived on her doorstep having bought the grand estate nearby. They were married within days and spent many long years together, raising a family of happy children.'

My hand is on my chest and my eyes have turned into heart-eye emojis. 'That's so romantic. A real fairy tale.'

'It's too long ago to verify, petal. It might just be an old wives' tale. You know how these things go over the generations.'

'I think it's true. There's something romantic about Elderflower Grove – it deserves a story that's not all ghosts and doom and gloom.'

She immediately asks if I've seen any ghosts, but I don't want to get off the topic of romance yet. 'How about Josie? Was she married? Seeing anyone special?'

I don't expect her laugh to echo through the shop. 'Josie? Married? Seeing anyone? Oh, you are funny.'

'She never talked about a man?' I prod, thrown by her reaction. Even her best friend doesn't know who Guillaume was?

'A man? Oh, heaven's no. Josie couldn't be doing with menfolk. She hated them.'

'Never? Not even when she was younger?'

'No. She was proudly single, always had been. Never wanted to conform and get married like the rest of us girls did. She thought we were quite silly to look for husbands and want babies.'

It's a perfect opportunity to do some digging on Carey's behalf. 'Did Josie ever have children?'

'Children? No, of course not. Josie hated children. She could never see why we wanted them. I used to play with my dollies and dream of the day I'd get to hold a baby of my own, whereas on the rare occasion that someone gave Josie a doll, we'd soon find it headless in the river. She had the maternal instincts of a postbox.'

If Carey's right, that could explain why she gave a baby up for adoption.

'What about … unwanted pregnancies?' I'm on thin ice here, probably too close to the line of acceptable questions to ask *and* ones that aren't going to arouse suspicion, but Gracie might be our only hope of figuring this out.

She repeats my question like she doesn't comprehend it. 'Josie was never pregnant. She would've hated the thought. Why? Have you found something to suggest otherwise? You haven't been inside, have you?'

'No, no, of course not. Just trying to understand her better.' I backpedal as fast as I can. 'She was an interesting woman, that's all.'

'Her honey was unbelievable. We used to sell it here in disguise. She thought her reputation within the village would put people off, so we labelled it "local wildflower honey" and didn't say where it had come from, and the villagers fell over themselves to snap it up and quickly started coming back for more. It gave Josie a real boost, and the revenue from it paid for some much-needed repairs on the house.'

Honey espionage. Each thing I hear about Elderflower Grove is more surprising than the one before.

'And you stayed in touch with her until … the end?'

'I'm a pushy old bat, if nothing else. She was my best friend and I wasn't going to let her push me out of her life, no matter what. I always said she could hide from the rest of the village, but not from me. She was very secretive about Elderflower Grove. Her friends were never invited over. Although she would occasionally join us for shopping trips and days out, she would always meet us outside and upon return, would insist on being dropped off here and walking home by herself. Any vague suggestions of it being a nice day to swim in the river were quickly shut down. But she did change. At a point in her fifties, she became withdrawn. She pushed us away. She stopped coming out. And not long after that, she gained employment from her beekeeping experience and started going away for months at a time. I never knew if she was home or not, and I'd see her so seldomly that we drifted apart.'

'What you said the other day – about Josie still being alive? Do you really think she could be running the Nectar Inspectors?'

Gracie sighs. 'I don't know. I'm probably repeating myself, but who *else* would do it? Who else would care about Elderflower Grove and those bees, *and* hide their own identity? It doesn't make sense unless it's Josie, and of course, it doesn't make sense at all if it *is* Josie. How did she escape the fire? And where is she?'

I shake my head in sympathy – both questions I keep asking too. 'Do you have any ideas of where she might've gone?'

'None at all. If she'd escaped the fire, she would have gone to someone for help. Me, probably. I was the closest person to her and I don't live far. And why would she disappear? She *must* have died, but there's always been a niggle in my head about it. There's something that doesn't make sense there, make no mistake.'

At least she thinks so too. I hesitate on what to say next because I don't want to kick off the next round of village gossip, but the local council leader, Kingsley Munroe, chooses that moment to stroll past the window, and Gracie hisses like a cat.

To my surprise, she grabs a stick from behind the counter and rushes outside, chasing him down the street, brandishing it in his direction. It would be quite concerning if it wasn't so utterly hilarious to see a pensioner dressed as a bee screaming obsceni-ties at a smartly dressed middle-aged man.

'The nerve he's got to show his face around here!' She's out of breath when she comes back in and slams the door behind her. She strokes the stick lovingly. 'This is my beating stick. All the Little Kettling shop owners have got one. If he has the guts to come near us, he knows full well he'll be on the business end of it.'

'What's he done now?' I ask, suspecting that a list of his crimes might be so long that I'll need a cup of tea to see me through.

'I'll tell you what he's done now. Always destroying things. You know that gorgeous big oak tree on the village green?'

I nod. It's the first thing you see when entering Little Kettling, right behind the 'Welcome to Little Kettling' sign. It must be a couple of hundred years old, and it maps the arrival of autumn as its leaves change colour and squirrels run up and down its branches gathering acorns.

'He wants to tarmac over that patch of grass and he's been trying for years to claim the tree is a hazard, and yesterday, one of the residents noticed an orange cross spray-painted onto its trunk at the base – the council symbol for a tree that's had weedkiller injected into it. He couldn't get it done with paperwork, so he's underhandedly murdered our beautiful tree. How could anyone do such a thing?' She looks like she's about to cry.

'That's horrific. Surely he can't get away with that?'

'People like him get away with everything. That's what's so wrong.'

'I'm not sure hitting him with a stick will help …'

'I don't mind. I'll happily be arrested. Someone needs to show him the damage he's doing to our village. He hasn't been bothering you, has he?'

'I haven't seen him once.'

'Good.' She gives a sharp nod. 'Of course, that probably means the horrible knickerbocker glory is busy doing other things, like cutting down more wildflowers. He's had more verges strimmed overnight. Imagine doing such abhorrent things that he can't even do them in daylight hours, he has to send his minions out to cut down every flower under the cover of darkness.' She sighs. 'No matter. We'll keep re-sowing our wildflower seed bombs in every available space. We'll sow so many that he won't be able to keep up with us. *Our* bees will have plenty to forage on under my watch!' The vehemence in her voice is impressive. I never knew squabbles over flower verges could get so serious.

'What do you think will happen to Elderflower Grove now?' I ask her to see if the villagers know about the significance of the approaching seven-year marker from Josie's death.

'Happen to it?' She looks confused. 'Absolutely nothing, I would imagine. It's in limbo, isn't it? I suppose it's in the care of some solicitor or other, but with no family and no heirs, it's doomed to stay that way forever. I do hope you'll come back next spring, you're the best beekeeper we've had for years.'

The bar for beekeepers must be set very, *very* low. But it does prove Carey's right. They *really* haven't a clue that anything's going to happen to Elderflower Grove. The news of the theme park nearly bursts out of my mouth, sentences spilled all over the counter, because *she* would be first in line to do something about it. She'd rally the locals. She'd protest. Maybe she'd find a way to stop it.

I bite the inside of my cheek *hard*. I can't betray Carey's trust like that, even though telling the villagers is the best chance we've got of stopping it.

Another one of the Nectar Inspectors comes in, and Gracie introduces me before they start gossiping, and I take the opportunity to mooch around the shop, looking at the local craft things on offer: handmade clay flowers, dainty bee-themed jewellery, and felted animals and gnomes, the display table dotted with painted stones, and a stand of handmade occasion cards that all revolve around bee puns. The Elderflower Grove honey is arranged in a seriously depleted pyramidal stack. There's a glass case of fresh pastries made by a local baker, so I pick out two cinnamon buns for me and Carey and take them to the counter.

Both Gracie and her friend eye me.

'Two?' Gracie asks cheerfully as she rings them up.

'All that honey gives you a hearty appetite.' I pat my stomach and laugh, even though they don't. 'One for now, one for later,' I add when it becomes clear they expect an answer.

I pay and make a hasty exit, and wander back along the leafy streets, passing grassy verges that were full of wildflowers only a few days ago, now strimmed down to ground level.

When I get inside the Elderflower Grove gate and walk up to the courtyard, I stop in surprise. There's a pair of oversized glasses resting on the gargoyle's nose. It's got Carey's sense of humour written all over it. Who *else* would do something like that?

'So he can see out again,' Carey calls, unseen from one of the window frames. I laugh at the throwback to yesterday morning when I tried to scrub the moss from his eyes.

'I'm sure he'll appreciate it, although I'm not sure even Specsavers could sort that one out,' I call up, feeling like I'm speaking to the house itself. 'And you just happened to have a pair of oversized glasses about your person?'

'It's amazing what you can find in Elderflower Grove when you most need it.' He appears at one of the second-floor windows and smiles down at me. 'Thought I'd better start treating inanimate objects with the same reverence you do.'

'Don't call him inanimate out loud, he'll hear you.' I grin at him and he grins back at me, until we've been grinning at each other for an abnormally long time, and he suddenly turns serious.

'You have no idea how glad I am to see you.'

I go warm all over. That's *so* nice. I'm glad to see him too. Maybe I'm not the only one feeling *something* here.

'I got breakfast.' I hold up the bag I'm carrying to hide the fact I'm red and blushy and unsure of what to say.

'Yeah, thank god you're here.' He inclines his head to the left. 'You've got a swarm.'

All the warmth I was feeling instantly dissipates and

disappointment punches me square in the chest. *That's* why he's glad to see me.

'Is that bad?' I ask, even though the terms 'bees' and 'swarm' are unlikely to fill anyone with unbridled joy.

Even from this distance, I can see the perplexed look on his face. 'Er, yeah, if you don't want to lose half the hive, that is.'

My blankness must show because he says, 'You look like you need coffee with that breakfast. Rooftop in five minutes?'

I nod and hurry around the side and up the steps to the roof.

'Morning, bees,' I say quickly as I scramble the beekeeping bible out of my bag, desperately try to find 'swarm' in the index, and rush to open the chapter on the right page. My eyes scan over the opening lines. Something about when the hive gets overcrowded, the queen bee leaves and half the bees follow her, while the remaining bees have to grow a new queen. Something I should have noticed signs of in the last few days and been prepared for. Brilliant.

Carey's quicker than me and appears on the roof before I've got to the part that explains what you're supposed to do about it, and I hastily slam the book shut and hide it underneath my bag.

'Good morning, Queen Bee.'

'Good morning.' The nickname makes me smile every time he uses it, despite the rising panic that he's expecting me to do something about this swarm.

He swaps a coffee for a cinnamon bun and sits down on the bench to clink our mugs together. 'So, let me get this straight, you're a beekeeper and you've never dealt with a swarm before?'

'Well, yeah, I've *dealt* with them but never in this situation.'

'I believe bee swarms are the same anywhere.'

'Oh, right.' I glance at the edge of the book sticking out from under my bag. I *really* need a moment alone with it.

'They're on one of the elderflower trees. You'll be able to reach them from a stepladder if you want to start a new colony or you could just let them go and find somewhere else to live.'

142

'What would Josie Garringham do?'

'Well, judging by the fact there are sixty hives on her roof, it doesn't seem like she's ever let a swarm go, does it?'

I haven't got a clue what he's talking about.

My face must be more traitorous than I think, because he says, 'Do you want to read your book? You seem a little rusty.'

'Yes! Rusty! That's it! I've been out of the beekeeping industry for a while. I should refresh …' It feels awful lying to him, but what else can I do? I should have admitted I wasn't a beekeeper from day one, and now it's even worse because I've been lying to him for the ten days I've known him, and between harvesting five hundred jars of honey and the inside info he's told me, I *should* have been open with him too. There's no reason to have hidden it from him, and now the reason is solely because I *have* hidden it from him.

'They're over there.' He uses his mug to point in the direction of an elderflower tree at the edge of the courtyard, and I eat the last bite of the cinnamon bun and walk across to the corner of the rooftop, keeping a safe distance from the hives when I'm not suited up.

On a low branch, there are literally *thousands* of bees in a cluster, crawling all over each other. The branch is way below roof level, and it's like looking down on a huge, pulsating mass.

That's a bee swarm? What on earth am I supposed to do with *that*?

That is a *lot* of bees to have to do something about and I haven't a clue where to start. The thought makes me feel quite queasy.

I go back to the bench and pick up my coffee mug again.

'You say I'm brave, but you're incredible to deal with that,' Carey says with a shudder.

'You ever been stung?' I get the impression he's regretting the decision to come up here, but I quickly realise that talking about bee stings possibly isn't the *best* way to get someone's mind off the mass of bees on the other side of the roof wall.

'Yeah, when I was younger. Wasn't a good experience. Not something I want to repeat anytime soon.'

'I'm sorry.' I'd guessed as much because his fear has to come from somewhere. I go to reach out, intending to slide my hand over the top of his and squeeze it, and then realise what I'm doing and pull it back.

Maybe I should let them go. It would certainly be the easiest way, but my mind is flooded with images of those poor little homeless bees. What will happen if they don't find somewhere else to live? They'll have no way of surviving without a decent hive to make their honey in.

Bees probably don't understand the concept of abandonment in the way we do, but still. I don't want to let thousands of bees die because I'm intimidated by the prospect of dealing with a swarm. This job is supposed to be about saving bees.

To buy myself some time while I figure out what's best to do, I tell him about everything Gracie said this morning, including being certain that Josie never had a child.

'Maybe it's true.' He sounds demoralised. 'Maybe she didn't and I'm totally wrong. It's just that as soon as my dad said it, Elderflower Grove came into my head and ...'

'Gracie wouldn't necessarily know. Your dad was adopted very young, right?' I wait for him to nod and then continue. 'Josie wouldn't have wanted the villagers gossiping about her, and Gracie didn't see her regularly, she could easily have been pregnant without anyone knowing.'

'Yeah, I know, I just ...' He sighs and leans forward. 'I was so *sure*. It was an answer to why I'd always been drawn to this place, and the more time I spend here, the more I wonder if I'm wasting my time. What hope do I have of finding a grandmother on the basis of living in Hampshire and keeping bees? If it's not Josie, that's it, I have nothing else to go on. Another failure.'

'Care ...' This time I *do* I reach over and let the backs of my fingers trail against his sun-warmed forearm.

For just a second, his fingers slide over the top of mine and then he pulls back sharply. He downs the rest of his coffee and shudders because it's obviously still too hot. 'I'm going to carry on looking for proof. Far, *far* away from bee swarms. I'll leave you to get suited up and … prepared.' His eyes are on the not-so-hidden book, leaving me in no doubt that he realises I was cramming like the last moments before a school exam, but I appreciate him not saying anything about it as he disappears back inside the house.

I sit there and read the chapter from start to finish, rereading key points, thankful for the step-by-step instructions. I put the suit on, take a spare nucleus box from the Honey House, and a cardboard box to catch the bees in, and the bee brush, and head downwards again.

There's a stepladder leaning against the side of the house, and I shout a thank you and go across to the elderflower tree where thousands of bees are currently clinging on to a low-hanging branch in a monstrous, pulsing clump.

I gulp. To think people do this as a relaxing hobby.

Instead of giving myself time to think about it, I repeat the things from the book in my head.

I lay a ground cover sheet down, set the ladder against the tree, and climb it. I steel myself, hold the box underneath the mass of bees, and give the branch a firm shake. A huge number of the bees fall into the box, so many that I nearly drop it under the unexpected weight. I give the branch another shake, and then lean over to sweep the remaining bees off with the brush.

The bees are like liquid, they slide and move in waves, like stirring wet cement or a builder manipulating plaster onto a wall with a trowel. It seems terrifying to see this many bees all at once, but they should be at their most docile now, and so full of the honey they've eaten before leaving the hive that they wouldn't be able to tilt their abdomens enough to sting me even if they wanted to.

When I'm certain that all the bees are in the box, I climb down and tip it into the spare hive box, a nucleus colony now. I leave a gap when I put the lid on, allowing a space for any stragglers to get in.

Later on, I'll come back and take the nucleus box to the empty hives we found at the other end of the estate, and the bees can move in there, but for now, a feeling of elation washes over me. I did it. I removed my first swarm like a real beekeeper.

Back on the roof, I'm desperate to check on the other bees, but it's best not for them to be disturbed more often than necessary, so I return the bee suit to the Honey House and go down the steps into the manor.

Carey's downstairs, going through a small room at the back end of the house, one where the lights don't work because it's so close to the fire-damaged area that the electrics were frazzled beyond repair.

'Find anything?' There's a tall window letting in light, and he looks up and shakes his head.

I've never been in this room before, but it's a sad room. Even so many years later, the acrid smell of soot still hangs in the air and blackened debris crunches under the soles of my shoes. No one ever came to clean up Elderflower Grove after the fire, presumably because without an owner, there was no one to pay for it.

It was some sort of office once. There are the twisted metal remains of what was once a filing cabinet and the charred stumps of a wooden desk's legs. The metal frame of a burnt armchair sits in front of the window and I go over to look out. Ivy has crept in and taken over the window frame, obscuring the view of buttercup meadows and the trickle of the river towards the point where it leaves the grounds of Elderflower Grove.

'I can imagine Josie sitting here for hours.'

'I can imagine her filing important paperwork in this cabinet and now look at it.' He toes at the metal remains with his shoe. 'Anything paper inside would've gone up in flames.'

'We should clean it up. Give it some much-needed attention.'

He scratches his head and leaves a smear of soot across his forehead, then goes to wipe it and leaves a bigger streak. 'Why?'

I go over and reach up to brush it away and he ducks to let me. 'Because it's so sad. You've cleaned up the living room, kitchen, and bathroom, but the rest of the house is still such a disaster zone that the fire could've happened yesterday. It's sat here alone and unloved for seven years. It deserves better.'

Somewhere above us, a pipe contracts inside a wall, making a muted clang. We meet each other's eyes and giggle nervously.

'Well, I don't have time for cleaning. I have a couple of months to strip this place apart piece by piece, and if I can't find anything in that time, then it's over. All this will have been for nothing. No point cleaning something that's going to be bulldozed in November.'

A gust of wind howls through the empty window frame and Carey side-eyes me nervously.

I doubt it means anything, but it isn't otherwise windy today, and I imagine it was the house's version of a cry of pain.

'We're going to do everything we can to stop that.' I speak upwards to what remains of the ceiling. 'But if you can help us, we'd be extremely grateful.'

I elbow him when he doesn't add anything. He coughs when my elbow connects with his ribcage and looks upwards too. 'Oh yeah, *extremely* grateful.' His voice is dripping with sarcasm, and he looks back down at me and speaks out the side of his mouth. 'Kayl, it's a *building*.'

'Oh, shush. I've had less sentient work colleagues than this building. You got any cleaning supplies?'

'In the kitchen, but you're wasting your time.'

I shrug. 'I can clean and look at the same time. If we could clean it up, maybe we could give it a fighting chance. Prove to someone, somewhere, that it's *not* an unloved and abandoned wreck.'

He goes to protest, but I can sense his eyes on me as I pull a spare hairband off my wrist and tie my dark hair up in a high ponytail, and set off for the kitchen.

He follows. 'I'll come with you. Got something to show you.'

We walk back through the downstairs rooms together, and when we reach the kitchen, Carey points to a book on the table.

'The Flower Fairies!' I squeal in delight. 'Where did you find that?'

'I didn't, Elderflower Grove did.'

I run my fingers over the green cloth hardback with gilt lettering. It's a first edition of the combined books in one volume from 1927, well-read with a spine that's threadbare in places, and I feel like I should have white cotton gloves on before opening the cover.

'I went to get a book from the library last night, and when I opened the door, it knocked against something, and this was lying on the floor, obviously fallen from some shelf or another. Quite a coincidence after we mentioned them the other day, right? And yes, I said thank you.'

'Good.' I grin at him and call out, 'Thank you, Elderflower Grove.'

He stands behind me as I start looking through the delicate illustrations and their accompanying poems. His hip is against my back, and his breath sends goose pimples dancing across the nape of my neck, and being at *this* close proximity makes it difficult to concentrate on anything but his exotic apple aftershave and the warmth of his body.

He ducks even closer, his chin almost on my shoulder as he leans down to read it. 'Is there an elderflower one?'

I leaf carefully through the old book, the pages yellowed and crisp with age, cracking noises suggesting they might detach from the spine if moved too vigorously. It feels magical, like if I glance up at the right moment, I'm going to see a fairy flitting away. Carey doesn't move, his breathing shallow and quiet, ghosting across my ear.

The elderflower fairy page is more well-worn than the others, the illustration of the yellow-winged fairy wearing a white dress is almost rubbed away by little fingers, and I can imagine a young Josie reading it under the elderflower trees.

'Wow,' Carey murmurs, sounding spellbound.

He goes to touch it but I smack his sooty fingers away, loving the way he laughs, and I struggle to take my eyes off him as he goes across to wash them and rubs a wet kitchen towel over his forehead too.

I miss his closeness as I read through a few of the other fairies for flowers that grow on these grounds, and he stands at the side of the table, looking at the pictures as he dries his hands. 'I think the building wanted you to see that.'

'So you *do* think it's slightly more than just a building then …'

He doesn't give me the satisfaction of a response, and I reluctantly close the book for now. I go to retrieve a mop and bucket from the pantry, and before I've looked through the cleaning products, Carey's taken it from me, filled the bucket with warm soapy water, and carried it back towards the office room. A real gentleman.

I take a broom and a dustpan too, a couple of cloths, and a few bottles of cleaning products, and as I leave the kitchen, I can't help glancing at Carey's mattress on the floor, folded-up sleeping bag, lamp, bottle of water. My eyes fall on the books piled beside the mattress. Facedown and open on top of the pile is *Pride and Prejudice*.

'So when you said you went to get a book, you didn't mention it happened to be my favourite book …' I say when I get back to the sad room. 'Quite a change from Stephen King.'

He's abandoned trying to get into the filing cabinet and is scanning the floor, moving debris aside with his foot. 'I've seen the TV adaptation but I've never read any of Jane Austen's books. I wanted to read something you like.'

'Aww.' I push my bottom lip out, but something warm fizzles

inside me. I don't think anyone's ever read a book solely because I like it. I don't think anyone's ever liked *me* enough to do that. 'But are you enjoying it? That's the main question.'

'I am, actually. I can see the joy of escaping into a different time.' He glances out the window, as if to indicate how bad things are out there sometimes. 'I didn't think I'd be able to stand reading the old-fashioned language for long, but you fall into the cadence of it. When I close the book, I want to speak the way they do. Walk around in a top hat, bowing occasionally, saying things like, "I hope I see you well" and sending people my *very* best compliments.'

He does a perfect impression of a Regency hero and finishes with a bow, tipping an imaginary hat in my direction.

I'm sure he was intending it as a joke, but he's ridiculously sexy and it makes me go a bit tingly. 'Well, you're already very good at swimming in lakes.'

He laughs and tips his imaginary hat in my direction again. 'Well, you have great taste in everything else, so I figured I'd enjoy it.'

'Says the man wearing a Gremlins T-shirt,' I say, appreciating his T-shirt today, which has got Gizmo on the front.

It takes me a while to realise we've been standing here holding each other's gaze for an unusually long time. I shake myself and grab the mop with such force that I lose my grip and send it clattering to the floor with such a bang that it feels like it makes the house itself jump.

'Sorry,' I say to it, and I like that Carey doesn't say anything about it.

My ex used to poke fun at my little habits in a derogatory way, but Carey doesn't. There's a lot to be said for a guy who's respectful and kind, and I don't remember when I looked at him, but I find myself holding eye contact with him again until we both turn away sharply.

I get on with the cleaning with an enthusiasm that's usually reserved only for chocolate and cheesy Netflix movies, but it feels good to be doing something for Elderflower Grove. It's something I can control in an otherwise out-of-control situation. I can't change what people want to do to Elderflower Grove, but if we can get them to realise it isn't *that* damaged, that it could be saved with less effort than they thought, maybe we could persuade them it would be worthwhile …

I sweep debris into the dustpan and deposit it into an empty bin bag, and then start mopping, revealing a stone floor, brushing away the burnt remnants of the carpet that once covered it. I go back to the kitchen to pour out filthy water and refill the bucket a few times, and Carey moves on to another room, convinced there's nothing to find in this one.

I'm convinced of it too, until I start scrubbing a cloth over the soot-blackened bricks of the wall, and my cleaning picks out an anomaly in the mortar that wasn't visible with the layer of soot covering it.

With the blackness being washed away, I uncover a hole between the bricks, and when I shine my phone light in, there's something in it.

My finger snakes in as I wriggle it loose. The tips of my finger-nails are shredded by the bricks as I pull out a blackened metal tube centimetre by centimetre. 'Carey, I've found something!'

He nearly falls over himself as he barrels back in and stumbles to a halt mere seconds before he crashes into me. He shines a torch into the hole as I struggle to get the rusty lid off the tube.

'So cleaning was a good idea after all then,' he says, more to himself than to me.

'It might not be anything yet.' Years of being locked away have done the seal no favours. Eventually the lid bends far enough that I can break it off. I brush the soot off my hands and peer inside. It's some sort of paper, rolled up to fit in the narrow tube.

I hold it out, but Carey shakes his head. 'You read it.'

It feels like we're teetering on the edge of something and *this* could be the answer. I don't breathe again until the paper is in my hands. I'm expecting a birth certificate for Carey's father or adoption papers or something, but it's …

'Josie was in debt.' I'm panting from holding my breath for too long as my eyes run over the paper. 'To the tune of £75,000. This is a final warning from a bank loan. If she doesn't set up a repayment plan within a month of this letter, they're going to repossess her assets.' I hold it out to show him. There are numbers scrawled on the top in Josie's shaky handwriting. 'It's dated in the September before she died.'

He takes the paper and scans over it, but he seems remarkably unsurprised.

'How did she get into *that* much debt?'

He shakes his head. 'At a guess, the upkeep of this place. Stately homes like this cost a *lot* of money to run, and I'm guessing beekeeping isn't a highly paid job?'

'It'll be a while before I buy my first yacht,' I mutter, the familiar guilt of lying to him washing over me again. 'Everything we think we know about Josie is based on assumptions – that she was a wicked old witch, and that she was rich. We're wrong on the witch part – she was lonely, broken-hearted, lost without Guillaume, but she wasn't cruel or nasty. Maybe we're wrong on the money too. You don't get into that kind of debt if you can afford not to.'

His forehead furrows as he looks at the letter.

'What are we missing here? Where are these people, for a start? This was sent nearly seven years ago. They *haven't* repossessed anything. All right, maybe they can't with Josie missing, but then it would be owed to them from the estate, wouldn't it? So Elderflower Grove *wouldn't* technically belong to the council, it would belong to the creditors and would have to be sold to pay off the debt. And why go to such lengths to hide this letter?' I shake my head. I can't make head nor tail of it.

He hands me the letter back and I look over it again. It's yet another thing that doesn't add up. 'What if it was an insurance job?'

He laughs. 'You have a seriously vivid imagination.'

'I'm serious. Josie hasn't *hidden* this letter – she's preserved it. If she wanted it hidden, she'd have let it burn in the fire. She's painstakingly hidden it in a heat-proof case for someone to find. She wanted this to be seen. By us or by someone else, I don't know.'

He glances back at the hole between bricks and sighs like I've got a point, and the more I think about it, the more sense it makes.

'What if Josie really did start the fire? What if she was going to claim on the insurance to get the money to cover the debt?'

'But why? How? You can't get any benefit from insurance money if you're dead. And if she somehow didn't die that night, well, the police *might* have noticed if a missing woman put in a huge insurance claim.'

'What do you think these numbers are?' I point to the hand-written numbers at the top of the letter.

'I have no idea.'

'Because they might be online login details.' I get out my phone and type in the website address.

'No way. You can't be serious. And you can't put them in and expect it to work. No one writes stuff like that on the letter they came with.'

'Maybe they would if they were an elderly lady who struggled with remembering things. Josie was alone here. She probably wouldn't have thought twice about leaving sensitive details like passwords lying around because who was going to see them?'

'That would mean she must've had a computer or a tablet or phone of some kind. Nothing's ever been found.'

'Then maybe she took it with her,' I say with a determined grin as the logo for the bank appears on my phone screen, unchanged from the one on the letter so many years ago. 'We're missing something, Care. I know you feel it too.' I look at him and he turns away.

'I don't think we should be doing this. It's not our place to get involved in Josie's financial worries. You've got a point about hiding the letter, but ... whoever she wanted to find it, it wasn't us.'

'Maybe it wasn't anyone. Maybe it was someone who loved Elderflower Grove as much as she did. Maybe she knew that some time in the future, Elderflower Grove would show this to someone who could help.' I press the 'existing customer' button on my screen.

'Kayleigh, don't.'

'Why not?'

'Because it's private. She wouldn't want two strangers poking around in her bank account.'

'Says the man who's quite happy to read her personal letters and tear her house apart looking for something, but you think *this* is crossing the line?'

'That's different. I thought they might tell me something about my father.'

'And this might tell us something about Josie and what happened to her.'

The website wants a membership number – the twelve-digit number scribbled on Josie's letter, and then a passcode, the shorter number scrawled underneath it. 'Two letters of her memorable word?'

'How on earth should I know? If you get it wrong enough times, it'll probably lock you out.'

I try the 'i' and 'm' from Guillaume, and let out a whoop when it accepts them. I half expect a siren to go off or something, but the blue circle goes around and starts loading the main page.

'Is this going to flag anything up? Is anyone going to be monitoring her accounts and notice that someone's logged in?'

He sighs. 'I doubt it. Honestly, Kayl, this is a cold case. It's not like an active murder investigation. No one's monitoring it. There is absolutely *no* doubt that Josie died seven years ago.'

'Yes, there is.' I meet his eyes and then look down at my phone screen. 'The account balance is zero.'

'I don't know what that means.'

'It means the debt has been paid. The £75,000 Josie owed seven years ago has gone.'

'Wiped out because she's presumed dead?'

'They wouldn't do that. It would still have to be recovered after she died. And Josie *isn't* officially dead yet – no creditors could take anything until she is.'

'A mistake then? Either the letter was sent in error or that balance is an error.'

'Maybe.' I navigate into the statements section, but it won't let me see any further back than two years, and there's been no account activity at all in that time.

'Maybe she'd fallen victim to some kind of fraud and the bank refunded her. That's possible.'

'Anything's possible,' I mutter, concentrating on the fine print at the bottom of the statement page. 'It says you can request a paper copy of every annual statement on record to be sent to your registered address for £2.50 each. I'm going to request the missing years.'

'You're wasting your money.'

'Fine. It'll be worth it, even if all it shows is the debt being a mistake. And I don't think it was. Something's going on here, something we don't understand yet, and I think Josie put that letter there in the hopes that *someone* would understand one day.'

'Fine.' He folds his arms and watches while I put in the order for paper statements to be sent here.

I'm convinced that accessing Josie's bank account will flag up something somewhere and I expect a police car to come whizzing up to the gates at any second, but I keep glancing at Carey, who returns each look with steely blue eyes. Something niggles at me about why he's so against this. We're invading Josie's privacy by being here. It was too late to worry about that once we'd read the first letter. I want to know what happened to her, but trying to find out is like trying to find a needle in a haystack if you're blindfolded and the haystack is on Jupiter. *Anything* is worth a try.

'I'm going to carry on. You know, find something that might actually help as opposed to hacking into bank accounts.' He goes to walk out and then stops in the doorway. 'I think the house likes you, you know.'

Somewhere on the floors above us, a pipe bangs like the house agrees and we both glance upwards. 'It's felt different since you got here. It didn't like me. It felt cold and closed off, but now it's brighter, warmer, and more welcoming. It wants to share its secrets with you. Or I'm losing my mind, which is a distinct possibility. It knows you're the one who saved its life. And yes, I do realise how weird it is to talk about a building being alive.'

'Maybe it's the cleaning.' I try to brush off his compliment even though it makes me feel all melty inside. 'Elderflower Grove has been unloved for a long time. It needs to feel like someone's looking after it, like someone cares. It was loved once. Maybe it had given up on ever having anyone to love it again, and now it's starting to open up and trust someone again.'

As the words come out of my mouth, in my head I'm thinking, 'For god's sake, Kayleigh, you sound deranged. It's a *building*,' but I can't stop myself. It feels like the house is alive. It has a personality. It has scars. It had a loving owner once, but now it's been abandoned for years. I feel a connection with it. We've all been hurt, we've all been alone and felt like we'd never find love again. Elderflower Grove understands that. It's more than *just* a building.

I expect him to say something incredulous and sarcastic, but instead he gives me a sad smile. 'I know the feeling.'

I stare at the empty doorway for a long time after he's gone back to what he was doing.

Chapter 10

Romans used honey instead of gold to pay their taxes.

'Great tits.'

I know he means the birds, but I nod towards his *Morph* T-shirt anyway. 'Yours look particularly fetching today too.'

Carey laughs loudly, scaring away the birds that were eating from one of the many feeders he refills every day. 'I've just realised what that sounds like out of context. Great tits – the bird with a name that you're never sure is a species, a compliment, or a sleazy observation.'

I giggle because there's something eternally good-natured about Carey, and he isn't one for lewd comments like that. We've stopped to watch the birds at the side of the house, where there's a collection of hanging feeders on the way towards the maze.

'I assure you, I only meant the birds in this case.' He hesitates for a moment. 'Oh, wait. That wasn't meant to sound like you have not-great tits. I'm sure they're very nice tits.' His eyes drift downwards towards my chest and quickly back up again. 'And not blue tits. Or crested tits. Or bearded tits, for that matter.'

'Or long-tailed tits?' I suggest, laughing.

We're standing too close, the sun-warmed skin of his arm

touching mine, and I'm laughing so hard that I'm almost leaning against him.

He snorts. 'I'm going to shut up now. For someone who was trying not to insult you, I've spent and inordinate amount of time going on about tits. Even if *they* are great tits.' He nods to the birds again, but leaves the innuendo hanging in the air, and it feels nice to be a little bit flirty with someone. It's been a *long* time since flirting was on my radar.

'No, *they're* blue tits.' I nod to a little blue tit leading a family of fluffy lemon-coloured babies from the sunflower heart feeder to the peanut feeder.

This area is on the far side of the house, completely out of sight from the road, which is good considering Carey seems to be on a one-man mission to feed every bird in the Hampshire area.

I've been slightly wary of him since his objections to the bank statements, but there's something infinitely good about a man who's got more bird food than people food in his kitchen cupboards, and I can't help glancing up at the soft look on his face as he watches sparrows and robins bickering over the tastiest mealworms.

He lifts his arm and drops it around my shoulders, briefly surrounding me with the scent of his tart apple aftershave, and then he pulls away and we carry on walking.

'Careful, stinging nettles.' Carey puts an arm out to stop me, whips out the bottle of weedkiller that's hanging from one of the belt loops of his jeans, and gives them a good dousing with it.

It seems like much longer than seven years since anyone was out this way. Once you get past the bird feeding area, the ground disappears, lost to masses of cow parsley, thistles, and willowherb. Carey's got the machete again and he's slicing a path for us.

The edge of the maze is overgrown and the intricate metal-work of the double-gate entrance that was once shiny silver is now rusted through in parts and one side is attached only by the bottom hinge so it hangs at a limp angle.

As usual, Carey pushes it open and walks in without a second thought. The elderflower hedgerows that form the walls of the maze have gone haywire and some branches are tall enough to meet in the middle and form a darkened tunnel.

'Aren't you coming?'

'Yeah, I just …' I peer in worriedly. 'Don't you worry about what might be in there?'

'Only if it's another angry duck.'

I laugh so hard that I momentarily forget how daunting it looks, and Carey holds his hand out to me. 'I promise to protect you from any enraged avian life. Or Bigfoot.'

The ground was once stark grey stones, which are now dulled with moss and clumps of grass growing in random places, but sprays of pretty white elderflower blossom dangle from the trees above our heads, scenting the air. Even this far out, a few bees are busily filling their leg baskets up with yellow pollen.

Within a few steps, the tunnel recedes and the blue sky is above us again. The overgrown hedgerows go upwards instead of outwards, and the late-June sun shines down. Stones crunch under our feet as we walk, our hands swinging between us because Carey inexplicably hasn't dropped mine yet.

'If fairies live anywhere in Elderflower Grove, it's going to be here,' he whispers. It's definitely a place for indoor voices. 'Makes me feel like a kid again. Like this is a playground and I can forget about everything outside of these walls.'

I let my fingers trail across the sprigs of elderflower that jut across the path. It doesn't feel daunting now. It feels magical. There isn't a sound out here and the silence makes me feel more serene than I have in years. 'Maybe it *will* be yours one day.'

'I love your can-do attitude, you know.'

'Me?' I say, like he might be talking to someone else.

He nods, giving me a soft smile. 'Nothing fazes you. You really believe we can do this. That there's a way to save this place.'

'I think the beekeeper job came up at the right time. I was

meant to be here this summer. So were you. Meeting you, Care …'
I'm not sure how to end that sentence. 'Well, let's just say that
Elderflower Grove would've been a much different experience
without you. You have a way of making things fun. I would've
been too scared to explore without you. *Everything* fazes me,
but you push me to be brave. To walk headfirst into unknown
situations where an angry duck could be lurking around every
corner.' I smile at the sound of his laugh. 'And look at this place.
It's so romantic. I mean, not that we … not in *that* way, you
know …' I trail off.

He gives a sad laugh. 'No worries on that front. Romance
and I aren't on speaking terms. I'm dead when it comes to love.
Never, ever again.'

'Aww, everyone says that until they meet someone else.'

'And *everyone* says *that* until they realise I'm serious.'

He sounds so despondent that I squeeze his hand and tug
it towards me. 'You know you can't say that and not elaborate,
right? That attitude doesn't come without being seriously hurt.
I know you were married …'

He glances down, first at me and then at our joined hands.
'Yeah, I seem to keep slipping up in front of you. I don't know
why I keep telling you things I never intended to tell you. Must
be your superpower or something.'

Instead of answering, I squeeze his hand again. The only sound
is the crunch of our feet on the gravel path, and the hitch in his
breath as he builds himself up to saying something.

'I was married for thirteen years. I thought we were happy. And
then one night over dinner, she told me matter-of-factly that she'd
fallen in love with someone else. He made her feel young and fun
and giddy, and insinuated that it was my fault for *not* making her
feel like that anymore. It totally blindsided me. I hadn't had even
an inkling that there was anything wrong or that she was unhappy
in any way. She was so callous about it. She talked about him like
I was one of her girlfriends, giggling and fawning over her new

crush on a twenty-one-year-old toyboy, without a thought for my feelings or that I was hurting and shocked. I felt like I'd been discarded. Like an object, cast aside. *I've had enough of that one and I want a new one.* There was no … I don't know … desire to save the marriage? After thirteen years, you'd think there'd be some regret or sadness or something, but she was stone cold and unemotional. I begged to know what I'd done wrong, offered to go to couples counselling, move out to give her space, anything she wanted, because I didn't think such a long relationship could be over just like that.' He snaps the fingers of his other hand.

'Maybe you didn't do anything wrong. Having an affair was *her* choice, not yours. If someone makes that choice, they don't get to blame the person they're cheating on.'

He sighs, and I disentangle my fingers from his and slip my hand through his arm instead, and squidge up closer to him. I want to pull him to a stop and force him into a hug, but I settle for giving his forearm a squeeze and letting my fingers rub over his warm skin.

He glances down at me and squeezes my hand against his ribs. 'You haven't heard the best part yet. She texted me two weeks later and told me we'd be getting back together. Turns out that for the twenty-one-year-old, the excitement of an affair with a married woman was only there *before* she left her husband, and now he didn't want her so she was coming back to me.'

'Wow. Did you …'

'Are you kidding? Not in a million years. She made me feel like a toy – something she could drop when it suited her and pick up again when she felt like it, so I did the sensible, mature, adult thing and sent back three laughing emojis.'

Even though the situation isn't funny, his deadpan tone makes me laugh. 'I'd have been disappointed if you'd sent anything *but* three laughing emojis.'

He looks down and meets my eyes and we grin at each other. Suddenly, he reaches up and pokes a finger to his own cheek.

'Jeez, I'm smiling. I *am* smiling, aren't I?' He laughs when I nod in confirmation. 'Thanks, Kayl. That's the first time I've smiled about anything to do with my marriage in many years.'

I fight the urge to reach up and cup his jaw and let my thumb run over his dimples. Thankfully we reach a dead end of the maze and have to double-back before I have a chance to do anything regrettable.

'We did talk later, but I would never go back to someone who could do that. It was a simple divorce – no kids, no pets, she kept the house. A load of forms and a hefty fee, and that was it, the end of thirteen years of happiness like it had never happened. I was devastated. She wasn't even vaguely bothered. You'd have a similar amount of emotion after chucking an old wardrobe on the tip.'

I squeeze his forearm tighter and press my chin against his upper arm. 'I'm sorry.'

He turns and nudges his chin against my hair. 'Thanks. And thanks for listening. You're the first person I've ever told what really happened. It was over two years ago now, and I still feel like I'm … I don't know. Waiting for the other shoe to fit? I still lie awake at night going over every moment of the last few months, searching for signs I missed or things I did wrong. I thought family man was my future. When you're in a long-term relationship like that, it's easy to imagine the rest of your life – kids, dogs, family time, school runs, and weekends of playing in the park – and then it was gone in a flash. I went from having the rest of my life planned out to staring into the abyss, alone, and thinking, *What now?* What have I got to look forward to? Being alone forever?'

We turn another corner of the maze and come to another dead end, and go back and take a right. 'You *will* meet someone else though.'

'No, I won't. That's the point. I can't do it again. I can't spend another thirteen years of my life with someone only to be thrown away like a tin of out-of-date tuna you find at the back of the cupboard, starting to rust and too old to even feed to the cat.'

His analogies are really something else. It makes me giggle *and* squeeze his arm tighter because no one should be left feeling like tuna. I knew he'd been hurt, but I can't imagine how you begin to get over something like that.

Another dead end. We turn left and follow a spiralling pathway between the bright green leaves of elderflower hedgerows. I'd be scared of getting lost for good if I was alone, but I feel safe with Carey. There's something about his confidence and his way of plunging headfirst into unknown situations that's inspiring, and makes me wish I was a bit braver in my life.

But I also think about what he said the other day about no one caring about him. This is obviously where it springs from, and the thought makes me squeeze his arm and pull his other hand over and cuddle it to me, the fingers of my left hand closing over his. He turns his hand over until his fingers slot between mine, and then lifts our joined hands to his mouth and presses a kiss to my knuckle. His jaw is clean-shaven, his skin smooth against the back of my hand, and my grip on his arm tightens because he makes my knees feel decidedly wobbly.

So wobbly that when he releases his grip, I'm still holding on to him too tightly and I stumble towards the hedgerow, but as I go to put my hand out, the hedge suddenly stops, and we're staring into a clearing.

'The centre of the maze!' Carey says.

'The wishing well!' I shriek in delight, loud enough to frighten away Bigfoot if he *is* lurking here.

I let go of his hand and dash towards it. It's *real*. It's always been said there was a wishing well that granted wishes, but no one ever *really* believes things like that, do they?

'Well, well, well …' Carey says over my shoulder, making me laugh out loud.

'Do you think anyone has *ever* arrived here and *not* said that?'

'*Well* spotted.' He laughs too. 'Good point, *well* made.'

There are four entrances to the circular clearing, and the path from each of them intersects in the centre where the well stands. The gravel here is brighter and less weed-ridden than the rest of the maze, and there are decoratively scrolled white benches at each curve, and behind each one is a funnel-shaped patch of grass that's been taken over by daisies and buttercups with dandelion clocks standing tall above them. In the centre of each one is a small fountain made of marble. The well is old grey stone with a peaked roof above it.

'It's like a fairy tale. Like the grounds of a handsome prince's castle.' I go red as soon as the words are out of my mouth, even though he doesn't react if he's got the insinuation that *he* is the handsome prince. 'I could see Jasmine and Aladdin or Belle and the Beast strolling through somewhere like this.'

The wall around the edge of the well is wide and flat and I sit down on it, looking around the circular clearing. It's like emerging into a different world, much like the feeling you get when walking through the front gate, but even more secluded. A world within a world within *the* world. It's the most romantic place I've ever *seen*.

He flops down on the wall beside me and leans back on his hands, his fingers touching mine where they're stretched out on the smooth stone.

There are so many dandelion clocks blowing around that it looks like we've entered a snowstorm, and we sit in silence for so long that I lose track of time, imagining the love stories that must've been shared here over the years. Did Josie and Guillaume know the paths of this maze like the back of their hands? Did they bring lunch and sit on the benches, listening to the fountains burbling? Was there water in the well back then?

It's dry now, and there's a cold burst of air rising from the depths of it, tickling the back of my neck, and Carey leans backwards, shining the torch on his phone into the endless black hole. 'There's something down there.'

My mind fills with possibilities of monsters that could be existing down a well, but he's on his feet instantly, and then on his knees on the wall, leaning so far down that I want to curl my hands into his T-shirt just in case. No one should lean *that* far over a god-knows-how-many-metres-deep well.

He shines the torch down from different angles, and eventually stands upright again, and I can't help breathing a sigh of relief. How does he have no fear of stuff like this?

Carey laughs when he spots the look on my face. 'Something glinting, Kayl. Not something that wants to eat you for lunch.'

'I knew that,' I mutter as I peer over from a safe distance. 'Well, whatever it is, it's lost for good now. Good luck getting that out.'

'We don't need luck – we need a rope. You can hold the end and I'll climb down. I'll run back to the house and get one. Won't *bee* a minute.'

'Carey! I was being sarcastic!' I call after him. He can't *seriously* have gone to get a rope. *No one* would be mad enough to climb down there.

I walk around the path of the clearing, my feet disturbing gravel so rain-washed that it could almost be sparkling. At one path intersection on the opposite side to where we came in, almost in the shadow of the manor house, there's a stone on the ground, naturally shaped like an imperfect heart. I crouch down and run my fingers over the smooth rock. It's been placed here, almost like a plaque, but there's nothing written on it. It's totally out of place with the symmetrical design of the area, and it wobbles like there's something underneath it.

I get both hands around it and heave until it's rocking on one edge, and then inhale sharply when I realise *why* it wasn't lying flat. My hand sneaks out to take the thin metal tin inside a polythene bag. I undo the tight seal and pull out the folded-up paper inside.

My dearest Guillaume,

This is the spot where you proposed. I found this stone on the riverbank and I wanted to mark it in some way, even though we knew we could never marry. I never expected it to end like this.

Forever love,

Josie

I knew there was something special about that stone. And another letter, hidden out here, perfectly preserved ... For what? Did she expect Guillaume to return and go to their memorable places? Or did she want someone, anyone, to stumble across it one day? If she had no one to tell her stories to, did she tell them to Elderflower Grove itself in the hopes it would pass them on one day?

Carey's already tying a rope around his waist when he enters the clearing. 'Found one and only took four wrong turns on the way bac— Are you okay?' His face turns to worry when he sees me on my knees in front of the stone.

I nod and hold the brittle paper out.

'Knew we could never marry?' he repeats as he reads it. 'Does that suggest it was some sort of forbidden relationship?'

'Yes, but what? They were too old for parental disapproval. Why would they be unable to marry?'

He hands it back to me and I fold it exactly as it was and look up at him. He's got a selection of ropes looped over one arm and a headlamp strapped around his head. 'You can't be serious.'

'How else are we going to know what's down there?' He walks back to the well and secures the other end of the rope around the post holding the roof up.

'You're *seriously* going to abseil down into a well just because there's something glinting down there? It's probably a stone.'

'It's worth looking. If you wanted to hide something, down a well is the place to do it.'

166

'Yeah, because no one's daft enough to look!'

'Good job I am then,' he says with a cheerful shrug, doing some elaborate crossover thing with the rope under his thighs.

'Have you seen *The Ring*? There's a ghost thing in the well and it climbs up after the girl when she falls in. It gave me nightmares for months!'

'We're not in a Japanese horror film. The only thing likely to be down there is algae.' He peers in. 'And no angry ducks, with a bit of luck.'

He really does have a penchant for throwing himself headfirst into places no one sensible would venture into. He sits on the wall and swings his legs over the side, gives the rope one final tug, and then nods to the knot around the post. 'Keep an eye on that end, will you? Shout if it starts to unravel.'

'Oh, because that's *fine*,' I mutter, wondering how anyone can have a fear of bees but *not* a fear of climbing into wells. 'Guillaume could be dead down there! He could not have disappeared but fallen down the well! Maybe Josie murdered him and the trauma made her block it out?'

'You have a remarkably macabre mind for someone so sunny.'

'Sunny? Me?' I'm taken aback by the compliment.

'Yep. This is what I was saying earlier.' One side of his lips pull up into a smile, revealing the dimple at the edge. 'Spending time here with you has given me something to look forward to. I've been down since the divorce, and my dad dying last year, and losing my job. I've spiralled. I've felt like giving up a few times. It's been a rough couple of years.' He waits until I meet his blue eyes and then continues. 'You burst into my life and fire-pokered me back into living too. Seeing you every day is like that tingling feeling when you've been to the dentist and the sensation starts to come back into your tongue, but without the nasty pain bit. I've been numb and it's hard to climb out of that black hole, you know?'

My hand is over his and squeezing so tightly that there's a

167

decent possibility I've broken his fingers. My other hand touches his shoulder and trails down his arm until I reach the warm skin below his T-shirt sleeve, and it jolts us both back to reality.

'That would have more impact if you weren't *literally* climbing into a black hole,' I say as he pulls his fingers away and shakes them to get feeling back into his hand.

He flashes a sarcastic grin my way. 'I just wanted you to know in case I don't make it out alive.'

I smack his shoulder and he laughs as he flicks his headlamp on and lowers himself over the side, gripping the rope and using his feet to walk down the wall step by step.

'Have you ever done this before?'

'Nope!'

'Carey, in the nicest way possible, there is something seriously wrong with you.'

'Thanks!'

He never fails to make me laugh at the most unlikely moments. I concentrate on the knot securing the rope to the post, but it seems solid. I shine the light from my phone downwards instead, watching the top of his head disappearing into the darkness until there's a thud as his feet hit the dry stones at the bottom of the well.

'Oh god, there are bones! So many bones!' he shouts up.

I shriek in horror. 'Seriously?'

'And … rustling … Wait, what on earth is that whooshing sound … Oh, hello, are you a Japanese ghost thing?'

I roll my eyes. 'It's not funny!'

His laugh echoes up to me. 'It's hilarious. The scariest thing down here is some leftover autumn leaves from last year. There's also a dead frog, but I don't *think* it's haunting the well by night. We'll have to listen out for ghostly ribbiting.'

I can't stop myself giggling and I'm not sure if it's relief at him making it down there in one piece or the term 'ghostly ribbiting'.

'There's a shedload of money down here!'

'Money?' I ask, presuming he's joking again.

'Well, coins.' There's the clang of metal on stone as he picks them up and shines his torch on them. 'Old coins that aren't in circulation any more. Nothing valuable, but some so old they outdate Josie.'

'What would coins be doing down a … The wishing well! They must be coins people have thrown in to make wishes.'

'It must have been open to the public once then. There's no way these are all Josie's, without even taking into account the dates on them.'

He's quiet for a few moments and I listen to his footsteps echoing as he bends to pick something else up.

'Oh, wow. Kayl, you're going to want to see this. Can you take our lunches out of my rucksack and use the other rope to lower it down?'

'Don't do anything stupid.' Maybe it's a bit late to say that to someone standing *in* a well. I push myself off the wall and go across to where he dumped his bag and unload our picnic onto the nearest bench.

I tie a thinner rope onto the handle, wrap the other end of it around my hand, and lower it down to him. I listen to the sounds of him collecting up whatever he's found, and the weight gradually gets heavier as he loads things into the empty bag, and I pull it back up again.

'You haven't put the dead frog in here, have you?'

He laughs. 'No, I thought I'd leave that down here. Unless you think it'd make a fetching new hat then I'll bring it up on my head?'

'I'm not going to dignify that with a response!'

I can't remember the last time I laughed so much. Carey is effortlessly funny, and knowing what he's just told me explains *so* much about the way he brushes off compliments and seems so warm and open and yet closed off and secretive. Feeling discarded like that must really do a number on your self-worth, and I wish I was brave enough to tell him how lovely he is.

169

I haul the bag onto the wall beside me and unzip it, feeling the weight of what must be a couple of hundred coins. Some of them have got mud caked onto them, and some are so old and weather-worn that they're almost completely smooth or irregularly shaped where the edges have worn away.

'There's an engagement ring,' I say in surprise when my fingers sift through and find a plain gold band with an empty setting for a diamond, that part obviously lost to time and whatever other elements exist down a well.

'Read the inscription!' he calls up.

J and G – forever love. My heart melts in my chest. 'It must've been their "thing". That's why she signs off every letter with it. How did it get down there?'

'Well, considering there's no decaying skeleton or detached finger bone with it, I'm guessing she threw it down here. Maybe she was angry when he left.'

'Maybe it was a wish. Maybe she dropped it into the well in the hopes that Elderflower Grove would answer her wish to bring him home.'

'And you wonder why I think you're like sunshine.'

My heart melts again for a different reason.

'All these coins.' The metal is cold against my fingers. 'Wishes from days gone by. What wishes were people thinking of when they threw them in? Did they ever come true?'

He's stopped moving around for a minute. 'You really believe in magic?'

I look down, but he's looking up and the light from his head-lamp blinds me. 'A wishing well at the centre of the maze is like a part of every child's favourite fairy tale. You can believe anything is possible here.'

He's quiet for a few moments. 'You know what, I'm in. Let's do it.'

'What?' I say in surprise. 'Open up to the public?'

'Yes. You're right – anything feels possible here, and we've got one final chance to save Elderflower Grove. To hell with the council. It's wrong for anyone to destroy this.'

I let out a whoop of joy and then realise quite how weird this situation is. 'Carey, I think you should know this is by far the strangest conversation I've ever had with a man standing down a well.'

'I sincerely hope it's the *only* conversation you've ever had with a man in a well.'

'I feel like Lassie is going to turn up at any moment.'

He laughs as he starts making his way out, gripping the rope and walking up the side of the well, no ghosts from Japanese horror films following him. Hopefully.

'*Well*, that was fun.' He clambers over the edge and flicks the headlamp off.

'And you still haven't exhausted the supply of well puns.' I grin up at him. 'Do you really think we can do it?'

'Firstly, I guarantee I will *never* exhaust the *well* of well puns.' He flashes both eyebrows. 'And secondly, your love of this place is inspirational. The joy you find in every little corner … I haven't found joy in anything for a very long time, and being here with you makes me see the world differently. So let's do it. Let's tell the villagers what's going on. Let's throw open the gates. Let's share Elderflower Grove with the people who make up stories about it. We can block off the house because it genuinely isn't structurally sound, and you and me can get the gardens cleared up between us. It's June now, we've got about five weeks until the summer holidays, so what if we aim for the middle of July?'

I nod so enthusiastically that my head might fall off.

'We'll start by cutting down the weeds and clearing the pathways to make it safe for people to walk around. Lop off any low-hanging branches on the trees. Cut this hedge back to being neat and tidy. A bacterial treatment to clear the water of the lake …' He stops when he realises I haven't taken my eyes off him for ages. 'What?'

'Just you. Your enthusiasm. The fact you're a landscaper – a gardener without a job, and what Elderflower Grove needs above all things is a gardener. Tell me this *wasn't* fate.'

Before he can answer, there's a hollow clunk from down the well, and we both look dubiously into the hole.

'Well, either Elderflower Grove agrees or something down there had a delayed reaction to being disturbed.'

'My money's on the dead frog.'

I smack at his arm and he laughs and steps closer, bending down to look at the collection of coins. 'We should take them back to the house to clean and try to date them. We could do an exhibition of them.'

'We can't take these. They were people's wishes. They're down there for a reason.'

He raises an incredulous eyebrow. 'One of these has got 1905 stamped on it. I really don't think that person's still around to care about their wish coming true.'

'It doesn't matter. You can't take a coin thrown into a wishing well. That goes against the whole spirit of the thing.'

'I've just gone to the trouble of gathering all those up, and you're going to make me put them back, aren't you?' He waits for me to nod, and then the look on his face softens so much that it doesn't sound like a bad thing.

He leans down so his elbows are on the stone wall and we go through the coins one by one, but there's nothing we can tell from them, other than the oldest one is a guinea from 1803 and the most recent is a farthing stamped 1958, and then eventually Carey puts them all back into the bag and hands it to me. 'Go on, you do the honours. Good karma or something.'

I keep Josie's ring just in case we need it for anything, and then I upturn the bag and we both watch as the avalanche of coins falls back into the well, a metallic clanging echoing up as they hit the bottom. 'I wonder if any of them ever came true.'

'The rumour must've come from somewhere.'

'Look at you being all positive.'

He stands back upright and grins at me. 'I would've walked off with those coins without a second thought. You make me want to be a better person.'

I push myself up to my feet too, and before I can chicken out, I throw my arms around his waist and pull him into a hug.

I thought he might react with horror, but his arms encircle me and he squeezes back just as tight, if not tighter.

'What's this for?' he murmurs, his chin moving against the top of my head.

So many possible answers, and I'm not sure if I'm brave enough to say any of them. 'Because you didn't die. Because no Japanese horror film ghost chased you back up. Because of everything you told me earlier. I'm trying to be as brave as you are and this is a good start.'

'I think "reckless" is the word you're looking for. And believe me, Kayl, you don't want to be anything like me.' His lips press against my forehead. 'If it takes bravery to hug me, I really am doing something wrong.'

'No, you're not. You're lovely, Care.' How's that for bravery? I turn my face further into his chest, hiding it in the Morph picture on his T-shirt so he can't see how burning red I've gone.

He does a half laugh, half scoff, half sigh. His arms tighten around me, but I forget about my embarrassment and pull back far enough that I can look up at him. Our eyes lock, his bright blue, and I can't stop myself reaching up to trace my finger along his smooth jaw.

'Their loss.' I say the words so quietly that I'm not even sure they've come out until his mouth turns into a smile and his features sort of droop in a disbelieving way.

He breathes out softly, his fingers dancing up my back, his other hand comes up to stroke through my dark ponytail, and I can feel magic sparkling in the air, like every moment of the last three weeks has led to this point. I push myself up on tiptoe and his hands tighten, his head lowers, and his eyes close, and … the headlamp that's still around his forehead clonks into mine with an audible bang and we leap apart with such force that I nearly lose my balance.

'Oh my god, I'm so sorry.' Carey rips it off. 'Are you okay?'

'Fine.' I rub my forehead and start laughing as adrenaline floods me.

He's got a red mark on his forehead at the point of impact and he rubs it and stares at the lamp in his hand accusingly.

'I'm sorry.' He eventually turns to me and when we meet each other's eyes, he starts laughing too. 'I don't think there's ever been anything more on brand than that. Try to be romantic, end up with concussion instead.'

'It's fine.' I'm still trying to catch my breath because I'm laughing too hard. 'Some things aren't meant to be.'

His eyes meet mine and the atmosphere turns serious. 'Yeah. Definitely for the best.'

'Right.'

'Right.' He picks up his bag and puts the headlamp in it, and goes across to the bench where I left the picnic.

I should be grateful to the headlamp. No matter how caught up I got in that moment, carried away by the romance of this beautiful garden and touched by the way he opened up to me, it would have been a huge mistake to kiss Carey. I'm not ready to trust another man or let anyone in again yet, and sometimes it feels like I never will be.

The easy atmosphere returns as we work our way through our sandwiches and share crisps, watching a bumblebee visiting each daisy and dandelion flower in the section of grass behind us. Carey rests his arms along the back of the bench and lays his head on them, and that familiar urge to reach across and touch the straight hair that falls forward at one side returns, so I sit on my hands to keep them to myself.

When the afternoon sun is much further across the sky than

174

it was this morning, we stand up to leave. He pats himself down to make sure he hasn't left anything behind.

'Oh, I almost forgot. I grabbed these from the house.' He pulls two coins out of his pocket and balances them on his fingers as he holds them out to me. 'Thought you might want to make a wish.'

'Aww.' I push my bottom lip out because he's thoughtful in a way most men who've been in my life aren't, and although I want to close my fingers around his and squeeze tightly, I settle for taking one of the coins and enjoying the tingle as my fingertips brush against his.

We both go back across to the well, and I turn the ten-pence piece over in my hand.

'Here's to Elderflower Grove.' He knocks his coin against mine like we're making a toast with glasses of Champagne instead of pocket change, and we look down into the well. It feels significant somehow. This is a wish we'll never get to make again, and although I thought he'd be keeping his distance after earlier, when our hands are hanging side by side, his fingers tangle with mine.

'On three,' he whispers, starting a murmured countdown, and we both drop our coins in at the exact same moment.

I wish to save Elderflower Grove.

Chapter 11

Because of urban beekeeping, it is estimated that
honeybees outnumber the residents of London
by thirty to one in the summer months.

'That's an odd hill,' Carey says as we make our way back. We've stopped at the edge of the maze and we're looking through a gap that leads to the back of the Elderflower Grove estate, even more overgrown out there than it is on this side of the manor house.

He points out a huge hill that's totally swallowed up by the surrounding trees and plants. 'It looks man-made. The rest of the garden is flat, there's just a random mound there.'

His gaze lingers on it, but it's too inaccessible to even think about. If it's been seven years since any maintenance was done on the front side of the estate, it looks like it's been about twenty since anyone ventured in that direction.

'Go on then, I opened up to you, now it's your turn,' Carey says as we carry on trying to find our way back through the maze. He inexplicably hasn't let go of my hand yet and he tugs it encouragingly.

I groan because I knew he was going to ask, and it's something I gloss over and change the subject whenever anyone brings it up, but it's different with Carey. Something makes me want to be honest with him.

'I was with someone for eight years. Lived with him for seven. Long story short, I started my own business and he took all my money, savings, investment, brand name, motivation, and trust in any other human being in existence.'

'Was this something to do with the candles?'

'Yeah.' I sigh, still wanting to back out of telling him, but I'm also touched he remembered that. 'I loved scented candles. I've always had a thing for them, always had too many, more than I could burn in a lifetime, you know? And that led to me having a go at making my own, and I gave them to friends and they loved them, so I made a few more and tried selling them online, and people bought them. People I didn't know, who had no obligation to be nice to me. I got great reviews and I got customers messaging me to ask for different scents, and it became an unintentional little business. I hated my real job and it got to the point where I could afford to go part-time and put extra work into the candles. My ex said we needed to register it as a company. He was a business guy and I knew absolutely nothing about that side of things. He already owned a couple of businesses, so it was easy for him to set it up in his name, and I let him get on with it because he knew what he was doing and I didn't. It never crossed my mind not to trust him. We'd been together for a few years by then, and as far as I was concerned, we'd get married and have kids one day.'

He squeezes my fingers and I squeeze his back because it echoes what he said this morning.

'The business did really well. I started supplying a couple of local shops, I went to craft fairs, and it got to the point where we had to hire someone to help keep up with online orders. I used our garage as my workshop, and I was cleaning up in there one day and I found a used condom and, well, let's just say it was definitely *not* used with me. He was sleeping with the woman we'd hired to help out with the business. All the times he couldn't come to craft fairs with me because he was "working" were because he was seeing her. All the times he'd offer to help her take the online orders to the post office and I thought he was just being gentlemanly … And when we split up, the business was all in his name and even though I'd put *my* money into it, there was no way of proving that, so he kept it.'

'Oh, Kayleigh, I'm sorry. That's awful.'

'It was my own fault. I invested all my savings into buying stock and equipment and more options to offer a wider range, and I didn't do anything to protect myself. I made my stupid candles and trusted him to have my best interests at heart. I don't even think it was intentional on his part. He expected me to turn a blind eye to the cheating and he was angry when I ended things. He'd put up with my "effing candles" for so long, and he'd done the paperwork side of things, and it was in his name, so why shouldn't he keep it? I don't think he even wanted it. I mean, what the heck is he going to do with a business called Kayleigh's Kandles?'

'What did he do with it?'

'The woman we hired has kept it going online, kept the brand name, although I did notice they lost the contracts for the shops I supplied, and I've got to admit I've taken a little bit of vindictive glee in reading their Etsy reviews that say how much the candles have gone downhill in the last few months and aren't like they used to be.'

He laughs out loud. 'Good. I'd have been disappointed if you hadn't.'

I force a smile, but there's never been any glee in it, vindictive or not.

'Can't you start again? Kayleigh's Kandles with the real Kayleigh? I'm sure you'd quickly get your loyal customers back, and—'

'I've got no money, no supplies, and no space. My ex had a

178

garage. I've got my mum's spare room which barely has space to scooch around the bed, and my mum yelling at me not to get wax on the carpet. And it's not just that ...' I swallow hard, and appreciate that instead of pushing me in any way, he untangles our fingers and manoeuvres my hand until it's hooked through his arm and he can squeeze it tightly against his ribs.

'I haven't looked at a candle since. I haven't even got my own collection out of the boxes in my mum's spare room. I'm constantly stepping over reminders of my biggest failure.'

'Starting your own business and being successful at something you love is a *huge* accomplishment. You should be proud of that. It isn't your fault that you trusted someone you loved and *he* turned out to be untrustworthy. Any decent human being would've ... I mean, I don't know much about business either, but companies can be divided and dissolved or one partner can buy the other out. *You* didn't do anything wrong.'

'Thanks, Care.' My fingers rub his forearm. 'I've never told anyone before. I try to pretend it never happened and hide from the embarrassment of being thirty-six and having to beg my mum to take me in again because I did nothing to protect myself. Everything was *his*, you know? I moved into his house. I let him deal with the financial side of everything and I just went along for the ride.'

I've got a vague idea of where the exit is and we're gently meandering in that direction. It doesn't seem to matter if we ever get out of here or if we end up walking round in circles until nightfall.

'Life has spiralled out of my control in the year since it happened. I feel as if I have no agency over my own life, like decisions are made for me and my time is not my own. Life whizzes past while I stand and watch, desperately trying to find a job, to get out from under my mum's feet, applying for jobs I don't want and have no experience of, being rejected over and over again. It's like I had one chance to make something of myself and I blew it. I can't remember the last time I enjoyed anything – except reading, because I can lose myself in a book and pretend life is better than it is for a while.'

I can feel him watching me. I keep my gaze steadfastly ahead because I'm likely to cry if I look into his kind eyes.

'And then this came up,' he says softly.

'Yeah. But it's just another book, isn't it? A fairy tale. A place where you can escape the world for a while.'

'Feels pretty real to me.'

We've reached the tunnel of trees that lead to the gate, and he stops, pulling me back. 'You're an amazing beekeeper, Kayl.'

'No, I'm not.' I want to tell him everything. I've told him stuff I've never admitted to anyone before, but I still can't make myself tell him this one simple thing.

'Yes, you are. You think you're not brave, but you kept going. You didn't give up, and you found this job that was clearly meant for you. You're fantastic with those bees. Fantastic with this house, these grounds. Even inanimate objects *love* you.'

In the middle of what could've been a serious moment, I burst out laughing and his eyes twinkle in the late-afternoon sun, and I'm *this* close to trying to kiss him again now the headlamp is gone, and I'm sure he feels it too, because he shakes himself and marches into the tree tunnel.

'The meeting of the Elderflower Grove broken hearts club is now adjourned.' He lifts one half of the gate aside and lets me go through first.

I can't help smiling as I squeeze past him. 'Poor Elderflower Grove. It's had more broken hearts than happy ones recently.'

He lifts the gate back into place and gives it a pat. 'We'll leave you *bee*. Goodbye. *Bee* well.'

I snort. 'You've reached new heights. That was a bee pun *and* a well pun in one.'

'I'm glad you think I did *well*.' He unexpectedly holds his hand out and I slip mine into it as we make our way back past the house.

180

'Oh, *there* you are!'

As soon as we emerge from the undergrowth near the court-yard, my mum's voice makes me scream in fright.

It takes me a few moments to locate her, standing outside the gate with her arms through the railings, allaying the sudden fear I'd left the gate open for anyone to walk in. There's a man with her, but I don't remember which one it is. Malcolm or Martin or maybe Martcolm or Talcum Powder or something, I can't keep them all straight. Thankfully it's *not* the same one I had that unfortunate encounter with in the kitchen.

'I've been calling you for ages! Where have you been?'

'Oh, we were just exploring.' I gesture over my shoulder.

Mum makes an 'ooooooooooh' noise. 'Who was that? Were you with someone?'

'This is Ca—' I go to make the introductions and turn around to introduce Carey, but he's gone. I stare at the empty courtyard in surprise. He was one step behind me. I don't remember my hand falling out of his, and yet it feels as cold as if I'd never been holding it.

'Did you see him?' I turn back to her.

'Well, I thought I saw a flash of something, but it might've been a trick of the light. Him, eh?' She does the 'ooooh' noise again and waggles her greying eyebrows.

'Oh, not in that way.' I glance behind me again. He has liter-ally disappeared.

'A "him" and a "we" all at once. Are you seeing someone?'

'No, definitely not.'

'It's not one of the ghosts, is it?'

I do a false laugh and look behind me again. While it's extremely unlikely that Carey's a ghost, he's certainly good at disappearing. 'No, I'm alone. Trick of the light. There was a big bird. An owl.' I point towards the nearest tree.

'At this time of day?' Mum's boyfriend asks, straining his neck to see. It's odd referring to a sixty-something-year-old man as a 'boy' anything, but manfriend sounds even creepier.

'Never mind all that, what are you doing here?'

'We were walking this way and thought we'd drop by to say hello. Aren't you going to let us in? I'd love to have a poke around inside. I bet there's all the old witch's spells and cauldrons in there.'

'Can't do that. The house is unsafe. But you might be able to look round the grounds sooner than you think.'

'Oh, you're no fun.' My sixty-six-year-old mother actually pouts at me. 'I'm just trying to support you in your new job.'

'Thank you, mother dearest, but I'm doing just fine. The bees are keeping me very busy.'

She turns to her boyfriend. Bloke-friend, maybe? That sounds better. 'I don't know what she was thinking. Getting a job as a beekeeper when she's never even seen a be—'

I squeak and try to shut her up because I have no idea where Carey is, but he *must* still be within earshot. He couldn't have got any further away without being seen. Unless he did literally turn into ectoplasm, which is *really* quite a disturbing thought.

'You're braver than me, love,' the bloke-friend says. 'Couldn't pay me to go near 'em. Horrible stingy things.'

'You need to marry that Mr Darcy fellow.' Mum flaps her hand in the direction of the manor house. 'If you got your nose out of those books, you might find your own "man of good fortune" with a house like this. There's plenty of them around, you know.'

'Mr Darcys?' What's the plural of Darcy? Darcies? Darcii?

'Stately homes, silly. Some of them must have lonely, uptight occupants in need of a wife. You should look.'

'I've got my hands quite full with this one. A couple of million bees and not a Mr Darcy in sight.'

'Shame.' Mum nods sagely, like Elderflower Grove *not* being occupied by a fictional character from 1813 is the only reason I'm not married to one. 'Well, if you're not going to let your dear old mum poke around inside, we must get on. We're off out for a meal and then the cinema.'

'Have a nice evening.' I wave them off, watching as Mum slips her hand into the back pocket of the bloke-friend's jeans, and his slides around her and holds onto her hip through her summery dress. Maybe I shouldn't be so hard on her. It's been fifteen years since we lost Dad, and she deserves to find happiness again. I just wish she didn't have to look in *quite* so many places.

I wait until they're out of sight and then turn back to the empty grounds. 'Carey?'

No answer.

I start making my way back up to the house, and then scream in fright when he pushes himself up from a crouching position behind a wild raspberry bush.

'What are you doing?' My hand is on my chest to try to stop my heart beating straight through my ribcage.

'I can't let anyone know I'm here, you know that.' He shakes his left hand.

'Yeah, but …' I point back to the empty road. 'That was my mum. She wouldn't have told anyone. And she now thinks I'm dating a ghost.'

'Better for her to think you're dating a ghost than dating me. Not that we're … you know …' He shifts awkwardly from one foot to the other, still shaking his hand.

'No, of course not,' I say too quickly, probably sounding so horrified that it comes across as an insult. Dating him would not be *that* horrific a prospect, were either of us interested in that sort of thing. Which we're not, obviously.

He shakes his left hand again and winces.

'You okay?'

He nods to the space behind the raspberry bush. 'Plunged my hand into a patch of stinging nettles. Don't worry, it'll be—'

'Aww, Care.' To avoid touching his hand, I reach for his forearm and lift it up so I can see. A patch of bumpy redness is spreading across the side of his hand from the base of his little finger on his palm, and around the side to his outer wrist.

I *should* say something about it serving him right for hiding

183

in bushes, but instead I hold up a finger to stop him moving and step backwards to where there's a clump of dock leaves growing.

I pluck two, crush them up, and he lets me lift his arm again and rub them gently across the redness.

He raises an eyebrow. 'You know that's an old wives' tale, right?'

'No, it's not. The dock leaf sap evaporating from the skin relieves some of the burning sensation.' It's been years since I had a close encounter with a stinging nettle, but I remember my dad always plucking a dock leaf and rubbing it on the area. A paradox of the great British countryside that dock leaves always grow near nettles.

'Kayl, it's fine. I'm a landscaper. Part of my job is to rip out stinging nettles, I've got on the wrong side of them more times than I can count.'

'Right. And *my* job is take care of you—'

'Your job is *not* to take care of me. I don't need any—'

'For as long as I'm the beekeeper here, I have a responsibility to all persons on site,' I bluster on, not bothered about whether it makes sense, but absolutely determined that he's going to let himself be looked after for a minute.

He laughs, and while I'm almost positive he's going to pull away, instead his eyes close and he lets me rub the leaf gently up and down the side of his hand, the fingers of my other hand wrapped around his arm to hold it steady, not quite sure if the close proximity is having the opposite effect of steady on me.

It feels too intimate, and I know Carey's not used to this sort of thing, but I look up at his face turned towards the sky, appearing peaceful and relaxed, and that familiar urge to kiss his clean-shaven jaw fills me again.

'You can't hide forever,' I say after a while, my voice as gentle as the way I'm still rubbing the leaf over his hand. 'If we open to the public, people are going to know you're here.'

'No, they're not. I'll stay well clear whenever the gates are open.'

Disappointment stings me harder than the nettles have stung him. 'I thought it was something we'd do together.'

'It is. But I don't want a public-facing role. Between us, we'll get the garden back to how it used to be, and we'll put a gate on the staircase to the roof and block up the windows, put some of that construction barrier metal fencing around the back where the fire damage is most severe. I'll stay inside and carry on with what I'm doing – trying to find a way to prove that Josie was my father's mother, because *that* is the only way we're going to save Elderflower Grove.'

'But you have to be around. We don't have to tell anyone you're staying here or mention anything about Josie. If we're telling the villagers about the theme park plan, no one has to know it came from you. Why does it matter if anyone sees you here?'

'It matters, trust me.'

Trust. Not my strong point recently. I don't know what it is about Carey. Half the time he seems infinitely trustworthy, and half the time, I get a sense there's something he's not telling me, but I don't know what it could be, and I'm convinced it's all in my head. Carey's the first man I've got close to since my ex. It's pulling at old wounds and I'm seeing things that aren't there.

The dock leaf has practically disintegrated and I've been rubbing his hand for so long that any nettle sting would've eased by now anyway. 'So did my old wives' tale work?'

'Little bit. Although I'm fairly sure it was something *other* than the dock leaves that has done the trick.'

I grin so loudly that I'm sure he can *hear* it.

'Thank you.' His eyes flick down to his hand and then back up to me. 'Been a long time since anyone …'

'Yeah, I know. Been a long time since anyone … for me either.' I deliberately leave the space blank.

'Well, I wouldn't recommend sticking any body parts into stinging nettles, but know I'll be on hand with the dock leaves if you do.'

185

'The knight in shining armour of Elderflower Grove.'

He laughs, but it doesn't reach his eyes. 'I wish I was.'

'Elderflower Grove doesn't need knights. It needs a gardener and a beekeeper. It *wants* to be saved. All it needs is someone who wants to save it. We can help each other.' I look at him pointedly. '*All* of us.'

Chapter 12

*Bees have two stomachs – one for eating
and one for storing nectar.*

'A theme park!'

I'm doing a hive inspection a few days later when I hear Gracie coming down the road before I see her. I quickly push the last frame back into the super and put the roof on, but she's already rattling the gates by the time I've ran down the steps and to the end of the driveway.

'A theme park, I tell you!' She shakes a wrinkly fist at the sky as I unzip my bee suit hood and open the gate, but instead of coming in, she waits for me to step out onto the pavement.

Gracie is dressed in a yellow-and-black-striped T-shirt with 'Livin' La Bee-da Loca' printed on the front, and she's clutching a massive laminated poster of Kingsley Munroe. She slaps it onto the gate, rips cable ties out of a packet with her teeth, and ties it into position, all the while muttering about evil men and legal torture methods.

I haven't even had a chance to say hello when she whips out a can of red spray paint, and squirts a giant 'no entry' symbol right across Kingsley Munroe's face, the deely bopper headband bouncing around in sharp, angry jolts.

'Good afternoon.' I'm trying not to choke on the spray paint fumes.

'No! No, Kayleigh, it is *not* a good afternoon! He wants to turn this place into a theme park!' She brandishes her fist at the sky again.

'So I've heard.' I take a wary step back. I've never seen an octogenarian quite so livid before.

'We've all heard! I couldn't believe it when I saw that document this morning. Josie would turn in her grave. It's not *his* to sell!'

'It's not anyone's, it's—'

'Oh, twoddledoddle, I can't be doing with all these legal loopholes. That morally defunct bloodthirsty badger is *not* having Elderflower Grove – not on my watch.'

'That's why we're opening up the gates. We want everyone to see what it's like. There's more to this place than ghost stories and ghouls.'

Even in the midst of her anger, her ears prick up underneath her banana-yellow hair. 'We?'

'Me and the bees, obviously,' I say, proud of my smooth save.

Carey's out by the lake somewhere, laying paths through the wildflower meadows, and I hope he doesn't wander into view anytime soon.

'Do you know he's had another tree? That beautiful sycamore behind the café has got the same orange cross sprayed onto its trunk this morning and it wasn't there last night. Murdering trees under the cover of darkness!' She growls towards the sky, like Kingsley Munroe is up there or soon will be, if she gets her hands on him. 'And those beautiful hedgerows that were just coming into flower along the roadside, he's gone and cut them down too. Oh, trimmed to a reasonable height will be the excuse, it always is, but it just happens that as soon as the wild roses and privet come into flower, he sends his minions out to cut them down. He even stripped the fruit trees of blossom this year because the apples pose a public health risk by falling on people's heads. Have you ever heard anything so ridiculous in your life?'

She's got a walking stick over her arm, although I get the feeling it's less about needing assistance to walk, and more in case she happens to bump into Kingsley Munroe while she's out and about.

'Have the Nectar Inspectors heard anything about what will happen to the bees?'

'No!' she bellows, making me wonder if there's a vacancy for a town crier anywhere and if they'd be keen to give her the job based on saving money without the need of a megaphone. 'I emailed the bee yesterday but she didn't know where they'd go. I doubt any of us would know *anything* without whatever kind soul it was who put those notices through our doors.'

I'm ninety-nine per cent sure it was Carey. There was one through Mum's letterbox this morning, and a few neighbours were outside chattering about it, and then there was one under the gate of Elderflower Grove when I got here too. So the secret is out. Little Kettling knows about the proposed theme park on the site of this beautiful estate.

'Some of the residents have got CCTV and those fancy-schmancy doorbells, they're checking them to find out who it was and give them a great big kiss.'

This time I do burst into inappropriate laughter. If it *was* Carey, he's not going to be over the moon at the prospect.

'We're not going to let him get away with it.' Gracie bangs her stick on the ground, and it takes me a few moments to realise she's gone back to Kingsley Munroe and not the mysterious overnight whistleblower. 'We're going to have a town meeting tomorrow. I suggested tonight but most people are so angry that the only suggestions would involve dismembering him, and that's nowhere near painful enough.'

'I still haven't seen him around here.' I nod to the new poster

189

on the gate. From everything Gracie's said, I expected him to be checking up on me all the time, but he's not been by.

'Did you tell the bees to sting him if they see him?'

I laugh. 'No, but I will.'

'Good.' She gives me a firm nod and starts muttering to herself again. Hell hounds and being fed to hyenas come up. 'Relocating Josie's beloved bees after all this time. I won't stand for it! I'll chain myself to the gates before I let them bring their bulldozers in here. Someone my age would certainly get a bit of media attention.'

I have no doubt that it's *not* an empty threat.

'Without Josie, Elderflower Grove has got no one to stand up for it, to speak with its voice.'

'It's got me and Ca— er, Carlton the gargoyle,' I amend quickly. I really am the worst at not telling people things I'm not supposed to tell them.

She peers through the gate, trying to see up to the courtyard.

'You are going to come in when we open the gates, right?'

'Yes, I think s—'

The sound of a clatter reaches us across the grounds, and I can picture Carey dropping a stack of the decking boards he's using, but Gracie spins around, her eyes searching through the trees for the source of the noise. 'What was that?'

'Must be the ghosts.' I do a nonchalant handwave.

'Ooh, have you seen any?' She sounds excited rather than angry for the first time since she got here.

'Not that I know of. Do you know of any I should be looking out for?' I ask because although I'm 99.7 per cent sure that Carey's not a ghost, you never know, do you? If any hot thirty-eight-year-olds have snuffed it here, it's *probably* not beyond the realm of possibility.

'Only my dear old Josie …' She looks up at the house again, and the afternoon sun disappears behind a cloud, and for just one second, it seems like the house blinks at her, and she steps backwards in alarm.

The hairs stand up on the back of my neck, even though it was nothing more than a change between light and shadow. It makes me think of Josie and the secrets she kept. 'What was Josie like when she was alive? Was she good for her age? Did she still have all her wits about her?'

'Oh, sharp as a pin, petal. As prickly as one too. She was older than me but she made me feel like a decrepit old donkey. I always said it was getting around in that big old house that kept her fit. That and all the honey she scoffed. She never had a thing wrong with her. You'd have thought she was still in her sixties, not her nineties. I don't think she even knew the name of her GP, whereas I see mine more often than I see my husband. I had to give up driving years ago, but Josie was still going strong, pootling about in her little car right up until the day of the fir—'

'Josie had a car?' I'm so surprised that I interrupt. 'Do you know what happened to it?'

She looks blankly at the empty driveway, like it used to be there. 'I haven't a clue. First time I've thought about it in years.'

She obviously doesn't recognise the significance of it, but it sets the cogs turning in my mind. Where is the car? Could it be something the bank repossessed? Or could there be something more important about its absence?

The thought of the bank reminds me of logging into Josie's account and I glance up the road for any sign of the postman. The statements I ordered should have been here days ago and they haven't arrived.

There's another bang from out in the grounds, and Gracie looks worriedly in that direction, and I tell her about the wishing well to distract her.

'When we were kids, we learnt the paths of that maze off by heart. People used to think dandelions were weeds, but I thought they were the most beautiful flowers ever. A lovely source of pollen when other things are scarce in early spring, and then the little puff of magic that each clock represents. Most of those dandelions are probably there because of me and Josie making wishes and blowing the seeds away, trying to get them all in one single blow, thinking our wish wouldn't come true if we didn't, like candles on a birthday cake.'

I'm surprised to see her eyes have teared up. 'We can't lose this place, Kayleigh. I know I come across as a mad old bee-obsessed bat, but Elderflower Grove brings something special to Little Kettling. I've always thought there was magic in these grounds. Josie would be happy if she knew what you were doing. She'd like people to have one last chance to look at it, even if that's all there is. Because honestly, I don't know how we can fight Kingsley Munroe. Elderflower Grove doesn't belong to us.'

'It belongs to the bees,' I say. 'Maybe they deserve a voice.'

'Maybe,' she says sadly, and then perks herself up and pats the satchel hanging at her hip. 'I must dash, plenty more posters to put up.'

I watch her toddle off, stopping to accost a dog walker at the end of the street, and then I go back inside and close the gate behind me. I should go back to the roof before I lose track of which hive I'm on, but the desire to go and check on Carey is palpable, so I make my way through the trees, towards the source of distant hammering.

'You're good at this,' I say as I approach. We're in the field next to the lake, but instead of traipsing across masses of wildflowers, Carey's put down a path made of wood that meanders through the forested area and to the edge of the lake, blends in with the greenery, and will stop people trampling the flowers.

'Good afternoon, Queen Bee.' He's on his hands and knees and he looks up at me with a grin. 'Gracie, I take it?'

'Either you've got the ears of a bat or she's got the voice of a dragon.'

'Voice of a—'

I cut him off with a laugh. 'This looks amazing, Care. Anyone would think you were a landscaper.'

'Once upon a time.' He looks down at the decking he's laying. 'Hadn't realised how much I miss it.'

I ignore the urge to go across and rub his shoulder comfortingly for purely selfish reasons. He looks *good* in that black Garfield T-shirt.

'This decking was just lying there when I walked into one of the outbuildings yesterday, like it was waiting for me to find it, and I could've sworn it wasn't there before.'

'Elderflower Grove helping us to help it.'

'I'm starting to believe that.' He sits back onto his knees and swallows from the water bottle he's got with him.

'Did you know Josie had a car?'

He shrugs. 'Why would I know that?'

'No, I mean, it's not here, is it? We'd have found it. So where did it go?'

'I don't know. Maybe vandals saw an abandoned car in the abandoned driveway of an abandoned house and thought no one would miss the abandoned thing?'

'Or maybe she took it. Maybe she got away in it. But wouldn't someone have flagged her up?'

'This is not a murder enquiry, Kayl. There was no "all ports warning" sent out. Josie was never missing – she's presumed dead.'

'So no one would've been looking? She could have simply driven away and no one would know.'

'Hmm.'

'You pretend to be uninterested, but you're looking particularly tired today. Could it be anything to do with being up all night delivering leaflets?'

He mutters something unintelligible, his eyes not leaving the ground. I wait for him to repeat it in a decipherable way, and prod when he doesn't. 'So was it you?'

'Was what me?'

'The sheet of paper through every door in the village. Just happens to be the exact same one you had.'

'I don't know what you're talking about.' Despite his words, he's trying valiantly to hide a smile – and failing.

'They're looking at CCTV, you know. They're going to find out.'

'Well, they won't see me,' he says with another shrug.

I decide not to push him any further. I don't know why he did it without telling me, or why he won't admit it, but I'm almost positive it was him.

Even though I could stay and watch Carey all day, I'm in the middle of a hive inspection and I refuse to let the bees down by being as awful at this job as I thought I would be, so I say goodbye and head back towards the rooftop apiary.

I'm prising apart each section of hive, lifting down the first supers that are already getting heavy with the weight of honey, and taking out each individual frame in the brood box, checking for the presence of eggs and capped brood. There's plenty in each hive, loads more bees ready to hatch and strengthen each colony, and my untrained eyes even manage to spot the queen in a few of the hives. I don't see any signs of mites or illnesses, and I do the whole thing without referring to the book once.

It feels like I'm finally getting the hang of being a beekeeper. It's the best job I've ever had, and I never, ever want to give it up.

Chapter 13

If a hive needs a new queen bee, the workers can create
one. They select a young larva and feed it royal jelly,
and the larva will develop into a fertile queen.

June has turned into July and we have barely two weeks until opening day. It's hard to believe I started this job five weeks ago – it feels like I've been here for years, like I've always known the ins and outs of a beehive, and like I've never *not* known Carey, but at the same time, I have a sense of things balancing on a knife edge, like one wrong move and everything good that's happening is going to slip through my fingers and crash down like a house of cards.

'This is fun,' he shouts from the other side of the hedge.

'It's certainly not a way I imagined spending an evening a few weeks ago,' I call back, even though as summer evenings go, I've definitely had worse.

We're in the maze trimming the hedge into submission. Carey's shown me how to use a hedge trimmer, and he's on one side and I'm on the other. The rest of the grounds are looking better than they were. Carey's repaired cracked concrete, cut down brambles and spiky thistle plants, doused stinging nettles with a homemade chemical-free weedkiller that won't harm the bees; the lake is looking cleaner, and between us, we've cut paths or laid walkways that meander right around the estate. There's plenty more to do, but Elderflower Grove is looking better than it has in years.

'What time is it?' Carey calls over the whirr of the hedge trimmer.

My hands are occupied so I look at the sky. 'I don't know, about eight maybe?'

'Oh, hell, I've gotta go. I've got a date.'

The hedge trimmer tilts in my hands and I accidentally scalp a neat corner. My stomach plummets. I had no idea he was dating, and the strength of how sick I feel takes me by surprise. I thought … I don't know what I thought, but I definitely thought there was something between us, something that wouldn't have made him want to go on dates with other women.

There's a crunch of gravel and he appears around the corner of the hedgerow.

'A date?' I swallow hard and turn around with the most false smile I've ever pasted on. 'I thought you didn't date.'

'I don't, but sometimes a real vixen comes along and makes an offer you can't refuse.'

My mouth falls open in shock. 'Carey! That's a really disparaging way to talk about a woman!' I can't hide my surprise because he's always seemed so respectful and well-mannered.

He grins, clearly not understanding the magnitude of this. 'You wanna come?'

'Are you seriously inviting me on some weird sex threesome thing with some sort of dominatrix?' I stare at him. I never thought he'd be the type for anything kinky. 'No! That would be very odd, and third wheel-ish, and quite frankly, extremely disturbing!'

'Okay, your loss.' He strides off through the maze, leaving me staring after him with my mouth still hanging open.

After everything he's said about his past, I *never* thought he'd be into casual sex or that he wouldn't realise how disrespectful this whole conversation is to women.

He's either been replaced by a pod person in the last ten minutes, or he can't mean what I think he means.

'Wait!' I chase after him as he hurries back across the grounds. 'Where are you going?'

'Gotta collect some stuff from the house.' He turns back to look at me. 'And make myself look presentable, of course. Wouldn't want to disappoint my lady friend.'

'You're way too young to use the term "lady friend".'

His laugh echoes back to me as he goes inside, and I stop in the courtyard, torn between going after him and going home to cry into a tub of ice cream. He's not *mine*, I know that, but I didn't realise how upset I'd be at the thought of him seeing someo—

He reappears with a rucksack over his shoulders. I'd expected him to change clothes or something after a day of garden work, maybe a quick shower, but he's still wearing the same Moomins T-shirt and jeans he was wearing earlier, and he hasn't even run a comb through his hair to get the bits of hedge out of it.

When he reaches my side, he holds his hand out. 'Go on. It'll be *satisfying*, I promise.'

I roll my eyes. I know they say men are led by their nether regions, but this is like he's turned into a different person. Even though I have serious doubts and I'm walking right back out if we end up in some BDSM dungeon where there's a woman with a whip, I slip my hand into his and follow him through the grounds.

'Carey, I think you should know this is very, very weird. To turn up on a date holding another woman's hand …'

'She won't mind, I promise.' He shoots that grin back to me again.

'Oh, good for her,' I mutter, sounding as childish as I feel. I *like* Carey so much, and I thought he liked me too but we're both holding back, but apparently he's *not* holding back on weird threesomes.

197

I expect him to head to the gate, but he leads me deeper into the grounds of Elderflower Grove, and a million scenarios flash through my head. Maybe a secret entrance, or maybe he's invited someone here, or …

Somewhere between the maze and the lake, further towards the back of the grounds than we usually go, he stops at a well-worn spot in the grass. There are trees just beyond, and a view towards Little Kettling, the lights from village houses shining in the darkening distance.

This just gets weirder. He shrugs the rucksack off and sits down. When I don't follow, he grins up at me with a finger on his lips, telling me to stay quiet, and pats the space beside him, and I sit down next to a patch of yellow pimpernel, its star-shaped flowers closed up at nightfall.

And no matter how weird this is, I *love* the way he shifts minutely closer until our legs are touching and my arm is pressed against his. He unzips the bag, but doesn't utter a word, and I'm unsure of what he's waiting for.

We sit there in silence for long, long minutes, and I'm warring with myself *not* to ask what's going on, and just as it's about to burst out of my mouth, there's movement through the trees and a flash of orange weaves between the trunks.

Carey nudges my thigh with his elbow. 'Told you I had a date with a real vixen.'

A fox appears hesitantly at the treeline.

It's a fox! A *real* vixen! Of course it is! I *knew* I knew Carey better than that! He isn't into kinky dominatrix threesomes! He's rustling food out of the rucksack for an actual real-life fox! I've burst into such hysterical laughter that the fox has shot out of sight, and Carey wraps his arm around me, tugging me into his shoulder.

God, I'm such an idiot. And now I'm *crying* with relief that he's *not* going on any dates. Actual tears. That's not embarrassing *at all*.

I'm still laughing too and his arm is tight around me, and

it's quite possibly the most humiliating sound that one human has ever made in front of another human. The fox is probably scarred for life too.

His lips press against my forehead and I turn my face away, over his shoulder, my damp chin pressing against his T-shirt, and I close my eyes and will myself to get under control. When I can face opening my eyes, my neck is stiff from the awkward angle and I creak as I face the right way again, my face burning red with embarrassment because there's no hiding *why*, is there? No one should be *that* relieved that a man they've known for a few weeks isn't going on a date.

I smack his arm. 'You knew what I was thinking!'

'Maybe I liked the thought of you having *that* many objections to me going on a date. Not that I could … I mean, I'd probably cry too if *you* went on a date. And I shouldn't have admitted that out loud. The crying or the …'

I'm glad he doesn't finish the sentence. I've embarrassed myself more than enough for both of us tonight.

The fox is sitting at the treeline again, flicking her tail and watching us warily, and Carey gives me a final squeeze and lifts his arm away. He pulls the rucksack nearer and goes through it. 'We've got cooked chicken, some fruit, and a cheese selection. Come on, lady friend, what do you fancy tonight?' He makes a noise to attract her attention and leans forward to pat the grass, making a deliberate rustling noise with the food packaging.

'I have a nightly date with her at eight. You're never usually here this late or I'd have invited you before. She's been coming for months. Since she was pregnant earlier in the spring.'

At his words, the female fox starts trotting across to us, and six fox cubs appear behind her. I want to squeal in delight but settle for an intake of breath instead. 'Oh my gosh, they're adorable.'

The group of fluffy, white-tip-tailed cubs bounce up to us, playfighting as they wait for Carey to throw them pieces of cheese. The vixen hangs back, keeping watch over her playful cubs.

Carey hands me a slice of apple and I hold it out, barely daring to breathe as one of the cubs comes and takes it without hesitation. Another one takes a piece of chicken from Carey's hand, and pulls it aside where the others can all attack it too.

'Come on, lady friend,' he says gently to the mother fox, and in any other context that would probably sound creepy, but to hear Carey's gentle English accent addressing a fox … For the first time, I understand what it means when people say their ovaries have exploded.

God, this guy. I've never met anyone like him before. Everything feels right in the world when I'm with him, and tonight, I'm shocked by the depth of my feelings. I want to wrap my hands around his arm and never let go, like if I can hold on tight enough, I can somehow keep him.

The mother fox saunters across the grass, sidestepping her squabbling offspring elegantly, hesitating when she's near us, sniffing the air, and Carey holds a hand out and nudges me to do the same, and her pointed muzzle sniffs us, not close enough to touch, but whatever she smells must satisfy her that we're not a threat, because she sits down and Carey throws her some chicken.

She picks it up and takes it a safe distance away, and four of the cubs run at her and try to take it for themselves, but she growls and sends them racing back to their own food.

Even though I should be watching them, I can't tear my eyes from the mellow look on Carey's face. He pulls his knees up and rests his arms around them, and his wrist twists around in my direction and he holds his hand out.

I reach over and slide my fingers between his, something melting inside me when his clutch mine tightly, and he lifts our joined hands to his mouth and his lips press a kiss to my middle knuckle.

He looks clean-shaven from a distance, but close-up, the barest hint of his five-o'clock shadow grazes my skin as he holds my hand against his lips for so long that I'm out of breath by the time I remember to breathe again. I can feel his face heating up until he eventually moves our joined hands back to resting against his knee, and then lifts his elbow, inviting me to slip my other hand through his arm. My hand wraps around his forearm and gives it a squeeze, and he lets out a long, shaky breath, and I'm buoyed by the thought that I'm not the only one this closeness is having an effect on. His muscular shoulder is right next to mine and before I lose my nerve, I lean over and rest my chin on it.

His head instantly drops to lean against mine, and inside, I do a little happy dance.

I lose track of time as we sit there. His thumb making mindless patterns on the back of my hand, and my fingers rubbing over his forearm as we watch the foxes. The cubs are unconcerned by our presence, and once the food is gone, they carry on playfighting, yipping as they chase each other, and their mum watches on, fed up with their antics, probably needing a glass of wine and a hot bubble bath like most parents by this time of day. It's genuinely like she's come to visit a friend. One of the cubs comes up like it wants a fuss, and it lets Carey stroke it once before dashing off again.

'Thank you for sharing this with me,' I murmur against his shoulder, the words barely coming out.

He turns so he can speak against my hair. 'You were missing one of the best things about Elderflower Grove.'

He *is* the best thing about Elderflower Grove. Although the foxes are a nice touch. I hear them calling on summer nights but I've never seen one up close before.

'Kayl, I got you something.' His voice is rough and low after ten minutes of silence, and the vixen looks up sharply. 'And I don't want it to come across as presumptuous or pushy, and I've been waiting for the right time to give it to you, and there's never going to be a right time, so …'

He lifts his head and reaches over to unzip a pocket of the

rucksack, and I sit up straighter as he hides something in his palm and hesitantly hands it to me.

It's a silicone mould in the shape of a bee. A mould for making candles in.

'We have all that wax here,' he says in a rush. 'The bees have worked so hard on that. It doesn't seem right to throw it away. You don't have space at home, but we have oodles of space here. You did something amazing and someone else took that away from you, to the point where you can no longer see how amazing it was, and it shouldn't have ended like it did. You deserve to rewrite that ending. People would *love* genuine Elderflower Grove beeswax candles. I thought you might be able to sell some when we open, and Gracie stocks local crafts, I'm sure she'd be delighted to display some, and … If you want to, that is …'

I squeeze his arm with mine as I turn the little blue mould over and over in my fingers. It's such a thoughtful gesture, probably the kindest thing anyone's ever done for me, and he's right about the beeswax. There's a huge bucketful in the Honey House, still with drips of honey on it, and I noticed that Carey had put it outside so the bees would clean it, but I'd thought he was just tidying up. I didn't think he'd do anything like this.

'Do you hate me?' His teeth gnaw his lower lip.

I shake my head and go to speak, but I hadn't realised how perilously close to tears I am and all that comes out is a choked-off sob.

It's the fact he's so encouraging. My ex hated candles. The business was started because he was determined I couldn't have so many candles for no purpose. Something that made me happy wasn't a good enough reason. For Carey to support me because it's something I like makes my eyes well up again. For him to have even given it another thought, let alone done something like this …

'God, Care.' I swallow hard. 'You're amazing, do you know that? Thank you. Thank you for caring that much.'

He lets out a relieved sigh and a wide smile crosses his face. I've disentangled our hands to take the mould, and I'm still turning it over in my fingers.

It's an adorable little bee shape, a few inches wide, and for the first time in over a year, my mind is flooded with ideas of what I could do with it. Bee-shaped candles in all colours. Yellow-and-black-striped ones. Glitter. I could get an elderflower scent and sell Elderflower Grove candles that actually smell of elderflower. I bet they do traditional hive-shaped moulds too. I can suddenly imagine standing behind a table full of bee-themed candles on the driveway, packaged in little organza bags, the same labels as the honey jars, and a thrill of excitement shivers through me.

'I'd frighten the foxes if I hugged you as hard as I want to right now. And probably damage some internal organs.' I slip the mould into my pocket and wrap both my hands around his, squeezing as tightly as I dare. 'Thank you. That's the nicest thing anyone's ever done for me.'

He beams and the joy in his eyes makes the fizzle in me grow even stronger. 'You don't have to use it. I didn't mean to over-step. I saw it and thought of you and then I couldn't get it out of my head.'

'You're going to help, right?'

'No, I'm not.' He looks down and meets my eyes. 'I mean, give me a shout if you need help shifting heavy crates of candles, but I think this is something you need to do on your own.'

If I thought I melted before, I must completely liquefy now. The fact he understands that makes tears spring to my eyes again, and before I have a chance to second guess it, I've slid my hand up the side of his neck and pulled his head down until I can press a kiss to his cheek. Well, it was intended to be his cheek, but it ends up being the side of his face, just under his eye.

I stay there for too long, my lips pressed against his skin, the thumb of my other hand rubbing across his ear, and when I pull back, his eyes have closed and he makes a tiny noise of disappointment that makes everything inside me burst into a fluttery mass of fluttering flutteriness.

My cheeks flare red because I shouldn't have kissed him, but I can't tear my eyes away as he blinks himself back to reality and meets my eyes again, his smile looking daft and faraway, and making me feel as tipsy as if I'd downed a couple of glasses of wine in quick succession, and I nestle my head back on his shoulder and he offers me his arm to hold again.

His lips press against my forehead before he settles his head back on mine too, and I give his arm a squeeze. If we never move from this spot ever again, it will be too soon.

I don't know how much time passes before the vixen gets up, looks at Carey with a final flick of her tail, and yips for her cubs to follow her.

'See you tomorrow, lady friend.' He lifts his head and gives her a wink, and she and the cubs disappear into the trees.

I know we should probably move, but my hand tightens on his arm. 'We don't have to go yet, do we?'

'Got all the time in the world.' His chin rubs against my hair.

Although I like the sentiment, I hate hearing him say that because time is running out. It's easy to forget when we're cocooned in this little world, sequestered away from everything outside these grounds, but the summer is marching onwards and the months are running out. If Carey *is* Josie's grandson, we've found nothing to prove it yet. We've turned the house upside down room by room, and there is nothing to suggest she ever had a child. No baby toys, no keepsakes, no abandoned cot in the corner of an empty room, and no paperwork.

'I need to tell you something.' His voice makes me jolt in the silence. The sky is dark now, and the only lights are the glittering sea of windows in Little Kettling. 'You know when we met and you thought I was homeless?' He waits for me to nod. 'I am.'

I lift my head from his shoulder to look at him, but his eyes are on the ground. 'I let my ex have the house. I know it was stupid, but when that happened, I was smacked with a wave of depression like nothing I'd ever felt before. I went completely numb. I didn't want to split things, divide things, have a fair half of everything. I didn't want any reminders of what I'd thought was a happy life. I took the stuff I'd come with and my car and she took my name off the mortgage. With hindsight, I should've done things differently, should have thought more about the future, but I was barely functioning. I couldn't see a future. I didn't think I was going to get through it.'

My hand has tightened so much on his that it's actually quite painful and my chin presses harder against his shoulder.

'I went to live with my father, and earlier this year, I had to sell his house to pay the debt for his care costs before he died. So you were right. I *am* homeless. I'm not staying here because it's easier than commuting. I'm staying here because I have nowhere else to go. If I don't find something that saves this place by November, I'm living in my car. The family who bought my dad's house have been kind enough to let me leave it there. Couldn't park it here, it would arouse suspicion.'

I nod, knowing he'll feel it. 'What about your job?'

'I won't get it back now. Opening this place is the end of the line for me. And the villagers know about the theme park. My boss will know where the information came from, no matter what.'

'Then we'll stop. We don't have to—'

'Yes, we do. Because I'm not so morally corrupt that my job is worth more than a place as beautiful as Elderflower Grove.'

'You know, when we met, I also thought you were a drugs baron, money launderer, possibly a murderer, or actually dead, so this really is the better of the options.'

He lets out a burst of laughter, sounding surprised by it, and I disentangle one arm, slide it around his back and brush through his hair until I can pull his head down and kiss his cheek again because I'm so touched by his honesty that it makes affection bubble up inside me until it spills over.

I feel his face shift into a smile, and his shoulders sag in relief. I pull back quicker this time, but I let my arm stay around him, stroking his hair back, and his head tilts into my hand and his eyes drift shut.

'It's never going to come to that,' I whisper. 'If it gets to winter and we haven't found a way to prove your relationship to Josie, you're staying on my sofa.'

His eyes shoot open and he makes a noise of disbelief. 'Your mum will *love* that.'

'I don't care. You're not sleeping in your car. My mum won't mind – she'll love you. She wouldn't see any friend of mine without a roof over their head.' I don't mention that as a single man in his thirties, to be honest, he *could* be a money-laundering murderer and my mum would still have started planning our wedding before I've finished the introductions.

'Kayleigh …' His voice sounds thick and emotional and like he can't finish the sentence.

I squeeze his hand again instead. 'Are you okay now?'

'Yeah. Better than I ever thought I would be, somehow. This place …' He tilts his head back and looks at the multitude of stars twinkling above us. 'I believe in the universe moving to put people in the right place at the right time and we were meant to be here this summer, together.'

I lay my head on his shoulder again, loving the peaceful ease between us, the way he seems to *want* to touch me as much as I want to touch him. I feel giddy and like a teenager with a crush when the world is filled with endless possibilities, and I never want to be anywhere else.

The night air is warm and there's no breeze, and the world is silent enough that we can hear the trickle of the river in the distance. '*When I look out on such a night as this, I feel as if there could be neither wickedness nor sorrow in the world.*'

'I know you're quoting something but I don't know what it is.'

'Fanny Price from *Mansfield Park*.'

'It's a nice thought. If only it was true.' He sighs and his head drops forward. 'How do you always look on the good side? You always see the best in people, even after what happened with your ex.'

'Because he was just one person. There are others out there – good ones.' I knock my arm against his so hard that I nearly push him over, trying to get my point across. 'I don't want that to be the last relationship I ever have. I don't want the rest of my life to be tainted by it. I don't want my own bitterness to erode my chance of future happiness. He's already had eight years of my life. I don't want him to have the rest of it too. I'll always struggle to trust people, and believe me, I'll never go into business with anyone ever again, but it *has* to be worth trying again one day. Not *now*, not yet, but I don't want to be alone forever.'

'I always thought I did. Thought I was dead inside. Would never meet anyone again. But everything feels different here …'

'There's magic in the air at Elderflower Grove,' I finish for him.

'I feel like time stops here. We're in our own little world. Nothing that happened before matters here and nothing that will happen afterwards matters. It makes you appreciate the here and now. I've been looking on the dark side for too long, only thinking about what I've lost, not what I've got …'

'That's Elderflower Gr—'

'It's not Elderflower Grove, it's *you*, Kayleigh. I can't remember what life was like before I met you. I can be myself without fear of being judged. You like my childish T-shirts and daft puns—'

'I like *you*.' I'd never usually be so straightforward, but he needs to hear it.

He makes a choked-off noise, and then his hand is at the side of my neck, his fingers playing with the long hair that's escaped my ponytail, his thumb brushing my jaw, his grip strong enough to lift my head at the moment his lowers, and it's probably a good thing that his lips are on mine before I've had a chance to process what's happening, because I would have done an excited scream and it most definitely would *not* have remained internal.

It's the soft, gentlest, most tender kiss I've ever experienced. Nothing more than a touch of lips on lips. It lasts for mere seconds, my whole world centred on the burning fire where our lips meet and the heat of his thumb brushing gently against my jaw, and a wave of emotion rises through me. It's the opposite of the frenzied first kiss anyone would expect, but it feels so much more special.

It's Carey giving a part of himself he never expected to give again, and even though every part of me is screaming to wrap my hands in his hair, straddle him, and wrestle him to the ground, the only thing I do is let my fingers curl into his arm so hard that there will be ten crescent-shaped marks in his skin when I let go.

He pulls back reluctantly, his hand not leaving my jaw, shivers running through him and making me shiver too, although it's nothing to do with the temperature of the warm July night.

His forehead rests against mine and his breathing has gone shuddery. 'If time stops here, I wanted to do that before it starts again.'

I unfurl one of my hands and let it trail up to tuck his hair back and drift down his neck, and he shivers and leans heavier against me.

Everything feels different with Carey. We're both damaged. We're both healing. Maybe Elderflower Grove is too, and it makes everything that happens here feel different somehow.

I don't want this night to end, and I never, ever want this summer to end. And that's the problem with good things – they always do.

Chapter 14

Bees can recognise human faces.

'Good morning, welcome to Elderflower Grove.' It's the morning of July eighteenth when I pull the gates open, and I was *not* expecting the queue that's formed on the pavement and stretches down the road. Gracie is at the front of it, hopping from one foot to the other at a level not usually seen in octogenarians who use a walking stick. Wilbur is right behind her, followed by the other members of the Nectar Inspectors.

Everyone says hello and thanks me for doing this as they come in and disperse through the grounds. Some head to the right towards the river and the lake beyond, some meander towards the courtyard, looking disappointed that the house itself is inaccessible. Carey and I dragged out a couple of tables from inside, and one holds the wildflowers we've had to remove from paths and walkways, planted in little pots, and free to take if any visitors would like some for their own gardens. It seemed a good way to spread the Elderflower Grove love and leave a legacy.

Gracie heads straight over to the other table – this one holding a selection of yellow-and-black-striped candles in the shape of bees, and not only does she buy two herself, but she talks another villager into buying one and puts the money into the honesty box.

The thing that feels the strangest is Carey not being here. He's inside, of course, locked in by closed doors, barricaded window frames, and the temporary fencing we've put up at the back of the manor house to stop anyone getting close to the part where the fire-damaged bricks are crumbling, but this feels like a monumental day for Elderflower Grove, and he isn't part of it. For the past few weeks, he's been at my side, there to turn to for a warm smile or an identification of a possibly poisonous flower or stinging weed, and it feels weird without him. Wrong, somehow, and I still don't understand why. I thought he'd be here. Chatting to visitors about all sorts of plants and what we're doing with the grounds, excitement creeping into his tone as it always does when he talks about nature.

But it's just me, and I feel more alone than I thought I would. Carey should be taking credit for the work *he* did, and it bothers me that he isn't. All these people think I'm the one who's done this, but none of it would've happened without him.

Hours disappear as I spend time by the gate, answering questions about plants and fielding comments about what it's like inside the house and if I've seen any ghosts or been attacked by any rogue rubbish bins. A local news reporter rocks up with a microphone and a camera crew and I wish my hair looked marginally less like I'd been lounging about in the nearby hedgerows. Another reporter from a newspaper turns up and asks a few questions about the council's plans for the theme park and records my answers so he can type it up later.

By lunchtime, I'm surprised by how many visitors are still filtering in. The 'free to a good home' pots of pimpernel, wild violas, daisies, and forget-me-nots have completely disappeared, and I've seen people putting money into the honesty box instead of just taking them. People ask where they can make donations to the Elderflower Grove fund, and I direct them to Gracie, who is currently sharing a ghost story with a young girl who only wanted to know where the bathroom is and has probably wet herself by now.

'It looks wonderful, darling.' Mum makes me jump when she appears near the fountain in the courtyard. The concrete has been jet-washed so it's bright grey again, and although it's still cracked, there are no weeds growing through each fissure now, and the moss-covered gargoyle has kept his glasses on to make him look less threatening.

'It's so nice to see you happy.' She gives me a hug and inclines her head towards the rapidly diminishing table full of my little bee candles. 'And good to see you doing this again.'

The bee mould Carey bought me was a good way to ease back into things. It felt different to what I did before. Rendering the beeswax, melting it down and filtering it, felt like doing something good, and I truly appreciated how hard bees work and how much they bring to our lives. It reminded me of all the things I used to love about candle-making before it went wrong. And seeing the candles being bought is filling me with even more joy. They're small enough to fit in the palm of a hand so I've only priced them at £1, and there's still plenty of beeswax left, and will be tons more after the major honey harvest at the end of the summer.

'I have so many bee-themed ideas for candles,' I tell Mum. 'I was thinking we could do gift hampers with a jar of honey, a candle or some wax melts, maybe a honey drizzler or something, and packets of wildflower seeds to sow. Maybe I could team up with other beekeepers around the UK and offer different types of honey. The possibilities are endless.'

'It must take a special person to inspire that in you again.'

'No one special. Just Elderflower Grove itself. It's inspirational.'

She gives me a doubtful look. 'And how's that ghost of yours?'

'Ghostly,' I mutter, glancing up at the house before I realise what I've said. 'Oh, Mum, he's not a ghost. He's not anyone. Whatever you thought you saw was an owl.'

'You've been getting home so late every night. No one stays at work until 11 p.m. for an owl.'

'It's a nice owl.'

'It must be a very special owl to have dragged you away from hiding in your room.'

'I haven't been hiding … as such.' I probably have actually. When I moved back, everyone knew why. Everyone knew what happened with my ex. The sympathetic looks haven't inspired me to race out into the village and embrace life in Little Kettling. Staying at home and reading has been more my thing until recently.

'No man today?' I look around, expecting at least one to pop out at any moment.

'No, I fancied a bit of "me time".' She hesitates. 'And a couple of them found out about each other. I accidentally went to meet Malcolm when I'd arranged to meet Martin and they both turned up. They bonded and went off to watch a football match together, and now neither of them is answering my calls.'

'I'm sorry.'

'No great loss.' She reaches out to pat my hand. 'Between you and me, I haven't been enjoying myself lately. It's exhausting to keep up with so many dates. Plenty more fish in the sea, but I think I might stick to rockpooling for a while. I've had just about enough of fishing. I'm not sure relationships should be so much of a struggle. Maybe I should wait for someone to find me.'

'He's here, you know!' Gracie rams her walking stick down hard enough to create a few more cracks in the concrete as she approaches. 'I *knew* he wouldn't miss this opportunity to stick his oar in!'

At first I think she's talking about my mum's next man, but judging by her red face and snarling expression, she must mean Kingsley Munroe.

'I saw him by the gate! He looked at my signs and strolled straight through, the cheeky beggar!'

I'm unsure if she thought a laminated three-foot poster on a gate would actually deter him, but I'm unsurprised that it hasn't worked. 'Where is he now?'

'Licking his wounds, I hope! I gave him a right good whacking!'

It shouldn't make me laugh as much as it does, but the mental image of yellow-haired eighty-seven-year-old Gracie beating up the posh-suited slick man I've seen around the village is just too much. 'Surely you can't go around assaulting the poor man with a walking stick?'

'Poor man?' She bellows so loudly that the house itself shakes and several people turn to look at us. 'Poor man, Kayleigh? The evil, rotten, vile fellow is a menace to all known society *and* some unknown societies!'

I try to say it was a figure of speech, but Gracie's got her arms folded and is glancing between me and my mum, who looks quite taken aback by the outburst.

'Well, you saw him off, that's the important thing. Now Elderflower Grove is open to the public, he's within his rights to have a look arou—'

'And I'm within my rights to beat so many bells out of him that we'll be collecting his teeth from the riverbed.'

I bite my lip to stop myself laughing at my surprisingly violent friend.

'You must keep an eye out for him when I'm not here working security. He'll be up to no good, you mark my words!'

'I'll watch out for him,' I say, wondering what exactly she expects me to do if I do see him. Chase him off with a feather duster?

'Kayleigh's got enough mysterious men around here.' Mum's obviously trying to get her onto less aggressive topics. 'She's dating a ghost, you know.'

I groan and go so red that I look suspicious even though there's nothing to hide. Not *really*, anyway. I might've kissed Carey once, and since that night, there has been nothing more than hand holding and the odd cheek peck, so I'm certainly not dating him.

'I'm not dating a ghost.' I hurry to reassure Gracie. 'I'm not dating anyone, dead or alive.'

'Oh you're young yet, not so desperate that you have to date the undead. It's when you get to my age that the undead start to look attractive … Especially when compared to *living* eighty-five-year-old men like my husband.'

I laugh, even though I've never actually met Gracie's husband. 'Purely out of interest and for no other reason, you don't happen to know if anyone died here, do you? Handsome guy in his late thirties?'

'No, definitely not.' Gracie shakes her head. 'Although with the gates closed, you don't know what's been going on. Anything could've happened here …'

At my look of horror, she rushes to reassure me. 'I'm sure we'd have heard about it. Why? Have you seen a hot ghost? I'm going ghost hunting in that house if the dearly departed are gorgeous!'

'No ghosts.' I think. I mean, I'm ninety-nine per cent sure that Carey *isn't* a ghost. He's just very good at being invisible. I glance up at the house again, but I still don't understand why he's hiding. On what should be such a happy day, Carey's absence makes me feel lonely despite being surrounded by more people than Elderflower Grove has seen for decades.

My mum spots a friend from her yoga class and goes over for a chat, and Gracie rounds on me, pulling me closer to the fountain for some privacy.

'Have you heard anything from the bee?' When I shake my head, she continues. 'There was a Nectar Inspectors meeting last night – the bee led proceedings and it's very pleased. *She's* very pleased. It must be *her*.' Gracie winks at me knowingly. 'Who else would be so pleased with how this is going?'

I'm relieved. If the bee *is* Josie, I was half-expecting she'd be extremely angry at us, given how private she was and how closed off she kept Elderflower Grove. It's good to know she's happy at the thought of sharing the magic in these grounds.

'It had been ages since our last Zoom meeting with the bee,' Gracie carries on. 'It was like she knew she wasn't needed with you looking after things.'

'Oh, I haven't been …'

'And now we've *all* written to our MP, we've posted on our Facebook group, and our petition has got thousands of signatures. Someone threw eggs at Kingsley Munroe's house last night, although we don't know who it was. It wasn't me this time. I'd have thrown something much heavier and spikier than eggs.'

It makes me giggle again and she gives me a glare. 'And we never did find out who put those plans through our doors. Everyone checked their camera thingymajigammies but the person was completely disguised, had a mask on and a big hoodie pulled right down. It's a good job it was the middle of the night or a darkened figure coming up the garden path would've given a few of us quite a scare.'

Is this what Carey meant? When he said they wouldn't see him, I took it to mean that it wasn't him, but did he *really* mean that they wouldn't see him because he was in disguise?

'Still, what an angel, whoever it was. We would never have known otherwise, would we?'

'No, I guess we wouldn't,' I mumble, still trying to make sense of it. *We* knew. Carey knew but wouldn't tell anyone. He said his ex-employer would know where the information came from – does that suggest Carey is one of the *only* people who knew? And what changed to make him furtively let everyone in the village know in the darkness of the night? Or did it genuinely have nothing to do with him and I'm overthinking things?

Gracie has got her bee candles in a little bag, which she fishes out of her pocket and holds up. 'These are fab. I'd *bee* happy to stock them in my shop.' She laughs at her own joke and I laugh at how much she'd love Carey and his endless well of bee puns.

'They smell just like elderflower too.' She holds one to her nose and inhales, and then admires the sprigs of dried elderflower that some of the wax bees are decorated with.

I tell her about my idea for Elderflower Grove gift sets. I'm trying not to get overexcited at the prospect but I've already ordered a hive-shaped mould and a couple of different bee moulds. 'It'll be a great way to keep this place alive, even after ...'

'No. Don't say that. There will be no "after" – because we are going to win. I've been telling everyone to sign the petition. That plush Portaloo is not having Elderflower Grove, and don't you start acting like he's already won. He hasn't – he just wants you to think there's no point in fighting him. But there is. Because good will *always* triumph over evil, and that rotten man makes evil look *nice!*'

Gracie rushes off when she spots someone who hasn't signed her petition yet, and I look around at the vast number of visitors.

It's an opening day that couldn't have been more perfect if I'd dreamed it.

***

It wasn't just one day, either. It's the end of an opening week, and the steady stream of people coming through the gates hasn't diminished. Families are bringing dogs and picnics; one family even brought a cat on a lead, which certainly pleased a few of the dogs. People are spending hours walking alongside the river or sitting by the lake, feeding the mother duck and her troop of fluffy yellow ducklings, getting lost in the maze and making wishes at the well.

Everything feels different. The house seems brighter than it was. When you look up at it now, it doesn't feel cold, ghostly, or foreboding. It seems like it's glowing, like it's fallen in love with life again. Like it's happy.

The hives are busy, and the bees are buzzing merrily, seemingly unperturbed by the increase in visitors to their foraging grounds, and I've added extra supers to the top of most hives because the busy bees have filled the existing ones already. I can't imagine how much honey the end-of-summer harvest will bring in September.

It's 6 p.m. on Friday when Carey walks down the driveway towards me, carrying a bottle and two glasses.

'No stragglers.' He indicates the now-empty grounds. 'Thought we deserved to celebrate a good opening week with homemade elderflower cordial.'

He's been making it in the kitchen, following an old cordial recipe found in a drawer and written in Josie's handwriting. 'Anything's exciting with you. I've barely seen you this week.'

With visitors on the grounds, Carey's remained steadfastly inside. I've seen him every morning when I get here and check on the bees before opening, and every evening when everyone's gone and we walk around together to make sure there's no dropped litter or rubbish left behind. I'm surprised by how much I miss him and, even a few days later, it still feels wrong that he's not by my side, greeting guests, answering questions about gardening that I can only fudge an answer to, and proudly advertising for a new job because he's worked a miracle on these overgrown grounds, and he deserves *everyone* to know that.

'Missed you too, Kayl.' He bends to slide an arm around my waist and pull me to him for a quick one-armed hug, holding the bottle and glasses out of the way. His lips press all too briefly against my cheek, and then he pulls back and hands me the glasses while he unscrews the bottle. 'But it's been amazing to see. I never expected *that* many people, even in a best-case scenario, and it's got busier as the week has gone on. Posts are appearing on Facebook and that article was printed in the paper. All because of you.'

'*You* are the one who's done the lion's share of the work. You should be out here being celebrated for the fantastic gardener you are. People keep asking who's behind this and I have to

217

fumble some vague answer, and there's an article online about The Mysterious Gardener of Elderflower Grove. People genuinely think this has been done by a ghost, Care, but you—'

He sploshes the cordial into our glasses and drops an arm around my shoulder, tugging me into his side in one swift movement. 'Stop overthinking it. This is about Elderflower Grove, not us individually. Whether we save it or not, Elderflower Grove deserves to spend its last summer being enjoyed, and the people of Little Kettling and beyond deserve to spend the summer enjoying it. Cheers.' He knocks his glass against mine with a clink.

I sip the sweet, light, floral drink. 'You can add "drinks maker" to your CV too, this is gorgeous. Could do with some wine with it though.'

Instead of replying, he bends to slide both arms around my waist, his glass against my back as he hugs me to him and picks me up, spinning us in a circle. 'I don't think I need anything else to make me take leave of my senses when I'm with you,' he whispers against my neck.

My feet are currently off the ground and I'm sure there's a metaphor for sweeping me off my feet in there somewhere, but I start giggling like the elderflower cordial is the world's bubbliest Champagne.

He sets me down on solid ground but his arms don't leave my hips as he holds on to me.

His tongue wets his lips and his eyes are on mine. 'Didn't realise how much I'd missed you this week.'

My breath catches in my throat and I can't tear my gaze away from the intensity in his blue eyes. He swallows hard, and slowly, carefully lowers his head until his lips meet mine.

It's a world away from the gentleness of the last kiss. His five-o'clock shadow is burning in the tingliest way possible, and his hand has slid up my neck, his thumb brushing my jaw as our tongues tangle and the hand not holding my drink has curled into his Rosie and Jim T-shirt so hard that the fabric is likely to rip. One of my legs wraps around one of his in an effort to get *more* of his body pressed against mine, and one of us lets out a moan so obscene that if anyone walks past, we'll be done for public indecency.

His teeth sink into my lip and I mouth along his jaw, pulling him down until I can bite his earlobe and feel the way his knees threaten to buckle. It's like how much I've missed him this week has built up and built up, and finally getting my hands on him has released the dam, and now I can't get close enough or hold him tight enough.

His tongue is teasing, pressing, his fingers curled into my hip so tightly that I'm sure there will be five fingertip bruises there tomorrow and I don't mind a bit. My entire body is flashing with lust and my hand is clawing through his hair and down his neck, still trying to pull him closer. Half my cordial has tipped down his back and every time we pull back for even a second, it's too long and we dive back into the kiss.

We're both gasping for air by the time we force ourselves to pull away and his forehead rests against mine.

'Jeez, what did you put *in* that cordial?'

We burst into semi-hysterical embarrassed laughter. I can't remember the last time I kissed anyone so passionately, especially in broad daylight when anyone could walk by.

His lips find mine again, just for a peck this time, and that turns into pressing kisses in a line across my jaw and another gentle hug.

'Cheers.' He clinks glasses again when we pull back this time. 'Been wanting to do that for a while.'

'Me too.' This feels like a conversation that's long overdue, and you can't kiss someone like *that* without having it. 'I didn't want to push you. I know how you must feel about getting into another relationship.'

'It's not that. I mean, I guess it is that, but there's something else. Something I need to tell you.'

He looks up at the elderflower trees for an abnormally long time, longer than is normal when someone says they need to tell you something and then *doesn't* actually tell you, and I can feel myself getting tetchy and uneasy, and the post-kiss flush has dissipated to stiff awkwardness.

'Kayleigh …' He starts and then looks down, seeming unable to finish the sentence.

It plays into my fears that he's hiding something. There's something going on here that I don't understand. I've been unable to shake the feeling that there's more to this. I keep telling myself I'm self-sabotaging, seeing something that isn't there because of my past experience with a man – all those things people tell you when you're at the start of a new relationship and second-guessing every little thing, but this is different. There is *no* explanation for Carey's absence when anyone but me is around. 'What's going on with you? What are you hiding?'

He shakes his head.

I sigh and step away so his arm clonks down against his side with a hollow thud. 'All right, answer me something. *Are* you a ghost? Because, quite frankly, it's seeming like the most logical explanation at this point, and no, I can't believe I'm saying that either.'

He laughs awkwardly. 'No, I'm not a—'

There's a noise from behind us. A crackle and a sort of popping noise, and we both spin around to see an orange glow coming from the house and tearing across the rooftop.

I let out a scream.

Elderflower Grove is on fire once more.

Chapter 15

*A worker bee can carry a load of nectar or pollen
equal to eighty per cent of her own body weight.*

'It's on the roof! The beehives! The bees!' The glass I was holding shatters on the concrete as I start running towards the manor house.

'Kayleigh!' Carey calls after me, but I have to get up there. Nothing else matters. The gate he installed across the steps to the roof to keep visitors out is locked and it takes me precious seconds to undo it. I've never taken the steps so fast in my life, I jump them three or four at a time, out of breath and panicking by the time I reach the rooftop.

Acrid burning fills the air and black smoke billows up. The fire is blazing from the corner beehive, the furthest away, the flames licking so viciously that the surrounding hives have caught fire too. Over the crackling of the wood, there's buzzing, so much scared and angry buzzing.

The bees. The poor bees. They won't survive this. I have to stop that fire before it spreads any further. There's a fire extinguisher in the Honey House and I dig it out from under the sink, holding the heavy thing with trembling hands. I've never had to use a fire extinguisher before. I don't know how they work. I read over the instructions again and again, but my panicked brain can't take them in.

I'm already running towards the furthest hive by the time Carey reaches the rooftop.

'Fire brigade are on the way!' he shouts after me, pocketing his phone. 'Kayleigh, get back!'

'It's going to spread!' I shout. 'It's only burnt four hives so far – another few minutes and it's going to take the lot, this can't wait!'

I'm stung instantly as I dash towards the flames, but it doesn't matter. The bees are frenzied. Thousands of them are flying en masse, buzzing, probably disorientated by the smoke. The ones that have escaped must be petrified and I wasn't going to waste time putting the bee suit on. Nothing matters but stopping this before it gets any worse.

I glance back in time to see Carey disappearing through the door that leads down into the house, but all I can think about is the heat from the fire, so uncomfortably hot that if I stand here for too long, my skin will start blistering. I scan over the instructions on the fire extinguisher again as the heat builds. I pull out the pin, aim the nozzle at the nearest hive, and press the trigger. White powder fills the air, dumping on top of what little remains of the first hive. I move along, spraying side to side, the flames lessening but not stopping.

I'm stung again, multiple times, of course I am. I'm standing next to burning beehives without any protection on. I stamp out a flame that's licking across to another hive, trying to spread the one fire extinguisher too thin. There's not enough, and I don't remember seeing any others on site.

I'm coughing, choking on the smoke, when Carey comes back holding what looks like a carpet he's cut from the third-floor landing. It's wide and long, long enough to cover the burning hives, and he spreads it as he approaches.

There's so much smoke between us that I can barely make out

his silhouette, but I see him hesitate as I bang the fire extinguisher, trying to get the last dregs of precious powder out.

'Carey, bees!' I shout. He must be *terrified*, and just as I dump the fire extinguisher and go to get the carpet from him, he comes forward, walking through the cloud of bees.

Facing his fear to help. It doesn't matter what he's hiding. *That* is the kind of man you want – someone who will do something they're scared of to save the *thing* they're scared of. I see him wince as he gets stung too.

The powder has dulled the flames, and Carey is between the hives, getting in the centre of the burning ones. He throws the carpet across them; it's so large that it encompasses all four and covers them like a fire blanket. From his side, he kicks it inwards, and from my side I pat it down, cutting off the fire's oxygen, suffocating it, and stopping it in its tracks.

My heart is hammering like it never has before, and every part of my body is shaking. I can't imagine the devastation under this carpet. How many bees must've died. At least four hives are completely destroyed. It will be a miracle if *any* of the bees inside made it out. Four hives out of sixty, I repeat in my head. Undoubtedly there will be heat damage to the surrounding ones, but we've stopped it before it got further out of control. It could've been so much worse.

I glance up at Carey through the smoke, but he doesn't look right. He looks sort of dazed and a bit wobbly. 'Care, you okay?'

'Yeah.' He chokes the word out. Even his voice doesn't sound right. 'Going to—' He gestures vaguely across the roof behind him, and starts backing away, and I guess he's going to sit down because he looks like he needs to.

He collapses before he makes it to the bench.

'Carey!' If I thought I ran fast to get up here, it certainly wasn't as fast as I sprint towards where his body has landed facedown on the floor and skid onto my knees beside him.

He's still conscious, breathing fast, hard, and shallow, struggling to push himself upright with swollen hands. I get my hand on his shoulder, one on his elbow, giving him something to push against where he's struggling to turn over.

'Oh my god!' I jump back in shock. His face has swollen to twice its usual size, his eyes are puffed up, and his lips look like they're about to burst.

'Al-ler-gic.' He croaks the word so slowly that it sounds like it has eight syllables.

The bee stings. Holy hell. He's not scared of bees – he's bloody allergic to them.

And he can't breathe. He's gasping for breath. His eyes are wide. Terrified.

I've never seen anyone in anaphylactic shock before, but I know it's life-threatening. I have no idea what to do. What to say. How to help. I need an adult to take over. Someone older than me. Someone who'll stay calm. Someone who'll know what to do. I'm useless and panicking.

'—pen.' His entire airway must be closing because he can't get a full word out. 'Bag. Down …' He lifts a trembling hand and points downwards.

'EpiPen in your bag downstairs?'

He can barely move but he jerks his head and I translate it as a nod.

'I'm going to get it, and I'm calling an ambulance on the way.' It tears my heart out to leave him, but there's no other option. I've already scrabbled my phone out of my pocket. 'Stay calm. Don't move. I'll be back *now*.' I'm already on my feet, running across the roof and trying to dial 999 at the same time.

My hands are shaking so much that I nearly drop my phone. 'Ambulance, please!' I'm not intending to shout at the operator but my panic is rising as I slip-slide down too many flights of stairs, crashing through doors and banging into walls.

Elderflower Grove is too big. There are too many floors between the roof and the room Carey's been staying in.

'My friend's been stung by bees and gone into anaphylactic shock,' I say to the person on the phone when she asks for more details. 'He's collapsed, he can't breathe, and he's swollen up. We need an ambulance now.' I reel off the address as I finally make it to the ground floor and race to the room where Carey's stuff is.

There are too many bags. There's the rucksack he uses all the time and two other holdalls with clothes pouring out of them. It can't be the rucksack. I'd have seen it. The operator tells me an ambulance is on the way and asks if I want her to stay on the line.

'How do I use an EpiPen?' I ask, holding the phone between my ear and my shoulder as I go for the nearest holdall bag. It might be easier to have someone tell me rather than trying to read the instructions when I can't think straight.

I'm on my knees on the floor in front of the bag, hauling out handfuls of clothes and toiletries, dumping them on the floor in a pile. I've never even seen an EpiPen before. What does it look like? What if I miss it?

'Take the blue cap off, hold the EpiPen ten centimetres from the side of the thigh, and push it hard against the leg. You'll hear a click. Hold for ten long seconds, and then massage the area. It'll go through clothing, don't worry about that.'

I thank her and hang up, mainly because I don't have enough arms *or* concentration to carry on talking.

I haul out T-shirts, and jeans, and jumpers unneeded in the summer, and … a letter. A letter with Josie Garringham's name on the front. I turn the white envelope over in my hands. The bank logo is stamped on the back. What on earth is this doing in Carey's bag?

It doesn't matter. Nothing matters except finding the EpiPen. I dump the envelope with the pile of clothes and keep pulling things out. His bags are like portals to Narnia, and I'm convinced they're bottomless and if I stuck my head in one, there'd be a whole other world down there.

I've been gone too long. He's been alone on that roof for too long; anything could've happened in the time I've been piddling about down here.

'Help me!' I say in desperation to the house. 'I know you're a building, but for the love of *bees*, if there's anything you can do, keep him alive!'

Finally, finally, there's plastic under my fingers and my hand closes around a small case tucked into a corner. I unzip it and *finally* get my hands on the orange-tipped, blue-capped pen. An empty space in the case where there should be a second one, but isn't.

I scramble back up the endless stairs and burst onto the rooftop, expecting to find him unconscious or *worse*. I've been gone a matter of minutes, but it feels like days. I can't get to him fast enough. He's somehow managed to drag himself across the rooftop floor and is leaning against the bench in a sitting position.

'Oh my god, Care,' I murmur. It gets worse every time I look at him.

He's shaking, itching, trying to claw at his throat, and when I touch my hand to his head, he's freezing cold but pouring with sweat. An angry red rash has covered his arms and risen up his neck and into his cheeks, and I have no doubt that it extends under the rest of his clothes too. It scares me with how fast it's happened because it wasn't there minutes ago.

He lifts a hand, probably for the pen, but there's no way he can do it.

'I know what to do.' I kneel down beside him, push his leg slightly so I can access the side of his thigh, and quickly scan over the instructions again. 'Blue cap off, orange tip to thigh, press, hold— This expired in 2017! Carey, why the hell haven't you replaced this?'

He tries to say something, but it's unintelligible. I stare at the expired EpiPen in horror. I have to use it. I have nothing else. It might help, even so many years later, and I have to do *something*. He is literally going to die in front of me if I don't.

'Hold still.' I grip the pen in my fist and jab it hard into his thigh, just above the seam of his jeans. I count to ten and then count to ten again for good measure in case I did it too fast the first time, then I pull it away and massage the spot it went in.

I keep doing it for much longer than I probably need to, because it's an excuse to touch him and I can't bear to take my hands off him.

I'm shaking so much that it feels like my internal organs are vibrating, and now I've done all I can do, the adrenaline leaves my body in such a rush that I feel light-headed and like I might pass out too. Tears start streaming down my face and the floodgates open.

He's losing his grip on consciousness. His breathing is short, sharp, and shallow, his chest is making wheezing noises, and I can see he's trying to fight the rising panic.

His hand reaches out for me and I grasp it, swollen like a balloon, too much to even move his fingers.

'Why didn't you tell me?' I give his hand a squeeze. 'I'd never have let you get anywhere near those hives.'

He doesn't answer, he *can't* answer, and I push myself up to sit on the bench he's leaning against, and he shifts to lean against my legs instead, and I get the feeling he needs touch, something to anchor him. I won't let go of his hand, and my other arm is around him, giving his head something to rest against, rubbing his shoulder and upper arm through his T-shirt, unsure of where to touch that won't hurt him more.

I want to wrap both arms around him and squeeze him so tightly that I could keep him alive by sheer willpower, but all it would do is further restrict his airflow.

'Breathe. Just breathe. It's going to work. You've just got to hold on.' I bend so my head is resting against his, and breathe into his ear, in and out, in and out. I tap my fingers on the back of his hand in sync, trying to give him a rhythm to follow.

He manages to fold his fingers around mine, and his grip on

my hand is crazily strong, so tight that it hurts, but I'm not sure he can even feel it.

'Don't leave me. I don't want to die alone.' The sentence is stilted and barely audible.

'I would never …' The thought that he even *considers* being left at a time like this makes me burst into heaving sobs. 'You're not going to die. The ambulance is coming. You're going to be okay, darling. You *have* to be okay, okay?'

Too many okays for one sentence. And a darling. I don't think I've ever called anyone a darling in my life.

'You can't die on me when I'm falling in love with you. The universe wouldn't let that happen. We were meant to be here this summer. We were meant to meet. Elderflower Grove isn't going to let you go. And neither am I.' I bend forward and kiss his forehead.

His grip is going lax and his eyes are rolling back.

'Carey, breathe!' I yell at him. I rub his shoulder harder. 'Stay with me.'

Stay with me. I sound like I'm on a TV drama show. No one actually says that to people in real life. I never thought I'd be in a position to need to say something so dramatic and soap-opera-ish.

'This is all my fault.' I squeeze his shoulders as hard as I dare. 'I'm so sorry. I'm so sorry, Care. I should have realised this wasn't about a fear of bees. A real beekeeper would have. I should have taken safety precautions. I should never have taken this job. I never would have if I'd realised someone could get hurt like this. Why did that stupid bee offer it to me?'

'Because you made him laugh.'

Every part of my body freezes and the hairs on the back of my neck stand up. 'How do you know that?'

His eyes open into slits and find mine. His words are croaked and juddering. 'Because it was me, Kayl. I'm the bee.'

'What? How could this possi—'

His eyes roll up and his head drops forward.

'No! Don't you dare say something like that and then pass out! This is not the time for passing out, Carey!' With a hand on his forehead, I pull his head back upright and tap his cheek gently, trying to keep him conscious.

He groans, but he's not with it.

'You don't mean that. You couldn't possibly be. You don't know what you're saying.' Obviously he's confused and mixed-up. He's saying the wrong thing or I'm misinterpreting what he's trying to say. He *couldn't* be the bee I had an interview with all those weeks ago.

He grunts like he wants to elaborate, but he can't.

I press my lips against his forehead again, my tears dripping into his hair. Even his forehead feels swollen. 'It doesn't matter. Stay with me, Care. I've got you.'

He tries again to say something but fails, so he lifts a puffed-up hand uselessly and I catch it and rub my thumb over his swollen red skin.

Sirens. Sirens in the distance. 'They're here! Carey, they're here! And the gate's locked!' I swear. 'I've got to go and open it. Keys!'

I don't know which one of us had the keys, but thankfully they're on the next bench across, and I have to leave him again. He's fading in and out. His body is limp and he doesn't react when I have to get my legs out from behind him and prop him against the bench to stay upright.

I step across him and grab the keys. 'Listen to me.' I crouch back down and kiss his cold, clammy cheek. 'You're going to be okay. I love you too much for you not to be. Just hold on.'

I give his hand one final squeeze and force myself to let go.

The ambulance has stopped outside the gate by the time I get down there, blue lights flashing as I fumble with shaking fingers to find the right key. Two paramedics jump out carrying a stretcher and bulging bags.

'He's on the roof. Round the side, there's a staircase going up. His EpiPen had expired!' I call after them, relieved that they waste no time in racing up there.

The fire engine pulls in behind the ambulance, making me realise just how little time has passed. It's been twenty minutes, tops, since Carey called them for the fire, but it feels like hours since we stood down here, toasting to a successful week.

What a great omen that turned out to be.

A fireman gets out and I give him a quick rundown of what's happened, and as there's no immediate fire threat, they hang back and let the paramedics work.

I can hear them talking, hear them communicating with Carey, hear the names of different drugs, and words like 'oxygen' and 'blood pressure' and 'dangerously low'.

I've never bitten my nails in my life, but I've shredded a thumbnail as I pace the driveway, torn between going back up there or staying out of the way. There's not enough space and the bees are too upset to stand anywhere near the hives, and with two paramedics and Carey up there, I'll be in the way. The best thing I can do for him is let them do their job.

I've just reached the gate and am about to spin around on another pace when I hear my name.

'Kayleigh!' Gracie is scurrying up the road faster than a squirrel in Scotland. 'We heard sirens and saw blue lights. I told my husband it was Elderflower Grove and he didn't believe me. What on earth's happening? Are you all right?'

'There was a fire. My friend's been stung. I think he might be dying. They've been up there too long. He was practically unconscious. He couldn't breathe.'

'Oh my goodness, you poor thing.' She gives me a hug and looks worriedly up at the house. 'Another fire? Do they know what caused it?'

'It took the beehives. Some are destroyed.' I don't know if I'm crying again or if I ever stopped in the first place. I've all but forgotten about the bees with the Carey crisis, but it brings the thought of them back to the forefront of my mind. So much devastation. And why? How? It's been sunny today, but the bees regulate the temperature inside the hive, so what would suddenly cause it to burst into flames?

And then the paramedics are there. Carey's strapped to a stretcher, an oxygen mask obscuring most of his swollen face, and they're carrying it between them. I jump back into Gracie's space to give them room to pass, and as they open the ambulance doors and manoeuvre the stretcher into it, she makes such a pained noise that I must've accidentally trodden on her toe, and I'm about to apologise when I realise the noise is a growl.

'What is *he* doing here?'

She must be talking about one of the paramedics, and I'm about to say that I don't care who they are as long as they save Carey's life, when she suddenly brightens.

'Ooh, have you killed him?' She steeples her fingers together gleefully. 'Fantastic work, Kayleigh! Well done!'

'What?'

'You'll get brownie points if he dies!'

'*What?*' My mouth falls open in shock. 'What are you talking about? You can't say things like that. That's my friend. He's the one who's done all this to the gardens. He's been helping me with everything. He's been staying here. Living here, actually. He *is* the thing that you lot have heard going bump in the night. He's been fixing the place up, making it liveable.'

I've always known the saying of a face turning to thunder, but I've never seen it actually happen before, except Gracie's expression darkens so much that it turns into a category five hurricane. 'Tell me you're joking.'

'No, of course not—'

'That's Carey Paxton – the council gardener. *He's* the one who's been strimming all the verges, putting pesticide on the flowers, cutting down the hedgerows, and injecting weedkiller into our lovely trees.'

I almost laugh at how absurd that is. 'No, he's not. He lost his job. He may once have worked for the council, but he doesn't anymore.' Even as I say it, something niggles at me that he'd left out the little nugget of information that his old job was working for Gracie's most-hated man, but at least it explains why he knows the things he does and where his 'friends in the right places' come from.

'Kayleigh, he was strimming two days ago.'

'No, he wasn't. He doesn't have a job. He's been working from morning until night on the grounds here.'

'Oh, believe me, we *know* he lost his job as a garden designer. The company were *very* vocal about his misdeeds, but he didn't lose his job – he was demoted to the position of Kingsley Munroe's dogsbody. All this year, he's been the one you see murdering all our wildflowers and destroying every bee-friendly place we try to build.'

'No. No, no, no. He would never do that. He *loves* wildlife. He feeds birds and foxes. And he would never have had time, he's been here all day, every day.'

'It's being done overnight!'

I go to splutter a response, but it catches in my throat. I haven't got a clue what Carey gets up to at night, have I? It's not impossible that he's moonlighting, is it? I would never know.

'Oh, Kayleigh, you poor, sweet, innocent girl. You've been taken in by a minion.'

'There's no way.' I picture the little yellow things from *Despicable Me* and it almost makes me start laughing hysterically.

'It's my own fault.' Gracie tugs me into another hug, pulling me down until my head is squashed against her chest and she's patting my hair. 'I should have warned you. I should have foreseen that Kingsley Munroe would do something so underhanded. *This* is why you haven't seen him hanging around. This is why he's feigned disinterest in Elderflower Grove lately – because he's had a minion reporting back from the inside. And you've fallen for it hook, line, and sinker. You poor thing.'

The stretcher is secured in the ambulance, and the driver jumps out. 'You coming, love?'

It's a good excuse to pull myself out of Gracie's clutches, but I stutter to find a response. I don't know what to do, and he obviously hasn't got time for my dithering. Eventually, I gesture to the fire engine. 'I need to stay for the fire brigade.'

'Suit yourself.' He slams the ambulance doors, and within seconds, it reverses onto the road and screams away into the evening.

Two firefighters get out of their lorry and come over. 'All right if we go up and have a look?'

I nod, overwhelmed and lost for words, my mind reeling from everything that's happened today, and I feel like what Gracie's just said has made something inside me short-circuit because I can't process it.

'Carey would never do that,' I say as we stand in the driveway and watch the firemen make their way to the roof. 'He wouldn't report back. There has to be a mistake here. Crossed wires, mistaken identity, something. Anything.' I can feel my heart rate speeding up and panic rising. I can't have been taken in by another untrustworthy man. 'It can't be true. Carey won't even cut the head off a dandelion in case it's vital food for a bee. And I'm almost positive he's the person who put those papers through our doors that night.'

She ignores me and silence falls as the sound of the sirens fade.

'You've got some nasty stings yourself.' Gracie points out red lumps on my arms and hands and starts pointing at my neck before I bat her hand away.

'It doesn't matter. I'm not allergic like Carey is …' I burst into tears again. 'God, *why* didn't he tell me? Why say he was scared of bees but *not* say he was deathly allergic? I even made a joke out of it on the day I met him. I *asked* him why he admitted a fear when he could've just said he had an allergy. It seems so stupid now.'

Gracie doesn't have a chance to respond before the firemen traipse back down from the rooftop, looking grim.

'All out now,' one of them says. 'Don't envy you the clean-up though. Poor little bees.'

My eyes start watering again at the thought. I can't comprehend the scale of destruction. 'Can you tell what happened? How did it start? How can I make sure it never happens again?'

'I'd suggest not having arsonists on the roof,' one of them jokes.

The other one shoots him a glare. 'It was definitely deliberate, I'm afraid. Started at the corner hive nearest the wall and spread.'

Deliberate. It feels like I've been punched in the stomach. Who would do such a thing? And how? The manor house is closed off. There's one access gate and only Carey and I have the keys. 'No, it can't have been. No one's been up there. You must be mistaken. The honey must've spontaneously combusted or something.'

The second one laughs. 'That'd be a new one.'

'Unless honey is known for pouring accelerant on itself too, I don't think that's likely,' the kindlier one says. 'Make sure you put in a police report in case you have any further trouble.'

'Accelerant?'

'Traces of it on the floor around the hives. Nothing else it could be, I'm afraid.'

Gracie makes a scoffing noise. 'Oh, yes. A deliberate fire when Carey Paxton's on the premises. You don't need to be a mathematician to put *that* sum together.'

'No!' I turn to her in horror. 'There's no way.'

The firemen walk away. 'Make sure to replace your fire extinguisher, won't you?'

'Oh, I definitely will. We're getting at least ten, maybe more.'

'Was there anyone else here?' Gracie asks as we watch the fire engine pull away.

'No. It was just me and Care. But he couldn't … He wouldn't … And even if he had, he wouldn't have put himself in mortal danger to put the fire *out*. He did that to help me because the extinguisher wasn't enough. He wouldn't have bothered if he'd started the fire.'

She shakes her head, giving me a pitying look. And she's right, isn't she? Only two of us were here, and I was down by the gate. Carey *was* alone in the manor house before he came down with the elderflower cordial ...

But he would never ... No matter what his job is, or was, or whatever he's lied about, I can't believe he'd do that, regardless of the logic in the explanation.

'Oh dear, Kayleigh, you do look pale. Why don't we go inside and have a nice cup of tea? You look like you need one.'

I must look frightful. My hair has turned to bird's-nest chic from the heat of the fire, I'm drenched with both sweat and tears, and there's definitely soot on my face, arms, and clothes. A cup of tea and a sit-down sound like something from a fairy tale right now.

I nod mutely, and she locks the main gate and slots her arm through mine and drags me up to the house.

My hands are still shaking by the time we make it to the kitchen, and after I've washed my face with warm water, she pushes me onto a stool at the island and starts clanging around in the search for mugs and teabags.

I put my forehead down on the cool wood of the table and try to make sense of the tangled web. Carey working for the council. Carey reporting back on everything that's happened here. Carey being the minion who destroys bees' foraging patches in covert night-time raids. Carey being allergic to bees and nearly dying from helping to put out a fire that he apparently started. Just thinking about it makes me want to cry again.

Gracie pops two mugs on the table.

'He buys biscuits.' I point out the cupboard where he keeps them, like a packet of chocolate Hobnobs somehow means he's incapable of starting a fire.

Gracie retrieves a packet and sits down next to me, and it reminds me of sitting here with Carey on the day I met him, trying to decide if I trusted him or not. And I did. I trusted him

235

enough to fall in love with him. And I thought he felt something for me too, but how can he have if he's been here under false pretences all along?

'We'll get through it, Kayleigh.' She pats my hand. 'I'll help you clear up and replace the hives. Bees are surprisingly resilient little creatures, I know from my own beekeeping days. They'll be okay. I know you've lost some, but …'

'It's not about that,' I admit. 'I mean, it is, obviously, but … Carey. It doesn't make sense, and yet, so much that didn't make sense now does. Like you knowing his name. You knew him straight away. Even in the almost unrecognisable state he was in, you recognised him. Does everyone in the village know him?'

She gives me a silent nod and I thump my head down again. 'That's why he's been hiding. That's why he disappears every time there's someone other than me around. Not because he's a ghost – because *everyone* knows he's the evil council gardener. Everyone except me. And if any of you had caught sight of him before, his game would've been up. I've stupidly, blindly let him stay here, enjoyed his company, and every word he said has been a lie.'

'I'm sure you like him, petal, but you can't trust a word any of them say. That council is like a cup bubbling over with poison. It starts at the top and filters down to all the lowly minions.'

'But why? Why would he do it? Why would he move in here for the sum—' I cut myself off as I realise how much of this must've been a lie. He can't really think he's Josie Garringham's grandson, can he? That must be a cover story. It makes tears fill my eyes again. *None* of what he's said to me is true. Not even the reason for him being here. Searching for evidence of Josie being his grandmother … If she isn't, then what exactly *has* he been pulling the place apart to look for?

'Wait …' I jump off my stool and … well, I intend to jog but my legs aren't steady enough, so I hobble through the downstairs rooms to where Carey's stuff is and pick up the letter from where I'd dumped it with the pile of clothes. A very modern-looking letter. With a postmark dated the day after I put in the request for Josie's bank statements.

The statements that never arrived.

Surely the very fact he has this is damning evidence enough. What did he do? Intercept the postman and hide it from me? Pretend it never came? *Why* would he do that?

I go back to the kitchen and tear it open in front of Gracie, wanting a witness. Someone else to help me make sense of it. Pages of numbers and figures and financial terms I don't understand. The earliest of the statements first, detailing Josie's spending, her bills, her debt rocketing skywards. The bank loan she'd received and was unable to pay back. Then it goes blank. No use of the card. No more transactions. Not from the day of the fire onwards. The next four statements are blank.

And then there it is. A payment of £74,729. One lump sum.

Paid by our local council. Wiping out the debt. Ensuring that no one else had a claim to Elderflower Grove.

'It's an investment to protect,' I say aloud. 'The council have invested in this property. By paying off Josie's debt, they've essentially bought a share in Elderflower Grove, haven't they? They've staked a claim on it. That's what Carey's doing here. Making sure nothing goes wrong with their plan. He's not tearing the house apart to find evidence that Josie was his grandmother – he's doing it to make sure there are no other skeletons about to come loping out of the closet. Looking for evidence of any other potential claimants. In November, as long as there are no other claims on the estate – and by paying off the bank, they've ensured there aren't – ownership will pass to the biggest shareholder, our local council.'

No wonder he took this letter. The whole thing would've been exposed if I'd seen this statement. And it explains why he was so against me trying to get into Josie's account. Another thing that never made sense and suddenly does, and more than anything, I wish it didn't.

***

237

It's still daylight when Gracie leaves, just gone eight, and I take some food and walk out to Carey's vixen meeting point. I sit on the grass and she appears within minutes, watching me suspiciously, wondering where he is. Her cubs run and bounce and play, taking the cooked chicken and ripping it playfully between them, but the mother fox doesn't leave the safety of the trees, looking like she's ready to run at any moment. The irony of her trusting him but not me. But animals are a good judge of character, aren't they? Does she know something about him that I don't? I still can't get my head around it. He's seemed so trustworthy from the day I met him. So calm and laid-back and easy-going. Fun. A nature-lover who'd do anything for any animal who needed him, no matter how big or small. How can he be the opposite of everything I've thought he was?

Watching the foxes play makes me want to cry again, bringing back too many memories of the first night he brought me out here. That was *real* and unfiltered. It might've been the first time he'd *truly* opened up to anyone in years, and no matter the evidence, I cannot believe that was part of an act.

I say goodbye to the foxes and walk away.

The evening light is low but the sun hasn't set yet, so I pull the bee suit on, and face the hives. I can't bring myself to use the smoker tonight. We've all had enough smoke for one day. It isn't necessary anyway. There's no bee activity at all.

The bees are as subdued as I am.

I go to the nearest hive first, the very first one I opened when I arrived seven weeks ago. The bees in it are good-tempered and unbothered by being observed. It's the furthest one from the fire, and I was expecting it to be full of the usual buzzing now the smoke has cleared, but when I lift the lid off and take the two honey supers away, there's none of the usual activity. The bees are all gathered in the brood box, unhappy but alive, an angry hum at my interruption.

'I'm sorry,' I say to them. 'I'm so sorry, this is all my fault. I'm not a beekeeper. You've known it from day one and now I know it too. This job wasn't meant for me, and if I'd left well alone, none of this would've happened.'

I lift the supers back into place and put the lid back on. At least the furthest hives are undamaged, just traumatised, and probably gorged on honey because of all the smoke.

I check a few other hives and they're all the same. Clustered in the brood box like they would to survive the winter. Mourning the loss of their neighbours. Recovering.

They *will* recover, I tell myself. Bees are experts at fixing human mistakes. They'll be okay.

I'm checking the other hives to put off dealing with the destroyed ones. A scar on the rooftop. Four hives gone, another two full of dead bees that couldn't get out, burnt by the heat and melting wax.

I thought I couldn't cry anymore today, but my body proves me wrong. It feels disrespectful to sweep them into a bag, but I can't leave them here. Dead bees are likely to attract predators or spread disease to the other hives. I sweep them up along with the charred remains of the wooden hives. My mum comes over when she hears about the fire, and we take them into the woods and bury them underneath a tree.

All I can think about is Carey. He *couldn't* have done this. There has to be another explanation. No matter what lies he's told, no matter what his job is, that lovely man couldn't have been responsible for all this death and destruction.

The house feels dead tonight. It feels like a shell. Empty, hollow, and numb. I can't believe I ever thought it was anything more than a building. What I know above all else is that I should never have come here.

Elderflower Grove wasn't meant for me.

Chapter 16

*A bee's age dictates what job it does within the
hive, whether that's feeding the larvae, building the
honeycomb, acting as an undertaker or a guard at the
hive entrance, scouting locations, or foraging for pollen.*

There's something haunting about walking into a hospital.
Knowing that somewhere within these walls, people are facing
the worst moments of their lives. Trauma. Injuries. Pain. Surgery.
Death. No wonder people don't like hospitals.

I phoned last night, but I'm not family, and all a sympathetic
nurse would tell me was that Carey was stable. Whatever that
means. Maybe he's going to be housing horses shortly?

The hospital corridors are a maze and I have to ask for directions three times before I eventually find a lift and end up on the
right floor, following signs to his ward number. The same kindly
nurse checks he's awake and then sends me in.

I intend to go in full throttle. I want to yell at him for lying to
me. I want to plead with him to tell me he didn't start that fire.

What I actually do is take one look at him sitting up in the
hospital bed and burst into tears. There's an IV in the back of

his hand and oxygen cannulas up his nose, and he looks small and pale, the complete opposite of strong and capable Carey.

He looks momentarily alarmed, and then his face breaks into a smile and he shifts further upright on the bed. 'I didn't think you'd come. Or if you did, that you'd have Gracie's beating stick with you.'

I should have thought of that. A hospital is the right place to do it. 'Nah, it wouldn't be fair to beat an injured man. I'll let you recover first, then we'll see.'

He laughs, and I sniff and turn away to wipe my eyes and try to compose myself. I came here to get to the bottom of this, not sob all over him, but seeing him brings the terror of yesterday flooding back, and nothing seems to matter other than him being okay.

'Hey.' I walk across the room on unsteady legs and dump my bag on the visitor's chair. It's a small ward, meant for four people, but Carey is currently the only occupant, which is just as well considering my teary entrance.

I stand beside the bed and run my hand over the back of his, the one without the IV line going into it. 'How are you?'

His fingers close around mine. 'I'm okay. I'm pumped full of god knows what. Epinephrine, steroids, antihistamines. They're waiting for the drugs to wear off to make sure the reaction doesn't start again.'

'You look better.' I should yank my hand away. I should start shouting at him. I practised an angry conversation in my head on the way over, but all I want to do is hug him. Hold him. Prove to myself that he's okay. That he's not what Gracie says he is. That there's no way I've fallen for an untrustworthy man *again* and this is all a crossed-wires misunderstanding.

'I don't think the bar is set very high. That decomposing frog down the well looked better than I must have yesterday.'

It makes me snort-laugh and brings up the memory of him lying on the floor yesterday and my eyes fill up again. 'Is there any way I can hug you without hurting you?'

He smiles. 'Probably not, but I'll give it a go.'

There are too many wires, too many things monitoring his vitals, but he pushes himself further upright and leans forward, and I bend down and get my arms around his torso, burying my face in the back of his neck.

'Oh my god, Kayl.' His voice sounds thick and emotional, and his arms tighten around me so much that I'm not sure he'll ever let go. I let one hand reach up and pull his hair back, stroking through it until his lips find my shoulder, and I kiss the back of his neck.

He's wearing thin hospital-issue pyjamas, and he has a hospital smell of disinfectant and cleanliness, and lingering smoke from the fire, nothing like his usual gorgeous aftershave, but nothing matters except having him in my arms, okay and alive.

I can feel his breathing getting tighter, every breath still isn't deep enough, and I force myself to pull away and disentangle my arms carefully, avoiding the wires, and his noise of disappointment makes me smile despite myself.

I step back and look him over. The rash is fading and the swelling has gone down, but he still looks puffy in places, his eyes are sunken and surrounded by dark circles, and the red volcanoes from the bee stings are throbbing lumps on his arms and neck.

The atmosphere is awkward. He knows I know, and we both know we're avoiding the elephant in the room, and the elephant is the size of at least three whale sharks.

'How are you feeling?' I pull the chair nearer and perch on the edge of it, my bag digging into my back.

'I've had better days, to be fair.' He grins at the understatement. 'Feel like I've had a good squashing by a steamroller that reversed back over me at least fifteen times, but grateful mainly. Glad you were there. Thank you for saving my life.'

'I nearly got you killed. The first rule of beekeeping is never to approach a hive without a bee suit on, and I let you.'

'You didn't have yours on.'

'I'm not allergic to bee stings.'

He does a nonchalant shrug. 'That does help, yeah.'

I squeeze his hand, holding it up and resting my chin on it. 'Why didn't you tell me? God, Care, I wouldn't have let you anywhere *near* the roof. Why tell me you're scared of bees but not say you're allergic to them?'

'Because it's a weakness. You can control a fear. You can face a fear. You can push yourself through something you're scared of. You *can't* face an allergy. You can't fight an allergy. If people know, it's a weakness for them to pick on and use against you.'

'*Who* would use a deadly reaction to bee stings against you? And if there *are* people like that in your life, you need to get them *out* of your life sharpish.'

'Tell me about it,' he mutters.

'And why did you do that yesterday? You literally could have died, do you realise that? I thought you were going to, and you can put on the macho face now, but *you* thought you were going to as well. I was coming to get the carpet from you. You didn't need to put yourself in danger like that. I know you're reckless, but flipping heck, you *don't* walk into a cloud of angry, stinging bees when you know you could die from a bee sting.'

'I wasn't thinking about myself in that moment. I was thinking of you and the bees.' His eyes meet mine, still bloodshot and puffy around the edges. 'You needed help and I didn't want to be useless in that situation.'

'I'd rather have you useless and alive than helpful and dead!'

He doesn't respond, and I kiss his inner wrist where I'm still holding his hand against my chin. 'Do you remember much of yesterday?'

'Some. Not all.' His thumb nudges my chin up until I'm looking at him again. 'I remember you. You're stern when someone's dying in front of you.'

I give his hand a gentle tap, which would've been a light smack if he didn't look like a strong breeze would tip him over.

'It's not funny.'

'I know that.' He swallows hard. 'You gave me something to hold on to. I have never wanted to live as much as when you mentioned love. Kayl, I'm falli—'

I cut him off because I can't hear this now. 'And why the heck haven't you replaced your EpiPens? 2017, Carey!'

'Because for the past few years, I haven't cared if I lived or died.'

Tears blur my vision again and when the nurses check on him later, they're going to wonder where all the extra bruising on his hand has come from.

'What was the damage?'

'Four hives destroyed. And the other two closest to the flames …' The tears spill over and I'm crying again.

'I'm sorry. I'm so sorry.' With Herculean effort, he pushes himself up far enough that he can bend over and kiss the top of my head, and then sits back, panting for breath.

'It would have been worse if you hadn't done what you did. So thank you, even though you are more important than the bees. No matter how important they are, they're just bees. *You* are irreplaceable.'

Colour brightens his pallid cheeks. I need to ask him about the fire. I came here to confront him, but I don't want to lose him yet. I want to sit here and appreciate him being okay and pretend he's still who I thought he was yesterday afternoon, and remember the best kiss I've ever had in my life and not anything that came after it.

'Your lady friend missed you last night.'

'You kept our date?' His eyes light up. 'And yeah, that's creepy. I'm going to stop calling her that.'

I laugh, but it's a false titter, and he hears it just like I do.

He knows I know. If nothing else, he must realise the EpiPen was in the same bag as the bank statements. Maybe he wonders why I'm just sitting here, pretending our bubble hasn't burst when it clearly has.

Eventually, he clonks his head back against the metal headrest. 'Which one of us is going to bring it up first?'

He's always been braver than me.

'In my hazy, questionable state, I saw Gracie last night … Well, I wasn't really seeing much, so maybe I heard Gracie, and quite frankly, the *dead* could hear Gracie. She must've told you …'

And in that one sentence, he answers all my questions. 'She's right, then?'

'I should've told you, but I didn't know we were going to get as close as we did, and by the time I realised how big the lie had become, it was too late and I knew I'd lose you.'

'I don't understand what you're doing there. How can you do so much good for Elderflower Grove but still be the person who's going out under the cover of darkness, cutting down important wildflowers and injecting weedkiller into ancient, beautiful trees?'

'I never did that.' He raises the hand with the IV line in and winces. 'I sprayed the orange cross on the trunks to make it look like it was done, but I never did it. I bought them time. It'll be a couple of months before Kingsley Munroe realises they're not dying and orders it done again. The strimming I can't get out of. He didn't fire me after I messed up with that garden. He put me on menial jobs for the rest of the year, and if I'd behaved myself, I'd have had a chance of getting my old job back.'

'And haven't you?'

He snorts. 'I told everyone about his plans for the theme park. My job is gone because of that. I was trying to be a better person, Kayl. Trying to make up for the horrible things I've had to do.'

'You didn't have to lie about it.'

'I don't have anywhere to live. I couldn't lose my job as well. Elderflower Grove was somewhere to stay when I needed it most, and a summer there is giving me the chance to save up enough of a deposit to rent somewhere. The job cut came with a huge drop in income too. I *had* to do what he told me to. Please understand that. I expected him to sack me, but he gave me a lifeline – his

245

assistant had just left and he needed someone to step into the role of general dogsbody. I do all the things he can't bully anyone else into doing. If it wasn't me, it would be someone else.'

'That doesn't make it better. *Someone else* hasn't been lying since the day I met him. *Someone else* hasn't been staying out of sight and hiding when anyone's around, acting like a ghost because if anyone had seen him, they'd have recognised him instantly. *You* have.'

He thunks his head back again. 'I didn't know what to do. I didn't know how to tell you, and I knew it would be worse if you found out from someone else, and I was still trying to keep my job. None of the villagers could know I was there or they'd have suspected Kingsley Munroe was up to something.'

I'm not even sure that makes sense. Somewhere I've let go of his hand and now my fingers are twisting around each other where they're resting on the edge of the hospital mattress. 'What was your *real* job at Elderflower Grove?'

'We expected trouble this year. Kingsley thought the Nectar Inspectors would realise seven years passing was significant. He thought they might break in and try to uncover something to prevent him taking ownership, or chain themselves to the gates, or get the building listed status or something, anything, he didn't know, but he wanted someone to keep watch on the place at all times. He'd made a big investment in the property and he wanted to make sure nothing untoward happened.'

'He *is* the untoward happening. And so are you.' I drop my head down on my arms. 'Why have you worked so hard on something that *you* wanted to destroy?'

'I never wanted that. Everything I've said to you has been true. What he's doing is abhorrent. All I wanted for Elderflower Grove is what we've given it – to be loved again and appreciated by people who visit those beautiful grounds.'

'I'm sure you'll understand why I find that difficult to believe.' I stare at him until his eyes meet mine and then I look away sharply.

246

'And what about Josie? All of that about being her grandson was just a cover story, right?'

'What? No. No, of course not. As soon as my dad told me what he knew of his birth mother, I thought of her – the eccentric beekeeper from Hampshire. It was a twist of fate when Kingsley gave me this assignment. A legitimate reason to go inside Elderflower Grove and find out if my hunch was right. I thought if I could find evidence, proof in some way that she really was my father's birth mother, then I could stop what he was doing. I could save it.' He lets out a long sigh and his little finger twitches like he wants to reach out for my hand. 'You have to trust me.'

'How could I ever trust a word you say again?' I didn't intend to snap at him, but being told I have to trust him when *everything* has been a lie makes me bristle.

'And you've always been completely honest with me, have you?'

Instinctively, I want to bark out a 'yes!' and storm off, but I can't. His question leaves a charged silence. I can't deny it, can I?

'Well, I …' I start but stutter to a halt.

'Kayleigh, on the day we met, you tried to brain me with a copy of *A Complete Idiot's Guide to Beekeeping*. I'm not so much of an idiot that I didn't recognise it as a brand-new book and not some good-luck charm that had been carted around from job to job for years. It was bright and shiny without a crease in sight. Do you think I haven't noticed that you've had to read it every time anything to do with the bees comes up? You've got the hang of things now, but you couldn't hide how hesitant you were at first, and it was definitely more than being "a bit rusty".'

'I needed the job,' I mutter.

'So did I.'

All right, he's got a point there. 'What you said yesterday – about you being the bee? How is that possible, Care?'

This time he lets out such a pained groan that I start wondering if I should call for a nurse.

'I didn't want to die without you hearing it from me.'

Even after all this, I still expected him to say that was a mistake, his fevered mind playing tricks on him. 'I don't get it. *You* set up the Nectar Inspectors?'

'No. It hasn't always been me. Just this year.'

'Wait, so …' Of course. The computerised voice. The bee filter. *Anyone* could be behind it. It hasn't always been the *same* person. 'This year' needles at my brain and my skin prickles at the implication. 'If you haven't always been behind it … who has?'

'You have to promise not to tell Gracie. I sincerely fear she'll end up in prison for her reaction.' He doesn't even need to say the name.

'Kingsley Munroe?' I ask and he nods in response. 'Flipping hell, Carey. *Why*?'

'A diversion. A decoy. He's getting his hands on Elderflower Grove through dodgy, underhanded tactics. He has no real right to it, you know that. He knew the villagers were uppity and he didn't want them digging too deep. He thought if he set up the group to "save the bees" and convince the villagers that they were doing something good, it wouldn't matter how much good they did in the end, because he was in charge of it.'

'Wow.' It's so horrible that my brain can't process what my ears are hearing. 'Do you have any idea how devastated they'll be? They've been working for the enemy all along. They've been *helping* him to steal Elderflower Grove. That really is the lowest of the low. And you've supported that.'

'I had no choice. I needed my job.'

'You've made them look stupid. You've made us all look stupid. I work for Gracie's most-hated man without even knowing it.' I'm such an idiot. It's all smoke and mirrors. I have no idea who my employer is. 'And the money in the Elderflower Grove fund? Every penny they raise from the sales of honey and the other fundraising they do? That's just going to line his pockets, is it?'

His eyes close like he can't bear to open them. 'If I could change things, I would.'

I suddenly realise why Gracie must never know this. She will,

248

literally, kill Kingsley Munroe. And it's not just that. They think Josie is the bee. For as long as they don't know the truth, Gracie's best friend is still alive, and this is the final proof that she isn't. I can't comprehend how heartbroken she will be.

This is so nasty. Tangled and twisted and wrong, and Carey's right in the middle of it, and has been since the moment I saw the job advert. *He* must've come out from Elderflower Grove and stuck it to the gate. *He* must've conducted my interview from *inside* Elderflower Grove, and I never even had an inkling. The signs I missed that seem so obvious now. The 'baptism of fire' comment they *both* made. The first time he mentioned something about me making candles and I was *sure* I hadn't told him. 'So that Zoom meeting … that was you?'

He cringes. 'I'm sorry. This wasn't supposed to go the way it has. I didn't think I'd ever meet you. I certainly didn't think I'd fall in lo— Well, you were supposed to stay outside and I didn't think I'd be unlucky enough to get two beekeepers in a row who'd come poking around inside.'

'Why the hell did you give me the job? That interview was terrible. You couldn't have been *that* desperate.'

'Because of what you said. That feeling of needing to take back control and having no agency over your own life. You voiced what I'd been trying to put into words for months. My life had spiralled out of my control since I screwed up on that job. My time wasn't my own. I *am* a minion. My life is dictated by other people. You worded that. You felt the same as me, and I'd never met anyone who felt like that. I connected with you. It felt right, and then you mentioned Madonna's "Dear Jessie". It's how I've always felt about Elderflower Grove, like it would be walking into a lullaby, and I thought it was a sign.'

'If you've known I'm not a beekeeper since day one, why didn't you fire me?'

'Because it didn't change anything. That job was meant to be yours.'

'But now it changes everything. Even you helping me with that honey harvest. The way you said it was an oversight on someone's part. That's why you helped me – because it was an oversight on *your* part. Because *you* didn't fully explain the job expectation. Not because you're a lovely guy who wanted to help.'

'Oh, come on, it wasn't just that. I couldn't help with the hives, but you looked out of your depth and I saw a way I could help.' His hand moves towards mine again, but I pull mine back. 'And honestly, I liked you. You made me smile just as much in person as you had on the video call, and *that* had been a pretty difficult task up 'til then. I *wanted* to spend more time with you.'

It sounds nice, but the problem is that, no matter what he says, I don't believe a word of it. 'I need to ask you something, and this time, I *need* you to be honest with me.' I swallow hard. I can't believe I'm asking him this. 'Did you start the fire yesterday?'

I don't expect his eyes to well up, and I feel ridiculously guilty. 'Are you serious?'

'Yes. No. I don't know.' I risk a glance over at him and he looks so broken that I want to wrap my arms around him and squeeze tight enough to make him forget I said it.

'Do you *honestly* think I could do that?' Instead of waiting for an answer, he chews his lip and looks upwards, blinking fast. 'Wow. I must've become an absolute horror show of a person for you to even consider that …'

'I don't. I don't, Carey.' I go to touch his hand but pull back before I make contact. The rest of the words hang in my mouth, taking a long while for me to spit them out. 'But it was deliberate and you were the only one there.'

'Fair enough.' He gives one sharp, resigned nod, and I can almost see him shutting down. His body stiffens and I get the feeling that, if he was capable of it, he'd have got up and walked out at those words, but he pulls away instead, shifting minutely on the bed, moving as far away from me as poss— 'No, I wasn't.'

'What?'

'Kingsley Munroe was there yesterday. I ran into him on the third floor. I thought he was coming to see me and poking around on the way, but I didn't know how he'd got in. The main door was locked and the windows are boarded, so I figured he'd come down from the roof and one of us must've accidentally left the gate open.'

'I didn't. I had to unlock it to get to the fire.'

'I didn't eith— That padlock I put on the gate ... I got it from work. It's a standard-issue council one. Anyone who works there would have a key that would open it.'

'What did you do?'

'I escorted him out the back way so you wouldn't see him. You were seeing off the last of the visitors, and I went back inside and grabbed the drink and came down to meet you. I didn't go onto the roof. I didn't know he'd done anything.'

'It was him. It has to be. There's no other explanation.'

The silence is awkward and difficult. I thought Gracie was exaggerating how awful Kingsley Munroe is, but she clearly wasn't. How could he stoop so low to do something like this? And why? He got what he wanted when he paid off Josie's debt – a claim to Elderflower Grove. What did he think he was going to get out of harming the bees, other than petty revenge?

'So now we've established that I'm *not* a bee-murdering arsonist ...'

'You can't blame me for thinking the worst.'

'No.' He sighs. 'I can't.'

He sounds so dejected and looks crestfallen, and I fight the urge to give him a hug. Relief has washed over me at the realisation he didn't set the fire, but it doesn't change all the other things he's lied about. 'Even yesterday, even right before that incredible kiss, you were lying, hiding, sneaking him away so I wouldn't find out.'

'I've been *stuck* in my job. I couldn't lose the only income I've got. It's the only place I've worked since I was in my twenties – he's my only reference, and he's not exactly going to give me a

251

glowing recommendation for getting other jobs. I've been trying to help, Kayleigh. Trying to make things better at Elderflower Grove to make up for the things I *had* to make worse.'

'But you should have told me.'

Neither of us can argue with that point.

'There's nothing else to say then, is there?' he says when the silence has grown heavy.

He's right on that one too. And he can't get up and walk away, so it's my turn to be brave.

I shove the chair back so hard that it scrapes across the floor, the noise making us both wince. I pat his knee clumsily through the blue hospital blanket. 'I'm glad you're okay.'

I want to say goodbye, something to acknowledge that whatever we had is over, but I'm biting the inside of my cheek to stop myself crying, and I'm going to dissolve into a sobbing wreck if I try to speak again.

I walk across the room on stiff legs.

'Kayleigh …'

I don't turn around and look back. I can't. It would be so easy to hug him, to think of him yesterday and how scared I was of losing him, to convince myself that the good things he's done outweigh the bad because I *do* believe he's genuine in what he says, but none of it alters the fact that I can't trust him.

The ward door clicks shut behind me, closing on a summer I'll never forget for all the wrong reasons.

Chapter 17

Like humans with an empty stomach in a supermarket,
bees lose self-control when they're hungry.

It's more than a week later, July has turned to August, and I haven't been back to Elderflower Grove. Carey must be out of the hospital by now. He must be there again, and I can't risk running into him. I'm fooling myself by even thinking that I'm still the beekeeper there. I've had no formal notice of being fired yet, but it's not like the job is still mine, is it?

The bees can fend for themselves at this time of year, and after everything that's happened, so much human-caused damage, maybe they're best left to recover without a human sticking their nose in. The usual hive checks can be left for a fortnight at a push, but if I don't hear anything about a replacement beekeeper in the next few days, I'm going to have to steel myself into phoning the council to make sure someone is looking after them.

Mum has spotted that the gates have remained closed since last week. Elderflower Grove has nothing left to give at the moment.

I think nothing of it when there's a knock on the door and the sound of Mum's footsteps as she goes to answer it, and then calls up the stairs, 'Kayleigh, it's for you!'

At nine o'clock on a Sunday morning? I run down the stairs, expecting a courier with a parcel or something, and barrel to a halt when I pull the door open and Carey's standing there.

'Have you got a passport?'

'What?' I snap, my heart pounding from not *just* the run downstairs.

He goes to carry on and then hesitates. 'I appreciate that's a really odd question out of context, and I know I'm the last person you want to see.'

'Wrong. You're actually the last living creature I want to see. I would genuinely prefer a hammerhead shark to turn up on the doorstep than you.'

'That would be odd. And remarkably cramped. It's quite a small doorstep.'

My face betrays me by smiling. I fight it, but I can feel my lips twitching enough for him to notice it, so I purse them in an attempt to cover it, annoyed at myself for still finding him funny. 'What do you want?'

My voice is too sharp, too hard, and honestly the sight of him on my doorstep has set my heart racing. He looks like himself again, no swelling, maybe a little pale and with dark circles under his eyes, but a million times better than he looked in that hospital bed last Saturday.

He's grinning wildly. 'I found something, Kayl. I know where Josie is. You were right – she isn't dead. At least, she wasn't dead seven years ago but seven years is a long time in a nonagenarian's life … She's in France. We can be there and back in a day. My car's ready, but you've *got* to come.'

'Are you insane?' I stare at him. His hands are clasped together to stop himself gesticulating with them and he's grinning like he couldn't stop if he wanted to. 'After everything that's happened, you think you can turn up on my doorstep like it's all water under the bridge?'

His face falls. 'Well, no, of course not, but I … There's

something at Elderflower Grove that you need to see, and I'm not even going to tell you what it is because it's so unbelievable that you won't believe me, but—'

'That's the trouble with lying about everything – people stop believing you.'

He looks stung. Which is probably a poor choice of words considering what happened last Friday. 'I didn't mean that. I meant you seriously have to see this thing. This is about finding Josie. We're in this together, you can't give up now.'

He's still smiling, an excited smile, like he genuinely can't work out what the problem is. It's like he's had a memory lapse and everything that's happened since last Friday hasn't occurred. 'I'm not *in* anything with you. Nothing that happened at Elderflower Grove was real. You employed me under false pretences, and you've deceived the rest of Little Kettling too. You might not have been the captain of the ship, but you went along for the ride. You can't turn up here like nothing's changed. You're insane if you think I'm going *anywhere* with you, let alone on some wild goose chase to a whole different country.' I'm sure he can hear my gulp, but I have to be strong here. The sight of him looking so normal in his jeans and Pink Panther T-shirt is too much of a reminder of how scared I was of losing him last week and it's a battle with myself to *not* pull him into the biggest hug and never let go. I swallow again. 'Please go away.'

It takes all my strength to push the door closed and shut him out. The past two months have been the best time of my life, and it would be too easy to brush all of this under the carpet and go back, follow up whatever he's found and pretend everything's okay when it isn't.

'Kayl …' he calls through the door, and I peek out a corner of the frosted glass, waiting for him to leave. He stands there for an abnormally long time, and eventually turns and starts back down the garden path.

Before he reaches the gate, I remember something and yank the door open again. 'Carey?'

He turns around with that grin still on his face, and goes to come back but I hold up a hand.

'I want to know one thing from you. Have you replaced your EpiPens? *Both* of them?'

'Aww.' He pushes his bottom lip out and then rolls his eyes good-naturedly. 'Yes, I have.'

'Good.' I close the door with a click and push the handle up to lock it, my hands shaking from a mixture of the tension of seeing him and the relief of hearing that. I lean my forehead against the cool frame and take deep breaths.

Within seconds, there's a rap on the glass, but instead of waiting for me to answer, Carey kneels down and lifts the letterbox, pushing his hand through to hold it open from both sides.

'I'm not walking away. I'm not giving up on us, and *that* is exactly why. No one has ever cared about me like you do. No one's ever worried about stuff like that. Even when you hate me, you still ask me that.'

'I can hate you without wanting you dead,' I mutter.

He laughs through the open letterbox. 'Yes, you can, but you're going to hate yourself if you don't see this through and I'm not letting that happen.'

I don't respond.

'Kayl, listen, please. I know I've messed up. I know I've hurt you. I'd do anything to go back to the start and change it, but I can't. I'm trying to put things right. Kingsley Munroe is being charged for the fire. I gave the police a witness statement. The board of directors has already kicked him off the council. I think Gracie's going to apply for his job. The villagers know everything. I called a meeting of the Nectar Inspectors and took the filter off. They know it's me. And I know I have no right to ask anything of you, but I need you to trust me on this one last thing. This isn't about you and me – it's about Josie and

Guillaume.' The letterbox flaps closed and then something is posted through it.

A letter lands on the doormat and I bend to pick it up and unfold it.

This is the last wish I'll ever make. This is the last letter I'll ever write. The last time I'll ever see this beautiful place. I know where you are, Guillaume. I know where you are and I'm coming. I just hope I make it in time. I'm too old to go any faster. Please, to all the magic that exists in Elderflower Grove, let him still be alive by the time I get there.

Forever love,

Josie

Why am I crying? It's like the letter has broken something inside me. It *has* to be proof that Josie started the fire and disappeared that night. It's validation that everything I've thought since we found those hidden hives is right.

I yank the door open and stare at him, back on his feet on the doorstep now. 'It's dated the day before the fire.'

'Exactly.' He grins, and I can see the moment he catches sight of my tears. 'Just so you know, I *really* want to hug you right now and I know you'd thump me if I even thought about it, but it seems right that you know.'

It makes me smile through my tears. He's still the same guy, the same funny, quirky, kind Carey, and there's something about him coming here and bringing this to me. He was hurt when I accused him of starting the fire the other day, but I'm still his first thought when something like this happens.

'What do you say? Fancy a road trip?'

'No! I'll come to Elderflower Grove, but I'm not coming to flipping France with you, that's madness.'

'Okay, hypothetically, if you *were* to go on a spontaneous road trip to our European neighbour, what would you need and can you get it *now-right-now*?'

'I'm not—'

Suddenly the door is wrenched open from behind me, two hands are on my lower back, and my mum shoves me out the door so hard that I stumble forwards and fall straight into Carey's arms.

His arms wrap around me and he plants his feet wide to keep us both upright.

'Of course she's going with you,' Mum says to him and then turns to me. 'You're going with him. You're not too old for me to boss you around, and you're not coming back into this house until you've seen this through. No more moping around over gorgeous ghosts who aren't dead. You only need your purse, phone and passport, I'll run and get them.' She closes the door behind her and locks it. Actually *locks* it to prevent me getting back in.

'You can't do that!' I shout after her. If there was ever a good reason for not living with your mum, this is one of them.

His arms get impossibly tighter. 'Moping around, hmm?'

At least he didn't mention the gorgeous bit.

'Don't flatter yourself.' I push my hand against his arm to get him to release me, but the second my fingers touch his skin, they flex and linger, squeezing his bicep gently, reassuring myself that he's okay.

I make the mistake of meeting his eyes, still the same earnest blue as before, and something fizzles in the air between us. In the past few days, I've thought only of his misdeeds, so much so that I've forgotten the good things about him too. His lips are centimetres away from mine and my eyes are pulled to them like a magnet, and it would be so easy to …

Thankfully, Mum opens the door again and I push myself away from Carey as she thrusts a handful of things at me.

'Mum! I can't go on a trip with just a phone, purse, and passport.'

'I've got snacks, I've got drinks, I've got spare phone chargers and clothes and I know you've been dying to get your hands on one of my T-shirts. You said you wanted to be braver – give it a go.'

'I'm *not* going to France with you,' I grumble as Mum shoos us both away.

He's got a smirk on his face and he shrugs an 'I know something you don't know' shrug. It would be infuriating if he wasn't kind of adorable with it.

I'm determined to keep my distance. I am adult enough to walk the ten minutes to Elderflower Grove without saying a word. I will look at whatever he's found, wish him luck with it, and leave. Mum won't actually keep me locked out. Besides, how can I trust him on anything? Whatever he's got to show me is probably a dead frog or something equally thrilling.

Except … he's whistling as we walk, clearly more excited about something than he would be about a dead frog, and his cheerfulness keeps making me look over at him, and every time he catches my eyes and smiles, I feel those butterflies again.

It shouldn't be so difficult to stay angry at someone.

***

His car is in the driveway, an old-looking navy thing with the back seats folded down and the back full of stuff. He opens the passenger door and holds his hand out. 'Put your things in.'

'I'm not going to France with you,' I repeat.

He gives me a smug grin and lifts an eyebrow towards the car. I've put my phone in my pocket, but I've got my purse and passport in hand, seeing as Mum didn't give me the option of a bag, and it *is* a bit daft to continue carrying them just to be obstinate. I put them on the seat and he slams the door shut, grinning at me.

'What's got into you this morning? Why are you so smug?'

His grin gets even wider. He doesn't answer, but there's nothing unkind about it – he's like a kid you should tell off for being cheeky, but can't because they make you laugh.

259

He leads the way out past the manor house and around the outer edge of the maze. There's a yellow hosepipe coming from an outside tap at the side of the house, and we're following it along paths that look like they only exist because he walked them this morning.

We pass the maze and come to long, long grass, filled with poppies and ox-eye daisies. We're heading towards that odd hill he noticed from the maze a few weeks ago, but the mound of earth is gone, and in its place is …

I squint into the distance. 'What is that?'

He flashes an eyebrow at me.

'Carey, that's a …' It looks like a plane. No, it can't be a plane.

He flashes the other eyebrow at me, and I hurry him faster along the path. The morning sunlight is so bright that sunbursts obscure the view, and whatever the thing is, it's still surrounded by the rest of the mound, and it's impossible to make out from this distance.

It's the longest walk in history, and when we finally, finally reach the area, there's something emerging from the earth where the hill used to be.

'Oh my god.' I stare at the mangled wreckage of what is unmistakably an aircraft. 'It's a plane!'

He grins at me. 'No, it *was* a plane. Specifically, it was a French army plane flown during World War Two.'

The earth he's pulled down to uncover it is piled in heaps all around, a shovel driven into the nearest one. I walk around the wreckage. It's wet where it's recently been hosed down, and water is still soaking into the ground around it.

There's not much of it left. The crumpled frame of a nose part. Sections of wing that are all but burnt away, a tangled and twisted tail section, and even so many years later, the scent of molten metal is still in the air when you get close to it, combining with smell of fresh dirt where he's dug it out, and rust from being underground all these years.

'Well, we know there are unexpected things at Elderflower Grove, but this tops the rest of them combined. Josie had a *plane* buried in her garden?'

'It looks that way.' He's doing the smug grin thing again.

'But why? How on earth did it get here?' I look upwards like another plane could land on my head at any moment. 'It must have crashed here … and then someone … buried it?' This makes no sense. I look between him and the plane, and then realise what he's just said. 'Wait, if this is a French plane and Guillaume was French, do you think they could be connected?'

He raises both eyebrows, like he's waiting for me to understand.

'Oh! Could this be the accident Josie's referenced in some of her letters? When she's mentioned him learning to walk again, learning to dance, taking his first steps … What do you think happened? His plane crashed here, he fell in love with Josie, and just … never left?'

'I think it's possible,' he says with a shrug.

'Maybe it was like *Misery* by Stephen King. Maybe she tied him to a bed and broke his ankles and wouldn't let him leave.'

'Has anyone ever told you that you watch too many horror movies?'

'Not until I met you,' I say with a grin. 'How did you find this?'

'I was at the well yesterday. I made a wish to find a way to make things right again, and as I sat there, I felt something. I don't know what it was, but the back of my neck tingled, and I was absolutely convinced that when I turned around, there was going to be a ghost standing there. There wasn't, but I followed the feeling. I got to the end of the maze and saw this hill again. It bothered me because it looked so unnatural. When I walked out here, there was another one of those stones.' He points to a large, flat, river-smoothed rock that's half-buried by wet mud now. 'I found the letter underneath it. Josie used those stones as a marker, a way to acknowledge something happened in that spot. I came back this morning with a shovel, climbed to the top and dug it in, and it started falling away.'

He's looking so pleased with himself and he's got *that* smile on his face again.

'All right, what do you know that you're not telling me yet?'

His grin gets even wider and he beckons me over with one finger, then he digs around in his pocket and pulls his hand out with something large, flat, and metal dangling from his fingers. 'That soldiers in French army planes wear French army tags.'

'Carey!' I squeak and grab his hand, pulling it down until I can read the tag he's holding. 'Guillaume Dumont. We have a surname! We can look him up!'

Without letting go of his hand, I pull my phone out and navigate one-handed to the search engine and start typing in the name, hitting the wrong keys and swearing in my rush.

He laughs, and when I glance up at him, he's got that grin on his face again.

I put my phone away. 'You've already looked him up, haven't you? That's what you're so happy about. That's why you keep going on about France.'

'Guillaume Dumont. A pilot in the French Air Force in World War Two. Disappeared on a reconnaissance mission over England in March 1943. Missing, presumed dead. His aircraft was never recovered.'

'I think we've just recovered it.' My fingers are rubbing across the smooth metal tag in his hand.

'It gets better. Reported alive in 1979 when he handed himself in to French police. Kayleigh, he died at ninety-four-years-old on the twentieth of November in the year of the fire.'

'They had two weeks together,' I say, thinking about the letter he put through my door earlier. 'That's so romantic. Or, you know, completely tragic. We have to assume that Josie got there and found him after so many years of looking. She must've got answers to her questions. And then never come back …'

'His record says he's survived by a Mrs J. Dumont. And I've got a last known address … And no death has been recorded for

262

a Josie Dumont *or* a Josie Garringham. There's a chance she's still there.'

I squeal.

'So you're coming to France with me, right?'

'Of *course* I am.'

His face turns into a beam that could break the Guinness World Record for widest smile, and that's it. I throw my arms around his neck and finally let myself hug him. His arms tighten around me and lift me off the ground, spinning us in a circle before he puts me back down but doesn't let go.

'Kayl, can I say something?' he says into my neck.

I nod without letting go of him either.

'I'm sorry. I'm so, so sorry. I know I should have told you, and I know I should never have gone along with Kingsley Munroe in the first place. I've been totally numb. I haven't cared about what I was doing. And then you burst into my life and woke me up – literally and metaphorically. You made me want to live again – literally and metaphorically. You made me realise *why* I've always loved my job – and it's the opposite of what I've been doing recently.'

'I'm sorry I accused you of the fire the other day. I know you wouldn't—'

'It's okay.' He squeezes me tighter for emphasis. 'Who *wouldn't* have thought the same in that situation? I was upset, but not at you – at me, for becoming the kind of person where that was the natural assumption.'

'I'm sorry I lied to you about the beekeeping too. I didn't mean any harm. I know I should have been honest with *you*, but I wasn't, and then it was too late. I'm sorry.'

His lips brush over my neck just once, but we stand there for an abnormally long time, and it's only Carey's phone buzzing with confirmation of the Eurotunnel booking that makes us realise we need to get to Folkestone in two and a half hours.

'Care, can you afford petrol for this kind of trip?' I ask as we get in the car and snap our seatbelts into place.

'Well, no one's fired me yet, and I still have access to the Elderflower Grove fund, and I think this counts as important Elderflower Grove–related work and is an appropriate distribution of funds, don't you?'

'*Vitally* important Elderflower Grove work.'

Even though we're grinning at each other, as he sets the car in gear and puts his hands on the steering wheel, his forearms flexing with every movement, I can see the fading red marks of the bee stings.

I reach over and let the backs of my fingers rub gently over his arm. 'How are you?'

He goes to say something flippant but I cut him off. 'Just over a week ago, you were …' I can't bring myself to say it. 'How are you *really*?'

'I'm okay.' He looks into my eyes and then sighs when he realises he's not going to get away with a one-word answer. 'Kind of shaky. Shaken. Tired. Feels like a bad dream that never really happened. I haven't been brave enough to go back on the roof yet. I keep having flashbacks and getting emotional. Surprised by how desperately I wanted to live and how glad I am you were there.'

He holds his hand out and I hesitate and then take it, and every inch of tension drains away and everything that's been so wrong since last week dissipates in an instant. His fingers close around mine and his thumb rubs over them. '*Now* I'm fine.'

I swat at his thigh gently. 'Got your EpiPens?'

He laughs and lets go of my hand to point into the back of the car. 'That bag, pocket on the side.'

'Get used to being asked. Don't expect to ever go anywhere without me checking. Even if we never speak to each other again, I'm going to text you every year to make sure they haven't expired.'

'Us never speaking again?' He shudders. 'I don't like that plan.'

'I don't like that plan either.' I can't get the grin off my face and neither can he. We're idling in the driveway because he's smiling too much to pull out.

'Has that ever happened before?' I ask when he finally reverses onto the road, and I get back in after locking the gate behind us.

He knows I mean the allergy. 'Happened when I was younger – about seven, I think. I don't remember any of it, other than how scared my parents were. That was how we discovered I was allergic to bee stings. I've had to carry the pens around since then, but I never got stung again. A few years ago at work, I was redesigning a park where solitary bees were nesting in the ground and I didn't know and dug straight into the nests – that's where the other pen went. It was just one sting, the pens were in the bag I had over my shoulder, I stuck one into my thigh and within ten minutes, I was fine. They say you're supposed to go to A&E afterwards, but I didn't. I thought it probably wasn't as bad as it had been before, maybe I'd grown out of it, so thanks to Elderflower Grove for proving that one wrong.'

'You got any other allergies?'

'Not that I know of,' he says as we circle the roundabout that leads out of Little Kettling. 'I'm sorry I scared you the other day. It had been so long, and after the last time being a non-event, I didn't think it would be as severe as when I was younger. I thought I'd have plenty of time to run downstairs and grab the pen without you even knowing.'

'We're going to have to talk about the things you think it's appropriate not to share with people who lo— *care* about you.' I correct myself before I say something I can't take back.

He glances over at me and quickly swivels his eyes back to the road, leaving me in no doubt that he knows *exactly* what that was intended to be. He blindly holds his hand out again, and when I slip mine into it, he pulls it up until he can kiss the back of it. 'I'll share anything with someone who makes me feel as *cared for* as you do.'

Even though what I really want to do is pull over and snog his face off, I extract my hand and give his thigh a squeeze instead. 'Now let's go and find your grandmother.'

Chapter 18

*Bees have personalities. Some are lazy and some aren't.
Some are more sociable than others. Some will fly vast
distances and some are too timid to venture far from
the hive. Some are better at certain jobs than others.*

Just over four hours later, we pull up outside an apartment block
in Ardres, France. We're both grunting and groaning as we unfold
ourselves from the car and stand up straight for the first time
in far too many hours. It's late afternoon, sunny and warm, but
we're on a mission rather than a day trip. I send Mum a quick
text to let her know we've arrived safely.

From what I've researched on the drive over, it's an assisted-
living facility where people live independently with help from
regular care workers.

'Apartment Three, second floor,' Carey reads from his phone
as we go through the main door and up the first stairwell to a
narrow landing area with numbered doors for each apartment.
He's got the tin of Josie's letters under his arm.

We press the button for the intercom outside Apartment Three
and wait. We could be moments away from coming face to face
with Josie Garringham. After spending so much time in her home

and reading so many of her personal letters, I feel like I know her well enough that she could be *my* grandmother.

My hand is in Carey's without even realising it, and I definitely cut off his circulation as the intercom crackles and an elderly voice speaks. 'I'm not interested in whatever you're selling, go away.'

'Is that Josie Garringham?'

There's a long hesitation, and then the elderly voice responds. 'There's no one by that name here.'

'Josie Dumont then?' I try again.

'No.'

I meet Carey's eyes and his narrow like he doesn't believe her either, and then I think about how intimidating it must be for an elderly woman to have two strangers turn up on her doorstep.

'We don't mean any harm. I'm Kayleigh, the beekeeper at Elderflower Grove. This is Carey, the gardener. We've come looking for the original beekeeper at Elde—' The door opens so quickly that it makes me jump.

'My bees? They're still there?'

My eyes well up instantly. 'They're fine. As productive and buzzy as ever.'

'Are they on the roof?'

I nod as a tiny woman half-appears around the door. I don't expect *her* eyes to fill with tears too. Who knew the little creatures could cause so much emotion?

'They survived.' She says it as a statement, not a question.

'The villagers have been taking care of them ever since. Elderflower Grove honey is big business in Little Kettling nowadays. I've been the beekeeper there this summer.'

'How on earth did you two find me? It's been so many years. I never expected to hear the words "Elderflower Grove" again.'

'We found these.' Carey holds up the tin, and she stares at it for a minute before her watery eyes widen in recognition. 'We also found Guillaume's army tag. That's how we got here. We're not here to cause trouble – we only wanted to know what happened to you. And because we may as well jump in with two left feet – I think you might be my grandmother.'

His forwardness makes me smile, and we're both surprised when Josie Garringham starts laughing. 'I think that's *very* impossible, but you'd better come in.'

She pulls the door fully open, inviting us into a narrow hallway with mobility aid bars along both sides of the walls, and I have to force myself not to hug her, mainly because she's so petite and frail that I'd probably squash her. She's hunched over and using a frame to get around, and we follow her into a brightly lit living room with tall windows and a view of a canal and a bustling village beyond it.

Carey volunteers to make cups of tea, while Josie lowers herself into a rocking chair and I place the tin on her lap when she asks for it. 'How did you find these? I'd put them in a place no one could ever possibly look.'

I tell her where we found them. 'Some sort of death-something beetle—'

'Deathwatch,' Carey calls from the kitchen, making me grin.

Josie looks between me and the open doorway with a smile on her wrinkled face.

'Whatever it is, it's eating your floorboards. I accidentally put my foot through one, and in trying to free me, he uncovered it.'

'Ah, I see. Elderflower Grove wanted you to find them.'

The fact that she thinks that makes me feel so much more normal. I'm not the only one who thinks it's got something that most buildings haven't.

'I can't believe it survived the fire.'

'Because of her.' Carey reappears in the doorway carrying three cups of tea on a tray.

'I can see the house from my bedroom window. I saw the flames that night and called the fire brigade.'

'No wonder Elderflower Grove likes you so much. I'm not surprised at all that it would show you these.' She nods sagely

268

and then gives the tray Carey's put on the coffee table a look of disdain. 'I'll tell you what, you're no relation of mine if you're serving tea with no biscuits. There's a tin on top of the fridge.'

I laugh out loud given his usual affinity for biscuits, and help myself to a shortbread when he returns seconds later and sits down next to me on the grey two-seater sofa.

Josie sips from a daintily patterned teacup and runs her fingers over one of the brittle envelopes. She's so hesitant that I wonder if she doesn't want to be reminded of them, but eventually she takes one with shaking hands and unfolds the paper, her lips moving as she silently reads the words to herself. She puts it back and selects another one. 'Never thought I'd see these again.'

'Please tell me you found him,' I blurt eventually.

'He wrote to me from his deathbed.' She closes the tin and folds her hands on it. 'As I'm sure you've gathered from these – he vanished. Just as quickly as he'd burst into my life, he was gone from it. You can see how distraught I was. I didn't know who to turn to. He wasn't supposed to be there, and *no one* knew he was. He lived at Elderflower Grove for thirty-six years and no one ever found out.'

'How is that possible?' Carey asks.

'If you've got this far, I'm assuming you know just about everything. And I know where I buried that tag ...'

Carey and I glance at each other. 'A plane crash?'

'It was a lovely spring day in 1943. I was indoors doing some darning, I heard a plane overhead, I was getting quite annoyed because it was flying so low and interrupting my thoughts, and then there was an almighty crash outside. I ran up to the roof and all I could see was a huge plume of black smoke. The plane was on fire by the time I got out to it, and I could see the pilot, slumped in the cockpit. I pulled him from the burning wreckage. I was a nurse back in the day. I was confident in taking care of injuries. I was certain someone would've seen the crash and come straight away, but no one came. It started raining and I managed to drag him inside, the rain put out the fire, and still no one came. I didn't know what to do, to be honest, but I knew he wasn't one of *ours*. There was an injured enemy soldier in my house. He was in a dreadful state, badly wounded and barely conscious, and my training took over. I had my supplies on hand, I got what else I needed from the few shifts I worked at a field hospital weekly, and still, I expected someone to come. The wreckage of a plane was in my garden. I thought someone would see it or someone would've heard the crash and come to investigate. Days turned into weeks. He recovered. He was traumatised by the war and struggling with what we now know as PTSD. His injuries kept him bed-bound, but we played card games, we talked, and we read together. He spoke English well but couldn't read it. I told him about my library and he was determined to recover well enough to get up the stairs to see it one day. We were in love before he was strong enough to walk again. It was spring and nature took over the garden. The plants and trees swallowed the wreckage and hid it from view. He grew stronger. I had been alone in that big old place since my parents passed, and I'd never realised how lonely I was until he arrived. He lit up my life. He was the missing piece of my puzzle – the other side of my coin. He was happy too – for the first time in forever. He didn't want to leave, and I couldn't bear the thought of losing him. But he had walked away from the army in the middle of a war. He was a deserter. By not reporting the crash straight away, by taking him in and hiding him, he had deserted his post. If anyone ever found out, he would've been brought back to France and faced execution. In those days, desertion was one of the most shameful crimes a soldier could commit.'

I'm ashamed to say I hadn't even thought of that.

'Guillaume never left the grounds for fear of being found out, and I was never a very sociable creature, I was more than happy to hide away in there. I went out to do the shopping, I met my friends in the village, but I never allowed another person into the estate. I never told a soul about Guillaume's existence, even though I desperately wanted to shout my love from the rooftops. We were head over heels for each other, ensconced in our little bubble, away from the world. Elderflower Grove became our playground. We danced in the ballroom, we swam in the river, we ate picnics by the well, and watched swans raise their cygnets on the lake. We had everything we needed as long as we had each other. We cooked together. We dashed around the estate laughing until our sides ached. When he was strong enough, we buried the plane wreckage and let nature take over. When I got my first bee hives, he embraced them with both arms – not literally, he was dreadfully allergic to bee stings …'

I don't realise I've shifted closer to Carey until his fingers brush mine. 'What are the chances?'

'You too?' she asks.

'We had an … *incident* last week.' I knock my arm against his and he gives me a smile.

It's yet another echo of our story that I recognise in so much of what Josie's saying.

'He bolstered my love of them. The colonies expanded and swarmed, and he encouraged me to get more hives. Soon we were overwhelmed with honey, and it was his suggestion that we start selling it. It became a little business. He built the Honey House so he could stay inside and extract it while I went to the hives.'

Just like we did at first. Carey looks across and gives me a soft smile, just enough to make one dimple dent at the edge of his lip and it makes a little tingle run through me.

Josie pats the tin on her lap. 'We had over thirty years of blissful happiness. Neither of us ever wanted for anything. We had each other and we had Elderflower Grove. What more could we want? And then one day I went to work, and when I got back, he was gone.'

Even though I knew where the story was going, it still makes me shiver.

'I didn't know where he'd gone – what had happened. The house was empty. He'd left no note. He'd taken only the clothes he was wearing, and not a thing else. I was completely lost. Had he ventured out and realised there was a whole world beyond Elderflower Grove and I wasn't enough for him anymore? Had he been in a terrible accident and the authorities couldn't identify him to let me know? I searched the grounds in case something had happened to him, but I found no trace. I didn't know what to do without him. Life lost all meaning. My bees were the only reason I got up in the mornings. They became my companions. I told them everything and their humming soothed my soul. I spent nights lying awake going over possibilities. I started writing to him because I didn't know what else to do with my thoughts. I was hurt, alone, and bitter. Every time I went out, I expected him to be there on my return, but he never was. The only thing that kept me going was the thought that I'd see him again one day.'

'And you did?'

'I received a letter from him, thirty-six years after I'd last seen him. He was in a hospice. He had cancer and the doctors thought he had only weeks left. He said he'd thought about me every single day and he didn't want to die without seeing me again. It was an emotional reunion. He was in a bad way – very ill, hooked up to countless machines – but as soon as I saw him, it was like no time had passed whatsoever. I sobbed all over him and he sobbed all over me. He told me what had happened – one of the French army personnel had started hunting for deserters. I don't know how he'd got there, but he'd traced flight paths and happened upon Elderflower Grove. He'd watched the house. He'd paddled up the river to get in, and he'd found Guillaume and threatened to reveal everything. Guillaume returned to France to hand himself in. He didn't want to bring shame on me if it had come out, so he did it quietly and without fanfare. He thought it was better if I didn't know. He *wanted* me to be angry at him. He blamed himself because he wasn't brave enough to face the consequences before.'

'Did you forgive him?'

'Forgiveness never came into it. The only thing I wished for was more time. In the years since, I've come to be grateful for the time we had. Those years we spent together at Elderflower Grove were the highlight of my life. I would never have become a beekeeper without his support, and that led to opportunities to look after bees around the world. He *gave* me the life I had. He served a ten-year prison sentence when he returned here, and after that, he thought I was better off without him. He was ashamed of what he called his "cowardly actions" – both of leaving the army in the middle of a war, and in leaving me without a word. He was ashamed of his time in prison and he carried that shame with him for the rest of his life. He'd wanted to find me, but he felt too guilty to face me again. He didn't think I'd *want* to see him. He was certain I'd have moved on with someone else after so many years, but I didn't, of course. Neither of us ever did. Those last two weeks we had together wiped out all the years between. They were wonderful in the most bittersweet way possible. He was dying – there was no escaping that fact above all others. I'd brought some of his favourite books from home, and I sat beside his bed and read them to him, just like I had all those years before. The nurses got us some boardgames and he had to translate the French for me. He'd told everyone he had a wife back in England, so everything was set up for me here. He'd left this apartment in my name, he had savings that he'd left me to live on. I took his name so no one could ever find me. I wanted a clean break. I felt like my soul had been cleansed by finding him again. I was a different person. I didn't want to go back. I wanted to move forward with the years I had left.'

'Why start the fire?' I ask.

'I was in huge debt. I'd lost my job as a nurse, and my only income was from the honey and the blocks of beeswax I sold to crafters. It was a summer income that had to last the rest of the year, and Elderflower Grove requires a *lot* of maintenance. The whole place overwhelmed me. What had been the home of my dreams turned into a reminder of Guillaume at every turn. I hated the house instead of loving it. And Elderflower Grove needs that. It *needs* love. It needs happiness, and it wasn't getting that from me. The weeds got as prickly and nasty as I had become. The grounds got so overgrown that I couldn't get through them, and the letters from the bank got more and more threatening. His letter was a lifeline when I was drowning. I knew that when I left, I would never return, and I couldn't bear the thought of it being repossessed, or of anyone uncovering the secrets we'd kept. I didn't want anyone to look for me. I knew they'd presume I was inside, and after I was gone, the bank would be able to recover their debt from what was left of the estate. Maybe it seems selfish to you young folks, but Elderflower Grove had become my prison, and I wanted to hurt it.' She looks at us. 'I'm sure I sound like a daft old cow, wanting to hurt a building, but it isn't just a building, is it?'

I shake my head. My eyes have filled up again, and I haven't even realised that Carey's hand has slid over mine until he squeezes it.

She takes a sip of now-cold tea. 'Oh goodness me, I've been yammering for ages. Tell me about you two instead. You make a lovely couple.'

'Oh, we're not …' I extract my hand from Carey's and gesticulate between us, even though I have no idea *what* we are.

'Elderflower Grove threw us together,' he says.

'In my experience, it only does that for very good reason.' She taps her nose. 'Trust an old girl who's had her fair share of both love *and* heartbreak. Only a very special love happens in that strange old building.'

Our eyes meet again and his smile makes me wish we were alone, but I settle for knocking my knee against his.

Carey volunteers to make another round of tea, and I sense Josie's eyes on me. 'He's a lovely young gentleman.'

'He is. I think.' I sigh. 'We've had some issues lately.'

She looks towards the open doorway, rocking thoughtfully in her chair, and when she looks back in my direction, she can see right through me. 'Guillaume had done things that weren't good – what he had to do to survive – but I chose to see the best in him, because the only thing that mattered was that he *had* survived. People don't end up at Elderflower Grove for no reason. I think you see the same in that house as I do – trust it. It can see the good in people better than we can.'

How many times can you tear up in one day?

When Carey comes back, Josie takes her china mug gratefully. 'Now, lovely young man, about this grandmother nonsense. I assure you there's no possible way it could be true, but I'd love to know where the idea has come from?'

Carey gives her a brief rundown of his father being adopted and admitting in his final days that he wished he'd found his birth mother.

She shakes her head. 'I never had any children.'

'Not even a baby you put up for adoption? You don't have to hide that from us. No judgement, no ill will. My father had a wonderful life. All I know is that his mother was an eccentric beekeeper from Hampshire and I've always felt strangely drawn to Elderflower Grove.'

'I'm sorry to disappoint you, but it isn't me.'

He nods resignedly. I think he expected as much from her reaction at the door earlier.

'Well, there goes our only hope of saving it,' I mutter.

Josie sits forward faster than you'd expect a ninety-nine-year-old to be capable of moving. 'Saving it?'

We give her a summary of everything that's happened this summer, from the seven-year anniversary of her death to Kingsley Munroe and the fire last week. Even with him off the council, the theme park has other backers, and in paying off the debt, the council have staked their claim. There is probably no way of getting it reversed.

'The villagers like it?'

I almost laugh at the understatement. 'The villagers *love* it. They go crazy for your honey. Gracie's beating them off with a stick and rationing jars.'

'Oh, my dear old Gracie.' Josie puts a hand over her heart. 'The only thing I missed about leaving Little Kettling. You wouldn't believe the amount of times I wished I could call her for a natter.'

I tell her about the rugby scrum for miracle honey and people putting it on their bunions and all sorts. 'We have photos. Not of the bunions, thankfully.'

She beckons us over eagerly. Carey crouches at one side of her chair and shows her the photos of the grounds on his phone. 'Oh, my dear, it looks better than it ever looked. In the early days, I had a gardener who didn't do half as good a job as that.'

'See?' I mouth at him, smiling because he's blushing at the compliment.

I kneel beside her and show her the photos I've been taking of the visitors enjoying themselves, including a few of Gracie talking animatedly in her bee antennae headband and striped top as she cajoles people into buying my beeswax candles.

'She hasn't changed a bit,' Josie says.

'She's been brilliant. She's on a mission to save Elderflower Grove now. There has to be something we can do. Now we know you're still alive, there has to be a way we can stop it being torn down. The council might have a share in it, but they don't own it yet.'

'A share?'

When I've finished explaining to Josie about the debt being paid by the council, effectively a down payment to ensure Elderflower Grove passes on to them, Carey interrupts.

'There's something I need to tell you about that. I know you think I took those statements to hide them from you, and yes, I did, but I also took them because I wanted to investigate that payment. Everything Kingsley Munroe does is underhanded and … well, I don't know what the opposite of above-board is, but very, *very* below-board. Kayl, the council didn't make that payment – the bees did.'

'What?' I try to form a sentence but nothing comes out for a minute. 'How? Bees are not generally known for zipping in and out of banks, opening bank accounts, and how would they ever carry a debit card?'

He laughs at the mental image. 'Kingsley Munroe wasn't allowed to use council funds for that purpose. It was devious and scheming. He was trying to wrangle a stake in Elderflower Grove so he could take "donations" from future investors on land he didn't own. It amounts to fraud, which he's now being investigated for. The board of directors would never sign off on something so dodgy, so he hid that transaction inside the fund set up for Elderflower Grove. He used the money earned by the Nectar Inspectors' honey sales and fundraising efforts to repay the debt. It was never the council's money. The bees themselves effectively bought back Elderflower Grove. The council have no claim to it.'

I look between him and Josie, who looks as befuddled as I am. 'You're telling me there was £75,000 lying around in that account? The Nectar Inspectors have raised *that* much?'

'That much, and *much* more. I don't think you realise quite how big the end-of-season honey harvest will be. We got five hundred jars from three frames in each hive. By the autumn, you'll have added three or four honey supers to the top of every hive, and each one will be full. We're talking twenty to thirty frames full of honey from each hive in a good summer. *Thousands* of jars. This stuff has a cult following online. Gracie started taking international pre-orders in January. We had a deal with a posh London department store one year – they sold the stuff for fifty quid a jar. And then there's the fundraising. You've not lived in Little Kettling for a few years, so you've missed how much they've done. Fun runs and marathons, village fêtes, bingo and quiz nights, sponsored bike rides, head shaves, and all sorts of things. Gracie did a sponsored silence once and earned thousands. Can't imagine why.'

I burst into laughter despite the tears dripping slowly onto Josie's carpet. Josie starts laughing, and then her laughter turns to tears as well, and Carey rubs her shoulder comfortingly, and I hand her a tissue from the box on the coffee table.

'My dears, I didn't realise until the moment you knocked on my door that *you* are exactly who I've been waiting for. Elderflower Grove is yours. The two of you and all the villagers. I didn't realise how much they loved it. I hand it over to you collectively, with immediate effect. The paperwork will be with my solicitor tomorrow morning.'

'What? No, no, no, you can't do that,' Carey says.

'Consider it done.' She pats his hand.

'Josie, you can't …' I'm blinking back tears again.

'It's no good to me anymore, and I am still the owner. The beggars haven't declared me dead yet. Elderflower Grove deserves to belong to the people who love it. Can you give me a list of all the Nectar Inspectors' names and addresses?' She points to a sideboard for pen and paper, and Carey goes to get it and starts copying information from his phone.

'You can't just give it to us,' I say.

'Of course I can. What else am I going to do with it? We'll make it a fair split among the villagers, but I'd like you two to have the controlling shares. It has clearly chosen you as its new owners and you belong there, just like Guillaume and I once did.' She leans over to pat my cheek. 'All these years, I've been wondering what had become of it. I had a feeling it was okay. I'd know if such a huge part of me had indeed perished. I've always thought it would be sold by my solicitor when I shuffle off this mortal coil, the debt paid and any proceeds put into some estate never to be seen again. And then you two turn up – exactly who I needed without realising I needed it. Elderflower Grove belongs to the people who want it. It's a legacy in itself – and I think its next love story is right in front of me.'

Carey looks up from writing and gives me a wink that makes my heart feel like it's glowing.

We sit talking, reminiscing, Josie telling us stories of days gone by, until one of her health visitors turns up. She greets us in French and excuses herself to the kitchen, but we never intended to overwhelm Josie or outstay our welcome, so we take our leave, but not before swapping phone numbers.

'Do you ever want to come back?' Carey asks as we say goodbye in the narrow hallway.

'Back to Blighty with autumn on the way? No, thank you.' She shivers.

'If you ever do, give me a shout. We could pop over and pick you up anytime.'

'At my age?' She does a low whistle. 'I'm not long for this world, we all know that. Elderflower Grove isn't mine anymore. It's time to move on, leave the past behind, and let a new couple find their magic there.'

His hand grasps mine again, and I'm biting my lip to stop myself crying *again* as we walk away.

'Carey?'

We both turn around.

'At the risk of hugely invading someone's privacy and upsetting a dear old friend by sharing an old secret, what you do with this information is up to you, but there's something I think you should know. I'm not your grandmother, but Gracie *did* give a child up for adoption in 1947, a two-month-old baby boy.'

'An eccentric beekeeper from Hampshire!'

He looks confused. 'Gracie doesn't keep bees.'

'Yes, she does. Or she used to, anyway. She told me the other day.'

He grunts. 'Gracie wants to gut me and feed my intestines to angry ducks. She's never going to want to know that.'

'Her first husband died very suddenly and very young,' Josie says. 'Beekeeping had been his hobby, and she couldn't face doing

279

it without him. I volunteered to take his hives – so in a way, it was Gracie who gave me *my* start in beekeeping. She was nine months pregnant when her husband died. She couldn't face raising a child without him. She was heartbroken and distraught. She couldn't cope with a baby in the face of that grief. I'm sorry.' She says goodbye again and closes the door.

'And on that bombshell …' Carey mutters as we walk down the same flight of stairs we came up hours ago.

When we reach the car, I go to let go of his hand and go round to the passenger side, but he tugs me back. He holds his arms open and I can't hug him fast enough.

'You okay?'

'Mmm.' He nods. 'That was more intense than I expected. I don't know what to do with that. How do I walk up to the person who hates me more than any other currently on the planet – avoiding projectiles being hurled in my direction – and say her dead friend has told me she might be my grandmother?'

'I don't think she'd hold a grudge. If you tell her everything …'

'When I took that bee filter off … Let's just say, I didn't think an octogenarian would even *know* those kinds of swear words, let alone the inventive terms for what I could do to myself.'

I laugh and squeeze him tighter. 'You're a very difficult man to stay mad at, Carey Paxton.'

He grins against my neck. 'Do you speak from personal experience?'

He's asking if I've forgiven him, and while it would be easy to say something teasing, he needs a bit of reassurance tonight. 'Yes.'

He pulls back and his fingers graze my jaw and his head dips. My eyes close in anticipation, and … A car horn blasts in the next street, startling us both out of the romantic reverie we were lost in and he scrubs a hand over his face and pulls away.

The French sky is darkening as we drive home. He's quiet all the way, turning over the information about Gracie in his head, and it's after midnight when we pull up outside my house. A light is glowing from behind the living room curtains and I'm surprised Mum is still up waiting for us.

Carey gets out of the car when I do and hesitates as he comes around to my side like he's going in for a kiss goodbye.

'I can see how tired you are.' I reach up and brush his hair back. The thought of saying goodnight and letting him go is impossible. It's been such a crazy day, and I don't want to watch him drive away and go back to that huge old house on his own. It's not a night for being alone.

'I'm fine.' The two words trip over themselves and he shakes his head, trying to wake himself up. He's obviously shattered from the drive, the information, and still suffering the after-effects of last week. 'But I need to ask you something. Have you been as desperate to kiss me as I have been to kiss you all day?'

'*More* desperate, I assure you.' I feel flushed despite the chilly air at this time of night.

He grins. 'May I?'

I can't get the smile off my face as his lips touch mine.

It's gentle and respectful and over way too fast, and when he pulls back with a contented sigh, I slide my arms around his neck and pull him down into another hug.

'I'm not letting you go,' I say into his ear.

For just a moment, he hesitates, and I get the feeling he doesn't want to be alone tonight either, but then his hands fit on my hips and he protests. 'It's just down the ro—'

'For goodness sake.' My mum appears in the doorway. 'You're *both* coming in to tell me all about your day, and I'm not having him going back to that house on his lonesome. The kettle's on. He can stop on the sofa. No arguments. Hurry up before the moths come in.'

She disappears back inside and we glance at each other and start giggling.

'I see where you get your ability to strike terror straight into the heart from.'

I'm still laughing as I shove him into the house.

Chapter 19

Bees fly at a speed of fifteen to twenty miles
per hour, and cover about 55,000 miles to make
less than half a kilogram of honey. They visit
approximately two million flowers for just one jar.

It's been a few days since I saw Carey. The day after the road trip, I checked all the hives to see the bees thriving, and then he said there was something he needed to do and asked me not to come to Elderflower Grove for a few days. He keeps texting reassuring messages, but I'm starting to get tetchy about how many days it's been when there's a knock on the door.

Outside is a man in the full uniform of a letter carrier from the early 1800s. He's wearing a scarlet tailcoat with blue lapels and cuffs, brass buttons and a beaver hat, and he's holding a fancy-looking piece of card. 'Telegram for Miss Kayleigh Harwood.'

'Telegram?' *Telegram*? What year is it? Have we accidentally travelled back in time?

'Mr Carey Paxton formally requests your presence at a ball to celebrate the life of Miss Jane Austen, to take place at Elderflower Grove on the evening of August twentieth. Please give a response for me to convey.'

I've gone all hot and fluttery and it makes me laugh. 'Tell him he's an idiot, but yes, of course.'

'Very good, miss. The gentleman will send the carriage at seven.'

Oh my god. A carriage *and* a telegram. I feel like I'm living inside *Pride and Prejudice*, even if telegrams weren't invented then.

The man does a bow and thrusts the fancy card invitation at me, looking as embarrassed by his outfit as I am on his behalf. He's probably hoping not to run into anyone he knows – he'll never live it down.

'Look at what he's doing.' I thrust the invitation at Mum when she comes to see what's going on. 'I once told him I dreamed of going to a Jane Austen–style Regency ball, and he said if he ever owned Elderflower Grove, he'd throw one for me. *That's* what he's been doing for the past few days. When he said he had a promise to fulfil the other day, I didn't realise it would be one to *me*.'

Mum turns over the gold-edged thick card. 'You'll finally get to wear your dress.'

I will! And Carey knows that. I feel an overwhelming rush of love for him. I knew he was up to *something*, but I had no idea it would be something like this. Talk about going above and beyond based on one throwaway line I said to him weeks ago.

Although with all the honey I've been eating lately, it'll be a miracle if I still fit into my Regency-style dress.

The village is abuzz with talk of Jane Austen by the time the day of the ball comes around. Everyone is going and I'm aflutter to see what Carey's done to the house. I feel like Jane Bennet preparing for a ball at Netherfield Hall and hoping to dance with Mr Bingley as I get ready. Simple make-up and a Lizzie Bennet style up-do that I watched tutorials for on YouTube. My empire-line dress is made of silk taffeta in such a deep blue that it looks purple in some lights, with a ribbon of silver under the bust, and I miraculously get into it with only one seam having to be unstitched. It's the only dress I own, hanging in its garment bag in the wardrobe, being lovingly stroked every time I open the door, but never with an opportunity to wear it before now. I feel like an old-fashioned Cinderella going to the ball to meet a handsome prince. I pace inside the front door as I wait for seven o'clock to come around, and then there's the sound of horses' hooves clip-clopping on the road outside.

The carriage that pulls up looks just like the carriage Elizabeth and Mr Darcy go off in on their wedding day, complete with two white horses.

'Good evening.' Carey gets to his feet and lifts his top hat in my direction. He's wearing a full Mr Darcy outfit – straight black trousers, with a white cotton shirt, a pale blue silk cravat tied in a bow, and a navy frock coat with gold edging – although he's smiling a *lot* more than any Mr Darcy has in the history of adaptations. He jumps out and strides up the garden path to offer me his arm. 'May I escort you to the ball at Elderflower Grove, Miss Harwood?'

'You know you're insane, right? You didn't have to go to all this trouble.'

He smiles but doesn't break character. I slip my hand through his arm and I can't resist giving his forearm a squeeze.

I can't believe he's done all this. It's so sweet and thoughtful and yet another way he makes me feel important by taking an interest in the things that matter to me.

At the carriage, he holds his hand out to help me in, and even though I'm perfectly capable of climbing into a carriage without assistance, I slip mine into it and his fingers fold around mine just a little, and it feels exactly like the moment in the *Pride and Prejudice* movie when the camera focuses on Matthew Macfadyen touching Keira Knightley's bare hand for the first time.

When I'm seated, he sits beside me and gives the okay to the driver, who starts the horses trotting again, and I squeak in delight, even though it's not exactly a speedy ride.

He knocks his shoulder against mine, dropping character for the first time. 'You have no idea how much I've missed you.'

I reach across to pick up his hand and clasp it between both of mine, holding it tight enough to let him know how much I've missed him too. 'I can't believe you've done all this.'

'I wanted it to feel authentic. I know how much you love Jane Austen, and you've mentioned balls and your dress …' His other hand reaches across to rub the silky fabric covering my thigh. 'I'm sure this is *very* un-Mr-Darcy-like of me, but you look *incredible*.' His lips touch my cheek softly.

God, he's perfect. The actual Mr Darcy pales in comparison, and I wish we were alone so I could kiss him properly, the kind of kiss that requires more privacy than an open-top carriage, and I settle for holding his hand even tighter.

It really does feel like we've gone back in time as we trot through the village. Little Kettling has always had an old-fashioned feel to it, but the streets are quieter than usual today, and as we turn into the driveway of Elderflower Grove, I let out a squeal so loud that it frightens one of the horses. 'It's got windows!'

He's grinning so widely that he can't get any words out.

'This is what you've been doing? This is why you told me to stay away?'

'I wanted it to be a surprise. Thing is, Kayl, the new manager of the Elderflower Grove Conservation Fund thinks funds have been misappropriated in the past, and by funnelling hard-earned money into the correct areas, Elderflower Grove can actually save itself by being used as a venue for weddings and events, as well as its sideline in honey production and candle-making, and tonight is a little bit of a test to prove it can hold its own and that people will come and enjoy themselves.'

'Who is this new mana—'

His smile answers before I've even finished the question.

'You?' I throw my arms around his neck and knock his hat skewwhiff as the carriage pulls to a stop in the courtyard.

His arms wrap around me and he holds us both upright, laughing as I force myself to let go just enough to *not* suffocate him. 'I took it to the higher-ups of the council. Told them every-thing. Showed them pictures. Showed them mock-ups of what we could do with the gardens with a proper team on board. Showed them quotes from structural engineers to ensure the safety of the house and open it up properly. The council directors agreed that this space is one of the county's most valuable assets and deserves people who will restore it to its full potential. They asked me to oversee the project.'

I pull back and hold his smoothly shaven jaw, making him look at me. 'Do you have any idea how incredible you are?'

His face burns in my hand and he leans forward to kiss me all too briefly, and then climbs out of the carriage and holds a hand out to help me down.

The gargoyle has been scrubbed to bright grey stone with not a hint of moss in sight, and water burbles from his spout into the basin below. 'You've even fixed the fountain.'

'We've got a long way to go. Full restoration of the grounds will take months, and the structural repairs to the house will take even longer, but I wanted to start somewhere.'

I slip my arm through his as we go in the main door we opened so many weeks ago, the grand entranceway illuminated by lights that are making the marble floor glisten. We ascend a mahogany double staircase, which until now has been dusty and grimy, but tonight, the dark wood shines and the scent of lemon polish hangs in the air.

There's Regency-era English country dance music playing in the ballroom, and I'm surprised when we get to the top of the stairs. No wonder Little Kettling was quiet – most of the villagers are already here.

The ballroom is glittering. The high-domed ceiling has been cleaned, the three sparkling chandeliers have been repaired and hang at equal spaces down the centre of the room, and the walls are lined with gold-framed oil paintings of couples dancing.

'You can't have done all this on your own.'

'I had some help.' He inclines his head towards Gracie and Wilbur talking in the corner with a few of the other villagers. 'I called one final meeting of the Nectar Inspectors. Asked them for help in winning back the woman I've fallen in love with.'

'Care, you didn't have to d—'

Gracie catches sight of us and lets out such a squeal that the music cuts off abruptly.

'Three cheers for the knights in shining armour of Elderflower Grove.' She starts off a round of hip-hip-hoorays. She doesn't look like she's got any sharp objects about her person.

The whole crowd joins in and cheers for us, and when I look up at Carey, his face is as red as mine.

'Wait,' I say as it dies down and everyone is about to go back to their conversations. 'We should all toast to Josie Garringham. She's with us in spirit tonight. She wasn't always popular in this village, but she will never be forgotten. Three cheers to the love she found at Elderflower Grove.' I glance at Carey. 'And three cheers to the love that *will* continue to be found here because of her.'

Everyone does another set of hoorays, and I wish Josie was here to see herself being celebrated by the villagers. If I look hard enough into the ballroom, I believe I can see a young Josie and Guillaume spinning around one last time.

The music starts up again, and Carey holds his hand out. 'May I have this dance?'

I think the corners of my lips have actually split from smiling so much. I slip my hand into his once more, and he leads us onto the dance floor. The music has changed to a classical symphony that would've been popular in the 1800s, a slow dance with his arm around me, his hand curled into my hip, my head on his chest, both of us trying not to tread on each other's toes.

I don't know how many dances we go through before my feet start to hurt, and as I lean on the opulent burgundy wall while Carey goes to get us both a drink, Gracie corners me.

I've never seen her not dressed as a bee before, but she's

wearing a beautiful black dress with yellow roses sewn around the neckline, and in true Gracie style, she's still wearing a bee antennae headband, but tonight it's been sparkled up and covered in glittering yellow roses to match her dress.

'You've let him keep his vital organs then?'

'It was touch and go, but I couldn't murder my own grandson.'

'He's told you?' I say in surprise.

She nods. 'We're going to do a DNA test, but the timings are a perfect match. I'd be surprised if he wasn't.'

'And you're okay with that?'

'I am. You know what, Kayleigh, you like him and Elderflower Grove likes him. That's enough for me. He's proved a lot of us wrong in the past couple of weeks. It was a bit of a shock when he told me – unexpected, you know? It had never crossed my mind that my son had a family of his own or that he might've had questions about me. I knew he'd be well taken care of – better than I could've done at the time.'

I nod.

'And I spoke to Josie last night. I'm going out to France to see her next week.'

'That's brilliant!' I give her a hug, and she goes to dance with her husband, but not before telling me she wants more of my candles in her shop because the ones I gave her last week have sold out.

The next few hours are lost in a haze of dancing. It's exactly the old-fashioned ball I've always dreamed of going to, but the only person I'm dancing with is Carey. Apart from a quick shimmy with my mum when her favourite song comes on, there's no one else I want to dance with, ever.

'I realise it should've been Regency-style dancing, but honestly, who knows the moves?' he says in my ear as we slow-dance. It's been a long time since I even realised there are other people here too. My entire focus is on the gorgeous man with his arms around me. 'Maybe one day we can host a proper Regency-themed ball, with time-appropriate food, drinks, music, proper dress code, a dance teacher so everyone knows the steps … A real immersive experience. I've heard of Jane Austen–themed weekends; we could look into hosting those.'

My hand slides up his arm and over his shoulder and he shivers as my fingernails graze his neck.

He inclines his head upwards, towards the third floor. 'Can I steal you for a minute?'

The roof is locked up to prevent anyone disturbing the bees, and Carey produces the key from his pocket before letting us up the narrow spiral staircase from the third-floor landing.

There's a slight chill in air tonight. Late August always brings the first hint of autumn, and I can't wait for the end-of-summer honey harvest and to stand here and watch the elderflower trees turn yellow before the leaves fall. We've been dancing for hours and I walk across to lean on the wall and attempt to give my aching feet a rest.

In the grounds below us, the wreckage of Guillaume's plane is still uncovered.

'I thought we could make a feature of it.' Carey steps behind me and loops his arm over my chest, tugging me close to his body until I'm surrounded by his *very* non-Mr-Darcy-esque grapefruit-y aftershave. 'A display at the site of the crash. Share their love story. Some of the letters and what happened to Guillaume. I've got to admit I didn't even realise how much trouble he could be in for that. I was embarrassed by my lack of historical knowledge when Josie was telling us. It would be nice to share that with the younger generation. Wilbur's already said his granddaughter's class wants to come on a school trip here to learn about it. As long as there are no more costumes involved.' He tugs at the cravat, fiddling with it until it loosens. 'I've loved tonight, but thank god we don't have to wear these every day.'

I tilt my head against his chest until I can see his face. 'You look gorgeous, but I prefer you in a Wombles T-shirt.'

'Who *wouldn't* choose a Wombles T-shirt over a cravat and itchy shirt?' He ducks until his chin rests on my shoulder and cuddles me tighter, and we stand there for a good few minutes before he speaks again. 'The Nectar Inspectors agreed that the Elderflower Grove project manager should live onsite. They agreed that we should look at expanding the hives in the spring. Fill those ones at the end of the garden too. And they agree that we need an onsite beekeeper. Just in case of bee emergencies.'

'Of which there are many?' I raise an eyebrow and pull back until I can see his face. 'Are you asking me to move in with you?'

'Well, Josie gave us both a majority share, so we have a right to live here. And it's a heck of a big place for just *one* perso—'

'Yes, yes! A thousand times yes!' There has never been a more perfect time for a *Pride and Prejudice* quote.

He waggles his eyebrows. 'Which is the deciding factor – me or Elderflower Grove?'

I laugh. 'I love this place. But I love you more, Care. Every day here has been special because of you. This building is just a building, but *you* have made it feel like a home. You're the first person I think of when anything happens, the *only* person I want to share things wi—'

He stops the sentence with a kiss. One of his hands finds my hip and turns me to face him, his nose rubs against mine, and his lips seal tenderly over mine. Softly at first, but getting harder when my hand curls into his hair, the other on his shoulder, clinging on.

It feels like the first kiss where neither of us have held back, where there are no secrets between us, and I'm floating on a cloud of his aftershave and his smooth jaw, which is crying out to have kisses trailed along it, and he backs against the wall to hold us both up, and I really hope our favourite insects are asleep by now or there will be some blushing honeybees in the nearest hives.

Everything outside of him, his lips and his strong body feels far away. The noise from the party filtering up from below, the trickle of the river in the distance, the burble of water from the fountain all disappear to his soft kisses and gentle touch, and we're both panting for breath by the time we pull back. His forehead rests against mine and my hand caresses his heaving chest.

'So, that's a yes then?'

I lean up for another peck. 'Yes. But maybe I should repeat myself in case you didn't hear it the first time.'

He laughs and kisses me again, and when we come up for air, his arms encircle me and hold me tight against him as we stand on the rooftop of Elderflower Grove, looking out across the beautiful expanse of land that is somehow, kind of, ours for now.

I've always thought there would be something unexpected hiding inside the gates of this place. Maybe mermaids don't swim in the lake and fairies don't flit through the trees, but there is definitely something about Elderflower Grove that makes wishes come true.

A Letter from Jaimie Admans

Thank you so much for reading *The Beekeeper at Elderflower Grove*! I hope you enjoyed escaping into the grand old manor house and getting wrapped up in Kayleigh and Carey's romance, along with Josie and Guillaume's story!

One of the best parts of any book for me is the research aspect, and while this one required a *lot* of research, I loved every moment of it, and gained a whole new respect for beekeepers, and a wonderful understanding of bees and how important they are to all of us!

If you enjoyed this story, please consider leaving a rating or review on Amazon. It only has to be a line or two, and it makes such a difference to helping other readers decide to pick up the book, and it would mean so much to me to know what you think! Did it make you smile, laugh, or cry? Would you like to walk around the grounds of Elderflower Grove? What would you wish for in the well? What book would you most like to find in Josie's amazing library?

Thank you again for reading. If you want to get in touch, you can find me on Twitter – usually when I should be writing – @ be_the_spark and on Facebook at jaimieadmansbooks. I would love to hear from you!

Lots of love,

Jaimie

Twitter: https://twitter.com/be_the_spark
Facebook: https://www.facebook.com/jaimieadmansbooks
Website: https://jaimieadmans.com/

The Wishing Tree Beside the Shore

What do you do when 'the one that got away' now won't go away? In fact, he's so determined not to go away that he's literally chained himself to a tree.

Fifteen years ago, **Felicity Kerr** threw caution to the wind and kissed her colleague **Ryan Sullivan** under the ancient wishing tree along the coast.

When Ryan failed to respond to her kiss, Felicity was mortified that she'd read his signals so horrendously wrong and left Lemmon Cove for good.

But now Felicity's job brings her back to her hometown, and face to face with Ryan, who is leading a band of octogenarians rallying to save their beloved 300-year-old sycamore from being bulldozed by property developers.

The spark with Ryan is still there, but Felicity is guarding a secret and as much as she wants to join the protest by his side, she can't help but hold back.

Will Felicity be able to mend her broken heart and find happiness with Ryan beside the sea?

The Little Bookshop of Love Stories

Today is the Mondayest Monday ever. Hallie Winstone has been fired – and it wasn't even her fault!

Having lost her job and humiliated herself in front of a whole restaurant full of diners, this is absolutely, one hundred percent, the worst day of her life.

That is until she receives an email announcing that she is the lucky winner of the Once Upon a Page Bookshop!

Owning a bookshop has always been Hallie's dream, and when she starts to find secret love letters on the first page of every book, she knows she's stumbled across something special.

But Hallie's beloved bookshop is in financial trouble, and with sales dwindling, she can't help but wonder if she is really cut out to run a business.

Things start to look up when she meets gorgeous, bookish Dimitri and between them, they post a few of the hidden messages online, reuniting people who thought they were lost forever.

But maybe it's time for Hallie to find her own happy-ever-after, too?

The Little Vintage Carousel by the Sea

What if one moment could change your life forever?

Ness has almost resigned herself to being single forever, when she catches sight of the most gorgeous man she's ever seen on the train to work.

But just as she plucks up the courage to speak to him – he steps off the train and disappears into the crowds, without realising he's accidentally dropped his phone!

It's her 'glass slipper' moment, she's sure of it, she just needs to track him down – all the way to the gorgeous seaside village of Pearlholme, where she finds him restoring a vintage carousel by the sea . . .

Maybe it's finally time to follow her heart?

Acknowledgements

Firstly and always most importantly, Mum, this line never changes because I'm *always* eternally grateful for your constant patience, support, encouragement, and for always believing in me. Thank you for always being there for me – I don't know what I'd do without you. Love you lots!

Bill, thank you for sharing your beekeeping experience with me and answering my endless questions!

A big shoutout to some Facebook groups who support me tirelessly and are an absolute pleasure to be part of. If you're looking for book-loving groups filled with lovely readers who will be good for your soul (but terrible for your to-read list!) then I highly recommend joining The Friendly Book Community, Heidi Swain and Friends, Chick Lit and Prosecco, The Socially Distanced Book Club, and Book Swap Central. Thank you so much to all members and admins of these wonderful groups who put in so much effort to make little communities that are a joy to belong to!

The biggest thank you to an amazing author and my very best friend, Marie Landry. I look forward to talking to you every day. You never fail to make me laugh and feel loved, and you are *always* the highlight of every single day! And to Nancy – thank you for the continual love and support!

An extra special thank you to Bev for always writing lovely letters, always taking the time to ask about my writing, and for always being so encouraging and supportive and kind, even through your own hard times.

Thank you, Charlotte McFall, for always being a tireless cheer-leader and one of the best friends I've ever had.

Thank you, Jayne Lloyd, for being a wonderful friend through good times and bad, and for the emails that always make me smile!

All the lovely authors, bloggers, and readers I know online. You've all been so supportive since the very first book, and I want to mention you all by name, but I know I'll forget someone and I don't want to leave anyone out, so to everyone I chat to on Twitter or Facebook – thank you.

Thank you to the team at HQ and especially my fabulous editor, Belinda Toor. The past couple of years with you have been incredible – thank you for everything!

And finally, a massive thank you to *you* for reading!